THE ONE STAR GOODNIGHT

CHRISTOPHER DUFOUR

Christopher Dufour

www.du4writes.com

ISBN: 978-1-7334724-0-1

Cover design by Blue Canary Books (bluecanarybooks.com).

For Doug.

Forever.

CONTENTS

1.

PANHANDLE DREAMING

9:05, and I said to myself, Jack...take a day off.

Comfortably clad in the black velvet robe my sister gave to me for Christmas five years ago, I found a fresh pack of Camels on the coffee table and made no further move that could be classified as initiative. It's not that I don't like my job, but you can only spend so much time scrubbing brass instruments before you zone out into the netherworld of blue-collar labor. I figured since I'd already made my draw for the month, I could relax a little bit. Boss be *damned*.

Of course, in the repair shop, there's little more than lip service paid to the time-honored tradition of punching the clock, working nine to five and going home to meatloaf and beer. Finding the music store owner anywhere near his business could be a tougher task than attempting a rear entry maneuver on Bruce Willis. Besides, the off-season was kicking into high gear, marching horns trading in for the cobwebbed concert instruments locked away in band halls all over southern Mississippi. I put my loaf-life at two days before someone started complaining that little Robby couldn't squeeze a C-major scale from his trumpet and that it was my fault that the horn had degraded to useless while stashed in Robby's closet for the past eight months marinating in spittle and old lanolin.

My brief morning bout of guilty justification completed, I took in a deep lungful of bad habit and went to refill my coffee cup. They make these huge Styrofoam cups at the local supermarket for about fifteen cents apiece. I buy them in packages of a hundred and they last me forever. People call me lowbrow for drinking coffee out of Styrofoam instead of the proper mug, but the damn things keep the stuff hot longer than that porcelain nonsense from Woolworth's. Even though I lived comfortably for my money, I've never been able to shake the frugality my mother ingrained upon me as a kid. She was always after my sister and I about leaving lights on in the house unnecessarily and the like, but what can you expect of a single, divorced mom with visions of mink coats and diamonds in her head?

The thought of Mom and Jeannette and Texas filtered through me as I made my way back to *Headline News.* I really tried not to think about the old days much, cliched as that sounds. But, honestly, who do you know that *doesn't* wish for the old days? Old Days are cool, superior in most every way. Innocent? Maybe. Certainly more fun. Old Days meant everything being handed to you on a silver platter, even if it was only corn dogs and Kool-Aid. Old Days meant a plethora of things to do in downtown Fort Worth. Old Days meant *better.*

Melancholy at this hour could only mean one thing: Restlessness. Keep oneself occupied at all times lest the thinking begin, and damn the philosophizing that's ultimately to follow. I fished a datebook out of the stack of unpaid bills on the table and tried to find out what I needed to do today. Go to work was one thing, but we've been over that. I noted that my band had a gig in two weeks, and rehearsals were fast approaching. But not at nine in the morning. If I was going to have a day off, I needed to find something to do that didn't involve exertion.

Best-case scenario: Breakfast. Mayla would have been shucking and jiving since 5:00AM at the Griddle House with her bacon and eggs and to even think that I could cook better than that invited obscenity. My father grew up in New Orleans, and all his life he learned the art of gourmet Cajun cooking. Naturally, some of that passed down to me, and when I had the time, I could dish out a mean etouffee or some lumpy jambalaya. Bacon and eggs, though, were foods for all times of the day. Cajun would have to wait another month until crawfish were back in season.

I showered and disposed of the coffee remnants, reminding myself for the umpteenth time that I really needed to take the thirty minutes to clean up my apartment...*soon*. Maintaining a one-bedroom really presented little challenge, and you know something's wrong when you can actually talk to the mildew that's growing in the tub. However, by this time, breakfast had asserted itself as the dominant force in my life. A big stack of scrambled eggs with plenty of fatty bacon and hashbrowns, maybe a few chunks of ham in between, far more grated cheese than was acceptable for the son of an American Heart Association director.

As I was struggling into a pair of jeans and a khaki shirt that didn't sport too many wrinkles, the phone bleated for my attention. Probably someone from the store wondering where I was, and if that was the case, it was always better to deal with it and get it over with. The mental list of Good Old Fashioned Lies started gearing up in my brain as I reached for the receiver.

"Yeah?"

"Jack, what are you doing, baby?!" came the high-pitched catcall. I involuntarily reached for the phone's volume control, a habit of listening to generations of my Dooley relatives calling at odd hours of the day.

"Whataboutcha, Uncle Carter?" I said. "Little early for a social call, isn't it?"

"You know me, baby; if the phone's more than a foot away from me, I get the shivers. How's your schedule today?"

Uhhh, I groaned. *Hadn't really thought about it...* "Listen, Carter, if you need someone to wash the trucks again, why don't you call—"

"No, no, no more grunt work, Jackie." Carter's affable tone took an obvious nosedive, something I wasn't familiar with. "We need to have lunch."

"We do?" I ran a hand through the short, jet black curls in the mirror and snorted. "What's up?"

"Tell you about it when we get there. Chesterfield's at one?"

"You picking up the tab?"

"Don't I always, you cheap sonofa—?"

"Right. Okay, Carter, one it is. And don't keep me waiting while you're on the phone with some old high school buddy, huh? Charge that cell phone every once in a while."

"You got it, nephew. See you there."

As I hung up the phone, a momentary flash of concern flagged my mind. Carter Dooley made a life of the art of bullshit. The man could not keep the phone away from his ear. He owned a propane supplier company outside of town, which had grossed him some serious cash in the past twenty years. As the only Dooley in Mississippi with money enough to pay off family debts, he was something of an oddball. He loved fun, worshipped fun. Always out of town on some business trip with Aunt Dee, spending money and bringing home souvenirs for those of us less fortunate to actually get out once in a while. He had that Dooley way about him, the fast-talking, all-nonsense guy who believed business and pleasure were the same thing. You couldn't *not* like the guy, but like I said, he was a Dooley. We all have little foibles tucked away somewhere.

Going outside, I noted with some satisfaction that fall had finally decided to grace Hattiesburg, Mississippi. With November looking around the corner, it was nice to actually be able to go outside and not be beaten down by the heat which seems to linger for the better part of the year. Anyone who doesn't believe in global warming hasn't lived in southern Mississippi. It gets hotter every year down here, the heat waves last longer, and the humidity from a rapidly encroaching coastline sweats it out of you more days in the year than not. I think it's been about twenty years since Hattiesburg saw an extended cold spell, let alone snow.

The Little White Honda Civic groaned its daily protest as I started him up and headed out. I'll never understand the appeal of big, flashy cars. I see people driving around in Mustangs and BMWs, and I know those people will be mourning their cars' deaths in another two or three years. Nobody makes a car like Honda. The Civic was going on its twelfth year of life, and after the hundreds of thousands of miles I'd put on it, he still purred at forty-five miles a gallon. Granted, I'd had to invest in lots of motor work over the past couple of years, but it was worth it. The Little White Honda just wouldn't die. I'd even found an old used Sony CD deck at Hudson's for forty dollars a few months ago, and the sound of Huey Lewis or Men at Work in the morning through the Honda's tinny little speakers propelled me into a state of simultaneous calm and excitement. I rubbed the Saint Christopher medallion hanging from the rearview mirror and said my daily prayer of thanks to the Great Honda God for his generous offering to this most humble and lowly human being. You could have your Mustangs and BMWs. I'm still getting from point A to point B.

Hattiesburg wasn't the sleepy retirement community that all the fogeys still thought it to be. I lived on the west side of town off Highway 98 where all the growth and modernization was finally coming in, after so many years of social stagnation. About a mile back east, the old district became more distinct with its seventy-year-old buildings and 1960s deco street signs. The town exuded a rather confused image. On the one hand, you had the rich old golf-walkers descended from plantation-age depravity. The "leaders of the community" like you hear on the news, but within their own, still possessed of the same garden-variety racism, sexism, and assholery common to Mississippians, which, alas, confirmed the southern stereotypes that I suppose we're all trying to rise above. On the other side though, you had the college kids. The University of Southern Mississippi had been established in 1910, and while its original graduates had gone the way of the dodo, those silly Gen Xers of my generation were taking over. Southern – we don't say "USM" out loud, you fucker – billed itself primarily as a liberal arts-based university. I wondered then why my tuition had gone mostly to the football team that had done little more in my frame of reckoning than parade out onto the field and perform ballet.

Nestled in one of a hundred tiny but new shopping plazas, the Griddle House stood as the last bastion of the old regime in thriving west Hattiesburg. Forty years ago, when Mayla and her late husband had opened the place, the diner started out as a way station for sleepy truck drivers and recently paroled cons fleeing Parchman. Now it was the choice hangout of high school kids who thought they were big time by skipping school and smoking cloves. The truckers stopped in for a hearty meal too though;

Mayla's reputation was going on fifteen counties now at last count. I rolled up into the drive and walked into the oppressive scent of fried fat, tar-like coffee and stale cigarette smoke.

Okay, so there were some things worth a damn in Hattiesburg.

"Mister Jack!" Mayla's crow-like voice beckoned me from behind the counter. "Now, I know you been skippin' them meals again, boy! Just look at you, so skinny and limp!"

"I got tired of the word 'fat-ass' following me around so I invested in oatmeal, ma'am," I chided her, climbing into the chair, second from the register.

"You better watch that language, young man! You know I don't truck no foul mouths in my establishment."

I jerked a thumb at the longhairs cuddled together in a booth a few yards away. "So that's why you're letting in the poets, eh?"

Mayla snorted, putting down some silverware and a cup of coffee in front of me. "What am I gonna do, Jack? You remember I tried to call their parents one time a few months back? The parents don't even care. They say as long as they come home at night and go away in the morning, it's okay by them."

"Yeah, real models of Hattiesburg citizenry, huh?" I tapped the counter before she could set the menu down. "Three eggs, scrambled; double order of bacon; hashbrowns with the ham and cheese."

"One of these days, Mister Jack, I'm gonna get that menu down before you order," Mayla said, slapping my arm. "Be right back with it, honey. You want a paper?"

I looked at the morning edition of *The Hattiesburg American* and made a face. "Anything besides the toilet paper? I forgot my magazines this morning."

"Sorry, Jack. Newspaper's all we got."

"I'll survive then. Thanks, Mayla."

Out of curiosity, I slipped the front page from the newspaper on the counter and checked out the headlines. You know you're in backwoods redneck-ville when the spelling mistakes in the local paper are directly proportional to the number of syllables in the headlines. "Tree falls on lawyer's home," read one of the articles. Or how about, "Family of four arrested for indecent exposure at Super K-Mart". Before I'd even made it to the movie listings, I tossed the paper away and dug out the cigarettes in my jacket. It's trying being a master of the English language and having to put up with drivel like *The Hattiesburg American* on a daily basis.

Well... I say "master," but I only got the B.A. in English Literature and Language. Graduate work didn't appeal to me: the high unemployment figures for those completing a liberal arts degree in the south equally matched the number of people who thought they could emulate Tennessee Williams' career to a tee. Instead, I lucked into the allure of high-commission work at the band shop. I'd come to Southern with the intent of learning to be a writer or maybe even a filmmaker. When I saw that Southern's English classes started with "How to Write a Research Paper 101" and ended with "How to Document a Research Paper 401," I figured I'd have to settle for intellectual stimulation. After all, my father offered me a free ride through college if I went to Southern, so I wasn't about to argue with that. My attendance at "redneck central" as my mother called it caused plenty of friction in the family. I may have been smart enough or savvy enough to have gotten a scholarship to some swank Texas school, but there was something very appealing about spending time with my Dad on the first daily basis since third grade.

Not to say that Southern didn't have a couple good teachers and a few fun classes. I remember my second year there, I had this lady for American Literature who had a pretty tough reputation around campus as a hard-nose for papers and the like. She also had been called the college's most fervent feminist critic and made a separate income writing long essays on feminism in the most unlikely places of American literature: *Moby Dick, The Last of the Mohicans*, some Emerson and Whitman. As it turned out, discussion in this lady's class became a highlight of my tenure as a college student. We had similar interests in modern entertainment that nobody else enjoyed like *Homicide: Life on the Street* and *Twin Peaks*. Part of the fun in that class included seeing which one of us, the teacher or the student, could befuddle the rest of the class with hidden allusions to television shows they'd barely even heard of. What was her name…?

And yet after three years of the standard student's university education, there I was drinking bitter coffee and reading *The Hattiesburg American* in a breakfast hut seventy miles from the nearest art museum. Sometimes, it was enough to make me want to cry.

"Ya done wit' that?" a crusty old-timer in grease-stained coveralls and a cap that read "TIRES" said to me. I shrugged and passed him the paper, stubbing out my cigarette as Mayla delivered my bacon.

"Make more sense of it than me, pal," I told the man.

The guy stopped with the paper in one hand and a spoonful of oatmeal halfway to his mouth. "Huh?"

"Never mind..."

"Dooley!"

I looked over my shoulder and saw one of my close acquaintances (hard to call him a friend), John Lewis enter the diner. Lewis had been a member of the fraternity I'd sometimes affiliated with in college and had graduated into a lucrative career with some insurance salesmen of the same frat badge. Knowing the guy's penchant for not being too quick on the trigger, the value of even the thinnest of connections in Hattiesburg became a very stark reality. Lewis couldn't sell a video rental.

"Whataboutcha, Lewis?" I said, indicating the chair next to me. "You late for work too?"

"Nah, I'm officially, uh, 'out of town,'" he cackled, throwing his jacket over the back of the chair and loosening his tie. "I've got an appointment at eleven and, uh, didn't feel like sitting around the office all morning on the phone."

"Smart man."

"What about you, Jack?" Lewis grabbed a menu and began scanning it for something that wouldn't offend his tender sensibilities. "Aren't you supposed to be, um, buffing horns or blowing on them or something like that?"

"Fuck you. I'm taking the day off. And I don't have to puss about it either."

"Right." Lewis gave Mayla his order and performed what I've come to call the "Upper Gentry Maneuver." He made a show of running his hand through his crisp brown hair and checking the time on the extravagant watch on his wrist. You could take the redneck out of the elite, but not the asshole. Especially the educated redneck like Lewis.

"You still got that band, Jack?" Lewis said. "Midnight Hour or something?"

"*Twenty-five to Midnight,*" I replied, eagerly awaiting the sensation of the eggs and hashbrowns Mayla set down before me. "Yeah, we're playing Dewey's this weekend. You ought to come; bring your girlfriend. By the way, when are you two getting married?"

"Aw, Jack, cut it out! It's not enough I have to hear it from her, but you too? Shit, man, I'm not ready to get married. I'm still having fun just being able to, uh, drink and screw around at will."

I pointed a fork at Lewis. "Watch out there, bud. That's how my Dad got his third wife."

"And fourth child. How is the old man?"

"Fine. He's really getting into this whole home improvement gig with the new house. Half of a deck's built on the back so far, and he keeps saying he'll finish it as soon as he has time. What is that? He's got all the time he wants! The guy runs his own business, plays music when he feels like it, and does the family thing. How can you not have time?"

"It's a deck, Jack. That's a big thing to families, man."

"Then hire a carpenter. Look, I'm gonna walk out on that brand new deck of my Dad's—whenever he finishes it—and I'm going to fall on my ass when the wood breaks under me."

"Oughtta run your fat ass around the block a few times then, punchy." Lewis laughed at my deadpan look of annoyance. "Lighten up, Jack. Man, you never change. Are you always gonna be the, uh, social misanthrope?"

I shrugged, washing down a combo bite of eggs and hashbrowns with some coffee. "Somebody's gotta do it."

"Right, and in the meantime, you're not doing anything *about* it. How many times have you told me to get off my ass and do something? You're a fucking hypocrite, Jack."

"That's a big word, John. You been taking SAT prep courses?"

Lewis shook his head as his breakfast arrived. "I give up."

A few booths down from the counter, the soon-to-be-high-school-dropouts exploded in a vicious stream of curses and laughter. One of their cheap clove cigarettes rebounded off the men's room door and landed on the floor beside me, earning a stern grimace from Mayla. I stamped out the clove and kicked it under the counter.

"John, have you ever lived anywhere but in Mississippi?" I said.

"No," Lewis replied. "You know that. Born and raised in Long Beach."

"Okay then. Shut the fuck up until you've got some perspective."

"I've got perspective! I've been to New Orleans and Houston and Pensacola and...and Tampa. Sure, they're cool cities and all, but it's not *home*, y'know?"

"You want to stay locked up at home for the rest of your life, John?"

"That's not what I meant, dumbass. Seriously, what's... what's Texas got that Mississippi doesn't? Huh? You came from Fort Worth, right? What's so, uh, good in Fort Worth that pisses you off so much in Hattiesburg?"

I looked over Lewis's plate to where the guy in the "TIRES" cap was counting pennies on the counter to cover his bill. Downing the rest of my coffee, I made a clicking noise with my tongue.

"*The Fort Worth Star-Telegram*," I said.

October meant normal in-season fall weather that other people around the country had been enjoying for a while. Hattiesburg saw cold fronts less often than a Tennessee preacher saw a liquor cabinet. I valued the cool air more than I did in other places I'd been to, and driving around town with the windows down in my car allowed for the wispy, stillborn autumn winds to filter through my hair and skin like a cleansing force. I considered myself a closet intellectual, and October weather helped me to think. I didn't know what it was about the oppressive, lethargic heat of summer, but I did know that summer wasn't beach balls and swimming pools in Hattiesburg. As a matter of fact, I think the last public swimming pool was shut down in 1989 for excessive visitor defecation.

The Little White Honda cruised just above the speed limit, darting around retired salesmen's boat-like sedans and boom-box wannabe lowriders. I love driving. Cherish it. There's something about the freedom of getting into your own automobile and just cruising around with no destination in mind. I didn't own a car until I moved to Hattiesburg, so I figured that piece of my adolescence still required attention. I had a stack of CDs in the glove compartment bearing everything from The Police to the orchestrations of Angelo Badalamenti. No better time existed to listen to good music than when you're leisurely cruising down Hardy Street, October breeze in your face, little to no desire to do anything productive with the rest of your day. I found those kinds of days more and more frequent, and it affected my get-up-and-go. Today wasn't the first time I'd called in sick.

Breakfast with Lewis had jarred an old, untreated wound within me. I had been trying to find a way out of Hattiesburg for over a year, looking for anything, anywhere else. I'd considered going to work for a pharmaceutical sales company in Miami a few months ago, but salesmanship just wasn't in my blood despite the inherited Dooley characteristic of Influential Bullshittery. The only aspect of the job that appealed to me had been the travel. Since graduating college, I'd looked at advertising firms, recording studios, paralegal agencies, courier work, and countless shit jobs that would at least have given me the excuse to leave Hattiesburg. It all came down to money, really. I didn't have much, and I wanted a lot. Living was moderately cheap in Hattiesburg and jumping into the next tax bracket presented an alien situation to me. My apprenticeship at the music store would be completed at the end of the year, and I knew I could use that to find a better-paying position at a bigger store somewhere else in the country. The demand for skilled brass repair technicians exceeded the number of techs in the market. But I wasn't sure about continuing on in a field—as lucrative as it could be—that felt so much like a chore.

I had this friend back in Texas, best friend. We were so close as kids, so into the same things that everybody called us twins. We looked like some insane version of Abbott and Costello, him being tall and lanky and me the short, dumpy one. Yet up until our high school graduation, we'd been the best pals on the planet. No one could come between us. Almost like brothers. Rick and I grew up under the influence of pulpy, used crime novels and comic books, and from the outset, he'd always known that what he wanted to do. Now he was undergoing the initial field tests for consideration in the extended training program of the FBI Academy in Quantico, Virginia. Right outta college too, where many of his cohort had to bring to the table prior experience in law enforcement or advanced degrees in criminology or behavioral sciences. In another few years, I could conceivably see him heading murder investigations the likes of which would make Mulder and Scully blush.

It's not the same old thing, as the song went. Or so it seemed for me. Time had frozen for me in Hattiesburg. Rick was having the time of his life at Quantico, and here I was still pooping along in a twelve-year-old Honda with nothing but question marks on the dashboard. Maybe the police department didn't sound so bad after all. Then again, I couldn't really see myself as a sworn-in member of Hattiesburg's infamous DUI Task Force. I liked to think that I had a little more verve than the skills needed to pull kids over for drunken escapades.

I pulled into the broken-concrete parking lot of The Book Rack once I'd gotten downtown. The Rack had been some old lady's house years ago, but its proximity to the bustling streets and shops of the old town area prevented anything resembling a peaceful life there. She had parlayed her retirement fund into a small used bookstore and filled the house with ancient copies of *Farewell to Arms*, a plethora of pop sci-fi reads, and the most comprehensive collection of crime fiction I'd ever seen. Used books went for half of the cover price, although I'd gladly have paid twice that for the first edition paperback of Chandler's *The Big Sleep*. I'd discovered so much here in this little shop, and it remained my favorite hidey-hole in Hattiesburg.

"Morning, Jack," Mrs. Terrance, the day clerk (not the old lady), greeted me. "Looking for anything today, or are you just sniffing around again?"

"We'll see," I said, allowing that first whiff of decayed paper and acidized pulp to overwhelm me. Mrs. Terrance frowned upon my jaunts to the shop; sometimes I would just sit in a corner and look at all the titles on the crime and mystery shelves or flip through dog-eared pages for hours without buying anything. The owner didn't care one way or the other seeing as how I'd traded most of my childhood science fiction books for bountiful copies of Ellroy, Leonard, and Vachss. As long as I kept her shelves full and put in a gratuitous amount of cash from time to time, I could probably get away with snorting coke in The Book Rack. Well, so long as Mrs. Terrance didn't catch me. Come to think of it… I never saw Mrs. Terrance and the owner at the same time…

I noticed some new books on the shelf bearing Charley Kittlemeyer's name. Kittlemeyer wrote lots of detective stuff with a real neat blend of international spy flavor for the mix. His books were thirty-minute reads at best, but damn, were they fun. I think he had written over a hundred books since his first cult classic, *Star for Ichabod,* hit the shelves to moderate success in the forties. Word around the Internet said that Kittlemeyer emigrated from Germany, the brother of a high-ranking official in Hitler's foreign ministry. Nobody knew for sure, of course. Kittlemeyer's mystique was as pronounced as the brevity of his books. No one was even sure if the guy was still alive.

I thumbed through a copy of *No More Solutions,* which bore a few taped-together pages and a strong scent of decomposing pulp. The caption on the cover described this one as a story of Jake Kilgore, master sleuth star of other Kittlemeyer novels, who had finally reached his low point after years of political intrigue abroad. Kilgore didn't have the American flair that came with Philip Marlowe or even classic Mickey Spillane, but the character exemplified what was cool about the fifties. Kittlemeyer's Kilgore was subversive, decadent, and in no way a productive member of society. He farmed out his spy talents to any and all buyers, taking cases as big as the murder of a head of state or as small-time as finding out who had gotten some oil magnate's daughter pregnant. This kind of literature never saw widespread print in its time. People back then were too into white picket fences, Sunbeam-Oster appliances, and 2.5 kids. But now, this stuff was art.

No More Solutions looked like a winner, so I picked it up and a few others at random. Total cost for six Kittlemeyer novels came in just a shade of four dollars. I smirked as I handed Mrs. Terrance a twenty. Can't beat those fifties prices.

"You're the only customer we have who buys that rubbish," Mrs. Terrance told me as she was bagging up my spoils. "We'd have to have a bookburning if someone didn't come in and move it."

I scowled at the woman, pocketing my wallet and snatching the bag from her hands. "Yeah, give my regards to *Mister* Goebbels when you get home."

I left it at that before the old hag could get feisty again and beat a retreat to my car. Once inside, I hunkered down behind the wheel and rolled the windows low, fishing *No More Solutions* out of the bag, and opening up to Chapter One. With cigarette in hand, Hattiesburg disappeared as I assumed the alter ego of one Jake Kilgore, master sleuth.

2.

THAT FANTABULOUS FELLOW

I took a snide sense of satisfaction in noting that I was ten minutes late for lunch with Carter. By the time I was halfway through my new Kittlemeyer novel, I realized that I'd be spanked by lunchtime traffic in getting back west toward Chesterfield's. I got into the restaurant just as a large gaggle of Southern alumni laughed their half-drunken selves out of the bar and back toward the line of law offices and insurance agencies along the Broadway strip in the old town. Walking into the reception area, I threw my Banana Republic leather jacket over one arm and smiled at the hostess. Another two steps avoided the perky girl before she had a chance to delay me with weather babble, and I slipped into the dining arena.

I found Carter tucked away in a small booth near the kitchen. As jolly as a Dooley can get, Carter clocked in at a reasonable two-hundred even. Overweight but naturally big, Carter never made bones about being comfortable, and he blended in fine with all the other noontime golfers in the restaurant. He favored khaki pants with a tucked-in polo that featured a red crawfish on the breast. Loafers, no socks, just like my Dad. *"When you own your own propane company, Jackie,"* he'd told me once, *"you can wear whatever the hell you want to when you go to work."* Fine words to live by, I guess.

"Whataboutcha, Uncle C?" I slapped Carter's outstretched palm and we grasped hands. My chin involuntarily jerked toward the half-empty glass of Merlot in front of him. "Couldn't wait on me, eh?"

"I'm the one who's supposed to be late, baby; you're gonna kill my reputation," he replied, sloshing the wine around in its glass. "Want one?"

The waitress had followed me over, knowing Carter well and also knowing the kind of tip money he invariably held on his person. "Crown and seven," I told her. "And I already know what I want to eat. Custer filet, baked potato. Douse it."

"And for you, sir?" the girl said to Carter, who was studying the menu intently.

"Ummm," Carter droned. "Could you bring me some shrimp scampi and a loaf of that French bread y'all make so fine? And let's get some crab claws, too."

She thanked us for our order, told us our drinks were on their way and scurried back to wherever unskilled labor went in the kitchen when not hooking for tips. I peeled the cellophane off a fresh pack of cigarettes and fiddled with the dented, tarnished Zippo on the tabletop.

"What are we sitting back here for? We're always up at the bar."

Carter plucked one of my cigarettes away from me. "Didn't feel like the bar today, man. Know what I mean?"

"Not really. And get away from those. You're supposed to have quit. Aunt Dee finds out I'm feeding you smokes, I'm fucked."

Carter brandished the cigarette at me once he lit it. "Right now, I'll take the chance on your ass. I've been having nic fits bad enough to shake malformed turds out of my ass."

"Charming. How's things, Carter?"

"Ma-an! Crazy shit, baby, *crazy.* I've been working my tail off all week, and I'm still not caught up with all this nonsense at the office."

"Get that phone off your ear every once in a while, and it might do you some good, kaz," I chided.

Carter grimaced and made one of his trademark laughs that sounded like a cross between a seal and a fire alarm. "Not me, baby! That's why I got secretaries! I mean, come on... Expense reports? What are those?"

"See, this is you being you again. Remember that talk we had last month with Dad? I thought you were considering selling the company and retiring."

"Jack, as much headache as it'd relieve, I'm still not sure I want to." Carter's lively, bearded features crestfell somewhat, and he reclined in the plush booth with his wine. "You know how it is with me. What else am I gonna do?"

"Don't even start that shit with me, Uncle," I said, brandishing my Camel at him. "You went to goddamn Acapulco three times last year, and I can never catch you at home 'cause you're always on the coast on your boat. And with what you can net for DPI? Please. Ten million is plenty enough to sail you through to a lovely retirement in Destin."

"I know, I know." He put his face in his hands, and I could see some genuine traces of tension in the temples he massaged.

"There's just been... Jack, some funny stuff's been happening around the plant lately."

"Funny ha-ha, or funny oh-shit-Joe-Bob-dropped-a-match-in-the-propane-tanks?"

"Somewhere in between."

Carter fell silent as the waitress delivered our appetizers and drinks. I lost the cocktail straw and sucked down a little Crown and seven between smoke puffs. One thing about Chesterfield's, they made excellent mixed drinks. Most places in Hattiesburg still served beer in cans, and at the upscale joints like Fatheree's and The Hog, the bartenders watered down the drinks so much that it took all night to tie on a decent buzz. Fucking crime, it was.

"Okay, Carter, what's the deal?" I said, trading a cigarette butt for fried crab claw. "You sounded like a spy on the phone."

"Well..." It wasn't like Carter to hedge. Through his rhetoric of bullshit, always a clear, sometimes keen, sliver of rationale peeked out. He dipped a claw into the mound of butter on the serving plate and sucked the meat off quickly, discarding the bone. "I need your help, Jack. Something's going on around DPI, and I can't get an angle on it from the inside."

My own claw froze just above the marinara. "O-*kay*," I said.

"Honest!" Carter pleaded. "Listen, all bullshit aside, we're in trouble. I didn't catch it until accounting brought in the last quarter earnings, and they were *ground zero* compared to last year's figures."

"There should be obvious causes though, right?" I asked. "Accidents? Layoffs? Hell, customer drop-off?"

"That's what I thought, too, at first. So I went back and did my own audit."

I raised an admonishing eyebrow. Carter doing anything on his own meant he probably read two reports and called somebody else to do it for him. "Do tell."

"Y'know, we had *eight accidents* last quarter alone. That's pretty unusual for us, okay? I mean, *I* didn't even know about it!"

I couldn't help the smirk that flooded my face. "Where've you been the last three months, Carter? Destin, New York... Hell, you took Dee to Paris for your anniversary. What do you mean you didn't know? Of course you didn't know. You weren't even around."

Carter's fingers performed a pitter-patter dance on the tabletop. "I know, but my partners would have called me if something that glaring had been going on. So I checked through the daily reports, and didn't find a damn thing. There were only six accidents on record; three by the same driver, and another three by different drivers."

"And you haven't fired the three-timer yet? God, no wonder the company's taking a beating."

"He wasn't the aggressor in each case, and the insurance paid everything out so there was no reason to take it any further," Carter said. "But that's pretty bad luck getting sidewindered three times in as many months, eh?"

I smirked, swiping the last crab claw before Carter's greasy fingers could find it. "You know I don't believe in coincidence."

"Right." Carter paused for a moment as the waitress delivered our dishes. As my uncle pulled heavily on his Merlot, I dove into my baked potato with glee. Chesterfield's made a potato to put the Irish to shame. The spud split open like a cornucopia of sliced ham, bacon, mozzarella, cheddar, and chives. The steam from the thing enticed my mouth immediately, and I shuddered with anticipation as the filet's sauce mixed lazily with the melting sour cream from the spud. Insert appropriate food-eating cliché.

"Anyway, what do you think?" Carter said, once the waitress had left. "Is somebody fucking me in the ass?"

"We're not in prison, Carter," I said through a mouthful of fileted steak and potato. "But the same guy in three different accidents, none of which were his fault, sounds too damn easy for me. Once, okay, I can buy that. Twice? All right, *maybe* if the guy's got a personal problem. But you *know* what those drivers have to go through after stuff like that happens. It's a rare day when it happens three times. What's his dossier look like?"

"Henkel? Oh, he's a prince. Been a driver for ten years, no outstanding problems with procedure or drugs. He's one of the good ones in my stable."

"Is it possible Henkel could be responsible for the missing accident reports? The other two you mentioned?"

"Maybe..." Carter's eyes narrowed. "You think?"

"Who handles your emergency response? Did you call Duke?"

"No, you know your father and I don't do business on that level. The in-house team does all our safety work."

"Okay, forget that for a moment." I washed a load of steak down with the rest of my Crown and seven and smacked my lips. "Explain to me why the accident reports mean decreased profits."

"Well, first of all, it's a product loss," Carter said, dipping a forkful of shrimp into his tub of butter. "When propane spills, it's impossible to recollect it. That means the payment from the customer, whoever that might be, is frozen until a new shipment can be delivered. Then there's the Emergency Response Network baloney we have to go through with each accident, and that can cost us a lot."

"So the money is gone, the accidents aren't recorded, but you get an insurance payout." I frowned, watching Carter lap up the scampi sauce as he searched my face for some kind of answer. I had worked for Carter during the first year of my residence in Mississippi and on and off again since when he needed small jobs done quick. He had me delivering samples and picking up all kinds of stuff between his plants, and after a year, I'd seen all the Mississippi countryside that I cared for. Also, the thought of driving around with several containers of propane in an unprotected Honda trunk didn't really sit well with me, despite what Carter had been paying me.

Still, I had gleaned a basic understanding of the propane industry from Uncle Carter during that year. Dooley Petroleum, Inc. was the biggest propane supplier in south Mississippi and also extended its reaches into Louisiana and Alabama. Hundreds of small, independent propane distributors subscribed to DPI's services in order to bring cheap, safe propane supply to all manner of businesses and residences in the south. The neat thing about propane was that it cost half as much as gasoline or electricity. Carter's house out in the expensive Canebrake suburb received its heating and power from a privately built and operated propane plant under the grounds, personally installed by Carter's men. The problem with cheap fuel like propane though emanated from the fact that the industry didn't have a big lobbyist group. Legislation passed down from the government always keeled over to the gasoline and hard oil side of things, so instead of bowing up and getting politically active in that arena, DPI diversified into kerosene, jet fuel, and CO^2. If someone in natural gas had the gumption to stand up to the petroleum giants in Washington, we'd all be paying fifty cents a gallon for the fuel in our cars. That's no shitting either: my Dad used to convert his car to run on propane, and a tank of that stuff would last a month with heavy driving.

"Have you checked the money yourself, Carter?" I inquired. "I mean, looked at all your assets?"

"Sort of," Carter replied half-heartedly. Math had *never* been a Dooley strong point. We preferred working through the cracks of things like the IRS and financial law. "A lot of the company's assets are tied up in some weird stocks overseas. I don't know a thing about stockbroking, so I let my partners handle it."

"Stocks," I said to myself. "And the hard cash in the bank?"

"Declining. But I can't figure out where it's going. ERNI hasn't received payments for more than four accident responses, and the product replacement fees shouldn't have been as expensive as it's showing on the books." ERNI was the Emergency Response Network to which most motor carriers belonged, mandated by federal regulations in case shit went bad, as it sometimes does with hazardous materials.

"Carter," I said, grinning into my filet; "do you trust your partners?"

"Matthew and Craig? Shiiiiiit. What kind of dumbass question is that? Matthew and I founded the goddamn company together; you know that! And Craig's like a son to me!" Carter curled his lip and threw down his fork. "What are you getting at?"

"Look, don't get pissed with me, kaz," I said, wiping my mouth. "You asked for *my* help. If everything has to go through either you, Matthew or Craig, how do you explain all this?"

Carter threw up his hands in exasperation. "I don't know! You think I expected anything like this to happen to me when I got into the business? For Chrissakes, this stuff only happens to people up north. Nobody gives a shit about the petroleum industry down here. Even my competitors are the kind of people I'd invite over for a cold beer at a Southern football game."

"Really?" I said. "Any new competitors in the vicinity lately?"

Carter scratched his beard and fondled his wineglass. "Y'know, PetroJet bought out a few dealers in Magee last year. They're the only recent additions to the southern scene. But what would they know about stuff like this?" He rubbed his eyes tiredly and sighed. "I don't even have a word to call it. I keep calling it 'stuff.'"

"Don't call it anything right now," I said. "Who else knows about this?"

"Dee, Matthew, Craig, probably their families. I'm sure it's filtered down to the grunts, but how often do I see them?"

"Point taken." I speared the last bit of filet and popped it into my mouth, savoring the taste of a finely done piece of meat. Still, I'd pay for it later on. My genetics allowed for little in the way of fatty foods, and I'm forced to keep a hefty bottle of Rolaids in my medicine cabinet at all times.

"The way I see it, Carter," I said, folding my napkin; "someone's fucking with you. Could be one of the many people you pass off responsibility to when you should be taking care of things yourself. But that's a moot point now. How much are you in the hole?"

"Over seven-hundred grand," Carter breathed slowly.

"*Ouch.* Well, I don't see how I can help other than give you some advice. Sell this bitch before word gets out to the rest of the market that DPI's starting to flounder."

"I *told* you I'm not ready to sell!" Carter protested. "And besides, *if* someone's scamming me for money, I want to know who so I can take him down to New Orleans and work the fucker over with a tire iron."

"How poetic," I said. "So *what* do you want from me?"

Carter drained the rest of his wine and fixed me with a stare. "I want you to find out who's messing with my business."

The laugh escaped my lips before I had a chance to stifle it. "Carter, I'm just a brass technician. I don't know anything about looking into something like this."

"Listen to you. Remember that time when you framed that guy in your old fraternity for money laundering because he ratted on your boys for all that alleged hazing shit a few years back? People are *still* talking about that one, Jack. If you can do it one way, you got the other way in the bag."

I took a deep breath, remembering the incident in question. As it happened, the mook I set up had pissed off a lot of good brothers in the frat when he sang to the national fraternity about hazing. Three good pals of mine got expelled, and one had been in danger of criminal proceedings because of some other shady things he'd been running out of the chapter house. In exchange for a free ride through my pledgeship, I set the mook up with a phony laundering scheme connected to some of the dons down on the coast. There was never a dearth of cash on the Gulf Coast, and with all the casinos in the area, it's a foregone conclusion that there's bound to be dirty money lying around. A few well-placed calls to some friends of some friends, and the whistle-blower disappeared from Hattiesburg faster than a drop of rain in El Paso. It didn't get the brothers back in, but it felt good. Well, to some of us.

Carter seemed to think the fraternity incident made me an investigator, but in my mind, I was just a lazy old asshole smoking cigarettes and fixing brass horns. Investigation was my buddy Rick's purview, and he wasn't even family. Well, he wasn't family to the Dooleys, although I considered him more blood than most folks bearing the Big D on their linen. Regardless, investigation occupies the same continuum as the concurrent discipline of research, in which I *did* have some skills. Few people these days can operate a microfiche, but, man, I love that shit. Give me a dark library and a basement full of microfilm any day, and I'll find your huckleberry. I couldn't help remembering a line from the Kittlemeyer book I'd started reading earlier in the day: *"Step lively if you want to keeping stepping."*

I bit a fingernail, considering. Then I made the jump.

"It'll cost," I said.

"Name it," Carter said,

"Fifty grand, all in cash. Half up front, the rest on completion. Plus expenses as I see fit." I reached for the small notepad and pen

I always kept in my jacket. "And I won't guarantee anything short of a full track of the guilty parties. *If* I find them."

Carter's eyebrows slowly climbed the length of his forehead. "Fifty *thousand*? Christ, Jack, why don't you just ask for a goddamn private gold reserve?"

"Why don't I?" I said, deadpan. "Carter, you obviously want something more than simple criminal charges filed against the guilty here. If that means I have to start tailing people and hiding in dark alleys and going through bank records, then it's gonna cost. What's that you told me back when I asked you for that loan to go to Europe? Oh, yeah. 'It costs a little more for first class... *baby*.'"

Carter sighed and put his head in his hands. "You and Duke were right. I should retire."

"Whatever." I set the notepad down and uncapped the pen. "You in?"

"Of course, I am. What's the first step?"

"You let me worry about that. Now give me the particulars. What's this driver's name again? Helbert?"

"Henkel, Al Henkel. You want his jacket?"

I shook my head as I wrote Henkel's name down in my notepad. "Later. Who's in charge of PetroJet? Anyone you know?"

"Bill Finley, up in Jackson," Carter said. "The guy running the local scene in Magee is Fred Acheson. I think their plant's down in south Louisiana somewhere."

"Find out for me. Matter of fact, get me a folder on everything you can gather on PetroJet. Take it home with you, and I'll pick it up tomorrow." I scrawled a few more notes down, thinking ahead. "Have that twenty-five grand ready for me tomorrow, too. Do you remember the exact profit loss at DPI?"

"Uhhh, seven-hundred-twenty-three thousand and something," Carter said, searching his memory. "You want that too?"

"Nah, it's not that important now."

"It is to me."

"Actually, it is to your wife, Carter. Aunt Dee's always been the one with the sweet tooth for high society, right?" I winked at him from across the table, and Carter just lowered his head with a grunt. "Find out about those stocks too, but be discreet. Get me names and traders specifically."

"All right." Carter bobbed his head up and down. "You want a credit card for expenses?"

"Are you daffy? Hell, no. Open a new account at some pot-luck supper bank in Petal and dump about two grand in there. I'll get the numbers later, but make sure you and me are the only ones with access to it." I looked up for a moment. "And for Pete's sake, Carter, don't tell Dee about this. She's got a mouth on her the size of Manhattan."

Carter smirked and couldn't help but laugh. "Yeah, okay. Anything else?"

I reviewed my notes and was satisfied that I had enough for a starting point. "No, I think I can work with this for now."

"Nice notepad," Carter said, noticing the gold-emblazoned initials on the leather pad. "Your dad give that to you?"

"For graduation," I said. "I keep it on me in case I need to write shit down like song lyrics or something that just pops into my head. Comes in real handy."

Carter grunted again and looked at his watch. "I need to be getting back. When will you get started?"

"Tomorrow," I said, pocketing the notepad. "I need to get my shit together."

"See?" Carter accused, pointing a finger at me. "I knew you were the right guy for this."

I half-shrugged, some semblance of a grin coming to bear on my face. "Yeah, maybe. We'll see." I grasped Carter's forearm and shook it roughly. "Be easy, Uncle Carter. I'll be by the house tomorrow morning."

"Later, baby," Carter said, holding the grip for a moment more. "And, Jack? Thanks."

I returned Carter's infamous wink and grinned back, throwing my jacket on over the khaki button-up shirt. "Family's family, Uncle C. Holler atcha."

As I walked out of Chesterfield's, I mused on the little notepad in my pocket and congratulated myself on actually putting some ink in it for the first time since Dad gave it to me.

Sitting in my car, I ran through an endless repertoire of questions and puzzles in the wake of Carter's pseudo-assignment. If he was willing to pay fifty grand to his nephew for something like this, then the risk must be pretty big. I figured he wasn't exactly the clean angel himself, and limited police involvement would please him to no end.

I mused on the suddenness of it all as I sat there in the parking lot, watching Carter amble out of the restaurant and get in his Cadillac. Earlier that day, I'd been wallowing in the selfsame routine of life in Hattiesburg, and now I actually had the prospect of an out. After all, fifty grand could go a long way in some place like Fort Worth, for example. Something didn't sit quite well with me though, and I chalked it up to the jitters I always get when walking into a new situation with no guide. To be fair, I had never done anything like this before. Maybe the jitters were something else. Excitement. The New.

Heretofore, in every circumstance or event, I'd had somebody to help me along in whatever it was I was trying to do. Frank Vandy, my mentor at the music store, had invested several years of his personal time in training me to be a brass instrument repairman. My Dad had contributed a lot to my involvement in the band. More than one teacher at Southern had shepherded me through many a daunting research thesis. This time, however, Jack Dooley was on the back roads alone.

I looked into the rearview mirror, watching the calm positioning of dark brown eyes and age marks way too pronounced for a twentysomething man. The curl to the corners of my mouth was unmistakable though.

"Smile, you rat bastard," I said to my reflection. "It's yer berfday."

As I gunned the Honda and pulled out into traffic, I noticed the Kittlemeyer novel on the passenger seat. I had left it face down, open to the chapter I'd last read, obviously anticipating coming right back to it after lunch. The soft, thin paper gave no resistance as I dog-eared one page's corner and shut the book.

"Plenty more solutions where that came from, Charley," I said, and lit a cigarette.

I'll admit now to my complete lack of experience in anything resembling the criminal investigatory process at this point in my life. All the knowledge I'd accumulated over the years about people, motive, crime, investigation, and two-fisted fantasy fuckery came from an assortment of books and movies. Leonard taught me how to get away with robbery. Spillane taught me how to swagger (badly). Vachss taught me about scamming the establishment. Simon taught me the necessary steps in identifying the guilty and how to deal with them.

The one I would miss from this reflection at the time, however, was Donald Westlake. Or Richard Stark, to crack the knuckle appropriate of a bone break. It took me a lot of long years after that moment to read about Parker and the sixties and revenge. Probably could have saved me some bad moves. Alas.

What I *did* have to work with was a rednecked knowledge of the basic degeneracy of southern culture, my own all-points initiative in all things extraordinary, and a datebook with a lot of phone numbers in it. I had Rick Sears on the phone before dusk.

"Brother, brother!" Rick's excitable voice filtered back through the line. "It's not Saturday. Why are you calling me?"

"Nice to hear you, too, asshole," I chuckled. "How's life in the Army?"

"Man, there's a reason why you'd never make a decent government employee," Rick laughed. "Your GS-rating would be a negative number."

"Never mind that. Listen, you gonna be available on that end of the line for a while? I might need your expert insight for some shit that's going down here in the near future."

"In Hattiesburg? What did Ma Joe Funky get porked by the cow again?" Ouch. Rick colleged at Sam Houston State University in Huntsville, Texas. Pretty great school for criminal justice adherents. I'm still in the process of living that one down.

"Nice. No, I'm into something caper-ish for my uncle at DPI. You're the bright boy with the Quantico qual, so I figured I'd mooch talent."

"Nice to be appreciated. You know I've got it for you whenever you need it, brother, but what's the deal? You don't exactly sound like you're fixing trumpets."

I grinned. "I'm not. I'll be in touch when I need something. I'm just making sure you're not gonna be jungle fucking with the CIA on some silly-ass exercise anytime soon."

"Please. Yeah. I'll be here."

"Be easy, huh, brother?"

"Anytime, anywhere, Jack. Later."

Armed with the knowledge that my FBI connection would stand solid for me, I set about collecting the rest of my wits for the weeks to come. At that moment, there really wasn't much to do except clear my schedule and start making notes for the course of my work ahead. I'd come to cherish this personal conviction I have. It involves superiority in a way that may seem quite offensive to most people. But not to me. If you asked me, my only real criteria for judge of character centered on intelligence. Common sense, skill, even everyday people interaction. The man who couldn't distinguish between a subject and a predicate was the lowest form of life to me. The man who thought ambition was a four-letter word was useless to me. The man who beat his wife and ignored the growing hate in his son's eyes was the greatest example of the weak to me. In my purview, right then and there, Hattiesburg, Mississippi... I knew I could wade through these stubborn hillbillies and come away smelling of Old Spice and tequila. *These are slow, unimaginative people,* I told myself. *And that is my greatest weapon.*

I was so wrong.

3.

THE DOC AND THE DUKE

The way I figured it, a simple analysis of the problem would present me with more insight than any surveillance that the Hattiesburg Police Department would institute in this situation. Somebody was skimming money off of Carter Dooley's petroleum company. Over seven-hundred grand had performed a disappearing act that would make David Copperfield jealous. Accident reports in DPI's records indicated more physical losses than actually occurred, and of the four concrete incidents, a single man's name came up three times. Seven-hundred bills were a big motivator for anyone, even someone as financially secure as Bill Finley, CEO of PetroJet Chemical. Stocks made up the largest quotient in the DPI financial asset portfolio, and the plain fact of the matter is that none of the head guys at DPI worked hands-on enough to know what was really happening. That made it great grounds for an inside job, and all my warning lights put Al Henkel in a nasty red haze.

My instincts were something I'd never really considered worth a damn. For the better part of my life, I'd always relied on methodical analysis to get the heart of a problem. I suppose that was what made me a 4.0 student in college. Still, I envied people like Rick who were born with an innate sense about them that laser-pointed them to direct solutions in the most efficient and logical way, be it natural or environmentally-induced. Even before Rick went off to join the Bureau, he could make someone for a liar inside a minute's worth of conversation. He won a five-hundred dollar bet on the Oklahoma City bombing when it happened, guessing the day after the bomb went off that a pissed-off, skinhead, twenty-something white guy most likely masterminded the affair. At the time, I could've cared less. All I'd worried about was that the local television station had preempted *Star Trek* to cover the bombing.

I thought about all of this as I drove down 98 West to Canebrake. The private housing region was a Hattiesburg 'burb set up around this beautiful lake in the middle of a forest. Carter and Dee Dooley had lived there for ten years, building a New Orleans-style house on the northern bank that emulated the look and feel of those great, beautimous monstrosities you'd find in the Garden District near Tulane. Joining the Dooleys in Canebrake's litany of elite were doctors, lawyers, accountants, bank presidents, stockbrokers, and even a city councilman. Canebrake represented the ultimate facet of Harrisburg class division. For the right price, you could transcend the town-bound dunderheads and live the good life. I'm all for being around your own, but I still lived in the city limits. I didn't get to come out to Canebrake that much.

The rent-a-cop at the front gate let me in when he recognized the "ILDS" bumper sticker on my fender. ILDS was a phrase Uncle

Carter came up with a long time ago when he founded DPI. It reflected perfectly his worldview, and ILDS stickers littered everything from Carter's own vehicles to his company trucks to family cars. He even made hats, cups, polos, and all kinds of other swag with ILDS on it and distributed that swag far and wide. "ILDS" meant "I Love Dis Shit." Typical.

The access road ringed the lake in a semicircular pattern, offering drivers a magnificent view of the blue-on-blue water and the immense pines that shrouded houses all over the suburb. Tucked away in those thickets of straw and maple leaf were two-million dollar homes with BMWs, Mercedes, and Lexuses (Lexii?) parked in the driveways. A golf course stood a few miles back on the south end of the 'burb, and it would be a fine day in hell when the groundskeepers could speak anything other than a broken version of the English language.

Everything looked so white to me. White columns, white bricks, white mailboxes, white picket fences. White people. Whitey white folk. Perhaps the landowners intended this by design, or maybe it was just a common agreement among the Canebrake inhabitants. I grew up in a lower middle-income household with a single mom and a bratty sister, and our first house's lawn took ten minutes to mow. These houses could fit all three of the houses in which I'd ever lived inside their perimeters.

One thing that really peeved me about southern living was all the goddamn trees. I gave up picking leaves and straw out of my windshield wipers a long time ago when Mom moved us from East Texas to Fort Worth. East Texas might as well act as the gateway to the True South, for a lot of reasons, but mainly to me because of its piney woods. In North Texas, you can stand at the heart of any city or town and still see the vast plains beyond, the thin line where sky meets land. There was always a sense in Texas of something bigger than the place you stood, and the grandeur of suburban areas with the big city in the distance were a thing of beauty at night. Driving east from DFW along Highway 87 or I-20, at a certain stretch – Terrell-way but not quite Tyler – the plains of North Texas give way to sudden clusters of immense pine tree forests, blotting out the sun unless it's directly overhead. Similarly in Mississippi, if you wanted any kind of view of the land at scale, you had to barter a helicopter ride and take a camera.

Canebrake was particularly heavy-wooded, and even though I'd been to the Dooley house out there before, I'd found myself lost on more than one occasion. Fucking trees. You don't see environmentalists in Texas cuddling up to creosote bushes and bemoaning the use of paper products worldwide. If half the populace of Hattiesburg cared one way or the other, the tree-huggers at Southern would be hosting orgies all over the town.

Carter had left a note on the front gate of his circular drive that read, "Jack: Gone to lunch with Dee. Your package is on the kitchen counter." No such thing as trespassing or locked doors at Canebrake either. The place was too intimidating for any kind of real criminal activity, and enough neighbors looked out for one another's properties. The white backdrop created a perfect canvas on which to identify off-colored intrusions and justify hushed calls to the security gate and the local police. Nothing but a bunch of stereotypical white folk here at Canebrake.

I let myself in the back door and got a good look again at what Carter's travails in life had brought him. Immaculate furniture littered the sitting and dining rooms, hardwood floors keenly polished and adorned with some kind of Moroccan rugs. Bookcases lined the walls of the den with untouched copies of Tennessee Williams, Faulkner, and a multitude of modern southern writers whom Carter had never read let alone cared about. But their inclusion on the shelves was a must to maintain appearances. Absolutely *everyone* was doing it, after all. The John Grisham Effect demanded at least keepsake copies of *A Time to Kill*, *The Firm*, and *The Client*, especially leatherbound or special edition trade paperbacks that looked just *divine* on the shelf next to Faulkner. For fuck's sake.

Aunt Dee had designed the kitchen all in white (surprise!) with black and gray shade accents, from the microwave down to the tile. A small stack of manila folders bound by a rubber band rested on the counter island next to the stove. My name was written on the top folder, and I picked the package up and tucked it under my arm. I tipped my sunglasses down to the tip of my nose to look around at the veritable mansion spread out before me.

"One day," I told myself.

While I was in Canebrake, I figured I might as well run across the lake and say hello to Doc Faller. Faller had retired from his thir-ty-year teaching position at the University of Southern Mississippi last year after a long battle with the board of trustees over some material he had used in one of his postmodern culture classes. I'd taken Doc Faller's sociology course to fill out my electives, and the guy became a real treat to see morning after morning. He performed rather than taught. His doctoral thesis was a thing of legend in Mississippi: a two-hundred page diatribe on the effects of political office on the male and female genitalia. When the the-sis finally got picked up by newspapers in the seventies, seventeen outed Mississippi politicians had been forced to resign based on various inappropriate sexual encounters including five cases of infi-delity, two cases of undiscovered homosexuality (a big no-no in the public American south), and one very revealing case of bestiality. Doc Faller hadn't cared one whit about the ruckus he had caused, but after the mayor of Pass Christian offered him a bribe to pub-licly recant the thesis in an op-ed, the Doc finally saw the fun of it all. Since then, he'd made a nice profit on the side from consulting with lots of investigative reporters doing scandal stories and writing columns of his own in *The Gazebo Gazette* and *The Clarion-Ledger*.

By the time I'd enrolled in Doc Faller's Sociology 445 class ("The Penis, The Vagina, and All Things Southern"), the university had been out for the man's blood for some time. His prestige had faded away into prehistory, and despite his popularity with students, Faller had piqued the ire of more than one of the university administrators. Hundreds of students barged into closed hearings in support of the Doc, all of them protesting the board's investigation by running naked through the hearing hall. The Doc had gotten a big laugh out of the whole affair, but with the money he had stashed away from his jaunts with Koppel, Cronkite, and Jennings, he was ready to cash in his chips. So, much to the student body's chagrin, Old Doc Faller resigned from the college, bought a house at Canebrake and made a new name for himself among the masses of single women in Hattiesburg.

As I parked the Honda, I could see through the fronds in the front yard that the Doc was spending his afternoon out back by the pool. I walked around the house, careful not to tread too heavily on the steroid-enhanced grass that always seemed a little too green. Coming out onto the marble, three-tier patio around back, I saw the Doc sprawled in a lawn chair under an umbrella, *Hattiesburg American* folded before him. As I approached, I saw a pair of well-tanned buttocks beckoning from the other side of the pool. Shaking my head and squinting, I could make out a naked woman lying face-down on another lawn chair. A rather form-fit naked woman at that.

"Jack Dooley!" Doc Faller's gravelly voice shocked me out of my stupor. Obviously, he had seen me gawking at the inviting ass on his pool patio and had decided to have fun. The Doc towered over me at a cool six-foot-nothing, his sandy gray hair sticking up and out in many directions as was the norm. For an Irish guy, you'd expect Doc to have a ruddy complexion or a rough crimson sheen to his skin. Instead, he was about as tan as anyone down south, having spent plenty of time on the beaches of the Gulf Coast. I grinned sheepishly as the taller man pumped my hand, looking down at me through stylized Ray-Bans that cut a dark streak through his silver hair.

"Hey, Doc. I was in the neighborhood; thought I'd drop by."

The Doc jerked his head over his shoulder at the ass on the lawn chair. "Drop that?"

"I wish. Local girl?"

"Yup!" the Doc said proudly, jamming his hands into the pockets of his maroon morning pants. "She's some kind of secretary for this attorney downtown. I was too busy focusing on those tits to listen to the guy's name."

"Secretary?" We turned in tandem to observe the lounging woman, peering over the top ridges of our sunglasses like Chris Farley and Adam Sandler from that Schmitt's Gay bit on *Saturday Night Live*. "Doc, she's got to be no more than twenty. You sure she's not interning?"

Doc made a broad, toothy smile. "Like it matters?" he said.

"You are a dirty old man." I followed him over to a table on the veranda and took a seat while the Doc poured a viscous green concoction out of a silver decanter into two mugs. "Little cool to be sunning, huh, Doc?"

"Last day before the real cold weather hits, I figger," Doc Faller said, passing me one of the mugs. "Irish coffee, snapper?"

"You're too kind, Doc," I said, taking the drink. "Whiskey and ass, all on one lawn. I really ought to move out here some day."

The Doc gulped half his mug down and poked a hand inside his tank top to scratch at the wily hair of his chest. His thin yet toned shoulders bounced in tandem with the lazy shrug he offered me, and I took heart in knowing that the Doc found retirement more fulfilling than others of his ilk had.

"Ehhh," he groaned; "the bleedin' administrators keep trying to charge me for inappropriate behavior. Every time one of the old farts next door comes outside and catches me going down on a blonde, I *never* hear the end of it."

"More than I can say," I laughed, resisting the urge to blink from the Irish coffee's acerbic taste. "How you been, Doc?"

"Can't complain. I've been corresponding with some lad in D.C. who's all over this Congressional hearing they're having for that senator who lied on a police report about his sexual orientation. I keep telling him the guy's queer, but no one listens! Just you wait! Twenty-point columns in *The Washington Post* next month: 'Senator Found Gay But Not Guilty.'"

"Does it matter that he's gay?" I asked.

Doc shrugged. "It matters that he might have had something to do with the homicide of a gay lad. Jack, you look a little peaked, m'boyo. You feeling all right?"

"Aw, it's nothing," I said. "I'm getting mixed up in this private investigation for my uncle and his petroleum company. It's pretty hush-hush, and I'm still kicking around ideas on how to find an angle." I shrugged. "Industrial espionage-type stuff, I guess."

"Ah, an out for the Texan!" The Doc was one of the few people I'd shared my antipathy toward all things Mississippian. Doc Faller had a unique perspective on the whole thing, the son of a Northern Irish family who had been too poor to escape a rapidly declining economy and a deteriorating safety situation. The Doc was a well-known athlete, having sponsored his own immigration to the States through a boxing scholarship. While taking his course at college, we'd swapped many a tale about the old days for both of us. Funny how sometimes your professors turn out to be better friends than your classmates.

"I trust you're coming at this from an analytical angle primarily," the Doc was saying. "That's your big strength, y'know."

"Yeah, but I can't help feeling that I'm reading too much into this. I mean, after all, this is Hattiesburg, *Mississippi*. Not some gold coast haven for drugs and crime bosses like… I dunno, Chicago or Boston. Or Medellin."

"You'd be surprised, snapper," the Doc said with a warning finger. "Don't underestimate your environment to such a heavy degree. There's things about people down here that don't work normally like they do in more sensible places."

"What, are you Obi-Wan Kenobi now?" I couldn't suppress my laugh. "Doc, one of the rules in detective's lexicon is that there's usually no big mastermind behind a crime. If you think it's the victim's secretary or brother or love child, then usually it turns out to be so."

"Okay, let me go point-to-point with you then, snapper. What's the difference between a redneck and a hillbilly?"

"A redneck has some grasp of reality," I responded, one eye narrowing in thought. "He knows that he's a wannabe in some sense, that there's something more than his own rotten life out there. A hillbilly's just ignorant."

The Doc folded his legs up under him on the deck chair, a Cheshire grin plastered on his face. "Then why do so many rednecks stay rednecks? Why don't they rise up out of their primordial muck of engine grease and chewing tobacco to become, as you so see, *respectable* citizens?"

"The redneck cannot grasp the edges of ambition," I said, adopting the Doc's own professorial tone. "He has a basic understanding of what's out there, but cannot understand why he can't be a part of it. Thus, the redneck stagnates."

"And if our theoretical redneck *did* grasp the concept of ambition in its entirety?"

"Then he'd..." I pinched my eyebrows together in confusion. Fucking Doc Faller. "What are you getting at?"

"If you take the very same typical redneck and put him in a sound booth with one of these rich esquires out here at Canebrake," the Doc said, "then listen to one of them on the phone, you wouldn't be able to distinguish between the two."

I shook my head and grimaced at the Doc's logic. "That's environment though, Doc. Most everybody born and raised in the south talks like that on one level or another."

The Doc slammed his whiskey mug on the table with satisfied grunt. "Exactly! See what I'm getting at?"

I put a finger to my lips, considering the old-timer's words. "The enlightened redneck is he who can use his stereotyped appearance to deceive others."

The Doc leaned back in his chair and dug a cigar out of his pants pocket. "Or...?"

Now it was my turn to shrug. "I'm not seeing it."

He winked at me. "You'll figure it out, snapper."

My mug shot up in salute, a half-serious look of praise and adoration on my face. "To the Irish goes the credit, Doc. Cheers."

The Doc clinked mugs with me and took a moment to semi-regurgitate some of the phlegm that characteristically got stuck in his basso throat. "Jackie, you need any help, just yell. Things can get kind of stale in this burg sometimes."

My grin matched the Doc's inch for inch. "'Preciate ya, Doc."

Checking into the bank statements Carter left for me in the folders, I found that he had indeed deposited twenty-five-thousand dollars in a single account at the SouthBank branch in Petal. Another phone call and some finagling with a woman behind the desk got me the account numbers on a second account at Deposit Guarantee (affectionately referred to as Desperate Guaranty by the locals), care of one Jack Dooley, containing a grand. The lady told me I could come pick my ATM card up anytime after one. I had to give it to Uncle Carter. When he wanted something done, he didn't fool around.

My next stop that Saturday afternoon was downtown Hattiesburg. Fifty years ago, the brick buildings and tight one-way streets exuded a harsh bustling of business and commerce. Some of Hattiesburg's oldest corporations began their lives downtown, from Sacks and Son Supply to First National. With the great move west in succeeding years, downtown had slowly degenerated into a breeding ground for vice and decay. Once-great buildings leaned precariously to one side with condemnation notices plastered on their windows. Street signs remained in a constant state of disrepair. The only places worth mentioning downtown anymore were the police station and the Forrest County Court House.

I drove down Main Street past a row of legal offices belonging to some of the more hotshot Hattiesburg attorneys. A lot of them received kickbacks from the mayor's office to revitalize the region, but honestly... tax lawyers and paralegals aren't exactly the best choice for deterring the lowlife element of downtown Harrisburg. My course took me past the only other saving grace in downtown nowadays, the California Sub Shop. Owned and operated for generations by a family whose name I couldn't even pronounce, the diner was tucked away on the corner of First and Pine. It drew people from all over the city for its ham and cheese sandwiches, seafood platters, and fried mozzarella sticks. I got a kick out of eating anywhere with an actual serving counter, so the phrase "I'm going to California!" had become something of a minor urban catcall in my small circle of acquaintances and family.

Crossing the train tracks into the seedy part of town, I veered away from a potential crack deal at a broken down auto shop and turned north. A large collection of warehouses sprang up from the deterioration in this section of town. The East Shipping Company had been physically inactive for decades, but the East brothers, Thom and Danny, had turned the joint into something much more. A relic of sixties interior decoration, the brothers rented out office space for a hundred bucks a month and used the money to show a profit on the books. The secondary source of income for the brothers had proven quite prosperous and allowed Danny, the junior of the two, time to get into his favorite pastime: restoring East's fleet of broken-down shipping trucks.

Danny East, a guy I'd only met once or twice, was himself the subject of another small urban legend in Hattiesburg. Across the street from the East building was a large lot where a bunch of state housing projects from the fifties had sunk down the social ladder to gang-controlled territory. The criminal element in that part of town remained a constant source of nuisance for all Hattiesburg residents, but not so that it warranted organized attention from the authorities. The cop shop stood only a few blocks away, and yet anyone could drive down South Pine and choose from a lively collection of drugs, hookers, and/or guns at any time of day (although...go at night, if that's your thing, brah). The boys that controlled the lot adjacent from the East building called themselves the Smokies. I figured the name originated partly in spite of the police, but more than likely had obvious other connotations.

A few years ago, a big story went down when the Smokies got involved in a homicide that took place in their lot. Making a show for the press, the cops set up snazzy flashing lights and questioned everyone even a slight shade away from white. I didn't know if the Smokies actually killed the victim, but from the way the cops janked them around, it looked like most of the major muscle movements were bogus. Danny East had been watching the entire thing from the truck yard, and when the cops finally left (minus any arrests, mind you), he'd walked over to the Smokies lot to strike up a conversation. Imagine a guy in greasy coveralls with one of the most obnoxious southern accents in the state walking into a crowd of pissed-off black guys and then *asking* them for a favor.

Luckily for Danny, the Smokies' leader lived up to none of the traditional gang stereotype. Def-J, as he was called on the street, had listened with interest while Danny illustrated the security problems about maintaining a business in what had become "gangland" in Hattiesburg. Strangely enough, this had made sense to Def-J. You see, Def-J possessed a degree in accounting, the result of a hard-earned education at the University of Southern Mississippi. With affirmative action singing its swansong at the time of his graduation, Def-J had parlayed his know-how into business on familiar home turf. Returning to where he'd grown up, the African-American Merit Scholar had assumed control of the Smokies after ratting out their former leader for narcotics trafficking across state lines to the state police. After that, Def-J had spent months providing the Staties and the Hattiesburg police with information leading to arrests all over town on narcotics, murder, prostitution, and other unsolved crimes.

While the general gang populace of downtown Hattiesburg scratched their heads and wondered what the hell the college boy was doing, the cops gradually came to understand that Def-J was doing their job for them. In return, they left him alone. In less than six months, Def-J had consolidated the Hattiesburg gang element into a single, organized band, purged of liabilities. Instead of finding a decent job in the private sector as a CPA and paying Uncle Sam regularly for his toil, Def-J was now taking home cash money with no strings attached. This money had paid off his student loans, had funded his sister's move to Colorado, and had bought his ailing father a remodeled home in a run-down projects lot across from the East Brothers.

So it had been no real surprise when Def-J agreed to Danny's proposal. In exchange for the Smokies' eyes and ears on loan for his building's security, Danny had appeared as a witness in court and gotten three Smokies off a bum murder rap. The relationship hadn't ended there as Danny frequently paid one or two Smokies to help him out on the truck lot or maybe clean the building's windows up from time to time or perhaps wash his car.

Danny's brother Thom, raised in the era of segregation and lynchings, had little love for Def-J's posse. Like many of the white folk in Hattiesburg, he liberally used the words "jig" and "afro-hound" and one or two more that I don't need to repeat. To him, Danny's relationship with Def-J had just become another opportunity to slight a people whom he did not understand nor care to respect. Thom would have shit himself had he figured out that Def-J's annual income almost tripled anything Thom made for himself. Thom would sometimes go outside the office to find one of the younger black kids in the neighborhood and offer him a fiver to "Go wash my car, boy." Although, he used worse terms, and that always lead to a dust-up that someone had to defuse. Most times that was Danny, always on the lookout for his aging older brother, but sometimes it was a guy named Duke...whom we'll get to in a minute.

I drove past the Smokies' lot and saw a group hanging out on the front porch of the only house still fit to live in on the lot. Def-J's father lived alone inside, nursing some illness that no one could convince the man was fatal. Still, one of Def-J's proclamations to his flock was that his father was to be waited on hand and foot. The Smokies frequently took turns in house upkeep and shopping trips for the old man's necessities. I waved pleasantly as I pulled into the East building's parking lot. A few of the gang-bangers (many of them no older than I) waved back, vaguely recalling that I was related to one of Mister Danny's residents upstairs.

People could learn a lot from The Smokies. I'd rather hang around guys like them instead of the sort I'd encountered in places like Canebrake or The Mahogany Bar. It's all a matter of station, I think. Not class or social stratification, mind you, but more of Darwinian evolution. The fat cats of Hattiesburg may end up living their years in relative comfort, but it was people like the Smokies who had become accustomed to the true tests of life that so many of us try to ignore. And when you get right down to it, you can never really count on help from the upper gentry in Hattiesburg. They'd just as soon sell you out to protect their own ass than speak to you politely. But with folks like the Smokies, you knew that there was an unspoken bond of trust and mutual respect. Most of the Smokies would lay down in traffic for Def-J, and some would go a lot further than that. Ask me, that's real respect.

With only three rooms currently operating in the East building, the brothers saw little point in maintaining anything but the bathrooms. I walked past the receptionist's counter as I entered, raising a cloud of dust from the decades-vacant desk as I swished by. A 1986 issue of *Playboy* rested on the desk nearby, so old that no one even bothered to stop and flip through it anymore. Bushy. Following dim lighting upstairs, I ambled down a corridor of empty offices until I reached one whose placard read, "Dooley Consulting Services."

As usual, my Dad was engrossed in a tense game of *Air Force Pilot* on the computer. When I entered, his concentration faltered, and I heard the distinct computer-generated noise of a splash-down from the speakers. Dad smacked the desk in frustration and bounced backwards in his chair, fixing me with a harsh glare.

"I had the Red Baron in my *sights*!" he exclaimed.

"My heart bleeds," I said, plopping down into a sofa too old even for mothballs. "Whataboutcha, Pops?"

Like us all, Duke Dooley fought an uphill battle with hypertension, weight, and life. He made up for it by just being *him*. On the phone, no one could tell us apart. In filling out to adulthood in the past ten years, I'd taken on Dad's rackety, carcinogenic-plagued voice. Unlike me, however, Dad's once-chestnut hair had gone to grey, and the wear lines on his face and hands showed just how hard this guy had worked his ass off to make good on his responsibility to his kids. Still, Duke had that backstreet, jive-talking way about him that had survived the fifties, sixties, seventies, and eighties...not to mention three wives and four children. I make a habit of not getting into fights and scraps and the like; don't think for a minute that I actually enjoy pain. But fuck with my Pops, and I'll surgically remove your jugular with a coat hanger.

Duke, of course, was not Dad's real name because...come on, right? He had Carter to thank for that. Growing up, John Wayne movies entranced Dad, especially the World War II oeuvre. *She Wore a Yellow Ribbon, Sands of Iwo Jima, Flying Leathernecks, Hondo, The Sea Chase...* Dad could name 'em all from childhood jaunts to the movie theater and the drive-in. Carter, more of a car guy than a movie guy, nicknamed his little brother Duke and it's stuck ever since.

"Bobbin' and weavin', baby!" Duke said, popping a Vantage Ultra-Light between his teeth. "Y'know how I was bitchin' last month about slow business? Christ, I can't keep up with it all now."

"Prolly help if you laid off that World's Greatest Fighter Pilot alter ego of yours," I said, joining him for a smoke and nodding my head at the computer.

"Bite me," my Dad said with a chuckle. "One day, now, I'll be *training* those boys over at Camp Shelby."

"Camp Shelby's for the infantry, Dad. The only planes in Hattiesburg are up on blocks behind some portly fella's fixit joint."

"Whatever. What are you doing here?"

"Need a favor." I got up and opened one of Carter's folders, removing Al Henkel's driver qualification record and company dossier. "You ever heard of this guy while working DPI's safety seminars?"

Duke took the file and glanced over it, checking the photo and shrugging through a squint-eyed stare. "Looks like all the other drivers out there: wineheads. What's the deal?"

"Carter's got me looking into something for him around the plant," I said, leaning on Dad's desk and tapping a half-inch's worth of ash into an ashtray. "He thinks there's something fishy about this guy's previous accident reports. He hasn't told you?"

"No." Dad frowned, looking into the manila folder I'd opened before him. "He hasn't told me anything, that son of a bitch."

"Watch it," I cautioned, smacking his hand away. "He's a son of a bitch, so are you. Anyway, he wants me to keep this on the down-low, so forget I told you, huh? You want any more, go talk to Carter."

Duke Dooley grimaced and allowed a slow chortle to build up in the back of his throat. "What, you're an *investigator* all of a sudden? Neat-O."

"It's just something to do, and it pays nice, too." I sank back down onto the sofa and rubbed my eyes. "When's DPI due for its next safety renewal?"

"January, I think," Dad said after some thought. "You want to handle it?"

"Can I?"

Dad shrugged. "You still have the certification. Saves me the trouble, too. I go out there, and Carter and I end up sitting on the office porch drinking cold beer and shooting the shit."

I rolled my eyes and put my cigarette out. "Hard times."

Duke and Carter Dooley grew up in a working-class New Orleans neighborhood before moving to Meridian, Mississippi, where both attended high school. Two years apart, the Dooley brothers shared favor for bullshit, trickery, borderline graft, and good times. Carter had introduced Duke to everything a boy should and should not do in New Orleans, from early adventures in brothel review to peeling tails and sucking heads off crawfish in the French Market. Carter possessed the head for business, always figuring out ways to game systems and make money while also having a big time of it. You could always find Carter sweet-talking somebody out of some shit and drinking a cold beer while tooling around in his baby blue '55 Chevy, and that description—free of hyperbole—stuck with Carter from adolescence to today.

Duke, on the other hand, fell in love with music as soon as their daddy bought him his first Beatles record, and he immediately eschewed school for the drums. Duke found natural aptitude with percussion, and he joined a band in Meridian to record and play. He dropped out of high school to tour with the band, The Summertime Blues, and went on to write and record a couple of EPs that sold modestly alongside sixties acid rock acts. To Duke, the sixties music scene offered more reward than a job behind a desk somewhere, and he reveled in the life, even getting as far as recording some fill-in sessions with Skunk Baxter, Walter Becker, and Donald Fagen at Muscle Shoals for Steely Dan. It was at Muscle Shoals where Duke learned to chase the dragon, something that still blows my mind given his current career vector.

Growing up, Duke taught me how to sing and harmonize as early as he could. He would roust me from bed early on Saturday morning to go get donuts and chocolate milk at Shipley's, and in the car, we would belt out two-part harmonies on everything from "Rikki Don't Lose That Number" to Toto's "Hold the Line." He introduced me to Yes, pre-*90125*, which excoriated my young mind on the bizarre sounds of prog rock... but we never listened to Rush. Duke could still be picky.

"Yeah, sure, do the renewal," said Duke presently. All the piss kits are downstairs in the shed. You remember how to do all the paperwork?"

"Yeah." One corner of my mouth surfed north as I chuckled. "And I better get started this week if I'm going to finish by January."

Duke made a loud noise of affirmation and slapped his armrests. "I knew it! You just want into DPI's files about that Henkel guy."

I shrugged nonchalantly. "So sue me if I'm a tricky bastard. It's your fault, motherfucker."

"It's the mailman's fault, shithead." We shared a bout of laughter, and Dad got up to retrieve a couple of Miller Lites from the fridge. Popping the top on one and handing me the other, he said, "What else is happening, Jack? You still seeing that girl?"

I growled on the normally off-limits topic of Jack's Love Life. "Who?"

"Y'know, that one you met months ago at Dewey's."

"Crys?" I had to take a quick gulp of beer to hide the discoloration of my face. "Uhhh... haven't talked to her in a while."

"Really? She was neat; you two hit it off great."

"Let's drop it, Dad, okay?" I shifted uncomfortably on the couch and changed the subject before he had a chance to answer. "How's Vickie and the baby?"

"Same as usual," Duke said with a nicotine-induced cough. "Elmo gets sick, Vickie's head explodes. Loses her mind, whether it's justified or not. I'm beginning to think it's some kind of sustained PMS thing."

"You mean Post-Masturbation Syndrome? I hate when that happens."

"Yeah, me too. Nah, everything's fine. That damn deck's gonna have to wait until a few of these customers pipe down. Fall's always the fun time of the year."

Dad's company, DCS, dealt in safety consultation with a number of petroleum and trucking companies in the south. People would pay him to come down to their truck farms and inspect vehicles, make sure they were in compliance with federal Department of Transportation regulations, and drug test all the drivers. Afterwards, a fat two or three grand landed in Pops' pocket. Pretty easy way to make money, what with ever-updating regulations frequently posted on the DOT website every couple of months. But when you have these ancient, decrepit fly-fishermen running trucking companies who can't comprehend a VCR much less the Internet, "easy" can be substituted with "scam." They actually make certifications for what Dad does.

DCS provided the financial backbone on which Duke's true passions lie: music and cars. The best thing I inherited from that man was a nuanced appreciation for and ability to play music. Oh, he wasn't a virtuoso by any stretch of a very limited imagination, but that guy *loved* to play percussion. He used to play drums exclusively, and he still did from time to time when his band needed him to, but Duke had found much more fun in the congas, bongos, and timbales. He beat on a beautiful set of blonde wood Toca congas and bongos with a Tito Puentes-inspired rack of timbales next to them. Around this setup, Duke hung every possible percussive instrument he could find: tambourines, maracas, shakers, a vibraslap, chimes, cymbals, all kinds of stuff. It took him goddamn hours to set the whole thing up every gig, but his crowds loved it. He would toss maracas and tambourines to the ladies in the crowd, entreating them to sing along with him on "Brown Eyed Girl" or "Sweet Home Alabama." Standing up made it easier for Duke to engage with a crowd, and this was the secret for most musicians:

we mostly do it for the crowd, no matter how damned introverted or OCD we may be. Duke rocked it.

Back when I first came to Hattiesburg and moved in with then-single Duke Dooley, the old man certified me with a computer-generated HazMat license and sent me off to do half his work. Like what I'd been for DPI, I got to travel a lot and make some easy cash collecting piss and filling out paperwork. Okay, so it's not investigating possible industrial espionage, but whaddya want? I was fresh out of high school, for Chrissake. Also: money.

I sloshed back a little bit more of my beer and set the remainder down on Dad's desk. "I gotta run, Pops. I'll let you get back to kicking hell out of the Germans."

As I turned for the door, Dad put on an introspective face as he regarded the computer and joystick. "Y'know... actually, I think I'll hunt some Russkies this time."

4.

FIRST DANCE

I arrived at Dooley Petroleum, Inc. by nine-thirty, Monday morning. A lot of the secretaries up front knew me from the old days of my couriership for Carter, so deception presented a unique challenge. Under the auspice of freelance work for Dooley Consulting Services, I wore my best denim shirt and khakis and even broke out the loafers. If I had to wear a tie, I'd decided, it was going to be a cool one, deception be damned. The black and white Looney Toons tie I'd dug out of the back of my closet completed the picture. Enter one Jack Dooley, safety consultant for DCS, doing his Uncle Carter a favor by coming early on DOT annual renewals.

DPI occupied a large site in the neighboring town of Petal, nestled inside a thick grove of tall pine. The train tracks running parallel to Highway 11 separated the plant grounds from the highway, and just over the berm, one could see the intricate latticework of silvery pipes and rusty storage tanks that composed the bulk of DPI's on-site propane distribution equipment. Further back on the lot was the motor pool, a squat warehouse with four red and white DPI tanker-trailers in the yard outside. Carter's other fifteen trucks must be on the road, much to my gratitude. I wanted a look at Henkel, not Country Joe Motherfucker and the Cockblockers.

The main office had evolved from a single mobile home in the eighties to a collection of patchwork trailers, painted and linked together in a way that provided plenty of office space. In another decade, the office additions could get out of hand without better planning. The haphazard double-wide organization with its series of interconnecting wooden balconies and walkways spoke of local flavor, a Bobby Joe or a Jimmy Ray who could fix you up just right, Mister Dooley, sure'n you know it. It reminded me of this joint on the Florida-Alabama state line called, wait for it... FloriBama. Similar concept: FloriBama featured bars constructed from modular living options like your double-wides combined with shacks, tin roofs, and whatever else could be pasted together to accommodate the beach-bound Gulf Coast rats that habited the joint. Great shrimp though.

I went in the back door where the porch adjoined the drivers' ready room and into the kitchen. From here, a newcomer had access to Carter's office, the dispatcher's room, and the records dump, where all the secretaries stacked unused paperwork and files. As soon as I entered, I saw Carter at the kitchen table talking to someone on the phone. He nodded to me when I flashed my tie at him and gestured with the briefcase in my hand.

I hunted Craig Hauser down in the dispatcher's office. Hauser had gone to school on Carter's ticket after an injury knocked him off the player's list for the Seattle Seahawks. Uncle Carter had a habit of taking young men under his wing and building them up into experienced, hard workers. In Hauser's case, Carter had found an invaluable part of the team at DPI. The six-foot-six father of two, dressed naturally in slacks and a golf shirt, was directing a driver query over the horn when I found him.

"Jackie!" Hauser yelled once he was done and turned the radio back over to the dispatcher. "Long time, buddy!"

"And then some, Craig." I let his hand crush mine in the handshake and managed to conceal my wince. "It's that time again."

"Already? Damn, I thought we just re-certified everybody."

"Well, your renewal date's not until January, but with the time it takes to test all your drivers, I figured I'd get an early start this year." I shrugged half-heartedly, gesturing with my briefcase. "Dad was too swamped to cover y'all this year, so I offered to help him out."

"Good man!" Hauser escorted back into the records room with that wide-ass grin that seemed to be a requirement for employment in DPI's upper echelons. "Have at it, Jack. Whatever you need, just holler for us, okay?"

"Cool. How's things?"

Hauser shrugged. "Winter's charging up, so we're getting ready for that season again. I'll be on the road for a while at the end of the month, doing the customer thing."

"Better you than me."

"Yeah, pity you didn't get any of those bullshit genes that Carter and your Dad have. How've you been?"

My inner deadpan face looked at the camera. "Can't complain. Hey, me and the band are gigging at Dewey's Alley this week; make sure you drop by. And bring Melinda if you can find a babysitter."

"If you guys are still playing '867-5309,' I'm on, buddy. Heard y'all had a good show out on Dauphin Street last month."

"Didn't suck. Three bars in as many days can get kinda old after a while, but it *was* Mobile. I don't care what you and my degenerate uncle keep saying: Dauphin has Bourbon Street beat for class."

"You'll get taken to task for that around here, Jack," Hauser chuckled, punching my shoulder lightly, which still fucking hurt because I'm weak as shit I guess. "By the way, Mardi Gras's coming up. You coming down for the parade?"

"Carter still marching with Pete Fountain?"

"You bet. We're supposed to be dressing up as Egyptians this year. If you want space, let us know soon so we can book a room. If we don't do it now, The Provincial will be full-up by February."

"I'll let you know, Craig, but thanks for the offer."

"You betcha, kiddo. Tell your Pops I said hi."

"Will do, Craig. Say, do me a favor and get a notice to all the drivers that I need drug tests from 'em, willya?"

"Can do, buddy."

Hauser left me in what looked like the ass end of records hell. File cabinets stacked on top of each other were overflowing with files and folders, columns of paper littered the floor, and the table in the middle of the room was ankle-deep in general stuff. With a sweep of my arm, I cleared the table (and several weeks' worth of dust) and set up shop.

Within the briefcase were all the essentials needed for a safety consultant. Multiple copies of driver safety test papers, Social Security and Mississippi Driver's License guidebooks, and of course, a lot of little transparent baggies with urine cups and sealant. It would be a while before any driver checked in with me; most of the backwoods populace of rural Mississippi hadn't yet gotten used to the fact that the federal government could legally subpoena their urine if they drove trucks carrying hazardous materials. While I had the time, I decided to check the files around me.

The disorganization was worse than I'd expected. Accounting files and accident reports were recorded in different places, and I couldn't discern where all the damn personnel records had been stashed. It would take me all day to go through this shit by myself, but the alternative was less desirable. Working with one of the high school intern girls back here would lead to all sorts of gossip about what I was doing, and I didn't have time to entertain some post-pubescent teenager who had stars in her eyes for a man, money, and children.

I accidentally happened upon a logbook of debits that had been lost under a pile of shipping invoices on the floor. The book wasn't up to date and only included a few details, but it was a start. I settled in to read and dug a Camel out of my pocket.

According to the book—which was actually a product delivery/pickup log for the entire company—DPI showed a good net profit from hard propane sales in the past three years. The general cost of delivery ran around two- to three-hundred dollars per truck plus stipends for the drivers. A fully loaded truck delivering a shipment from DPI to, say, Foxworth in Jackson, would gross a good grand when all was said and done. Figure in state and federal taxes and an additional miscellaneous cost (which usually meant "boss's take-home"), and a net delivery could come out at about eight-hundred. For an average twenty deliveries per day per truck, that was a nice haul for DPI.

The last fifteen entries in the logbook caught my attention: They were all logged in by Al Henkel. Henkel had delivered and/or picked up a total of twenty-seven-thousand water gallons of petroleum from March to July. After that, the book remained mysteriously blank. I took a legal pad out of my briefcase and scribbled this information down, including the dates of each shipment and their destinations. Maybe nothing, but then again, murder cases in places much loftier than Hattiesburg had been cracked on less.

I spent the next several hours poring through documents, invoices and logbooks, gleaning little more than a reminder of why I hadn't followed the family into the petroleum business. Tons of useless minutiae filled DPI's records room, paperwork and half-scribbled receipts that amounted to a whole tomb full of nothing in the final analysis. I recalled that Mississippi had some kind of documentation law for certain companies over a certain total grossing dollar, this from my tenure as Dad's assistant at DCS. Obviously, the stellar cast of national merit scholars in the secretarial office dumped everything back in the records room until a certain statute of limitations was reached, at which point the whole room was probably cleared and burned. Once again, southern living at its best.

It was almost one o'clock before I got my first driver. Stashed in the records room, no one had the slightest hint I was even on the premises, and that was just fine with me. In the hours of paper trailing I'd done, I'd found little of what I actually needed for the job, but it was still only the first day. The driver's appearance that afternoon made for a good break in the routine, keeping me fresh while I filled out safety reports and saw to it the guy filled each plastic cup with just enough urine to test. Some guys get in there and piss all over the cups and hand them back without cleaning them off. It's those sorts of drivers for whom I want to add a little pure cocaine to the sample.

I took a break after the drug test and called Pizza Hut to deliver me something to eat. While waiting around in the kitchen, I had time to go over what I knew already. Frankly, it was skinnier than a teenage model. Because of a complete lack of computerized technology and able clerical personnel, DPI had become the perfect place to hide a paper trail. There was simply too much disorganized paperwork to sift through in one sitting.

Carter came in to drop me a line while I was snacking on pizza. He had the good sense not to bring up the real reason I was there, so we tossed around some casual conversation about Mardi Gras and the band. Just before it looked like he was about to cross into sensitive territory concerning the job, Carter's cell phone rang, and he disappeared back into his office to get back to doing what he did best. I'd have time to chat with my uncle later. The last thing I needed was Carter's ebullient voice broadcasting the details of my investigation all over his office.

I smiled politely and said hello to all the people who trounced through the kitchen while I was eating. The majority of time though, I was tight inside my head. I kept trying to draw a link between DPI's stocks and the money loss that accounting was showing. Seven-hundred grand sure was a long way to go on missing money, but when I compared it to the costs of accidents that I had gleaned that day, it fit pretty well. I made a note on my legal pad to get a hold of Carter's stock portfolio and have it examined.

By four in the afternoon, I was beginning to think that my stakeout would have to extend to another day. Surrounded by stacks of yellowed paper, pens, legal pads, and half-eaten slices of pizza, the fatigue of deskwork started to catch up to me. My eyes felt heavy in their sockets, and a dull ache in the back of my head would surely begin the uphill climb to a migraine meltdown by the end of the day. I had three drivers' samples to deliver to the testing laboratory that Dad used, and I figured I might as well start packing it in.

There was a knock on the cheap wood frame of the door. "'S'cuse me?"

"Yeah, what?" I grumbled, shoving notes into my briefcase.

"Mr. Hauser said we all had to come and piss in the cup again," the lanky, fortysomething man at the door said. He was dressed in the usual DPI trucker's uniform: red jacket and matching hat over whatever the individual felt like wearing, which in this case meant a coffee-stained T-shirt and jeans that had to be older than me.

My disdain for this guy and his ilk would have gotten the better of me if I hadn't gotten that one important question in under my breath. "Yeah, right. Who are you?"

"Al Henkel," said the driver, extending his hand.

It took a moment for me to register the exchange, but I followed up with a gracious shake of the hand and a totally bogus smile. "Mister Henkel! Good to see you, sir. My name's Jack, and I'm just updating records for the DOT renewal coming up in January. As you can see from the state of this room, it's better to get started early."

"Yeah, I don't see how them girls up front find anythin'," Henkel said, sitting down across from me at the table. "'Course, that computer stuff'd make things easier, but who's gonna learn it?"

"Right you are, my friend," I said, grinning at myself. I took out one of the legal pads and flipped to a page where I'd scrawled down Henkel's personal information. "Just a few questions, Mr. Henkel, then we'll get you on your way."

"Yeah, I got to drive home tonight," Henkel said, fumbling with a can of Skoal. "You got somethin' I can spit this in?"

I almost concealed the revulsion that time. My face remained pleasant, but nothing could have stopped the crawling of my flesh. I held out an empty Coke can to him. "Here you go. Now, Mr. Henkel—"

"You can call me Al," Henkel said, smiling through the large indentation of chewing tobacco under his lip.

"Al, then. All right. Now, I came across two different addresses while I was updating your folder. One at the Mark IV Apartments here in Hattiesburg and... Delphinus Street in Biloxi?"

"Yessir," the trucker said. "I stay up here when I got a big schedule on me, but my family lives in Biloxi."

"Ah, I gotcha," I said, writing on the pad. "Makes it tough on the family, huh? You going back and forth all the time?"

"Sorta," Henkel said indifferently. "But the kids gotta eat, y'know?"

"I do indeed. All right, now about these accidents on your jacket here. It says you were involved in six in the past year?"

"That's wrong." Henkel's aloof demeanor changed slightly as his eyebrows pinched together. He leaned forward in his chair, working his mouth around the lump of chew. "I only been in three. And they weren't my fault. Someone hit my truck every time."

"Really?" I said, exaggerating the disbelief on my face to a comic degree. "Wow, that's some kinda bad luck you got there, kaz."

"Yeah... Kinda."

"But, hey, if it works..." I nudged his foot under the table. "Pretty easy to scam off a DOT inspection, huh?"

Henkel shrugged. "Guess so."

I frowned slightly and pretended to write something down. Either this dimwit was genuine proof of what inbreeding had done to southern society, or he had been coached by a very clever person. Recalling the Doc's words from a few days ago, I allowed for the possibility that Henkel himself may even be the clever one.

"All right, Al, just a few more questions. How often do you deliver to PetroJet?"

"PetroJet?" Henkel's brow became a unibrow. "Um... not ever, I think."

"You think?" I tapped the pen slowly on the table in front of me while I held Henkel's eyes. "In all those deliveries you've done over the years, you've *never* been to a PetroJet facility?"

"Well, I..." Henkel looked away suddenly and then back at me. "What's this got to do with safety certification?"

I shrugged and scribbled some more on the pad. "Like I said, records are for shit around here, Al, and I'm just trying to clean up a little. You understand, right?"

"I s'pose..."

"You work any other jobs, Al?"

"Uhh... No."

"Ever been convicted of a felony in a work-related accident?"

"No!"

"Ever been treated in a hospital for a work-related injury?"

"Well, I was up at Forrest General back when I had my last accident. Messed up my neck kinda."

"Uh-huh... Okay, Al, that's all." I stood up and handed him one of the piss kits. "Now if you wouldn't mind squirting a few drops for me. You know the drill."

Henkel snorted and spat into the Coke can. "Isn't this drug testin' thing like an invasion of privacy or somethin'? I heard 'bout that on Sally Jesse one time."

I put my hands in my pockets and looked down on Henkel. "Does it matter, Al? Because DPI's policy is if you don't pee, you don't drive. *Capice*?"

Henkel snatched the drug test kit from the table and stood, shuffling off to the bathroom. "Still think it's pretty much an invasion of my privacy."

"Look at it this way, Al," I said, getting fed up with the whole routine by then. "If you want an alternative, I can go out to my car and grab the broomstick and the pine cone in my trunk. And when I come back, all you have to do is bend over."

Technology is a beautiful fucking thing.

Once safely entrenched back at the home base, I spread all the data I'd collected on my dining table and switched on the computer. For the duration of Carter's gig, I would have to be careful about communication. Being discreet always helps in any situation, but in a case like this, a telephone record could leave incriminating evidence behind. I'd learned my lessons well from Andrew Vachss's infamous Burke.

I opened my e-mail program and propped some of the notes I'd taken up on a work clipboard beside the monitor. The Gateway had become obsolete the year after I'd bought it, but with some upgrades here and there, I'd managed to turn the thing into an asset that I would do well never to lose. I'd become so dependent on computers in the past couple of years that if the country was suddenly to suffer an electrical breakdown or somesuch disaster, I'd probably be the first citizen to head out to the local gun club and start plugging customers. Organizing my approach to what I'd learned so far that day, I set out to write a message to an old friend in Texas.

TO: Deckhead ["user.address@unknown"]
FROM: Saint Jack ["jdooley@netdoor.com"]
SUBJ: Armitage's Heroes

Deck,

Need some help. Dig up whatever you can on a Hattiesburg, MS resident-- Al Henkel, SS# 563-23-8572. Also has Biloxi address, 354 Delphinus St. Bank records a plus.

```
Also need total hack on following corps:
PetroJet Chemical, Dooley Petroleum, Inc.
(DPI).  All relevant data pertaining to
financial records.  Stockholdings a must.

BTW, how did the DFW caper pan out?  Hope
everything's cool out west.

Down on the Upside,

Jack
```

That done, I made sure all records of the e-mail transmission were erased from my computer's master memory files. The recipient of my message was a stickler about deck jockey procedure, and I wasn't one to object. The question mark known only as Deckhead had once made me a lot of money in Dallas.

The subject line tag of "Armitage's Heroes" went back a very long way in Fort Worth, Texas. The phrase had been hacker code for back-channel favors between partners in the game. Deckhead and I had actually gone to high school together, but instead of entering society balls-first as I had, Deck had dropped out of school and begun what society liked to call a life of crime. To Deck, however, what he did was art. Sequestered in a shanty cyber café in downtown Fort Worth, Deckhead had groused a collective of some of the finest hackers, console jockeys, and general cyber trash on the market. His first caper netted a cool ten grand from the local police department's gratuities fund, and everything had been uphill since. Things were very different in cyberspace, and Deckhead had ambitions to be a master in the game some day. This is back when the hack game still didn't make headline news and before the days of cybersecurity firms and anything more formidable than

Norton Antivirus. Pre-Heartbleed even. Mitnick was probably still phreaking people for short cons and hadn't yet hit a hard roll. "Hacker" was just a pop culture term for the same kind of grifter from Ye Olden Days, the days of literally writing your own driver's license on paper and getting it stamped by someone with no other method of identity resolution. Networked computing just made it easier to do if you knew the right routes, and Deckhead did. Guy was no joke.

Unlike those of us who went to college hoping for some shot at a good job, a house and 2.5 kids, Deck assumed a Zen-Jedi role in life behind a computer. I'd kept in touch with Deck over the years, even helped him pull a few scams when he needed partners. The man owed me a favor, and the cliche of honor among thieves was very much alive between us.

My next message was a little less official, but for all intents and purposes, just as discreet.

TO: Brother Rick ["dsears@electromail.us"]
FROM: Saint Jack ["jdooley@netdoor.com"]
SUBJ: What You Need

Rick,

Remember our phone conversation the other night? Need some info. Al Henkel, MS resident, SS# 563-23-8572. Criminal record? DOT info good start.

You have any ins to the SEC? IRS? Let me know. Have a project involving stocks and bonds. Corporate stuff, too. How do you do industrial espionage? Enlighten a brother.

May need legal docs on PetroJet Chemical and civvie file on Bill Finley, national. See what you can dig up. History of big business? High roller? Think *Wall Street*.

Hope life in Behavioral Sciences is treating you good. Give Nia my love.

Down on the Upside,

Jack

The preliminary report from Puckett Labs said that Al Henkel was clean for traces of amphetamines, cocaine, marijuana, and alcohol. There was a note attached from the medical officer that Henkel had a prior medical history with liver dysfunction, but all state records came up dry when it came to follow-ups on the initial diagnoses five years ago. I found my notepad and scribbled this intriguing bit of information down. Dad would want Henkel's recertification for work drawn up as fast as possible and mailed back to DPI, but I shoved the papers in a desk drawer. Let the hick sweat it a little.

I sat back in the neck-high captain's chair I used as a work seat, my eyes unfocusing on the blank screen in front of me. Henkel looked beautiful on paper so far. There wasn't anything that I could use to further the probe that percolated in the back of my mind, but I hadn't really expected anything. I needed to gauge Henkel as a suspect, and based on the interview, the man had something spawning cobwebs in his closet. The only real lead I'd come up with was the dual address, and that put a nice smile on my face. A trip to Biloxi would be a nice diversion from Hattiesburg if I could work it in.

With my feelers out and a preliminary plan to take a look-see at PetroJet later in the week, I called it a day and accessed the daily Internet edition of *The Fort Worth Star-Telegram*. Online newspapers made me stop saving change and instead fostered actual charity in my heart as I cast those forgotten dimes, quarters, nickels, and pennies into whatever collection box sat neglected on convenience store counters where I traded for smokes. I bookmarked papers from all over the country including *The New York Times* and *The Washington Post*, as well as interesting online magazine editions of *Entertainment Weekly* and *TV Guide*. Deckhead fresh in my mind, I absently wondered when the Catholics would canonize their first digital saint. Things had come a long way since the days of Walter Miller and the blessed Saint Liebowitz.

The phone beeped in and interrupted my slack-jawed navel-gazing. I snatched up the portable from its cradle and settled back into my chair. "Hello?"

"Jack?"

I froze. Not her. Not now. *Shit.*

"Hey, Crys..." I mumbled, running through the multitude of excuses to make this a short conversation. "Um..."

"Don't say anything, Jack," she said, her silk and honey voice reverberating in my ear. "Something's wrong. I can tell. You haven't called me in weeks..."

"Crys, listen," I said. "It's just... There's been some stuff that's happened lately—"

The sigh was a thing of ghostly apparition and whispers. I involuntarily shuddered, unable to comprehend the sheer reality of what Crys brought to my life even in things as simple as a telephone call. "Crys, I…"

"Jack... It's fine. Take your time. You know how to find me."

The line went dead, and I listened to the dialtone for a moment. The emptiness filtered into me in the wake of her call. I finally clicked the phone off after minutes of statue-still introspection. As always, it couldn't have been something *simple.* No. It had to be her.

The usual rules didn't apply to Crys. The usual way I approached women didn't factor into my feelings for Crys. Nothing had been easy from day one... although it certainly had been *nice.* Nice. A lot of people take that word for granted. I yearned for *nice.* And with Crys, things had been *nice.* For a while. For a change. I would face up to those weeks Crys mentioned for the rest of my life, and in every dark moment henceforth, I would know forever the depths of cowardice.

I am a fool. I am a louse. I am everything undesirable, detestable, and despicable. I know this. I embrace it. I cherish it. It is who I am.

And it didn't matter to *her.*

Crys.

Damn.

5.

CLOCK IN AT 8:05 WHEN THE BOSS AIN'T AROUND

I dreamed of malevolent, tribal creatures and scores of newly-minted dollar coins. The crusty remains of mud kept creeping around the edges. Light became a thing to be envied, and I couldn't sit up. And there was a really cool Sinatra tune playing in the background; "The Lady Is a Tramp," I think.

I awoke to the scent of fresh coffee, the timer on my coffee pot having initiated the spurt and drip of dark roasted delightfulness. Coffee makes for a much better alarm clock in the morning than any loud-ass beeping thing or one of the local hillbilly radio stations. Sweeping the last vestiges of the murky dream from my mind, I sidled out of bed and groped into a pair of plaid day pants, read: pajamas (don't judge). The bedroom made up one-half of the apartment, sharing the east side with the bathroom. As I stumbled over a half-full hamper of dirty clothes and a pair of Reeboks on the floor, I caught my reflection on the closet mirror.

"Smile, you fuck," I said. While mornings aren't the best time to be self-critical, I couldn't help but chastise myself for the umpteenth time for the burgeoning rubber tire around my middle. I wasn't overweight…yet. Much. I tried to visit the local gym whenever I had a chance, but the old Dooley love handles were in full effect that morning, offset by the standard family barrel chest and shoulders. My raven black hair had gotten styled overnight into a duck's ass, and the slant-eyed appearance of my eyes put the timer at two hours before I was fully awake.

I stumbled out of my bedroom and into the other half of the apartment. The Greentree complex had some very good one-bedrooms, and I had been lucky enough to snatch one with a balcony when I'd originally applied. The living area was dominated by the entertainment center on one end; television, VCR, DVD player. I worship my entertainment. What with all the CDs and DVDs, sometimes I found single living to be almost bearable. That morning, I chose a thoroughly scratched Barenaked Ladies album and went to fill my mug.

The living area was separated from the dining area by my desk, a mish-mash affair of veneer wood tables and used stereo cabinets. Upon these sat my computer, printer, telephone, and all manner of Post-It notes with everything scrawled down from movie times to "If you're a guest, FUCK OFF!" A small dining table sat further back in the area, just in front of the kitchen. No matter what people said, I loved the apartment. A made-over relic from the '70s, it still had the green stove and trampled tan carpeting. Add to that the multitude of hand-me-down dinnerware and furniture that occupied the place, and I felt that I truly had something here that I could call Jack Dooley's even in spite of the reuse. Granted, it wasn't where I wanted to spend the rest of my days, but it was home. For now.

Filling a water-cleaned *X-Files* mug, I lit the first cigarette of the day and walked out onto the balcony, a great song about alcohol spewing from the speakers behind me. The *last* thing I needed right now was to tie on a drunk. I'm not overly alcoholic, but unlike the other members of my family, I don't do well with too much liquor. That particular distinction had earned me the nickname of "Puke Boy" back in my college days.

The sun had just peeked over the top of the Number Six building I lived in, casting pale morning light on the rest of The Greentree Apartments. Quaintly organized, the place was relatively isolated from the rest of the town, surrounded only by I-59 on one side and an open, grassy field on the other. It wasn't uncommon to find some of the welfare families' kids frolicking in the field in lieu of any public park. I noticed with a slight shiver that autumn had fallen, and soon the days of hot chocolate and fall season premiers would dominate the days and nights of the Hattiesburg public.

I wished I had the time to finish reading my new Kittlemeyer novel, but there was a lot to do in the coming days, and I didn't want to waste time. It was literally time to face the music, and I told myself that first priority today would be to visit the music store and let everyone know I was going to be out for a while. I don't consider myself a slacker, despite my generational pedigree. I took my responsibilities at MS Music very seriously, although nobody else seemed to.

As the early morning haze of sleep started fading away, I managed to clear my mind and focus on my objective. Henkel. I had to follow up on Henkel and quickly before he had a chance to sweep his tracks into the dust. He may not be guilty of anything at all, but if I'd learned anything from Special Agent Rick Sears, it was that you took absolutely no chances with an investigation nor cut corners. Be thorough, but be swift, he used to tell me. Rick Sears. He's my hero.

I looked down at the parking lot as a loud, exhaust-spewing truck slid into the space next to my Honda. The unwashed vehicle sported placards and advertisements for pest control, and a bundle of pesticide equipment sat in the pickup's bed. A somewhat hulking fellow got out of the truck, zipped up his white jumpsuit and retrieved a spray bottle from the back. As he approached my building, he looked up and saw me on the balcony.

"Mornin', sir," said the pest control man. "Mind if I spray?"

"Sure, come on up," I said. "Little early, huh?"

The guy shrugged. "Lot of apartments."

"Yeah."

I went back inside and unlocked the door for him, pulling on a black T-shirt as I turned down the stereo. The exterminator entered my apartment, Southern Pesticides placards sewn in unbalanced fashion all over his jumpsuit. He nodded amiably to me and went off to deliver his scentless stuff to the nooks and crannies of the apartment.

I raised an eyebrow in thought, watching the guy squirt fine mists of pesticide into the corner behind my entertainment center. "Hmmm..." I said.

"Sorry 'bout the early hour," the guy said. "I got seven complexes to spray today, and my wife gets bitchy when I come home late."

"Pity that," I said, eyeing the man's movements. Something tugged at the awakening nerve centers of my brain. Then... the first smirk of the day. 8:05, Dooley. Way to go.

"Hey, buddy... You wanna make a hundred bucks?"

MS Music stood on the corner of North 39th and Hardy, the second site of the company since its foundation thirty years ago. While the owners performed the day-to-day office work downtown in the old building, sales and repairs went through the Hardy street location. The store did a modicum of sufficient business, but the Jacksons had been forced to shut down well over twenty of their other locations in Mississippi following the Recession in the '90s. Now, the Hattiesburg store competed only with stores in Biloxi, Meridian, and Jackson for top profit stats. Thanks to the quality of personnel in the Hattiesburg store, we'd surfed the envelope in highest grossing dollars for the past five years.

Yet, all good things come to an end, as I hear so often these days. The repair shop where I worked had been whittled down to only one full-time technician. Frank Vandy, who had renovated and rebuilt the repair business fifteen years ago, was eyeing better horizons at his own private shop down on the coast. Our woodwinds technician, Chris Baker, put in the most time at the shop, delving into string repair and little bit of brass as the need arose. He was a man with a family, and he needed that commission, not to mention MS Music's generous benefits package. Baker wouldn't be going anywhere in the near future. And then there was me, of course.

I walked in the back entrance of the two-story building and saw a couple of high school kids unpacking boxes full of new guitars and keyboards. The grunt work always fell to the low boys on the totem pole, and Mr. Jackson had it in his head that high school kids were perfect for that job. It still flummoxed him to that day why he couldn't keep any of the kids around longer than a couple of months. Minimum wage will do that to part-timers, but it's hard to convince a Canebrake kid of that single facet of a good work ethic. In the bosses' minds, you weren't eligible for a higher wage or even a small commission on sales until you had put in at least three years at the store and graduated high school.

I walked past the piano and drum studios upstairs en route back to the band shop. The dull blue carpeting and wallpaper ended as soon as you saw the piles of instruments stacked outside the shop. The Jacksons figured that since we of the manual labor class dealt with acids and other nasty things up in the shop, why should we care about decent interior decoration? Well, we didn't. Everything in the shop was organized in a utilitarian manner, as it should be. Frank was fond of saying that while the outside world flitted around with the bosses and other folks running the sales departments, we got the real work done upstairs in our little dungeon.

The shop ran a tight rectangular space down the south end of the building. Huge windows allowed the bathing sunlight to naturally light the interior and the long multi-purpose workbench sitting directly under the windows. My bench, little more than a beat up desk with some hastily drilled holes to rack screwdrivers and other tools, sat just to the right of the main workbench and windows. On the other side of the room, two other benches... more professional models with rubber coated tops, drawers and stools...faced a wall of holed board from which hung all manner of horn parts, tools and supplies. Each of the pro benches sported a custom-made sax jig, thick black bars of welded steel with rubber stoppers to suspend saxophones in the air for easy access and manipulation in breakdown and repair.

Further on down the shop stood the main vise in the middle of the floor and flanked on either side by the soldering table and cabinets holding even more parts and supplies. Old, abandoned brass instruments hung from the walls, waiting to be given life once again on the occasion someone found the time for personal projects. A dent machine sat in the corner, a squat jungle gym affair with several protrusions that ensured any user a full upper body workout. The only reason my arms and shoulders were as tight as they were was because my mentor had originally started me out doing tuba dentwork on the dent machine. Two doors on the far wall led into the buffing room, which contained Mongo, the aged buffing machine that typically tried to eat your arms on a daily basis, and the chemical room: a depository for the wash basin, lacquer baking oven, and the large vats of degreaser solution and acids we used to clean brass.The shop looked like a mechanic's shop, for sure. The floor was pockmarked from years of fallen solder and streaked with hardened glue and fiberglass. Board-covered walls held rack space for boxes of spare musical instrument parts and hangers for tools. Between this workman's mess, we pinned pictures of our, the technicians', work: before-and-after photos of a 1932 Conn tenor brought back from the dented dead; an article from a magazine about how we had saved the show for a noted Swiss French horn player visiting Hattiesburg on a symphony tour who had accidentally cut his valve strings. My personal contribution to the character of the joint came just above my own desk where I'd thumbtacked a four-color poster of the Justice League of America, artwork courtesy of the great Kevin Maguire. Of course, even though he was hardly ever up there anymore, the shop just wouldn't be complete without the grey little guy at the sax bench.

"Jack-*san*!" said my brass mentor as I ambled into the shop. "Where you been hiding at, man?"

Frank was a short guy, but stocky and well built. Unlike so many Mississippians, Frank took a rather Zen approach to life. Not only had the man taught me how to make money fixing horns, but we'd also shared lots of philosophy between each other, sometimes over the propellant of great weed that Frank got from the coast. He convinced me to read *Zen and the Art of Motorcycle*

Maintenance when I only had eyes for Andrew Vachss, and Frank embodied that book. If anyone could understand the criticism I unconsciously spewed about Hattiesburg, it was Frank Vandy. So it should be no real surprise that he was actually born and raised up north in Pennsylvania.

"Been busy with some shit for my uncle, kaz," I said, plopping into a chair next to my workbench. "Might have to take an extended leave of absence from the shop for a while."

Frank had a dusty tenor sax on the jig over his bench, and he finished clamping a new pad in one of the keys. The area around his bench was full of tools. Pliers, hand torches, glue sticks, key cup seaters, dent balls, knuckle tools, Dremel wheels, pencils with cigarette paper glued on the ends to test pad settings. The casual observer would call the band shop a haphazard arrangement of junk and tools. No one but the techs knew where everything was and how to use it. This came in handy when nosy customers came in trying to figure out how we worked our magic on the deceased and ailing horns in front of us.

"Money-type gig?" Frank asked, pulling a used saxophone pad out of one of the pockets on his apron. As he inspected the decayed thing, he half-turned on his stool to face me. "You finally found something better than the old repair biz?"

"Maybe. Cash-wise, it's a peach. Fifty grand if I get the job done."

"Wow! Not bad, Mister Dooley. I suppose no one around here cares one way or the other if you're out."

"When has scheduling ever mattered a shit to the bosses? What are you doing up here, Frank-*san*? I thought you'd cut back to Thursdays and Fridays?"

"Ahh, the slow season's affecting the Brass and Lacquer Shop, too. Some cheese-eater from Virginia welched on a ten-sousaphone overhaul I had lined up, so I'm out about thirteen grand for the next two months. I figured I'd come up here, do some sax work for the store and for the make-up. I was gonna ask you to come down to Pass Christian and help out since you get such a hard dick for sousaphones. But, oh, well. Hey, hand me *da kine*."

I frowned to see what Frank was talking about. He made a hammering motion with his fist, and I retrieved a small, sanded mallet from my own bench rack. He winked at me as he took the tool and went to tapping a small dent down on a tone hole. "Just about got you trained in the Bermuda talk, Schoolboy."

"Every time you ask me for *da kine*, I keep having this horrifying vision of you making jerking off motions and asking for some KY," I laughed.

I propped my feet up on my bench, kicking a horribly twisted trumpet lead pipe out of the way and knocking over a sealed can of cork cleaner. I was glad to see that my absence for the past few days hadn't altered anyone's desire to avoid cleaning the shop. We worked better in filth, actually. Start cleaning things up and who knew what disasters might befall us.

"So you're up for the duration then?" I asked. "Good, 'cause I don't know how long I'm gonna be out on this DPI thing."

"For fifty grand, I'd go ahead and quit, Schoolboy," Frank said, waving his hand torch at me. "That's your hop-skip-and-jump back to Texas, hey?"

I shrugged with a groan. "Ehhh, I dunno. I'd tell you more, but it's kinda hush-hush now. Tell you the truth, Frank, I feel like I'm working out of my ass. I've never done this kinda shit before, and I keep thinking I'm going to fuck something up and get everybody sued."

Frank set down his tools and lounged against the bench, scratching some of the dust and grit out of his wizened, close cropped hair. "Hey, man, if you have the aptitude, that's half the job."

"In theory," I countered. "You know how much I dig on those crime novels and TV shows and shit like that. Funny thing is, I've got my bud in the Bureau to bounce ideas off of in case I'm shaky. But the fact is, I'm just a skilled labor worker in a shit town with nothing better to do."

"You're selling yourself short again, Jack. Remember when you were down and out about school? All worried about getting that 4.0 and being the star pupil of Southern Miss? What did I tell you then?"

"Frank, that's—"

"*What* did I tell you?"

The sigh came out as a cough. "'If it's a done deal in your mind, reality will soon follow.'"

"And I was *right*, wasn't I?" Frank got up and grabbed an apple out of his lunch sack. "Jack, we've been over this before. It's all in your head, man. It's all in your head. You can't *guess* whether or not you can do the job, you have to *know*."

"And knowing is half the battle!" I giggled, sending Frank into a paroxysm of laughter.

"And the other half is the kung fu grip!" he replied. "No, seriously. You did in two years what took most of my other apprentices four to learn about brass repair. And that's not even your *calling*! You set your mind to it, and you did the work, paid your dues, and now you're making sixty percent of every ticket you write up. That's a hell of a gig for somebody your age."

"Yeah, yeah, yeah. And I've got a prolific dick, too. Whatever."

Frank took a bite out of his apple and crunched some of the juicy fruit around in his mouth, eyes unfocused as he reasoned something out in his mind. "Jack, what it comes down to is this: What's your bag? I'm a sax man. I love my sax, I love working on my sax, and I make good money working on other people's saxes. You remember what I told you about what I said to my wife before we got married? 'You can ask me to do anything in the world, babe, but you can never ask me to give up the pot and damn sure not the sax.' That's *my* bag. So what're *you* gonna do?"

I swiveled around in my chair to face my mentor, folding my arms across my chest while chewing on my bottom lip. "I want to *be* somebody."

"Do you?" Frank continued munching on the apple, eyes steady on me.

I sighed and looked away. "Yeah."

"Then get the fuck out of here and find your bag, Jack. Mississippi is a class-A shithole for somebody like you." He waved his hands in the air, and his eyes got real big. "I'm only here because I like to fish! If the fish weren't so good, do think I woulda left that cream of a gig I had in Bermuda?"

I offered up a lopsided grin. "You left Bermuda because the pot cost too much."

Frank cocked his head to one side and harumphed. "Okay, granted. But the point is, my calling was that sexy Selmer Mark VI tenor sax and a big wad of smoke on the side. That's not your calling. We all have our different callings, Jack, and you've *got* to figure out yours."

"Yeah, I know..." I exhaled. "Anyway. How's the wife?"

"Joy?" Frank pitched the decimated apple core into an overflowing trashcan and sat back down on his stool. "You weren't kidding about that candle wax thing. She thinks I'm some kind of sex guru now."

"I told you! Candle wax freaks people out until they try it, but was I right?" I fixed him with a smirk and wagged a finger. "I can't tell you how many of the old frat gang got jiggy with that one. I mean, even Crys—"

Crys.

Dammit.

Frank frowned as he saw my face go blank; little Jack Dooley floating off to Nowhereland. He nudged my toe with his work boot. "You talked to her?"

"She called last night..." My voice came out a whisper, the cold thing happening again to my gut. I tried to find something to look at, to focus on. The busted, dented Conn alto on my bench wasn't doing the trick.

"Jack, listen—"

"Look, let's just drop it, okay?" I said savagely, unfairly. "I'm fucking sorry I even brought it up."

"All right, all right," Frank placated. "Just remember, Jack: It's only a woman."

I huffed, sprawling in my chair. "*Only...*"

Frank turned back to his bench and picked up a hand tool, fooling around with the regulation on his current patient. "Jack... go do your thing. I've got magic to work here."

I looked at his back and scratched at the grizzle on my chin. When Frank was in The Zone, nothing could stop him. He had preached to me on occasion about that ethereal state of being he reached sometimes while working on horns, a state where his body worked independently of his mind. At times, Frank could completely *go away*, just not be there while he was working on some ghastly large project like buffing the lacquer off an entire tuba. He claimed that he could work things out in his mind unconsciously before he attempted them in reality as he immersed himself in The Zone. The magic came in those periods when his eyes glazed over behind a sax jig, and his fingers worked at a rapid rate replacing pads and aligning keys. Meanwhile, Frank Vandy was somewhere else.

I bit my lip.

Somewhere else.

"Catch you later, Frank," I mumbled, shuffling out of the band shop. No reply followed me out.

Outside in the hall, I leaned against the wall and massaged my eyes. One of my (and Frank's) favorite songs floated into my head as I stood there. I heard a thunderclap through the cheap aluminum roofing on the building. Crys was probably at school at that moment. Uncle Carter would be on the phone. Somewhere in Texas, a beatnik was smoking dope. Sinatra rested comfortably in decaying satin and linen sheets. John Lewis was selling insurance.

"There's a little black spot on the sun today," I murmured.

The card read, "Bobby Guy, Southern Pesticides."

Irwin Fletcher I'm fucking *not.*

Or maybe I am.

The hip-heavy, leather-skinned lady behind the desk handed me the passkey and waved me away without even sparing a glance at the business card. "Bring 'em back when you're done."

"Thanks, ma'am," I said with the southern drawl that wasn't so hard to imitate after several years in the culture. The jumpsuit was riding my asshole, and I forced myself to not stop and diddle with my crack as I walked out of the apartment complex office and over to the nearest unit. Any other day, this would be humiliating as shit.

Compelling myself to ignore the itch in my backside, I spent an hour hosing down different apartments in the Mark IV complex. I didn't intend to spray all thirty units, and those I did would be happy to know that they got a free squirt of pesticide here and there. But before I headed over to #432, I had to establish the credibility of my Bobby Guy disguise.

I cased Henkel's apartment for ten minutes, making sure he wasn't home or nearby before I entered the unit. I only had to deal with one decrepit old lady who wanted me to stay for pot roast and turnip greens after I'd sprayed her apartment. I left an extra squirt of pesticide in her toilet bowl just to satiate my annoyance with her—that's right, *I showed her*—and I finally got out to Henkel's place. No one else in his unit was home, and I crossed myself for that. The Mark IV's aren't exactly apartments in which one hob-nobs with the upper middle class. Or even the middle class. Or class at all. Henkel's apartment was a simple efficiency unit, one large room with a kitchen and a bathroom. A bed took up most of the space inside, but Henkel had crammed in a small desk next to a few chairs and a television set. Half-eaten bags of hamburgers and fried chicken littered the floor in the kitchen, and a thick, dark liquid oozed inexorably out of a crack in the refrigerator. I suppressed the wave of nausea, set down my borrowed pesticide equipment and got to work.

The desk drawers were jammed full of papers and trinkets. I had to sort through stacks of Mardi Gras beads and depleted Bic lighters to find the folder where the good stuff lay. I got lucky in that case; Henkel must have been one of those people who was so afraid of the IRS that they saved every single receipt and check stub they ever saw. This particular folder was full of little yellow credit card receipts.

I opened my notepad and looked over the credit report Carter had sent me that morning. Henkel only possessed two credit cards, a Visa and a Shell card. The Visa must have been for his wife, because the list of purchases I had obtained from the Visa people included weekly doses of groceries and other domestic items. The Shell card stayed stable with gasoline purchases and the odd cup of coffee or Moon Pie. However, the receipts I found in the folder sported a Visa number that didn't match anything on Henkel's records.

Henkel's collection of Visa receipts included everything from hotel rooms in Alabama to fifty-dollar lunches at high-class restaurants. One hotel kept showing up in the stack, two weeks apart for each charge. I figured Henkel had himself some filly with a cocksucker's lisp in Birmingham, and I stuffed the hotel receipts in my pocket. Those could come in handy later on.

I couldn't find any checkbooks or bank balances that matched up with the credit card bills. The billing address on Henkel's second Visa was his box number at the Mark IV's, but the conspicuous absence of any stamps or envelopes in the apartment made me wonder how these bills were getting paid. I ruled out a forwarding address to some unidentified third party since Henkel had copies of the charge card statements month by month. Still...

In the second drawer I found stacks of check stubs and deposit tickets. A lot of them came out of a Union Planters in Jackson, but the occasional local bank in Hattiesburg or Biloxi popped up from time to time. The dollar amounts made my eyes water. Henkel was getting regular checks for upwards of about five grand a month, all signed by someone named Betsy F. Jones. These checks weren't business checks, and none of the stubs indicated anything other than personal transactions on the same monthly basis. But Jones's address on one of the stubs put her in Magee, Mississippi, and I stopped for a moment to consider the PetroJet angle.

If PetroJet was paying Henkel to run a scam on DPI, Bill Finley wouldn't want anything on paper that could be connected back to him. The most reasonable idea would be to establish a phantom bank account with one of Finley's close, upper gentry friends at one of the smaller banks in Magee, in this case, SouthBank. Henkel submits his reports or what have you, and Finley, or someone else at PetroJet, signs a check for Henkel to pick up the next time he drives through town. That story seemed forced, though, I thought. A fiction to fit the facts. Old Doc Faller had warned me against underestimating an opponent, but was Finley really capable of something this intricate? I wrote down the bank account numbers on the "Jones" check stubs for future reference.

The rest of Henkel's desk contained little in the way of evidence. I had assumed that Henkel wasn't smart enough to be involved in the stock trading that Carter had described to me, and when I didn't find any portfolios or investment reports, that theory became a fact. Still, I had enough to suspect that Henkel was involved in something paying a lot better than what he was making at DPI. I made sure I replaced every item I had shuffled through in its former place before closing up the desk. Then I set about wiping the desk down to erase any fingerprints I may have left behind.

I turned over the mattress on Henkel's bed and searched for any concealed cash or other incriminating evidence. Zilch. However, after going through the cabinets in the kitchen, I opened an unused cookie jar and found a .44 Smith and Wesson revolver wrapped in newspaper. A box of bullets rested beneath the gun and were strung tight by a collection of rubber bands. I sniffed the gun but couldn't detect any of the telltale signs of a recent firing. Henkel was careful, that was all. He probably had a license for the gun, but the fact that he was armed at all made me take a moment to myself. Guns changed the frame of the picture. Why would a truck driver have a gun stashed in his weekend pad? Who was he afraid of? Or was it simply a case of one typical southern American exercising his God-given right to bear arms?

A thorough run-through of the rest of the apartment turned up nothing else except a closet full of dirty clothes. I had hoped for a lot more, like some photographs or something. But the credit card receipts and check stubs pushed me further in the direction I felt like going. The whole thing stunk of money, and in southern

Mississippi, when the rich weren't adverse to the idea of bankrolling illegalities to be carried out by the not-so-rich, money became an eye-catching thing in terms of motive.

I read a book several years ago about a newspaper reporter who spent an entire year with the Homicide unit of the Baltimore Police Department. This nonfictional account detailed the reporter's observations of the meat and potatoes of death investigation and how detectives went about catching suspected killers. In the Baltimore detectives' views, motive boiled down to three things: money, sex, or drugs. Rick had told me after his first month at Quantico that the Bureau followed a similar investigatory strategy, although agents got more in depth with it and enjoyed stratifying the categories.

Money. That's the ticket, I thought.

I went over the apartment once more with a handkerchief just to be safe, and after a few squirts of pesticide into Henkel's nooks and crannies, I retired *Bobby Guy, Southern Pesticides.*

The rain came in sheets of alternating drops and droplets, spattering across pavement and intensifying the chill in the breeze. I like rain. When the pitter-patter of a good cloudburst hits the roof and window panes, I can relax to the soothing sort of music produced by the storm. As a teenager in high school, I had lived in a large, Spanish-style house on a huge hill in Fort Worth. The stucco roofing had made for a plethora of different waterfalls when it rained, and I remember spending some of my lonelier times underneath those runoff streams lost in thought.

I sat on my balcony with the rain blowing into me from multiple directions. Rivulets of water caught in my hair dribbled down my face, joining the soaked black T-shirt after their downward race. My bare legs were slick with moisture, and the chilly wind enticed goosebumps with each new gust. My mouth hung open at an angle, lips parted for nothing more than breath. The Zone, for me, took a lot more than a saxophone and buffing gloves.

I needed to think, to work some of what I already knew out into a logical pattern. The questions and the facts spun in a nuclear circle around my brain, attacked in random places by impulses from other subjects that had no bearing on the work. The analysis wasn't forthcoming, unfortunately, and visions of silky-smooth skin, cigarettes, and treble clefs kept invading my train of thought.

I snorted as the linkage I was looking for slipped away, or more to the point, never bothered to coalesce. My clothes were soaked through, and I had developed a slight shiver as the afternoon had given way to evening. Spitting rainwater out of my mouth and wiping my moist eyes, I shook my head in frustration.

"Fuckin' rain..." I said.

6.

CREEPIN' IN THE BACK DOOR

The evening began with a quick meal of homemade angel hair pasta, Alfredo sauce, and a couple of lightly toasted rolls. With a quick shit, shower, and shave, I was completely out of the events of the day and into the night.

My first stop ended up being a choice between The Mahogany Bar and Dewey's. Having gotten out at such an early hour, I decided to stop in at the Hog and peruse the night's scene before moving on. The bar actually linked itself to two other establishments in the same complex, an upscale restaurant called The Purple Parrot and a more "common man" eatery called The Crescent City Grill. The Hog, sandwiched in between both dining rooms, made for an interesting collection of the swift-of-suit and the short-of-style. As usual, things were in full swing by the time I walked through the door.

Unfortunately, I'd forgotten that tonight was college night. I try not to associate with too many people my own age; most of them in Hattiesburg are severely lacking in the most perfunctory of social graces. Perky, nubile sorority girls in swanky silk shirts rubbed shoulder-to-shoulder against the multitude of khaki-clad, baseball-capped frat guys. Mike, the Hog's veteran bartender, was already rolling his eyes by the time I made it to the bar.

"Not your usual scene, Jack," the bearded fellow said, already setting a Crown and seven down in front of me.

"Forgot what day it was, Mikey," I replied. "You seen the old man?"

"He was in here a couple hours ago, rousting the locals for an across-the-street show. Someone you know playing Dewey's tonight?"

"Probably. I think Pops and I have finally cornered the market on the respectable music scene around here."

"Well, something's happening over there tonight. Lot of your dad's friends headed out that way a few minutes ago."

"Killer." I put a few singles down on the bar for him. "Hate to abandon you, chief..."

Mike tittered and pocketed the bills, his burly demeanor providing not the least bit of relief for the harried younger 'tenders rushing about behind him. "Throw one down for me, all right?"

I drained the whiskey in one gulp, blinking twice as I set the glass back down. "Always do, Mike. Be easy."

On my way out, I was accosted by a group of swaggering college-level barhops. You can always spot the kids in a Hattiesburg crowd: They're the ones standing up, clustered around tables and the bar with no real places to sit or languish. Ergo, space normally reserved for actual transportation purposes gets annexed to the kids. More than a few beer-stained shirts had crossed the threshold of the Mahogany.

"'Scuse me," I muttered, trying to ease my way closer to the exit.

"Jackie?" one of the frat boys said. "Hey, look, it's Doo-dis!"

"Doo-dis!" the scrambled cry came up from the group. I rolled my eyes and stopped in my tracks. Obviously, these were supposed to be people I knew. I only recognized one of the girls as a distant Tri Delt memory, and the bruiser in the Bulldogs cap could only have been Barry Bryce, one of my former comrades-in-arms at the Sigma Tau Delta house.

"Where you been hidin' out at, Doo-dis?" Bryce guffawed, cigarette delicately perched between the fingers of a hand already laden with draft.

"I graduated, dumb shit," I said, flipping a cigarette between my teeth. "You know, the thing where you actually *stop* going to school?"

"Listen to this!" Bryce yammered, hammering my back. "Dude's tour of duty at Southern is just like his sex life: He's in, he's out, he's asleep."

The Tri Delt I had recognized giggled coquettishly. "Oh, come on, Barry. He's at least out and about now. More than I can say for you."

I offered the girl a lopsided grin by way of thanks. "Right. What's shakin', Bryce?"

"The usual!" Bryce proclaimed. "Must I go into such raucous detail with the ladies standing right here?"

"That's a good word, Bryce. Raucous. You finally pass the ACT?"

Bryce's hangers-on "oohed" and "aahed" at the perceived insult. Thing about Bryce was, though, he knew I didn't make verbal statements without some element of truth to them. I was probably one of a very select group of people who knew that Barry Bryce's hotshot lawyer daddy had bribed a Hattiesburg Public Schools official to change the scores on his son's ACT so his boy could get into college. He was three years older than I and had been in school even before I'd arrived at Southern. I hate to gloat, but...

"Pardon the brevity, kids," I said, shooting a stream of smoke up and out of everyone's faces. "I've got a thing."

"You playing tonight, Jack?" the Tri Delt asked.

"Nope. But somethin's going down at Dewey's, or so Mikey tells me." I fanned the air before me. "And it's *mucho* leaner in the air over there. See ya."

"Wouldn't wanna *be* ya!" Bryce hollered with a final backslap.

"You wish," I muttered, quickly extricating myself from the crowd.

Dewey's Alley sat crunched between a Pizza Hut and some insurance sales office, its spacious deck and wooden building extending out back from 38th Street toward a creek. The bar had undergone a plethora of name changes in its fifteen-year history as a sometimes-restaurant, all-the-time bar. The current handle arose from a twisted legal dispute between the bar's owners and a rival nightclub in Biloxi. Rather than waste the dough fighting the courts, the owners cashed in on Hattiesburg's finest and their favorite hangout. DUI Alley, as it was called by the locals, extended from Chesterfield's west down Hardy Street all the way to I-59. The police patrolled this area like vultures, each one determined to bring home a higher quota of DUI tickets than his partner. With their own television spot for the "DUI Task Force," the Hattiesburg Police Department stood as the single police organization in the nation to write the most DUI's last year. Being harmful toward business and all, the bar owners on 38th Street had put up a new sign in defiance of the HPD: Dewey's Alley, with the unwritten challenge on the sign, "Come get us, you lazy fuckers."

I dropped a fiver at the door and sauntered into the smoky, dimly lit bar. I immediately recognized The Jive-T's on stage: Four friends with whom I worked at MS Music that shared an interest in old acoustic songs and reefer. An instant after that, Dad's voice beckoned to me from our customary table near the stage.

"Hup, hup, *ho*, Jack! Whatcha know?"

"Same old thing, Pop," I said, plopping into a chair between two other similarly-minded musicians. "Hanging with the jokers tonight, are you?"

Jeffie Nils and Steve Burns comprised two-fifths of southern sensations 25 to Midnight. We made for an odd group, I had to admit. Jeffie, the completely uncharacteristic drummer, decked himself out in Polos and khakis, bulging muscles and sporting a neck thicker than a wrestler's. Steve—or Stevie Ray Burns as I liked to call him—was just plain sloppy, always dressed in some variation of a stained white T-shirt under an open dress shirt and rumpled pants. Add me to the mix on stage with my Huey Lewis-inspired suits (as well as our Russian bassist and sugar-addicted sax man), and you could host a freak show based solely on appearance.

"Watch it, watch it," Steve droned, stamping out a cigarette and needling his beer bottle. "We're off tonight."

"Yeah, so I get to poke at you more often," I said. "What's up, fellas?"

"Taking bets on which Jive-T has the biggest buzz tonight," Jeffie crowed. "My money's on Lightsey."

"Gotta be Tom," I said, indicating the glassy-eyed second-string guitarist, stage left. "Tom's always stoned."

"Yeah, yeah," Steve said. Steve, Tom, and Chad, the Jive-T's front man, shared a house on the edge of town. You haven't experienced the pot craze down south until you've walked through their kitchen.

"How's that deal with Carter, Jack?" Duke grilled me.

I waved a negative hand across the surface of the table. "Ixnay, Pops. I'm taking the night off from work."

"New job?" Steve inquired.

I offered Steve a deadpan. "Steve, what did I just say?"

"Night off?"

"Right."

Steve made a face and took a swig of beer. "Well, okay."

I fished a wad of bills out of my pocket and inclined my head toward the bar. "I'm running dry here, fellas. Anyone need a topper?"

Jeffie bounced his bottle on the table. "Shit, if you're paying—"

"I'm not."

"Cheap bastard."

"Yup."

I left the gurgling bunch at the table and sidled up to the bar to begin the difficult ritual of flagging down a 'tender. The Alley's bar was about thirty feet long with only two bartenders running all over the place trying to placate the customers. Add to that a complete absence of waiters, and the bar got a little crowded at times. Thankfully, the highest concentration of people started at the other of end of the bar, and I found room to lean up and attempt to get someone's attention.

"I'm sure it will be a while," the girl sitting near me said, sipping a modest cocktail. "I've learned to just order a tall one and drink slowly."

My eyes involuntarily swept over the lady's figure, taking in the cream-colored blouse and skirt, crossed legs and all. "Well, I just got here. I don't have anything to waste my time with."

The lady flipped a heavy head of brownish-blonde hair over her shoulder, offering me a full view of her face. Big brown eyes capped off a thick-lipped smile that spoke volumes about her class. She wore little makeup, letting her tanned and toned skin speak for itself. The conservative earrings confirmed my classy theory, and another pass over her legs had me thinking upper in a bad way. Mighty nice for a ginjoint like the Alley.

She pushed her drink toward me slightly, reaching for a thin pack of cigarettes in the vicinity of a lithe, ringless hand. "You can tug on mine, if you'd like." Her voice like cocoa; no trace of accent.

"Now, I couldn't do that," I said, letting the grin invade my face. "I might have cooties, after all."

The bartender—he who had paid 25 to Midnight's bill in the past—slid the beer o' choice down to me and pointed at the tip jar, where my dollars soon went. I clinked my bottle against the girl's drink glass and winked.

"Besides, it's old home week every week for half-ass musicians in this joint."

I grinned a goodbye and sauntered back to my table, where Steve had begun sharing a rather lurid tale of his sexual exploits with one of the MS Music owner's daughters. My eyes lingered momentarily on the girl at the bar, hypnotized by the shock of dirty blonde hair flowing over her shoulders. *Huh*, I thought."Little overdressed for the Alley, isn't she?" I intoned to Duke as I sat down. He lit up two cigarettes, passed one to me and squinted to where I was looking.

"That's a problem?" he said.

"Seems more like a Mahogany kinda girl."

"Probably was at some point tonight. Mike said he was sending as much business this way as he could for the boys."

"Speaking of which... *'You been creepin' in the back door!'*"

Chad and the Jive-T's had launched into a backbeat original tune that all of us in the musical family of bands had dubbed "Creeping in the Back Door." It was a great song, well executed by Chad on his own and with the larger band. I don't even remember what the original lyrics or title were; "Creepin' in the Back Door" had just become too sticky to replace with the truth. Chad, strumming a gorgeous blonde Martin acoustic, heard my acknowledged bastardization of his original tune and winked at me, trying not to laugh as he belted the lyrics. The rest of the Jive-T's caught the slip, and each one found me at Duke's table. Tom shook his head and showed me his ass while Lightsey twirled a drumstick for me. Harvey, the band's three-hundred pound prodigy sax teen, tooted a low blow from a Selmer Mark VI saxophone.

The thing about the local music scene is that you have to keep it in the family if you want to make it. Duke Dooley was regarded as Hattiesburg's go-to guy for good music because he knew so many musicians. His band, Kabana, contained lots of guys from Meridian that he used to play with in Ye Olden Days, but they weren't limited to that lineup. He had frequently asked Chad or Steve to sit in, and I had gotten my vocal start with Kabana. The Jive-T's sprung up from Chad and Tom's mutual working association at MS Music; two fledgling songwriters looking to make a buck and get their music out there. Duke had the connections at Dewey's for the gig, and the duo had evolved into a quartet as time went on; a quintet when Steve found the time to play bass.

25 to Midnight was born from Duke's wish that a good party band rock the town to pieces. Until our formation, the casual bar hopper couldn't go anywhere in Hattiesburg and find good bands that covered new music and covered it well. So Dad had talked me into singing, rounded Steve and Jeffie up, and Jeffie had brought in Alexei from Southern. Vandy had done us a favor by calling in Dave Smythe, a middle school band director and a hell of a good

saxophone player who also supplied keyboards. Thus Hattiesburg now claimed original fun from the Jive-T's, old school classics from Kabana, and funky new covers from 25 to Midnight. We were really all a bunch of incestual whores, sitting in with each other's groups and filling in here and there when one bandmate couldn't make a show.

"We need to have a rehearsal before the show Saturday night," Jeffie said over the din of Lightsey's skin-beating. "I want to polish 'Same Old Thing' and that 'Jungle Boogie/Brick House' medley."

"I'm free Wednesday night," Steve replied.

"What about Alexei and Dave?" I said.

"I'll call 'em and check," Jeffie said, unconsciously tapping the tabletop in his drummer's nervous fashion.

"I may be in and out this week. I've got some work I need to do. Just leave me a message if we're on."

"How's that going, by the way?" Dad asked.

"Slow right now." I took a swig of Amber Bock and grimaced. "I've got the certification paperwork in my car from my day at DPI. Drug tests are at the lab."

"Yeah, they faxed me the results this morning." Something in my Dad's eye told me there was more he wanted to ask me about the work out at DPI. I made a face that told him we'd have to talk about it elsewhere.

"Who was that girl you were talking to up there, Jack?" Steve asked, nodding back at the blonde at the bar.

I shrugged. "Dunno. Didn't have time to ask."

"So go get all up on that shit, bitch," Jeffie teased. "I see those calluses on your hands."

"Blow me. I've got standards about picking up women in bars."

"Yeah, those standards are one, pussy out; and two, run home for a quick jerk," Steve laughed. "Getcha hand off ya dick, Jackie."

I flipped Steve off and eyed the blonde again. She remained where I had encountered her before, quietly sipping her drink and paying the Alley's clientele no mind. I smacked my lips and quirked an eyebrow at Dad.

"What do you think, Pops?"

Duke just took a swig of his beer and winked at me. I drained the rest of my beer and clinked the bottled against Duke's. My Dad. Never one to judge. Always one to bullshit. Certainly one to enlighten another if you had the time to listen. I stood and bowed slightly to the guys at the table.

"I need another beer anyway," I said with a grin.

"Get me one while you're at it," Steve said.

"I'll get right on that, your majesty."

The smoke content of the air had shot up a few parts per million by the time I returned to the bar. The unaccustomed patron would find his or her eyes watering over in a few short minutes, but seasoned smokers like myself and the blonde breathed easily and clearly. Once I had threaded back through the crowd to the bar, I noticed that the girl had a fresh White Russian to accompany two more empty glasses.

"Get that for you?" I said, sliding my empty bottle down the bar.

She looked at me, surprised to see me. Her wide eyes slowly gave way to a mellow smile.

"I was about to do the same for you." Milk and honey voice. Ouch.

"Amber Bock," I told her. "What are you drinking?"

She made a tilting motion with her head accompanied by a slow blink and a quick purse of the lips. "It's a White Russian. Do you like those?"

I lifted an eyebrow and peered into the milky drink. "On occasion. More of a summer drink though, y'know? White Russians, bushwhackers, Doo-Ladas and the like."

Her eyes pinched in tandem with a furrowed brow. "Doo—what?"

"Doo-Lada," I said slowly. "Like pina coloda except with a Doo. It's a family thing. My dad makes these really good mixed drinks he calls Doo-Ladas after himself."

Her face lit up when she chuckled. "How flattering of himself."

"Yeah, I thought so. See that dumpy guy back there in the old hat? That's Dad."

"You favor each other. You've got his cheeks."

I fought the rush of red and ran a hand over said overly cherubic cheeks. "Gee, thanks."

"Don't be embarrassed," she said, sliding another long cigarette from her pack. "I like your cheeks. Guys like you should be proud of their faces. They're very striking."

"I'm not sure how to take that," I said, flipping my Zippo out to light her up. "*Striking* as in, 'I'm gonna hit you, you're so ugly?'"

This time she really did laugh, blowing smoke in a curly-cue pattern from between her red lips. "Not at all. *Striking* as in... striking. You know. Attractive." She wiggled her eyebrows at me. "You can't have an imperial like that and not be striking."

I grinned around my Camel as I, too, lit up. "You call it imperial? Damn, everyone around here just thinks it's a goatee minus the mustache." I scratched the shock of black hair on my chin. "Striking, huh?"

"Yes," she said, tapping some ashes out. "Italian? No, wait. Portugese."

"Portugese? Where the hell do you get Portugese from? What do Portugeezers look like anyway?"

"Dark complexion, dark hair. Animated face." She shrugged. "I was guessing. What is it then? Italian?"

"I get that a lot," I said, easing onto a barstool next to her. "Junkyard dog, actually."

"Ah! Cajun."

"You said it."

I whipped out a fast hand and caught the bartender's attention. A few more shouts over the din of the music and I managed to convey the order. As I settled back into my conversation with the lady who'd thought I was from Portugal, I made a mock frown and blew a stream of smoke over her head. "Okay, what's with the twenty questions? You looking for someone to pick up your bar tab?"

She tittered again but not in an especially girlish way. She had that twentysomething way about her, but the way she sat, how she talked, all of it said *grown-up*. "Direct, aren't you? I thought this was how people met each other."

"In Hattiesburg? Before or after the ceremonial shagging of the goat?"

That one drew an extended laugh out of her. "Now I know you're not local. Seen a lot of bestiality around here?"

"I plead the fifth," I said with a smirk. "What about you? From around here?"

She shook her head. "No, I'm farther north. Jackson. Had some friends down here who got married last night. I'm killing time because I hate the drive."

"To Jackson? It's only an hour."

"Have you seen Highway 49 lately?"

"Point taken." I made an inquisitive face. "Irish?"

"Very good. Scotch-Irish, actually. I'm originally from Gulfport."

"Ah, a coast rat. Me, I'm Texas born and bred."

It was her turn to smirk. "You know how you know someone is from Texas?"

Now I just had to smile. "We'll tell you."

Laughter.

"Whatever possessed you to give Texas up for this place?"

I shrugged, half-heartedly. "Free ticket to school. Pops lives out here, offered me room and board for the duration so long as I gradumucated. Still trying to find a way out though."

The bartender delivered my Amber Bock, and the woman raised her drink to me. "To getting out of Mississippi then," she said. "Cheers."

"Yup," I said, clinking glasses. "Hey. What's your name anyway?"

The legs uncrossed and crossed again, her posture fully directed my way. "It's Liz."

"Jack," I said. "Glad to know you, Liz."

"Likewise." She inclined her head toward the bandstand as she took another pull on the White Russian. "Have you heard this band before?"

"The Jive-T's?" I said, listening to Chad belt out a particularly soulful rendition of "Blackbird." "Yeah, I work with a couple of 'em. We're all a bunch of inbred musicians here in Hattiesburg. Keeping the music in the family."

"Oh, you're in a band, too? What do you play?"

"Nothing, I do vocals. Mostly good old eighties tunes. Huey Lewis, Men at Work, The Fixx. Throw in a little Dave Matthews and Barenaked Ladies here and there to whet the crowd's appetites."

"Very impressive," Liz said, grinning at me. "Will you be sitting in tonight?"

"Shit, no! This is my night off. Come back Saturday if you want to see 25 to Midnight."

"Nice name. Ever play in Jackson?"

"Mostly at private functions. Frat parties, high school proms, that sorta thing. The clubs in Jackson are more privy to the whole alternative scene than we prefer."

"Oh, come now. A little Nirvana here and there could work wonders for your band."

"What? Don't blaspheme. Hold that shotgun-wielding crooner next to Morris Day and The Time any show, and I'll take the Pepsi challenge."

"Perhaps a little Pearl Jam then? Soundgarden? 'Jeremy spoke in class today?'" Her barely-concealed chuckles finally clued me in on the fact that I was being fucked with. I offered up a pair of pouty lips and snorted.

"Yuck. Jeremy's free to speak all he wants, wherever he wants. You can find me being the king of pain and acting the prick singing, 'De Doo Doo Doo, De Da Da Da.'"

Liz's face brightened as she giggled. "How cute. 'Every Little Thing She Does is Magic?'"

I took the opening. "Yes, she does," I said, sobering my jocular visage momentarily.

Liz paused, a whispery smile hidden behind her glass as she sipped out the rest of the drink and returned the glass to the bar. Delicate in her movements. Not precise or stilted but lithe.

"Listen," she said, opening her purse and rummaging through its contents. "I have to get home. Work in the morning and all that, right? But could I call you sometime? I do want to come back and see your band."

"Absolutely," I said, a genuine smile creeping up my cheeks. She produced a piece of paper and a pen, which I took and began scrawling down my telephone number. "If you can't find me at this, call MS Music. I work there."

Liz's face sold the amusement. "Why am I not surprised?" She took my number and stared at it for a moment. Then her eyes peeked over the paper and met mine. "It was great meeting you, Jack. Honestly."

"Back atcha, Liz. And I'll get the drinks, okay?"

She rose and slung her purse over her shoulder in one cool motion. Then she leaned over and pecked me on the cheek, her lips making that slight popping noise that you always remember as they planted just below my ear.

"Thanks, Jack."

I watched her stride out of the Alley with none of the hair-tossing or strutting you come to expect from girls in a college town. She fended off advances from others as she left, extending a single hand to ward off the predators and fixing each with lioness glares to keep them at bay. Liz spoke class to me, or so I thought. I admitted to myself that I wouldn't mind seeing her again. That part of my brain where fantasy and reality met started firing neurons, and I wondered if she would indeed call.

"Ball's in her court," I said, picking up my beer and heading back to Duke's table.

I wish I'd never met her.

7.

SADDLE UP

I was up early the next morning, jonesing for a severe case of The Breakfast. While the computer was warming up and a pot of coffee brewed, I dished up a skillet full of scrambled eggs with cayenne pepper and a few strips of bacon on the side. I shoveled ounces of the tummy-yummies into my mouth while I skimmed over the morning online edition of *The Fort Worth Star-Telegram.*

The mailbox icon blinked at me for a full minute before it got my attention. I opened it up and found plenty of things to throw a party about, particularly a reply from Deckhead on the Henkel probe.

TO: Saint Jack ["jdooley@netdoor.com"]
FROM: Deckhead ["user.address@unknown"]
SUBJ: Re: Armitage's Heroes

Saint Jackolas!

miss you out here, chief. all sorts of fun to be had. got the info you needed; check the attached files below. Henkel's got a record, federal. 2 counts of DWI in Alabama, charges suspended by order of a judge in Birmingham named Will Schiedle. hasn't filed a proper tax return in over fifteen years, although he keeps getting return checks. figure someone's skimming his paperwork. DOT's got a file on him, but it's pretty thin. get back to ya later with more.

stockholders' info on requested corps. included in the file. I can't make heads or shits out of it though, but that's just Deck for ya. you're the brains, stink :-P speaking of which, when ya comin back west? the crew could use your shit sometime. BTW, DFW caper was da bomb. tell ya about it sometime at the Gym holler at me if ya need more;
Deckhead

Just to be safe, I went ahead and downloaded Deckhead's file to my hard drive, saving it in an obscure directory under the games folder. As I wiped out his e-mail, I thought over Henkel's connections in Alabama. The credit card receipts I tied into a possible hooker fetish in Birmingham could be connected to the trouble Henkel had with the law over there. That may bear some looking into, but the more I learned about Our Man Al, the more I learned that the dumbfuck had his decrepit little redneck hands in a variety of cookie jars. It may have nothing to do with DPI. Therein lay the rub. If I was chasing my tail on this lead, I could be wasting a lot of valuable time. I hated doing that.

Deck's tax information was another red flag. I'd found dozens of receipts and credit statements in Henkel's apartment, but no tax returns. If he was getting checks from the IRS, then where was the paperwork? Rick had told me some years back about a fraud scam the Bureau worked where two high school kids stole bank account numbers and used them to hack return checks from the IRS. If kids could do that, then maybe the esquires of PetroJet were hiding some kind of payment scam in Henkel's returns. I made a mental note to mention that to Rick.

Waiting to digest the rest of Deckhead's hacks for later, I went on to the rest of my morning mail, finding a reply from my personal special agent.

TO: Jack Dooley ["jdooley@netdoor.com"]
FROM: Brother Rick ["dsears@electromail.us"]
SUBJ: Re: What You Need

Jack:

The things I do for you. :-/

Henkel's got a record at DOT, namely for a number of service violations in the past ten years. It's a wonder this guy can still get certified. In 1984, he was responsible for three separate propane spills in Texas, Mississippi, and Louisiana, and got sent up on marijuana charges for the Texas spill. The company he was driving for at the time, Carlson & Sons, spent a fortune on his legal defense, probably just to save face in the papers. He ended up with a minor rap, 2-4 with time served. Year after that, he was back on the road.

Here's the kicker: Somehow, all these records were sealed and wiped clean from Henkel's DOT jacket. I had to interface with the Louisiana NTSB branch to figure it out, but it looks like somebody dropped Henkel's violations in File 13. What that amounts to is that when any new employer runs an MVR or a DOT background check on him, he comes out smelling like daisies. I haven't figured out who authorized this yet, but I'm working on it.

Henkel had a whole slew of stuff in Alabama, most of which involved misdemeanor offenses like moving violations and soliciting prosties. None of this was on the job either. Lots of his stuff ended up on a judge's docket, Will

Schiedle. Schiedle was involved in a bribery probe a few years back, and I'm working on getting more off this guy. I think it's a lead you should look into.

No direct lines to securities fraud or industrial espionage on my end, brother. I'm mainly in behavioral sciences. I'll ask around though. Ind. espionage is a tough nut to crack for most of the lifers up here.

Bill Finley's another matter completely. High roller and then some. He's got investments ranging from charity work in hospices to the casinos in Biloxi. Comes from old money, inherited and re-invested. Guy looks like a saint on paper, but I smell differently. Too much of a bright sheen on someone this powerful down south. More details in the PetroJet file I put in the mail this morning. The fucker was too big to e-mail.

Nia says hi, wants to know when you're coming up for a visit. We ran into a local legend in Baltimore the other day. Remember Sgt. Landsman from Simon's book? I shit you negative, brother. The guy is *huge*. Keep me updated on the case; I'll help out whenever I can.

Whatever you need, whenever you need it,

Rick

I couldn't help but chuckle around the mouthful of eggs and bacon.

Two red flags from different sources equaled a lead in my book, and were Rick privy to Deckhead's info, he'd say the same. The Biloxi lead on Finley only gave me another reason to get down there and look into things. I checked my calendar and saw that the band had a show in Ocean Springs next weekend. Good timing. On top of that, I also needed to schedule separate trips to Birmingham and Magee.

The Schiedle angle might be a definite tie to PetroJet for whatever reason. Somehow, Henkel had become ice cream for hotshots with money, and way too many people were throwing cash his way to keep the hick out of jail. Either he had some certifications other than HazMat training or he had some photos of people in compromising positions. Either way, it was plenty of juice to fill the condom.

Deckhead's file took a full half-hour to print, and I passed the time by picking up my place a little bit. I even got real domestic and broke out the duster to wipe away all the little dust bunnies on the rack of action figures I had poised on the mantle shelf above the entertainment center. After I'd rearranged the pose on Marv (he came with interchangeable hands that sported a gun, a knife, a hatchet, and a decapitated head), I picked up the sheaf of papers from the printer and got out my notepad.

I started with the DPI records and immediately got a headache. The stockholder's report must have been written in German, and I couldn't even begin to decipher the pages of tables and graphs and their corresponding dollar amounts. Stocks are another language to me. I do not understand how they work, and I have no desire to learn. I tried breaking the information down by trading company names and abbreviations, and that helped a little. While I couldn't confirm anything due to my Jerry's Kids syndrome with numbers, it looked like a new stockholder, T&Bin, appeared out of nowhere last March buying small stocks from DPI here and there. The activity increased through August and then subsequently disappeared off the record table. I could find no listing for T&Bin after August 21st. By September, though, whole chunks of stocks weren't even listed in DPI's portfolio, and their total dollars in transition had decreased exponentially by October. I flipped to the back of the report to the corporation glossary and looked up T&Bin: Truman & Binnell. A private investment corporation?

I set the DPI report down and picked up PetroJet's. Skimming the columns page by page, I soon found T&Bin listed in over twenty different places with huge amounts of money next to their name. Over the course of a year, PetroJet's stock options had leaped from a six-figure portfolio to the millions. Trying to draw a connection with DPI's losses, I checked the PetroJet report against the DPI dates where T&Bin had appeared. Nothing. Although, on those same dates, there had been plenty of activity in the PetroJet account. From March to September, they had grossed almost $3 million from their stocks, and the company's own stock had slowly grown during that time. It looked to me like an easy place to hide seven-hundred grand in missing money, but I was an amateur at the trading game and following money of that size through all the pipelines in which it could flow.

The phone jumped into my hand while I sorted through my computer's address book to find a number. In a few short seconds, I had the connection I wanted to a stockbroker's firm in Tampa. A few more seconds after that, my cousin, David Novak, came on the line.

"How are you, Jack? I haven't heard from you in months."

"You know me, David. Avoiding family functions to the point of disownment."

He laughed, a bit stilted as I'd come to expect from the only immediate cousin on my mother's side that had gone on to a six-figure salary. "Keep it up and we may have to do New York again."

"Not on your life. Say, I need a favor."

"What's that?"

"I'm doing some work for Carter out here in Hattiesburg that involves a bunch of stock and investment stuff that's way over my head. Would you mind taking a look at it and giving me your take on a problem?"

"Sure. What kind of problem?"

"Don't want to say over the phone. Will you be in Tampa for a while?"

"Actually, I'm on my way to Birmingham in about an hour. I have to meet with a potential new client and pitch the company."

"Really?" I smirked at my reflection in the computer screen. "When you getting in?"

"I can't believe I'm doing this," John Lewis groaned for the fifth time, his knuckles tight on the steering wheel.

"C'mon, where's all that brotherly love and shit like that?" I said from the passenger seat of Lewis's Montero, fishing through my coat pocket for a cigarette.

"For the record I'd, uh, like to state that you *left* the fraternity, asshole."

"And I still get to reap the benefits, don't I?" I cracked the window and blew a small stream of smoke outside to join the rest of the highway that flew by me. "Don't mind if I smoke?"

Lewis glared at me. "Would it matter if I said no?"

The one thing I could always count on in a former frat brother is that they would always bend over backwards to do anything they could to help me out. Especially after the incident with the laundering frame and the hazing rat. So when I had called Lewis at his office, told him to come pick me up and drive me to Birmingham, Alabama, he had only bitched and moaned a bit. I felt somewhat guilty for using Lewis like I did, but only a little. He wasn't exactly the tightest whip on the hip.

On our way out of Hattiesburg, we had stopped by a local independent cellular phone dealer where I'd purchased a phone and a no-frills national hook-up with Carter's expense account debit card. By the time we had made it to I-20 in Jackson, I had called Jeffie Nils to let him know I wouldn't be making band practice, Rick Sears for a favor, and the Birmingham Municipal Court House to schedule an appointment with the honorable Judge Will Schiedle.

"I still don't understand why the hell you, uh, need me to drive you to meet a goddamn judge in Alabama!" Lewis complained, coughing in annoyance of my bad habit. "You don't think there's any insurance salesmen in Birmingham?"

"Sure there are, but none I know," I said, rifling through Lewis's collection of CDs. "What the hell is this shit? Celine Dion? Where the fuck are your balls, John? *Where are they?!*"

"Shut up, dammit. Explain to me again why I ran out of a heavy sale to, uh, sell insurance to this guy in Birmingham. Huh? Tell me!"

"You have to do a background check on each new client you pick up, right? Anything from medical records to liability claims in the past. That's to make sure the guy who just took out a life insurance policy doesn't have AIDS or something."

"Duh! But what?"

"Shut up," I ordered, leafing through the pages of Lynyrd Skynyrd and Dr. Dre CDs. "So that gives me an excuse to poke through this guy's dirty laundry."

Lewis shook his head and whined again. "You couldn't do this by yourself?"

I winked at him as I pulled a CD from the holder. "You give me legitimacy, baby. Be proud that you're worth a damn. Now *here's* what I'm fucking talking about. How many times have you listened to this? Once? Twice? This should be the only goddamn thing in your player, Lewis."

He made a face at me as I switched CDs and hit play. "That was a gift from my mother. She doesn't know anything about music."

As the Stone Temple Pilots' "Crackerman" started pounding from the Montero's able speakers, I stuck my tongue out and chuckled. "Think you got that backwards, pal."

"Has it ever occurred to you that, uh, this guy's gonna toss us out on our ass because he's never heard of us before? Usually, you see, it's the practice of the client to call *me* first."

"He has."

"He has?"

"Yup."

"When?"

"The other day. You remember, right? You know when that guy called on the phone?"

"That guy?"

"On the phone."

"He called me?"

"Exactly."

Lewis snorted. "I give up."

"Just use those natural salesman's tactics of yours, Johnny. 'Of *course*, we spoke on the phone, Judge Schiedle. You told me you'd be in at this time today and that you didn't have to talk on the phone. Yes, *sure* I'll take time to explain myself. As much time as my partner Mister Dooley here needs.'" I tapped the side of my head. "It's all in the brain, Lewis. The art of bullshit is your bread and butter, and with me riding shotgun, we got this guy in the bag."

My cell bleeped at me, and I fished it out of my pocket. "Hello?"

"Am I your bitch? You want me to dance for you now? Shine your shoes? You want me to smile atcha?"

"Rick!" I crowed, tossing my cigarette out the window. "What's the word?"

"I'd just like you to know that I spent my whole morning digging this shit up for you when I should have been trying to impress my unit leader with the keen investigatory competencies," Rick Sears snorted at me on the other end of the line.

"If you need me to send you a doctor's note, I *can* fake a pretty good subject matter expert, y'know."

"Whatever. Listen, Schiedle's got state-sponsored medical and an expired life insurance policy that he has yet to renew. I think it has something to do with alcohol abuse since he's listed as an attendee of a regular AA group in Birmingham."

"Gotta love those alcoholics. Moments of clarity are few and far between."

"You know it. Couldn't find anything on auto, although he probably has it since owning a motor vehicle in Alabama requires that the driver has limited liability. Driving record's clean, although I hit a brick wall when I looked into a blank month back in 1991."

"Drunk driving?"

"More than likely. I bet he had a judge friend of his cover it up, too."

"Cool. What about the bribery probe?"

"The specifics are a little sketchy, but Birmingham's new DA got elected on a platform of exposing corrupt state officials. Schiedle was named on his list of suspects, and it looks like the DA only did a little work on him. I'm still researching, but I bet a bowl of porridge to some dead body storage that the guy's dirty."

I snickered. Trading quips like this is what we do. "Work that PetroJet angle, Rick. I've got somebody looking at their stock records today, and I'll feed you the particulars when I get back to Hattiesburg."

"Good deal. Can I go back to being an FBI agent now?"

"I give you official permission to arrest my ass. You know how I love being manhandled."

"Too well. Watch those exaggerated lane dividers."

"Holler atcha, brother."

I folded up the cell phone and looked over at Lewis. "Schiedle's got state-sponsored medical and a non-renewed life. We think there's alcoholism involved and maybe a few DUI's covered up in his jacket."

Lewis looked at me like I had just beamed down. "We do? Jack, how do you know all this? Who was that?"

"A friend." I smirked again. "Kinda like you except... not."

Lewis shook his head. "Fuck me..."

We pulled into downtown Birmingham just after four o'clock, giving us barely enough time to find the courthouse, park illegally, and get inside. For the purposes of appearing the least bit respectable next to Lewis, I'd worn a black and grey golf pullover from the Warner Brothers store and maroon slacks. I felt like I wasn't betraying my own personal sense of style with Bugs Bunny swinging a golf club on my breast and still looking the part I was to play that afternoon.

It struck me as we entered the courthouse that I had been spending a lot of time lately in different personas other than my own. The one big advantage to being privately retained is that you *can*, in fact, impersonate another person or profession. It's almost essential that you're able to sell yourself as something completely different than yourself. I had a few teachers in high school tell me that I'd make a great actor. Although I never pursued it, I found it somewhat funny that here I was, years later, playing a part.

What scared me was how much I enjoyed it.

A receptionist at the main desk directed us to the judge's chambers, and we threaded through the throng of people in the courthouse's lobby. The floor bore a huge seal of the Alabama state flag and words written in Latin that I couldn't understand. I got the gist, though, glancing at the marble under my loafers as I walked. This place encapsulated justice and due process and all that jazz. Funny how the jazz sometimes usurped the justice.

Lewis and I passed through two high marble columns into a long hall of offices near the back of the courthouse. The inlaid floor soon gave way to more functional, and inexpensive, gray tile, flecked with decades of spilled coffee, shoe scuffs, and dust bunnies. An old guard wood veneer finish decorated the halls of the justices who deliberated behind those doors. Every so often, a plaque commemorating some honorable, deceased legal eagle would appear between the chamber doors. Lewis found the nameplate that read "JUDGE WILLIAM SCHIEDLE" and pointed with his briefcase.

"Is this him?"

"That's the guy," I said, clearing my throat. "Show me some action, baby."

Lewis grinned in spite of himself. "He'll never know what hit him."

We entered into a small receptionist's office adjoining the judge's main chambers in the back. A sprite young lady in glasses greeted us with a tired glance as she plugged away at a computer old enough to make a good party joke for Steve Jobs.

"Can I help you?" she droned.

"Hi, I'm John Lewis from Carrollton Insurance." Lewis handed her a business card. "We have an appointment with Judge Schiedle."

"Let me check," the secretary said, as if she didn't believe us. As she rifled through a day planner, I let my eyes rove the office. Nothing unusual at first glance. Secretaries are secretaries, as they say. Their jobs, and their offices, are interchangeable.

Satisfied that we had indeed passed her appointment check, the receptionist rose and knocked on the open door in the far corner of the room. "Your Honor? Your three-thirty is here."

A muffled grunt from the far room turned her back around, and she raised a limp arm backwards. "He'll see you now."

"Thanks," Lewis said, shuffling into the judge's private office.

"Hi," I said to the secretary as I passed her. The lines around her eyes told the story. She'd been locked in that office way too long. She couldn't even muster up a reply to me, settling for a slight twitch of the lips.

"You want a stick of gum?" I said, taking a pack from my pocket.

"Well..." She frowned slightly. "Um. Sure. Thank you. Hey, this is my favorite kind."

"No problem." I smiled again as she took the chewing gum, finally gracing me with something representative of her true personality instead of the paper slate on which her job drew her. It didn't take much, really. It never does. A kind word here. A selfless gesture there. And the door is open.

Of course, I had to swipe the pack of chewing gum from her desk while she wasn't looking to do it.

The Honorable Judge William Schiedle appeared like a fat tumor growing from behind his great oak desk. He must have weighed over two-eighty easy, most of it dripping off his jaw in folds of cheeky, liver-spotted flesh. Thin white hair grew in patches on his rotund head, and a pair of black dots set into the flesh covering the eye sockets watched us from behind a pair of inch-thick glasses. To say that the years had not been kind would have been a bad joke.

"John Lewis, sir," my partner said, immediately going for the handshake. "Good to meet you."

"Likewise, Mister Lewis," Schiedle replied, shaking Lewis's hand.

"This is my, uh... associate, Jack Dooley."

"Your Honor," I said, repeating the handshake.

"Well, Sherry tells me you boys are here from some insurance company in Mississippi," Schiedle said, exhaling as if the handshakes had filled his daily exercise quotient. "Are you here to sell me something?"

"That depends on you, sir," Lewis replied, sitting down next to me in one of the guest chairs. "When we spoke on the phone, I didn't have time to go into specifics."

Schiedle's face didn't change, but you could tell he was puzzled. "We spoke on the phone?"

"Yes, sir. You said you didn't have time to talk much. Uh, remember? Well, I'm here now to, uh, explain everything you need to know. That is."

I tried not to roll my eyes. Henry Fonda, John Lewis *wasn't.*

"Well, I'm afraid I have all the insurance I need, young man," Schiedle said, the traces of amusement visible between the folds of his cheeks. "I get it as a benefit from the state."

"Your Honor, it may seem like a benefit," Lewis said, opening his briefcase; "but I bet I can tell you some ways that it isn't."

I tuned out while Lewis went into his spiel. It gave me some time to evaluate Schiedle's surroundings and the numerous plaques on his vanity wall. LSU, Auburn, even Tulane was represented.

Although it was probably true, someone of a judge's stature wouldn't include the obvious remedial education at state colleges. Lewis didn't even admit to ever spending a semester at Jones County Junior College during a particularly hard year. A moose's head looked down on the three of us, passing its own form of judgment for the atrocities committed against its kind. A wall of legal texts and books ran down one side of the office. A few pictures of family and friends adorned the opposite wall, a copy machine next to the door. Late afternoon sunlight peeked through dusty old curtains in the window behind Schiedle.

The judge's desk sported reams of disorganized paper and documents. At least three legal pads in varying degrees of paper weight covered a two-by-three day planner. The planner itself terminally represented June of 1988 and contained plenty of coffee stains and scratch marks. I made a mental note of each item in the room for further digestion later, memorizing placement and content. Even the faces on the framed photographs got digitized as my eyes swept the place. I didn't by any means have a photographic memory, so I had to work extra hard at remembering details. Faces posed the toughest challenge, so I gave the pictures extra-long looks. I thought the one with the judge and a few other men drinking beer on a no-name golf course was pretty funny. Especially with the pissed-off black caddy in the background, a look I'm sure the judge never considered as anything other than subservient, the fucker.

"What I mean to say, is that we offer more coverage for less action on your part," Lewis was saying. "Did you know that we don't even require physicals anymore? Nope. Not even so much as a single visit to the doctor's office. You just get covered, Your Honor. And that's the bottom line."

Something about that line had gotten under the judge's skin, and he moosed back in his high-backed leather chair to contemplate.

"Really? In no way am I required to submit to any sort of medical evaluation pursuant to the contract's institution?"

"Not at all," Lewis said, grinning. "You see, we choose to err on the side of trust rather than stopgap measures like that. If you're in a car accident, for example, that's the first time we ever ask you if you've ever had driving problems before. And if you don't have an accident, we don't even care. Our job is to get you covered *first*, and worry about the details later."

"That's the truth," I said, piping up for the first time that afternoon. "See, I've got this friend of mine. Al Henkel's his name. One time, he had this accident in a truck he drove for a propane company. So he calls me and asks me what happens now, right? After all, I'm the one who sold him his insurance policy. So I tell him to do whatever he has to for DOT and all that, and then we'll step in and cover him on the rest of the deal." I grinned and chuckled. "Al's in pretty good hands, if you know what I mean."

Schiedle paused for a moment, sizing me up. I couldn't tell if he was annoyed with me, butting in on Lewis's most excellent pitch, or intrigued by the namedrop. After a few seconds, he sipped from his coffee cup and coughed.

"You know Al Henkel?" he said.

"Yeah, I used to babysit his kids," I said jocularly. "Great fellow. Wait. Do you know him, too?"

Schiedle stroked his jowls in mute consideration. "I've... made his acquaintance before. He drives for that Dooley Petroleum company out of Hattiesburg, doesn't he? Any relation?"

"Who me?" I feigned wide eyes. "No, sir, I'm from Texas. I hear that Dooley in Hattiesburg is native. Lots of them around, though, y'know? You should see the phone book."

Schiedle chuckled, ruling that I was, indeed, amusing. "Yeah, too many of that particular family. Boys don't know how to run their company. "Henk... *Al* came out my way a few years back, got into some trouble. Landed on my docket. Poor Dooley tried his best to bail him out."

"Really?" I narrowed my eyes. "From what?"

"DUI." The judge chuckled again. "You tell your friend that he'd best start shaping up. He's got a wife and kids after all."

"Ah," I intoned. "Will do, sir."

Lewis, impatient with what he knew nothing about, butted back in. "So do you want to see our plans, Your Honor?"

"While you're considering John's brochures, sir," I said; "you'll excuse me for a moment. Where's the restroom?"

"Down the hall to the left of the lobby," Schiedle said. "And close the door on your way out, would you, son?"

I winked at Lewis as I got up, pulling the door closed behind me. With Schiedle's confirmation of knowing Al Henkel, I had a little bit more to go on. Without going directly to the judge though, I needed another inroad to whatever was going down between the two of them. Hence, the Doublemint secretary.

"Hi again," I said to the secretary. "How's it going?"

"Huh?" she said, jerked from her paperwork and back into reality. "Oh! Oh, the usual."

"Yeah, I bet it gets pretty stuffy in here." I eased down into the seat across from her. "I had to take a break from His Honor in there."

My knowing grin produced a slight smile on the secretary's part. "You should try working with him. You know he's been divorced five times?"

"Wandering eyes?"

"And hands." She set her pen down and contained her smile. "My name's Sherry."

I picked up the nameplate on her desk and showed it to her. "Yeah, I figured as much. Jack. Want some more gum?"

"You bet. I can't seem to find mine. You know, why don't they make those sticks bigger? It's like, I don't want bubble gum because that's a whole different thing, you know? But these little sticks just don't last."

I passed her another stick and nodded. "Yeah, I know what you mean. So working for the judge isn't all that peachy, huh? I used to be in law school, and I would have died to have gotten a job like this."

"It's okay, I guess," Sherry said, unwrapping the stick of gum and popping it in her mouth. She lowered her voice conspiratorially. "There's better judges to work for, you know."

I snickered along with her giggle. "That bad?"

"You wouldn't believe some of the stuff that Judge Schiedle's done!" She looked around again to make sure she was safe before continuing. "He's a womanizer, a drunk, *and* an asshole."

"I hear he also was under investigation for bribery at one point," I slipped in.

"You know, I heard stuff from some of the other girls. Like, one time, this guy from the DA's office comes down to ask him some questions and subpoena some files and stuff? Well, the judge, he gets all mad and has me call all these people in town, like these big-wig folks that he knows. It was funny though, because the mayor called him back, like, the next day and told him to cooperate. He got *mad*. He got all mad and stormed out of the courthouse."

"No kidding?"

"No kidding! And then later that day, they say he had a wreck in his car." She pursed her lips. "But it was, like, nobody did anything. The girls told me that his case just kinda got 'lost,' you know?"

"Yeah, I bet."

"Later on, I couldn't believe it, but he actually threw a party about it." Sherry's eyes inflated to the size of twin moons. "A party! Can you believe that? He had all these big business friends of his come in from all over. Bankers, construction, petroleum..."

"Shiedle's got propane pals?" I asked, nudging her in the right direction. "I know a few propane dealers in Mississippi."

"I bet you might know some of these people then. One of them was a really, like, *impatient* guy from Jackson. All dressed up in really nice clothes. But I could tell he didn't want to be there. It was like the whole thing was beneath his consideration or something." She rolled her eyes and huffed. "Typical."

"Typical, yeah. You remember his name?"

Sherry tapped a pencil against her chin. "I think it was Finley. Something Finley."

I winked at her. "I'll be sure not to do any business with him in the future."

I had my connection.

After placating Sherry with some more small talk, I managed to get her out of the office. A quick jaunt to the restroom yielded a shortcut to the main lobby where I borrowed a courtesy phone. I rang Schiedle's office and told Sherry that she had an important delivery at the rear entrance. Keeping concealed down the hall, I waited until I saw her exit the office and stride off under a pitter-patter of high heels.

Once back at Sherry's desk, I moved quickly. Schiedle couldn't have been silly enough to leave records of his activity with Finley lying around his office, but I had to be sure. Besides, quite often the best place to hide things is in plain sight.

Sherry's file cabinet yielded nothing of value. Most of the documents I found sported fresh legal insignia, trappings of the court. I resigned myself to the fact that the paper trail was cold in that office, and I turned to Sherry's computer. Somehow, Sherry had managed to upload several new programs on the aging device, one of which was QuickBooks. I checked out the accounting program immediately, defeating the password subroutines with some quick alterations to the actual program. Deckhead had taught me a lot in Fort Worth.

The banking records in the accounting program appeared perfectly sound. As I scrolled through the list of companies and corporations Schiedle kept listed in his database, one icon glared at me with an accusatory flash: T&Bin. Truman and Binnell.

I accessed the T&Bin file and received a list of several credits made to Schiedle's private account. Each credit bore the name "SERVICES" in the category field, and the dollar amounts clicked home in my mind. I paused momentarily, allowing the numbers to slide and twirl, watching them dance inside the complicated morass of information I'd assimilated in the past few days. If I wasn't mistaken, the money matched up to some of the numeric information contained in PetroJet's stock report. What did this mean? Was Finley hiding his investments through Schiedle? Or could Finley possibly be paying off Schiedle through stocks? Why? Just to keep dinks like Henkel out of trouble?

The printer spewed out everything in the T&Bin file I could find. I rolled the paper up and stuck it in my back pocket, hoping no one would notice that it hadn't been there when I walked into the office. I would need David's help in untangling this mess of money and numbers, but I had some solid proof that Finley was involved in DPI's problems.

Returning the computer to its station-keeping screensaver, I left Sherry's desk and reentered the judge's office. Lewis and Schiedle both looked up to me, as if in query of my protracted absence. I grinned, patted my stomach and said, "Boy, those grits can kill a man."

"You don't need to be around for this," I told Lewis as we pulled into the Hampton Inn just off I-20. "It'll only take a minute."

"What, I have to wait around now?" Lewis protested as I jumped out of the Montero. "Jack, for Chrissakes!"

"Hey, you got a potential new client, Lewis. Be the man." I flashed him a businessman's thumbs-up and hurried off to the hotel lobby.

David Novak was waiting for me in his room, and we both paused for a brief handshake. David possessed the rugged good looks of a man raised to work on a Mississippi farm, but he had subtly refined his appearance since striking it big as a stockbroker. He was about twenty years older than I seeing as how my mother was the baby of four sisters. David's parents lived on a farm, his father a hardcore backwoods Mississippi farmer and carpenter, and his mother a part-time legal assistant for the mayor of Meridian. I felt pretty proud that he'd gotten out of his Meridian, Mississippi lifestyle early on and aspired for bigger things. Instead of turning radishes and picking carrots, David was making weekend trips to New York and Las Vegas and having the time of his life in the big city of Tampa, breaking stocks by day and buying and selling start-ups for fun between repasts. I could do so well.

"Don't want to keep you too long, kaz," I said. "Thanks for coming down on such short notice."

"Ah, I could spare the time," David said, pouring us both a drink from a recently liberated bottle of bourbon. "The guys I'm meeting with out here are taking dinner to decide on our offer. I'll probably drop in on them in a while and close the deal."

"Cool." I produced a thick sheaf of papers from the folder I had been carrying. "This is the swag. What I've got here are two different portfolio reviews; one from PetroJet Chemical, one from DPI. Now, I've got a hunch that these PetroJet fucks have been screwing around with Carter's fundage, but I don't know how."

David slipped on a pair of reading glasses and seated himself at the table. "All righty, let's see what we can see..."

The printer records from Schiedle's office plopped down next to the files. "These are some documents I've... appropriated. Tell me if I'm crazy, but I think there's a link between an independent investment firm in there."

"Give me just a moment," David said, eyes narrowing.

I sat on the bed and watched David Novak do his thing. He inhaled the numbers, the tickertape names, the dollars... like Vandy did at his bench. David could enter his own Zone, and like Vandy, he reveled in it. Where numbers and stocks meant nothing to me, David played with them as if in some kind of mental magic show. As I waited, I could see his deep green eyes shifting rapidly from to column to column, absorbing the data. I wished I could work on his level, put things together like he could. Granted, David may have been a dunce when it came to seeing patterns in words and phrases, as far as I knew. Numbers represented a challenge that I just couldn't overcome. It made me feel weak and stupid. I hated that feeling. And I greatly respected David for his ability. Or maybe envied him.

"Truman and Binnell," David said after ten minutes of laborious study. "I see where your hunch came from."

I sat forward on the bed. "What do you think?"

David leaned over to show me some of the numbers in DPI's portfolio. "See this? Truman and Binnell bought several stocks from your uncle's brokers earlier this year. These weren't actual shares in DPI but simple assets of the company finances. Stuff like assets created in limited scope mutual funds or hedges, or even shared retirement accounts that can be invested in different ways.

Under normal circumstances, I'd say that was a normal trade between parties."

"What makes it abnormal?" I asked.

"DPI later shows a net loss of over seven-hundred thousand dollars in tradeable capital. However, the loss isn't accounted for through any of the reported trading. It's just not there anymore. Now, take a look at this."

David switched the DPI report for the PetroJet report and pointed to T&Bin's listings in three different places. "Truman and Binnell show up all over PetroJet's report. More than likely, they're doing some sort of commissioned work for PetroJet; nothing contracted like PetoJet's primary broker. But if you look closely here and here... the numbers just appear. PetroJet's portfolio goes up an additional $3 million in the space of a few months. And *here* are DPI's missing stocks."

I frowned trying to keep pace with David's conclusions. "I don't get it."

"It looks to me like Truman and Binnell bought some phantom stocks from DPI for a pittance. The only reason I can explain the resulting upsurge in value in those stocks in PetroJet's portfolio is that they were somehow inflated. That's very unusual. I'll have to check into the individual stocks themselves and see what their operating record looks like, but that's only if they're publicly available. These could be private stocks and funds, but I can still make some calls to some of these banks they're working with and get names on accounts to confirm."

"What would DPI be doing with phantom stocks in the first place?"

"I don't know. You'll have to ask Carter about it. But it looks to me like the stocks were set up as some kind of relief fund. The money that disappeared from DPI's portfolio could either be part of a hidden relief fund or an intercompany payoff of some kind."

"Is this something the SEC would like to know about?" I hedged.

"Absolutely. At PetroJet *and* DPI. Now, let me show you something else." David picked up the QuickBooks logs I had printed from Sherry's computer. "This accounting file shows multiple payments to the owner of this program *from* Truman and Binnell."

"For services rendered or something, right?"

"Right, but the dollar amounts correspond to the initial value of the DPI stocks that Truman and Binnell bought. After the date of T&Bin's last activity on the DPI report, this account shows huge transfers of money between the owner and Truman and Binnell. Jack, it looks to me like this account owner is laundering assets for Truman and Binnell."

"Taking non-existent profit and turning it into hard cash?" I prompted.

David nodded. "Which later shows up back in PetroJet's portfolio at a very inflated value."

I shook my head, off-balance from David's rapid response. "Sum it up for me, David. What the fuck is going on here?"

David leaned back in his chair and took off his glasses. "Best guess? Someone at PetroJet found out your uncle's got a phantom slush fund in phantom stocks and bonds. They figure they can lift the money because the stocks don't actually exist on the NASDAQ. If Truman and Binnell are working for PetroJet, then they could have found a way to buy out those stocks from DPI. Don't ask me how; you're not supposed to be able to do that. Assuming they found a way, though, they transfer the value of the stocks from their reserves to this QuickBooks account. It keeps growing because DPI is still paying investment benefits on its phantom stocks. That money ends up in the account, perfectly laundered, and then somebody else nabs it."

"PetroJet," I concluded.

David shrugged. "There's no evidence of that beyond the fact that the total amount in the QuickBooks account just about adds up to the $3 million increase in PetroJet's portfolio." His eyes looked like they contained small exploding stars. "Where did you get this stuff, Jack? This could be a securities fraud case the likes of which could make some careers at SEC."

My lips pursed in abstract thought. "Don't ask. David, if I asked you to hang onto this and put together some kind of official investigation into the fraud, maybe a...documentation of a discovery...would you do it?"

David blew out a long breath and adjusted his tie. "It'll take time, Jack."

"I'm willing to wait. And can you keep it just between us? I don't want someone from the SEC knocking on your door."

"Neither do I... which is why I'm adamant to stay involved." He picked up the papers on the table and waved them at me. "This stuff alone is enough for a preliminary SEC audit. Not to mention the accompanying IRS audit that's sure to follow."

I rubbed my eyes. They felt like someone had glued blocks of cheese to the eyelids. "I just need this stuff worked out, David. I'm not smart enough to do it."

"You don't really believe that, do you? I know you, Jack."

"Okay, I can't do it *fast enough*, David! Something nasty's happening between DPI and PetroJet, and I don't want to be the only one without a chair when the music stops."

David averted his gaze, looking out the hotel room window. Finally, he carefully gathered the papers up into the manilla folder and tapped them down to arrange them.

"Okay, Jack. I'll see what I can do."

"If you turn something up, email it to me." I scrawled my email addy down on a scratch piece of paper for him. "Just get me a good overview of what the hell's going on and what's going to happen if someone forgets to zip up after they're done pissing."

"If? Or *when*?"

I turned to the door, a dark cloud squeezing behind my eyes. "Lot of people forget to zip their fly these days, David. Thanks, kaz. I owe you big time."

David grinned, running a hand through his bushy brown hair. "Then come hang out with me sometime. I have got to show you this new motorcycle I just bought."

I thought about Tampa. About warm waters, tall palm trees, neon lights in the dark.

"Sold."

8.

FIFTEEN MILES OF TRACK

I barely caught the phone, lunging out of the shower and dripping water all over the carpet.

"Yeah, it's me."

"Hello, you," said a silky feminine voice. "It's Liz."

"Liz!" It's almost hilarious how I get calls like these when I'm unprepared. "Hey, what's happening, girl?"

"Not a whole lot. I was just calling to see what time you guys get started tonight."

I grinned, casting a baleful look at the suit that hung in the closet.

"Nine o'clock sharp. You want me to put you on the guest list?"

The laugh reminded me of Natalie Wood from *Love With the Proper Stranger*. "What if I don't show?"

"Then somebody else gets in for free."

A clicking noise. Her tongue against her lips?

"See you at nine."

I had spent the intervening days on the down-low, reevaluating my options and going over what I knew about the case. What it came down to posed a serious problem to my working relationship with Carter, and I wasn't quite sure what to do about it. Confrontation between family and myself always ended badly. I just hoped there was some way to make Carter see that he had waded into a deeper muck than I knew how to deal with.

Before I knew it, it was 25 to Midnight.

Time to be a star.

We opened up with the same song we always did, that from which our holy name had been divined. Virtually no one recognized the song since it had landed rather unceremoniously on a B-side single from Sting's fifth album. That made it perfect fodder for a quintet of paranormally enhanced musicians with a sweet tooth for good music.

I swayed like an Arabian serpent, entranced by the sweet noise emanating from a turban-top's magic flute. The mic gripped firmly in one hand, I pranced across the stage clad in a green linen suit and white sneakers belting out lyrics that no one knew but everyone was growing to love. The driving snare and hi-hat behind me egged me on. Dave's creeping sax fill brought us into the chorus.

The bridge involved a sudden change to a different meter, and we smacked it like we were born to the rhythm. Alexei's potluck bassline propelled us, and Steve's shadowy guitar riffs held us off. By the time I had reached the penultimate note, we skipped back into the song's closing verse.

The crowd, first wary of a tune not familiar to them, started hopping to the beat. Lightsey, Chad, Harvey, and Tom returning the favor from the other night led the chant, clapping in time with Jeffie's snare. It was enough to get patrons interested, and ears began to turn our direction. The true *coup d'etat* wouldn't occur until the opening of the next song.

We ground down on "25 to Midnight" and immediately launched into the pickup tune. I joined Jeffie on percussion, grabbing a shaker and gyrating in time with his bells and blocks. At his count, the others jumped in immediately, and half the bar was on the dance floor. You can't resist, can't help but succumb to the opening rhythm of "Tripping Billies" by Dave Matthews. If you perform it right, this song teases a crowd's interest for a short moment before the sharp moment of realization washes over them that *Oh my GAH they're playing DAAAAAAAAAVE!!!* We delay the payoff of the opening notes as long as we can with an ever-building cascade of percussion, all of us picking something up to bang on in a cacophony of wood blocks, sticks, conga skins, and tambourines. When it was just right, Jeffie yelled the count over the din—"One! Two! Three!"—and we all came in on the song's bombastic opening riff. Dave had a music box fed to his Senhauser mic, giving his sax a backup section replete with trombone, trumpet, and baritone; and the layers combined with bass, guitar, and drums to nail a rhythm that everybody knew

We played like it was meant to be played, live and in full force. Jeffie added a precocious running double bass to the mix while Dave smoked the stage with the sax hits. The power and fury behind our rendition could not be denied, and the boys and girls at Dewey's that night swarmed to the stage to get closer to us. We didn't have an original tune between us. But it didn't matter. Every time we took the stage, it didn't matter.

We were stars.

The first set rolled on into "80s night," drawing in more of the bar's passers-by with Paul Simon's "You Can Call Me Al," "One Thing Leads to Another" by The Fixx, and Peter Gabriel's "Sledgehammer." By the time our funk medley of Morris Day and the Time's "Jungle Love" and "The Bird" played out, the entire house had exploded into a mosh of sloshing beer and shaking cigarettes in upraised fingers and hands. We closed out the set with a guilty pleasure, Stevie Ray Burns' nightly shining time, "I Want a New Drug."

"Stay tuned, folks!" I crowed through the mic, waving to the applause. "We'll be back!"

We retreated into the small box that adjoined the stage and the corridor to the restrooms. Jeffie yelped and cackled as he traded high-fives with Dave. I needed a towel. It never failed. I could be on stage in a towel and I'd still sweat half my body weight off.

"*Daaaaaayyyyyyaaaaaaamn!*" Dave Smythe, our resident Bostonian transplant, screeched, twitching like a crack fiend. "Did you *see* that *ass*? That ass inna *front*? Dooley, *fuck*!"

"Yes, mastah, yes, mastah," I said, panting. "Ease up on the sugar cubes, Dave."

"What was up with that guitar action on 'New Drug,' Steve?" Jeffie said, tugging on a water bottle. "When did you start pulling Pete Townshends with the guitar behind the head and shit?"

Steve's massive bulk shrugged in its way, and he reached for a cigarette out of my jacket pocket. "Oh, y'know. Saw that on VH-1 one time."

I smacked Steve on the back of the head and howled, keyed up from the energy between us. "Like a rocket to the stars, baby! The *stars*!"

"We should play that one again, yes?" Alexei intoned in his thick Russian accent. "They go crazy!"

"Either that or our slow 'Message in a Bottle' for the encore, 'Lex" Jeffie agreed.

"Let's mingle, gang," I said, leaving the side stage for the bar itself. "And try and book some more gigs this time. I didn't spend fifty bucks printing us up these snazzy business cards to frame and put on the wall. And no fucking bar mitzvahs, Dave!"

The lag time between sets always offered us a chance to hob-nob with the crowd and book new shows. I kept the band well-stocked with 25 to Midnight business cards, and thus armed, we waded into the throng to display our wares. Steve immediately found his girlfriend and began whining for a beer. Dave jumped like a pogo stick across the bar, followed by a stolid Alexei. Jeffie managed to snag a Canebraker he had been pursuing for a hot minute. Hopefully, that would lead to a nice private party out near the lake. They always paid well.

"Jackie, m'boy!" I heard Doc Faller yell as I neared the bar. "Quite a fine night up there, snapper! When are you going to please an old man with some Tom Jones?"

"Next set, Doc, I promise." I doffed my sweat-stained jacket and lit a smoke. "Are we sounding worth a damn tonight?"

The Doc, clad in an outrageous Hawaiian shirt and his customary glasses, guffawed briefly and handed me a Crown and seven. "Aren't you always, Jackie-boy? Keep this up, I may have to join your band. The girls are going crazy out here."

I met some stares from a few of Doc's mentioned women, and I gave them all waves and winks. "Doc, I *need* to be in the band to get laid. You can just *do it*."

Doc Faller clapped me on the shoulder and grinned from ear to ear. "Remind me to tell you how to do that some day, lad. It'll come in handy on rainy nights. Now go enjoy yourself. Off! Off!"

I let the Doc push me back into the crowd where a bevy of anxious faces and hands awaited me. I doled out business cards for a couple hopeful wedding shows, and I let the boys from The Jive-T's give me the usual ribbing. I heard the catcall from a tall table near the bar, and the grin immediately came into being when I spotted Frank Vandy. Talk about a cat who has absolutely no hangups about fashion sense. He was still dressed in his shop clothes: A dirty, soldering solution stained T-shirt and holed fatigues. I let him pull me over to his stool.

"You're making me look bad up there, Jack," Frank giggled, tugging on a rum and coke. "Used to be, I was *da kine* in this place."

"You haven't played up here since last year, Frank," I said. "When you were still sitting in with Kabana. Say, speaking of which, you wanna play a few?"

I could see the twinkle in Frank's eye. "Whatcha got for me?"

"Remember the last time you asked me that?"

"You want to?"

"Last song of the show. Promise. Go get your sax."

Frank made a high-pitched whoopee noise and bounded out of the bar. I shook my head, snickered and got back to mingling with the crowd. Even Barry Bryce, John Lewis, and some of my other old frat acquaintances had showed for the gig. You get used to a lot of the smoke people blow up your ass, saying things like, "Yeah, your songs *rock*, man! They *rock*!" But even if most of it is half-hearted, you grow to love it. I certainly did. It was like a drug. Feed me with your praise. Succor me on your worship. For I *am* Rock Star.

After a few minutes of bouncing off shoulders, someone jerked at the sleeve of my ornate maroon silk shirt.

"Should I have gotten a big sign that said, 'Vocalist over here?'" Liz said.

I couldn't contain my grin, and I sunk into the other empty chair at her table. Her smile bore faint traces of lipstick and hinted at immaculately white teeth beneath. She wore a loose-fitting silk shirt of her own, white, and some long black pants.

"Sorry, I don't hear too well, ma'am," I said over the din of the house speakers. "Thanks for coming."

"Are you kidding?" Her green eyes twinkled under the glint from the house lights. "I had to check out this hot-to-trot band I've been hearing about. I've been doing some checking up on you, Jack."

"Oh, boy, that usually leads to a conversation about lawyers," I said.

"Well, the lawyer in question said he really enjoyed your show in Pearl last month. Jim Metterlink?"

"Oh, yeah! That *was* good show."

"He seemed to think so."

"And what do you think?"

She sipped from a milky glass and let her eyes fade into an obvious appraisal of me. "I've never heard anyone with the guts to actually play '25 to Midnight.' I think you play it better than Sting does."

I was agape. "You actually have that single? Wow. I better kick you up a couple of notches on my Impressed List."

"Found it in a bargain bin." She shrugged. "I really liked *Mercury Falling* so I bought up all the singles. He always puts the neat songs on the singles. Do you have the one with 'The Pirate's Bride?'"

I hummed a few bars close to her ear so she could hear me, offering a chance to get a whiff of stellar perfume. When I caught the tune just right, I sung the chorus in a low voice.

Liz made an excited clap and squealed. "Do you play it?"

"Nah, never got around to it. But we've got a little 'New York State of Mind' coming up if you're so inclined."

"I can do Billy Joel. You guys are really good, honestly. You should make an album or something."

"Not much of a demand for a cover album by a buncha unknown Mississippi boys," I lamented. "Although, we can dream. We did cut a demo of about six or seven songs last year. Cheap stuff, but I guess you could call it album material. We'll never sell it though. The rights to the songs cost too much. Say, thanks for that. Really. Starving artists need their faint praise."

"Nothing faint about it," Liz said, and I could see that she was genuinely excited about our music. "I'm glad I came."

"I'm glad you came, too."

That could have been the moment. I could have leaned in, right there, and asked her to come home after the show. It would have been perfectly within the strictures of inter-gender mating rituals, and I think she would have been amenable to the idea. There was one problem, though. I'm a coward when it comes to sex. I'm a Sex Coward. It's not that I hated fucking by any means. It was just the assorted baggage that came along with a quick coupling. Do you ask her to stay over for breakfast? Do you ask her if she's seeing anyone else? Do you get in a hissy about how clean your apartment is? I could no longer tolerate the minutiae associated with hooking up. Even if everything turned out for the better, there was always something down the line that killed the relationship. And I always knew that it was my fault. And I hated that feeling. As much as I would have given for abandoning my solitary lifestyle, I simply couldn't manage everything that came along with it. Ask anybody I'd ever hooked up with. Ask Crys.

Crys.

Dammit.

Ergo: "Hey, you wanna have Griddle House after the show?"

Liz's face blanched, clearly confused by the tack. "Griddle House?"

"Yeah, it's a breakfast joint. Stays open all night. I have the worst jones for bacon and eggs after a show. It's some kind of disease, I think."

"I suppose I could do breakfast," she said, her angelic smile returning. "Is this like a date thing?"

I raised an eyebrow, mulling it over. "I dunno. Should it be?"

"What do you think?"

"What do *you* think?"

"I think you're trying to pin my honestly asked question directly back on my shoulders and thus totally avoid the point of my question in the first place."

"I think you may be right, Sherlock Holmes."

She giggled. "So...?"

I shrugged. "Well... I guess, why not? Huh?"

She tapped the table between us very rapidly. "Tell you what. We split the check and decide if it's a date thing afterwards. Deal?"

I couldn't stop the smile. "Deal."

Liz had the attitude. There was no doubt about it. Any sign of pretentiousness on her part disappeared on contact. I couldn't fathom a single game-playing bone inside her. My worst trouble with relationships stemmed from my complete intolerance for bullshit. I'd been in college. I'd played the games. I knew what to expect. And I was tired of it. Liz seemed like she felt the same way. In her position, I didn't think many of the girls I'd danced with at the fraternity would put up with my sweaty appearance right then. But Liz just seemed to glom right over it.

I pulled the sticky silk from my chest and aired out my body, hoping to curb the perspiration with a light breeze. What I couldn't tell was whether or not I was still worn down from the last set or having that conversation with Liz.

"You better get back up there, superstar," she said, and I realized we'd been sitting there silent for a good while. I offered her a sheepish grin as I stood.

"You're not going to abandon me, are you?" I asked, only half-kidding.

"Not if you play me a song," she replied.

"What do you want to hear?"

Liz pursed her lips and eased back in her chair. Her eyes searched the ceiling for an answer, and she twirled a finger in her ponytail. I couldn't move.

"Surprise me," she finally said.

"Okay." No witty retorts. No slick comebacks. Nothing. Just, "Okay."

I guessed it was enough.

On my way back to the stage, I bumped into my Dad. He had been chatting with Doc Faller when I slid by, and he reached out to halt me. He offered me a pained grimace as his fingers sank into the wet mesh of my once-pristine silk shirt.

"Damn, boy, you been swimming tonight?" he jabbed.

"Yeah, in the gene pool," I said, lightly popping him on the shoulder. "Hey, you heard from Carter lately?"

Duke shook his head, swapping my empty Crown and seven for a fresh one. "I suppose he's been working."

My eyes narrowed as I sipped the drink. "He'd better be."

Duke caught the look in my eye. "Find something?"

"Yes." My flaccid cheeks conveyed the disappointment. "Most unfortunately so."

My father lit me a cigarette and handed it over to me. "What do you need?"

I took a quick puff and exhaled into the collective smoke cloud hanging over the bar. "I'll let you know."

"You know where to find me."

"You bet. Thanks, Dad."

I turned away, wanting for one night to forget about the morass in which I had covered myself. Jeffie, Dave, Steve, 'Lex were waiting when I returned to the side stage. For one night, I could forget about things for a while.

I just wanted to be a *star*.

"All right, folks," I said after the applause had died down. "Thank you, thank you. One more, okay. Please give a special welcome to the Tracks of Sax... Mister Frank Vandy!"

By the end of the night, I had completely lost my perception of the workout on stage. My hair was slick with sweat, and my shirt clung to me at every corner and cranny. My throat felt like someone had poured a pound of gravel down it and washed it down with arsenic. By all rights, the show was over. But no one left Dewey's Alley without an encore.

Frank entered the stage and joined Dave at the sax mic, hefting Frankenstein, the baddest motherfucking Selmer Mark VI you've ever heard. Frank had built the sax from scratch, its name derived from the numerous other horns he had cannibalized to give birth to this, his greatest creation. I met eyes with each of my bandmates, looking to get their confirmation of the upcoming clincher for the evening. Jeffie traded his sticks for a pair of brushes, Steve quickly tuned his stratocaster, and 'Lex gave one of his tune toggles a half-turn.

"I promised someone I'd give them a song," I said into the mic. "Well... here it is."

25 to Midnight were renowned for their ability to inject subtle original touches to their set list. We had tossed out the flute and added an unstrained snare to make "Down Under" into a fat reggae tune. We cut together Kool and the Gang, The Commodores, and Will Smith for the funkiest funk this side of "Jungle Boogie." We spiced up "Pussy Control" with more rap action from House

of Pain and Digital Underground. But this one was our crowning achievement.

Steve struck the opening chords, belaying the original, faster melody in favor of a slow, mourning riff. Frank added a touch of tenor here and there, fueling the dirge with a downbeat jazz. Jeffie's brushes lightly touched his snare and toms. I took Sting's charter lyrics from "Message in a Bottle" into myself and changed them, alchemizing their construction and delivery to render back unto our audience a slower caress of each line, stretching out the vowels. The assemblage pressed against one another in front of the stage, raising their arms in tandem to sway in time with the slow, burgeoning leitmotif. As they moved, Steve added his higher pitched voice to the chorus, joining me as if in benediction to our congregation of disciples.

At each pause in between verses, I lowered my head and bowed to either Alexei or Dave or Frank. Each took a separate solo, bending the constraints of the song in favor of their own unique gifts. Alexei's callused fingers danced across his bass, eliciting chords and pops where none should have any right to exist. They flowed together in harmony with the mood we had established, harkening back to the haunting tragedy of what the lyrics initially meant. Once the audience had a chance to scream and holler for the Russian's superb ability, Dave broke into the mix. His Conn tenor sax cut through the dim atmosphere emerging from the speakers. Invisible notes on a sad psychedelia clef danced over people's heads. At last, we unleashed Vandy on the crowd, allowing the senior musician's mastery to overwhelm us all. I traded bemused looks of amazement with Jeffie, both of us astounded by the magic spewing forth from Frankenstein.

I found Liz's eyes in the throng after panicking from not seeing her at the table. But she stood and swayed along with the crowd, decorum forgotten as she mingled with the beer-slogged residents of the Alley. Our eyes met as I quietly came back into the verse. I could see her lips move in tandem with the words I sung.

Steve's backups came to support my own, building in intensity. Frank and Dave echoed the melody with a double tap to the sax. The crescendo became unbearable, waiting to be born, until the full weight of the band kicked in behind me, abandoning our tragic interpretation for the upswept tempo and power of the original. Jeffie lit up the sudden switch in tempo and intensity with a Stewart Copeland-inspired crescendo across toms and cymbals, abandoning the brushes in favor of full-on double-butted sticks. In the space of seconds, we had transformed our requiem into a battle cry. Bass thumped from the house amps, strings squealed their protests, downbeats plugged catches in silence punctuated by cymbal crashes, and my own voice roared the lyrics until the final smash. This was our Zone, and we could only get there together, the five of us in tandem, never apart.

Ladies gentlemen, 25 to Midnight's gift to the world: "Message in a Bottle," Mississippi style.

The crowd frenzied as the last note crashed down. Applause and cheers rang out from every direction, quashing my thanks through the amplifiers. I looked down to see Liz cheering and clapping as hard as the rest. When she caught my eye, she blew me a kiss, blossoming into a radiant smile. I kissed my forefingers and held them up to her, winking to show my gratitude.

Then I ran to get my jacket.

"Sloppy, sloppy, sloppy! Okay, try *again*, O music master."

"Jesus, go easy on me, okay? Gimme a minute to think."

"Time's up!"

"Okay! Uhhhh... 'No Sleep Till Brooklyn.'"

"Good one. 'New Orleans Ladies.'"

"Augh! Why didn't you guys play that one?"

"I don't have the voice for it. You should hear Duke's band do it, though. Lowery nails that mother."

"Okay, okay. 'Sexy Sadie.'"

"Beatles back atcha. 'Everybody Has Something To Hide Except for Me and My Monkey.'"

"God, what letter do I get to use on that long thing?"

"Only the last one. This is your game, girl."

"Dammit. All right, Y. Ummm..."

"Tick-tock, tick-tock..."

"Quit it! Ah! 'You Can't Always Get What You Want.'"

"'Typical Situation.'"

"'New!'"

"Uhhhh... goddammit!"

"Come on, superstar. Thrill me with your trivia!"

"W-W-W... Dammit! I give up!"

Her laugh mingled with mine as we recoiled from the game. Two plates of empty bacon and eggs sat in front of us. The ashtray mixed the butts of Camel Lights and Marlboro Light 100's in a gray-orange mush. A cola and an orange juice stood off against each other at the middle of the table.

"Ha! Got you!" Liz crowed. "'Where's the Love?'"

"Hanson?" I exclaimed in pure shock. "You bust me up with *Hanson*? Oh my God, may the angels and all the saints above grant mercy for your condemned soul."

"Guilty as charged." Liz blew out a cloud of smoke and stubbed out her cigarette. "I reach deep into my sinister bag to win."

"Serves you right, you evil temptress." I chuckled again and leaned my head back against the glass partition separating our booth from another. In the ensuing break of chatter, Mayla appeared at our sides with a pitcher of Coke and a pitcher of orange juice.

"Can I fill you up, kids?" she said pleasantly.

"No more for me, thanks," Liz replied.

"I don't think my body can take anymore caffeine, Mayla," I said, sticking my tongue out at my glass. "No amount of fetid stimulant can revive me from tonight's ordeal."

"You should be drinking something healthy like apple juice, Jack," Mayla intoned with a severe grimace. "All these bad habits are going to ruin your singing voice, young man. Your friend here has the right idea."

"I have the right idea," Liz asserted with a curt nod.

"Thank you for that idea report, Mayla," I said, letting a corner of my mouth curl upwards at Liz. "I'll get right on that."

"Now you go home and get some rest, Jack," Mayla continued, picking up our plates and clearing off the table. "It's nearly five o'clock in the morning, for heaven's sake!" "Yes, ma'am," I said with all the gusto of an annoyed schoolboy.

When Mayla finally left, Liz tittered quietly and tilted her head. "Mother?"

"No, she is not my mother," I quipped. "My mother *made* me drink caffeine. And *Kool-Aid*. God, the horror of Kool-Aid."

"Well, she's got a point." Liz looked at her watch. "It is pretty late. Well, early, I suppose. And I have to drive back to Jackson."

I played with one of the leftover forks on the table, staring at it so I didn't have to look at her inviting eyes. "Well... You could stay here if you wanted to."

When she didn't respond, I looked up, immediately blinking rapidly as her green eyes pored into me. "I mean, if you wanted to. I've got room."

Liz seemed to consider this, reaching for an empty pack of cigarettes and fiddling with the lid. "Can I bum a smoke?"

"Sure," I said, handing one over.

"Well, since you were so nice as to offer me this tantalizing little cancer stick, I guess you're safe enough." Her teasing eyes softened as they met mine. "You're sure it's not an imposition?"

"As long as I don't hear any cracks about the pad," I said, pointing at her in mock sternness. "It's a good pad."

"It's a bachelor's pad."

"But a good pad."

"We'll see."

"Yeah," I puffed, reaching for my jacket. "I guess we will."

"Listen... I don't want to..."

"I don't either."

"But this is still... okay?"

"I'm not complaining."

"All right. I just don't want you to be uncomfortable."

"I don't think that's going to be a problem, Jack."

She let her clothes fall off her revealing a lightly tanned body. Her arms bore the faintest traces of a gymnast's musculature, and her dirty blonde hair swished across the smoothness with a soft whisper. I had already showered, more for her sake than mine. I crawled into the bed and pulled the sheets over me.

Sitting on the edge, Liz peered at me over one shoulder, her hands bending behind her to tug at the clasp on her bra. "Do you mind if I take this off?"

"As long as its contents are not in any way, shape or form used to perpetrate madness upon my person," I said, holding a judiciary finger up.

Liz smiled as she let the bra fall away. "You never quit, do you?"

I tried not to look, unsure of what I should do as I always was in situations like that one. "It's a defense mechanism," I admitted.

"Against what?" She curled under the sheets, laying across one arm on her pillow to look at me.

I looked at my bare chest, my lips forming into a small line. "Against... everything."

She didn't ask for elaboration, didn't request a meaning. She simply ran a hand along my chest, moving closer to me under the covers. I felt her breasts press up against my arm, and I tensed for a brief moment.

"I'm going to kiss you now," she said. "If that's all right."

I looked into her sea green eyes, transfixed. "That's all right."

Her mouth melted into mine. I felt a drop of sweat cascade down my forehead. I let my hand sweep gently through her silky blonde hair. We broke apart slowly as if refusing to give up what we had finally shared. Her lips brushed against the hair on my chin, and I let mine drift across the ridge of her Grecian nose. The tension was gone.

"I'm not uncomfortable," she told me, putting her head down against my chest.

"I'm not either," I whispered, reaching for the light.

9.

YOU DON'T LOVE ME LIKE YOU USED TO

Arising at half past ten in the morning, I almost screamed when I found Liz dozing silently in my bed. As the previous night came back to me, I scratched my head and let the cobwebs fade away. I tried to be as quiet as possible getting out of bed and slipping into my robe, and doing that awfully. I even farted once because I couldn't help it – thanks, Griddle House – but thankfully, Liz slept right through it. I even had time to quickly spray some Febreze just in case my senses had dulled to the point to miss the potency of a Dooley Fart.

The coffee pot had already completed its morning work, and I fixed myself a cup while heating up the stove. Moving in a half-awake trance, I broke a couple of eggs on the skillet and started serving up an omelette. Guarding the cuisine's comeuppance between slices of green peppers, cheese, and mushrooms, I brought out another skillet to dry up some bacon. By no means was I some kind of master chef, but when it came to the essentials, I transformed into a machine. Twenty minutes later, with no feeling of passage of time, I had a fat, artery killer omelette ready to go.

I kept the stove simmering just in case Liz wanted something when she woke. Falling onto the couch, I ate directly off my coffee table. The television didn't show me much on late morning Sunday, and I settled with a *Real World Boston* marathon on MTV.

A mane of unkempt blonde hair peeked around the corner of the living area and the bedroom. "I smell something yummy..."

"Hey!" I said through a mouthful of bacon, egg, and cheese. "Did I wake you up? I'm sorry."

"No, no, it's all right." Liz swept into the living room, clad in a long Batman T-shirt she must have liberated from my chest of drawers. "Whatcha got cooking?"

"Omelette. Want one? I can serve one up pretty quick."

"Sit down, Emeril." She disappeared into the kitchen, and I heard coffee splash into a mug. "I'll just munch off yours. There's no way you should be scarfing something that big."

"I'm a growing boy. It's good for me."

"Yeah, tell me that again when we're digging crust out of your arteries. You have any creamer?"

"Amaretto in the fridge. There's some sugar stuff in the cabinet above you."

"Got it."

Liz sprinted to the sofa and snaked into a cross-legged position next to me. She had brought another fork from the kitchen and speared a section of my omelette replete with bacon bits and melted cheese. "Whatcha watching?"

"*Real World*," I said, nodding at the TV. "It's the one in Boston."

"Ooh, I love that show. I never saw Boston, though."

"It's pretty cool. This cast cracks me up. They have to do volunteer work at this kid's shelter, right? Well, imagine that for sec. You've got a buncha typical Gen X folks at a boys and girls camp in the city. The redhead got thrown out because she let some of the kids drink wine at a food convention."

"Lovely. I always wanted to try out for *Real World*. I just never could get past the whole live taping thing."

"I sent in a tape for that last crew. The one in Hawaii? Christ, did I have fun making that thing."

"What did you do?"

"Well, I interviewed myself. I filmed two separate pieces of myself, one with a goatee and one without. Me with the 'tee was me, and the other me was the interviewer. Asked myself all kinds of silly questions. Put this stupid pinata on my head for some reason. Just general silliness."

Liz tittered around a mouthful of omelette. "You'll have to show me that sometime."

I snickered and sipped my coffee. "How about...no? Not a chance. You'll have me committed."

"Such a man. Always afraid of commitment."

"If it involves a straitjacket and a regular dose of thorazine, you're goddamn right."

We finished off the omelette together, chatting intermittently between snippets of the antics on TV. A soft blue glow filtered in from the balcony door, hazy light escaping from the overcast sky. Our cigarette ashes mingled in the communal ashtray, and lazy loops of smoke floated upwards above us. Mornings like that were hard to come by, and I dwelt on it. None of the tribulations from the previous week intruded upon me, and I found myself a little vertiginous as Liz cuddled against me on the sofa.

"I could do this all day," I told her, wrapping my arms around her.

"Me too," she said. "I really don't want to go back to Jackson."

"I really don't want you to."

Liz squinted at the clock. "Well, I've got the rest of the day." She grinned and touched my chin, playing with the hair that grew there. "You have any plans?"

I smiled down at her. "I do now. What are you up for?"

"I don't know. What's there to do in Hattiesburg?"

"Beyond what we're doing now? Not much."

Liz's finger trailed along my jawline. "We'll figure something out."

The kiss made the morning, omelette and all.

We ended up catching a movie shortly after we left the apartment. The repertory theater wing at Turtle Creek advertised a long-awaited James Bond festival, and we rushed to catch the tail end of *From Russia With Love*. *Goldfinger* came next, and armed with popcorn, we let the film devour us. I found it hard to concentrate on the movie since Liz liked to let out a little moan whenever Connery walked on screen. I retaliated with a catcall as soon as Honor Blackman told us that her name was Pussy Galore. Liz laughed like a delighted schoolgirl.

On a whim, I decided to pull into Books-A-Million so we could grab a cappuccino. The bookstore contained rows of tables featuring hundreds of discarded or unsold novels. The place wasn't much more than a glorified flea market, but I'd come to enjoy the massive periodicals rack with its multitude of magazines, literary journals, and newspapers. Often, I liked to come in, grab a *Comics Scene* and read it over a mochaccino. Liz and I both decided on mocha sorbettos which we slurped obnoxiously on as we strode the aisles.

"I take it you read a lot," she said, tracing a finger over a dusty copy of some local author's forgotten first work.

"Much as I can," I replied. "But it's hard to get the good stuff around here. I'm reading this old, out-of-print series by Charley Kittlemeyer right now. Cold War spy type stuff. There's a used book store downtown I usually go to."

"I wish I had time to read more," she said. "The last thing I read was some piece of pop trash I got at an airport. It's shameful, I know. I should be delving into deeper things than medical thrillers."

I noticed we had strayed into the self-help aisle, and I picked up a book entitled *Men, Myth and Orgasm*. "There's plenty of that for the taking, if you're interested."

Liz chuckled and elbowed me in the ribs, snatching the book from my hands. She started skimming through it, her lips playing across the straw in her sorbetto cup. "Ah! Here we go. 'A Quick List of Your Man's Personal Myths.'"

I rolled my eyes and leaned against the book rack. "Do tell."

Liz cleared her throat. "'Number One: Men are and will always be the breadwinners in a family.'"

I made a noise in the back of my throat. "I have no problem sitting on my ass all day while the wife earns the bread."

"Strike that one." Liz turned the page. "'Number Two: There is no such thing as too much sex.'"

"Not in my apartment. I can take care of myself quite fine, thank you very much."

Liz slapped the book against my shoulder. "Too much information!"

"Hey, you read the question!"

"So there *is* such a thing as too much sex?"

I raised an eyebrow and folded my arms. "Maybe."

Liz poked me in the ribs again. "Come on, Dooley, fess up."

I eyed her carefully. "Okay, yeah. Too much sex sucks."

"Wow. They did break the mold with you." She eased against me. "Any particular reason why?"

"Yes." I bit my lip. "Bad experience."

Liz looked away. "I didn't mean to pry."

"No, it's okay. I mean, I never set out to make a secret about it. It's just not something I talk much about."

"Ex-girlfriend?"

"Yeah. I met her at one of our gigs. She was completely into me, y'know? I've never been with anybody who's always telling me things like how good I look or how cool I am. All the time, too. She never shut up. So after a while, I guess I started believing her."

Liz set the book back down on the shelf and took a sip from her sorbetto. "She wasn't wrong, you know."

I offered her a lopsided grin. "What am I supposed to say to that? Thanks? Seriously, I never know how to move on that particular issue."

She winked at me. "Just take it in stride and don't object. My powers of observation are both uncanny and infallible."

"Thank you for that uncanny report, Professor X," I quipped, and sucked quickly on my sorbetto straw. "Anyway, so one thing led to another, and we end up together. The next thing I know, it's like every day is Jack Day. I couldn't get away from her. She was everywhere. She asked me to come over all the time. And the worst part about it was, she lived with her parents."

"Ouch. Never a fun time."

"Tell me about it. And that wasn't all. Her parents were divorced but still living together."

"What? What kind of a situation is that?"

"One that's pretty fucked, if you ask me. Her mom was on pot like it was going out of style, and her dad was a recovering alcoholic." I shook my head and shrugged violently. "What was I supposed to think? That it was healthy?"

"She got addicted to you?" Liz asked.

"In hindsight, it certainly seems that way. I even tried to help, y'know? I thought that maybe if I could get her off the drugs and out of that house... I dunno."

"Maybe you could make a difference?" Liz touched my arm. "But she didn't want to."

"She said I didn't have any right to interfere with her life." My eyes unfocused, the books in front of me turning to blotches of indistinct color. "But she had every right to mine."

I felt Liz's hand on my arm, and I refocused. She peered neutrally into my eyes and applied a bit of pressure to my forearm. I never talked about Crys to anyone. *Anyone.* For some reason, I felt compelled to do so with Liz. Whether or not it was some kind of justification for my lifestyle or personality, I couldn't say. My father's Catholic upbringing would have told me that confession was a necessity, a cleansing purge of bad material from your soul. Duke never raised me Catholic, though, and I'd never gotten the impression that he'd been particularly adherent to the practice. But maybe the Catholics were right and I was just too thick and proud to admit otherwise.

"Listen, I didn't want to..." Liz's fingers touched my lips.

"It's all right, Jack," she whispered. "I understand."

The sorbetto cups landed on the floor, disgorging their contents onto the worn gray carpet. We wrapped each other in ourselves, faces pressed tight. An older woman paused in consideration of browsing down the aisle when she saw us. When our lips parted, I could look at Liz without shame.

"Thanks," I said.

She winked at me. "That'll be five dollars, buddy."

It was my turn to poke her in the ribs. "How about another sorbetto?"

Night fell quickly, and we abstained from another fat binge at a local eatery, choosing instead to come home. Liz had to get back to Jackson anyway, and I had things of my own to worry about. The Little White Honda parked next to her Camry, and we debarked for a final embrace under the stars. The clouds had finally given way to a true sky, and the moon shone a muted pattern down upon us from its fingernail lighting.

"Thanks for having me," Liz said, arms around my neck. "I want to come back."

"I want you to," I said, stroking the small of her back. "I might be up in your area this week. Can I call?"

"Without a doubt. I'm afraid we don't have anything as engaging as a Books-A-Million to entertain with in Jackson."

"I'm sure we'll find something."

"I'm sure you're right."

The last kiss lingered briefly on my lips, and she turned to disappear into her car. As I shut the door for her, Liz put her fingers on the window glass, looking at me with her emerald scrutiny. I tapped the window with my own fingers and mouthed a goodbye. The car pulled out of the lot and disappeared around the corner.

As I turned back to my apartment, I wondered just how far my luck would hold out this time. Historically, my track record with women looked a lot like a crime scene report. Too many unknowns but plenty of gory detail on the perpetration itself.

The real crime would be my remembering the analogy a month down the line.

10.
WARNING SHOTS

I received Rick's PetroJet file late in the day on Monday. I'd spent the better part of the day compiling my notes on the problem at hand and avoiding a call to Carter. As much as I wanted to crack that nut, confronting Carter about the slush fund David had told me about made me uneasy. As it stood, I ended up busy enough taking calls for gigs from people who had seen 25 to Midnight at Dewey's Alley Saturday night. Three weddings, a New Year's party, and a reminder from the girl at The Sand Bar not to miss our two-night show Friday and Saturday in Ocean Springs. During the phone call, I made a mental note to go down early and spend some time looking into Al Henkel's family.

The PetroJet file arrived in a FedEx box complete with two manilla folders, reams of copied paper, and Rick's own annotations. Rick knew how I liked to tackle a problem, so the information was relatively easy to absorb. I started out with a general overview of PetroJet, reading a summary of the company's origin in Jackson. Finley had taken a rather large inheritance from his Gulfport-born family and parlayed it into the propane company he worked for at the time, Caddo Parish Petroleum. Finley bought out Caddo, renamed it PetroJet, and then merged with another up and coming company called Jet-Prop. As I read, I figured Finley must be a pretty smooth operator. Merging one's company with another and then assuming virtually all financial control wasn't an easy task. Then again, if what I suspected about Finley's money-throwing skills was true, then I supposed the merger went easier for him than I assumed.

PetroJet incorporated in 1978 as a retailer, selling primarily propane but investing heavily in kerosene, butane, and jet fuel as the oil market became increasingly unstable throughout the eighties. By 1985, Finley had acquired a supplier's plant in Pearl and had turned that into his own fleet of distributor's transports. By this time, PetroJet was on the fast track to becoming the largest petroleum and alternative fuel distributor in the state of Mississippi, and by all indications, Finley had designs on expanding into Louisiana, Alabama, and Texas. The company grew exponentially until 1992 when the Recession bit into the propane industry's powerhouse performance as an alternative fuel source. I found an additional report from the Mississippi Department of Transportation that listed several transport sales from PetroJet to various out-of-state petroleum companies. Rick had attached a note to this report that read, "This is where I think he started going sour. Maybe decided he needed to go a little further than business as usual to make up for lost profits?"

The evidence certainly supported Rick's interpretation. After 1992, PetroJet liquidated most of its frozen assets and turned them into hard cash to funnel into new investments. Lots of older transports and trucks had been sold off as well as more than a few smaller retail outlets that weren't producing sufficient revenue. I assumed this must have been the time Finley got into corporate stocks. The dates matched up with what David had seen on the PetroJet stock report, attributing several cheap portfolio additions to huge increases in net worth the following year.

By this point in the file, Rick had attached another note that directed me to the second manilla folder. I delved into that one and found numerous IRS audit reports and a couple legal documents concerning transfer of ownership. Apparently, Finley had gone back to acquisitions in the late nineties, which caused me to grimace since the propane industry's hard times had certainly not gotten better by then. As a matter of fact, many smaller petroleum companies still showed financial woes affected by the bottom-drop of the nineties, and I remembered Duke telling me about a few of his old clients turning to a co-op plan up north as a stopgap measure against bankruptcy. Most of the big shots in north Mississippi, as part of the co-op, bought each other out and operated as a linked corporation. PetroJet Chemical, on the other hand, kept chugging along the track, buying back its lost retailers and adding a few more independent dealers from Louisiana. Everyone else, all the mom and pop shops who had been filling cylinders for decades in tiny towns across southern America, they got ate up by bigger national energy companies and a few internationals. Market consolidation was eating the life out of a historically small-town business and forcing some folks to accept payoffs they didn't want to get out of the way and swap their brand logos out with something more nationally familiar. From the data, it looked like PetroJet was headed in that direction...but how? As Rick rightly twigged, how does a small- to mid-sized propane business find the profit margin in its failing funds to start buying up these mom and pop shops?

One of the legal documents in the second file showed a list of acquisitions made by PetroJet in the past year. Fred Acheson's name came up, the former head of Wolverton Gas Company in Magee. Duke had told me that the Magee location was one of Finley's most recent purchases, and I wondered if Acheson had experienced any of the same financial problems from which Carter and DPI were currently suffering. I consulted my notepad upon remembering Henkel's connection to Magee, and I found a scribble that reminded me Henkel was getting his five grand a month checks from somewhere in Magee. Perhaps Acheson could help me track down Betsy Jones, the signer of those checks. Considering this, I tapped a pen against my chin and decided to hit Magee in the morning. I lurched for the phone.

"Dooley Consulting," the earpiece stated after I'd dialed in.

"What up, Pop? You killing any Russkies today?"

"Hey, Jack! Nah, I got swamped with bullshit again. Client up in Greenwood's bitching about a DOT audit that's coming down on him later this week. I'm going to have to pack up and go see him tomorrow."

"Cool. Say, how much business do you do with Fred Acheson in Magee?"

"Wolverton's? He was a pretty good client up until PetroJet bought him out. I think Bill Finley's got his own safety team in-house; that's why I got screwed out of the account. Haven't talked to Fred since the buyout."

"Do me favor. Call him up and tell him I'm coming to see him tomorrow. Make up some bullshit about the state board ordering a new round of audits in the area or some other shit. Like I need to follow up on old paperwork for our own files. I dunno, just some shit. I need to get up there and take a look at his stuff."

"I can do that. I don't know how well-received you'll be, though, what with PetroJet's safety team."

"Just tell Fred that I'll come take a look at his stuff free of charge. Hell, he probably misses seeing a Dooley every other month."

"Most people do. Speaking of which, I saw that girl from the other night at the show. You talk to her again?"

"Liz? Yup. We hung out Sunday."

"Coooool! Get back on that horse, boy!"

"What's my name?"

"There you go!"

"*What's my name?!*"

"Now we're talkin'!"

"Killa Magilla, Pops. I have to go and track down your dumbass brother."

"That oughtta be a shit and a half. I'll call Acheson as soon as I hang up. And see what you can do get in on that PetroJet deal, okay? I like multiple location companies."

"Don't hold your breath, Dad. And thanks."

I hung up and dialed the number for DPI. Taking a deep breath, I prepared myself for what I'd been putting off the last week. After wrangling a couple of secretaries, I finally got Carter Dooley on the line.

"Jack? Hey, whatcha know?"

"Meet me at The Hog in an hour, Carter. No bullshit."

A pause. "You got something?"

"Just meet me in an hour. We need to talk."

I hung up without waiting for Carter's confirmation.

Time to go to work.

I got to The Mahogany Bar just before rush hour, so the crowd wasn't as thick as I would have liked. Even still, I found a secluded booth off to one corner that was tucked under the TV screen. Terminally tuned into ESPN, a college football game replayed across the TV. I lit a smoke and ordered a drink. I had about as much interest in sports as I did in contracting malaria.

Carter breezed in about fifteen minutes late. I had already finished my first Crown and seven, and I waved to the waitress as Carter spotted me and sat down at the booth. With a wild-eyed greeting, he clapped me on the shoulder and smiled up at the waitress.

"Glass of Merlot and another of whatever he's drinking," he told her. Once she had taken the order and moved away, Carter leaned over to me. "So what's the deal, Jack? Did you find something?"

"I found all kinds of things, Carter," I said, trying to keep my voice level. "But before we get into that, why don't you tell me a little about this investment slush fund you neglected to warn me about earlier?"

Carter blinked then exhaled heavily and leaned back in his chair. "How'd you find out about that?"

"Don't be stupid, Uncle Carter. You hired me to look into this shit, and I looked. What is it? Some kind of emergency relief stash?"

"Something like that." We fell silent as the waitress delivered our drinks. She left, and Carter looked at the smoldering butt between my fingers. "Can I have one of those?"

I passed him a cigarette and lit it for him. "As long as Aunt Dee doesn't find out. All right, now let's hear it."

"Larry Fortinbras, you know him? Our CPA. Anyway, back when we were first getting started up, we figured we needed to put aside some money in case the plant exploded one day or somebody sued us for something. You know how we do things. Fortinbras sets up this hidden stock with one of our stockbrokers. It was listed off as a contribution to charity at a certain level so the dividends didn't come back reportable."

"I follow you," I said, taking a long drag on the cigarette.

"Anyway, the money went into a slush mutual fund. It sat there and just made money. After it got up high enough, we added it to the DPI portfolio as an acquired asset through the partners."

"To avoid any prying SEC eyes."

"Right."

"But with the fund stuck out in the open like that, anyone can see what it's about."

"Not if it's wholly owned by the company. Investors can *see* it, but they can't buy shares of it because it's not public. Other funds in DPI's portfolio are, but not that one."

I shook my head. "Jesus, Uncle Carter. You didn't think that was important when we first met? What the fuck?"

Carter swallowed some wine and raised his hands in abeyance. "I told you I don't deal with all that stuff anymore! That's why I have Fortinbras and the stockbrokers on the payroll."

"Well," I said, putting the ciggie out. "Here's what I've been doing while you've been out living the high life. I did a check into PetroJet Chemical's portfolio and found some jacked up trading. David Novak's looking over it right now."

"Your cousin?" He made a face at himself. "Well, one of your cousins."

"Yeah, him. He's running a comparison between yours and PetroJet's portfolios, and we think they're the ones who've been scamming your stocks. I can't prove it yet, but I'm working on it."

Carter folded his hands into one big fist. "How?"

"Your boy Al Henkel's the key. He led me to a judge in Birmingham that may have some under-the-table stuff going on with Finley. I think your invisible accidents are being staged to throw money from your slush fund into Finley's bank account."

"What?" Carter blinked rapidly. "How is that possible? I've met Finley before. He's a sonofabitch, but he's an okay operator."

I lowered my gaze. "Carter, you don't see things like I do. This guy's dirty. Trust me."

"Okay. So what are you going to do about it?"

I polished off the Crown and seven. "I'm going to Magee tomorrow to see if Fred Acheson was in a similar situation to yours when Finley bought him out. What *you* need to figure out is how you're going to deal with this guy once I put him on the stage."

"You can do that? You can prove he's into all this?"

"I can light him up like a Roman candle. But you've got to consider how this is going to look for DPI if and when I do. That slush fund's going to draw some pretty heavy federal inspection if you decide to turn Finley in."

Carter rubbed his eyes and set his elbows on the table. "Fuck. This is the last thing I need. I'm already up to my ass."

"I don't know how much further into this I can go, Carter," I told him bluntly. "If we start getting into actual industrial espionage, then the most I can do is gather facts and get out of the way. That's some hardcore stuff to deal with. The FBI's got its own department for things like that, and so does the SEC. If David Novak keeps looking into this stuff too, he's going to be bound to report it."

"Son of a bitch," Carter breathed. "I'll have to think about it. In the meantime, you'll keep looking into it? You still haven't told me where my money is."

"I have a feeling it may be gone, Carter. But I'm not finished yet, so give me some time. I'll let you know what I find." I looked at the empty glasses on the table and took out a wad of cash from my pocket. "I'll get this."

Carter just looked at me blankly. "Thanks."

11.

LEGWORK

The drive to Magee took about fifteen minutes longer than I'd anticipated, Highway 49 having undergone a slight repair outside of Hattiesburg. Acres of allergy-inducing trees, bushes, and grasslands sped by me as the Little White Honda cruised, and I fancied a little Billy Joel on the way up. I still whistled "The Great Wall of China" by the time I opened the door to PetroJet Magee.

The Magee location stood just off the highway service road, boasting a small but functional main office and a large truck yard. A dilapidated and rusting cargo tank rested on cracked chock blocks further back in the yard. Several brand new residential propane tanks joined a bunch of older, decaying models near the side of the office. One of Acheson's bobtails—the single-tank propane motor carriers—thrummed quietly as it prepared to make its delivery for the day. The sun had broken through the cloud cover, and a cool breeze filtered through the air. It was one of the few times during the year that the weather could actually chase away the Mississippi humidity.

I walked past rows of gas grills and space heaters on my way to the front desk. A portly middle-aged lady sat behind the desk flipping through a four-month old copy of *Glamour*. I had to tap on the desk to get her attention.

"Hi, I'm Jack Dooley from Dooley Consulting. Is Fred in?"

The lady looked up briefly then shifted on her stool to yell over her shoulder. "Freddy!"

"*What*?" came a ragged voice from the back.

"Somebody from Dooley Consulting's here."

"Well, *shit*!"

Fred Acheson sported the customary walk and talk I'd come to expect from small-time propane dealers. His sagging gut poured a good two inches over his belt. A pair of faded jeans adorned what could only be varicose-plagued legs. His face remained tanned from long days of outside toil, and a drooping moustache offset his flaccid jaw. The only out-of-place thing I could see appeared to be the stark white and gold PetroJet polo he wore, sporting the company name on the breast.

"Duke Dooley's own boy come to see me!" Acheson chuckled, making his way around the desk to clasp my hand in a vise-like clamp. "How are ya, son?"

"Can't complain," I said, forcing a grin and hoping he didn't pull my hand out of its socket. "Duke told me you up and went corporate on him."

Acheson slung his cap off his head, revealing a sweat-packed rim of brown hair and a permanent bowl-cut crease around his head like a cap-molded halo. "Aw, hell, it was just that time, y'hear? Your name's Jack, right?"

"Yes, sir."

"Cut that 'sir' shit out, son! It's Fred! Yer daddy's called me worse things in his day, and I can't expect any less from a Dooley."

I slung my car keyring around on one finger. "Our reputation precedes us. I guess I'm fucked."

Acheson bellowed hard, slapping my shoulder and leaving a sweat-stained grime print on the leather jacket. I tried not to curl my lip.

"You are Duke's boy!" Acheson hollered. "Come on back, Jack. Is there anything I can getcha? Coke or something?"

"Nah, I'm good, Fred," I said, following him back into a dusty little cubicle behind the front desk. The office sported piles of stacked documents and unused refuse. A huge moose head adorned the wall to my right, and I wondered if those things were the new thing in southern office decor. Fuckin' mooses, man.

"Yer poppa said ya had something to tell me about DOT audits," Acheson said, seating himself behind his tiny desk. "That they're getting uppity on us again?"

"Yeah, that's what we've heard," I said, taking the seat across from him. "Federal budget surplus means more money for agencies. DOT hears that and decides to put some more inspectors on the road."

"Sonsabitches. Jack, they came to see me about six months ago already. We got a pretty good bill of operation, but it weren't through nothing I did. Those damn PetroJet people came down and started throwing paper around. Drove poor Terry out of his mind."

Terry Wolverton had been one of the co-owners of Wolverton's LP Gas up until PetroJet's buyout. I remembered Duke telling me something about the man having too much fun at the casinos on the coast while Acheson had to put up with details. I couldn't blame Acheson. With that kind of shaft, I'd be a little incensed, too.

"I heard about that," I lied. "What's the deal with those PetroJet boys?"

"I tell you what, Jack, I'm getting sorry I ever agreed to sell out to Finley." Acheson reclined in his chair and scratched his armpit. "Sure, the money's been fine, but these guys have policies and paperwork and all kindsa bullshit they're trying to ram down my throat. It's a pain in the ass. Hell, *they* inspect us more often than DOT."

"No kidding?" I prompted.

"Yeah, Finley's actually on his way down right now to check us out. Bastard finally took some time from his busy schedule to review the operation. Can ya believe it?"

A flash went off inside my mind. I hadn't planned on going toe-to-toe with the head cheese himself. Bill Finley's arrival at Magee could turn my probe sour if I let on too much. I had no idea what the man was like, and to tip him off that someone was sniffing out his operation might hamper my results. Still, I pondered going straight to Finley about enlisting DCS's services, potentially giving me a closer look at his business. I half-dismissed the idea, though. More than likely, Finley would laugh in my face and introduce me to his faceless safety team from Jackson. If he found the time for me at all.

"Better not bitch too loud, though, I guess," Acheson rambled on. "He and his girls're the ones that sign the paychecks."

My left eyebrow twitched. "His girls?"

"Yeah, his wife and his daughter." He shrugged noncommittally. "I think his wife manages the bank accounts for the whole company, and his daughter's been getting into it lately. I think they don't know their asses from a tree, though, Jack. The way they do business is making me cry."

"You don't say?" I said. "Are they supplying you with all your gas?"

"That's the funny thing," Acheson said with wide eyes. "Sure, we get our regular shipments from the Pearl plant, but every once in a while, a DPI truck pulls in here and drops a load. I got no idea why, but Finley's sent us a private check for the driver that drops this DPI gas off every time. Usually, you go through accountants, y'know?"

"Wait. One of my uncle's trucks comes through here on a regular basis and offloads an LP gas supply?"

"Yup. I asked Finley about it one time, and he told me to shut up and do what I was told. Can you feature that? Son of a bitch..."

"Same driver from DPI? Every time?"

"Uh-huh. Al something. I think the checks are made out to Al Henkel, now that I think about it. There was also this time a while back when Finley made me come in at two in the morning to accept this guy's load. It was weird shit, Jack, I tell ya."

The engines ground to a halt behind my eyes. Henkel *was* working for Finley after all. And based on Acheson's story, it sounded like he supplied PetroJet with stolen gas from DPI. I couldn't figure how that would compare to the accidents Carter had told me about, but I knew there had to be a connection. Perhaps Henkel had falsified DPI's records in order to cover the loss of product. He'd have to do something in order to get away with that much propane and not be suspected of outright theft, but with the sorry state of DPI's recordkeeping, Henkel could easily falsify the pickup and delivery numbers.

Henkel's mystery check writers started to come into focus as well. I reminded myself to check my notes once I got back to Hattiesburg. Whoever had authorized those checks had to be working for Finley in some capacity. I just had to link them together. I mentally kicked myself for not remembering the name. Details like that broke cases, from what Rick had told me.

"So why sell out to this guy in the first place, Fred?" I asked, taking a different tack. "Wolverton's was in pretty good shape last time I heard, but I've been out of the loop for a while."

Acheson looked at his desk and fiddled with a half-empty cup of coffee. "Well, that was partly Terry's fault, I think. He always took care of the financial stuff, right. Well, he comes to me one day and tells me that he's invested a lot of our profit in the stock market. I told him he was one dumb fool for taking that risk. We stand a better chance of increasing made profit if we speculate on the gas market itself."

"In what way?" I asked, intrigued.

"Well, you look at the market and see that propane's... sixty cents a gallon, let's say. Somewhere down the line, you're gonna have a falloff or some kind of shortage, so the price always gets kicked up. Sometimes as much as forty or fifty cents a gallon. My idea dealt with buying gas cheap at sixty cents a gallon even when we didn't need it. Then when the market shot up again, we sell that same gas for a forty-fifty cent markup."

I could see the merit in Acheson's strategy. "Gas market speculation. Sounds reasonable enough. And you don't have to deal with outside federal regulation, right?"

"Exactly! Well, Terry, the dumb sonofabitch, he takes all that money and funnels it into the stock market. And guess what happens? *He loses his ass.*" He clapped his hands loudly together to demonstrate his point. "I mean, we took a goddamn hit, Jack. I never understood that shit in the first place, but when Terry came back and told me we was hitting the poverty line, I 'bout died. It was like all that money just up and disappeared, like it weren't never there in the first place."

"You don't know who his broker was, do you?"

"Naw, I never asked. I was too mad. 'Fore ya know it, PetroJet's on the phone offering us a pretty substantial pile for the business." Acheson threw his arms in the air and blew out an exasperated breath. "Terry all but jumped at it to get himself outta that hole. And I didn't have much choice but to go along. The market had stabled out at about a dollar a gallon, and there was no way I was gonna make any of that money back. We got fucked but good."

"Yeah, it sure sounds that way," I said, but not in any way referring to anything Acheson and Wolverton had done. It reeked of Finley. His brokers could easily have gypped Wolverton out of his stock money, especially if Wolverton had gone through Truman and Binnell. I would have to make another call to David to look into that angle.

"I guess things don't look good for me and Duke coming back to work for you then, eh?" I said.

"Like I said, the PetroJet boys made us lose DCS," Acheson sighed. "If I had my way, y'all would still be taking care of us. I liked y'all a lot better. Ya didn't wear suits all the time."

I snickered and flapped a lapel from my jacket at him. "Hey, we have our standards."

A commotion sounded off in the main office area behind me, and I turned an ear to listen in. I could hear the lady up front chattering in her whining voice to another voice. The second voice had a distinct air of refinement, not at all what I was used to hearing in Mississippi. It was male, probably older. I made out a little of the man's speech. It sounded like the lady up front was getting fired.

Oh, shit, I thought.

"Mister Acheson?"

I saw Acheson's eyes light up and swiveled my head part way around to see the visitors in the doorway. The man was decked out in a gray suit with tiny pinstripes, a maroon tie threaded from his neck. What looked like a gold pair of horns glittered from the man's tie clip. His eyes held a deep brown color that bore into everything in front of them. A few thin streaks of black jetted from the man's hairline back through a wash of silver. He didn't look at all pleased. What totally threw me for a loop though is that *I recognized him.*

The picture in Schiedle's office, I remembered. *He was one of the men playing golf with Schiedle in the picture.*

"Well, hello, Bill," Acheson said, rising to his feet. "Wasn't expecting you so early."

"I like to be extra-punctual, Fred," Bill Finley said, taking two steps into the room and denying to shake Acheson's hand. He looked down to where I was sitting. "Pardon me if I'm interrupting something..."

"We were just talking about you, Mr. Finley," I said, rising to my feet. He had about four inches on me in height. I stuck out a hand. "Jack Dooley, Dooley Consulting Services."

I watched as the reaction glimmered over Finley's face. I said before that my instincts were shit, but I could attribute the power of my identity to Finley's reaction. He blinked twice, and his mouth twitched. Then he recovered quickly and smoothly, grasping my hand firmly and deploying a smile I could only describe as snake-like.

"A pleasure, Jack." His voice had changed from obvious contempt to respectful and charitable, despite that gross-ass smile. "You must be Duke's son."

"Yes, sir," I said, plastering on the salesman's grin I'd picked up from John Lewis. "I've been doing a little work for him lately. Consultants are hard to come by around these parts."

"Indeed they are," Finley replied, still smiling... A bullshitter's smile.

"Say, those are some nice horns you got there." I motioned to the bull's head tie clip Finley displayed on his tie.

"A souvenir from the alumni at my alma mater," he said, genuinely showing pride.

I frowned then covered it. "U.T.? You're a Longhorn?"

"Undergraduate and MBA. Wouldn't trade it for the world."

"I hear you. Austin's some kinda place, isn't it?"

"I thoroughly enjoyed my time there." His face relaxed, returning to business. "Tell me, have you come to offer services to us?"

"Actually, yes, I did." I swept an arm out to Acheson who stood smoldering next to me. "Duke was going through his database and wondered why Fred hasn't called us in so long. Come to find out as I drive up that he's PetroJet material now. You've got a hell of an operation here, Mr. Finley."

"You did help keep Fred in compliance before we bought him out," Finley said, putting a hand on Acheson's shoulder and smiling again. "Unfortunately, PetroJet has its own safety team. We handle all of our compliance issues in-house."

"Yeah, that's what Fred told me." I made a face and tilted my head. "Damn shame. We were hoping to do some business with you, Bill. Can I call you Bill? Cool. See, DCS is starting to expand, and folks are having a hard time booking us in advance. Duke wanted to give all his old clients first dibs before he went all-out, so that's why I'm here."

"It's not that we don't appreciate the gesture, of course," Finley said. "I'm always happy to retain any professional contacts in the field. But I'm quite pleased with my own team's results as it is. Be assured, we'll call if there's anything you can do for us."

"Don't hesitate," I said, angling myself for a quick exit. "Mock audits, supplementary documentation, *accident* reporting..."

I dropped the intonation on the word hard, going for another provocation to elicit some kind of reaction in the guy. The word hung in the air for a few seconds so I could gauge Finley's response. By the way his smile remained fixed in place without a single tic a nanosecond too long, I could tell that I had gotten his attention. As the seconds drew out, though, I wondered if I'd overstepped my bounds. The last thing I needed was for Finley to actually *know* I was on his ass. Still, it was out there in whatever form he might take it, and I had a good chance to see exactly how sharp the guy was.

As it turned out, Finley didn't give anything up. He remained as solicitous as before, shaking my hand again in obvious dismissal.

"I shall definitely keep you and your father in mind, Jack," he said in benediction. "Thank you for coming by."

"Anytime," I said. I clapped Acheson on the shoulder. "Chin up, chief."

"Thanks, Jack," Acheson said, eyes downcast. "Tell your dad we said hello."

I got out fast.

An Exxon station stood just across the highway from PetroJet Magee. I pulled in and quietly made a show of filling up my car. I had to make three trips in and out of the store before enough time went by. Finally, Bill Finley exited the PetroJet office and made his way for a dark green Lexus in the parking lot.

I pulled a digital camera out of my car, one that I kept around to document accidents like truck spills when I was working for Dad. I snapped about ten pictures leaning over the roof of my car, making sure to get the license plate of the Lexus. As soon as Finley appeared in the doorway, a stout six-foot-four guy got out of the Lexus and walked around to hold the passenger side door open for Finley. He radiated ex-football player with the non-neck and dark suit that barely covered his physique. Whoever the guy was (and I suspected some kind of bodyguard for Finley), I didn't want him taking potshots at my head.

As the Lexus revved and pulled out, I slid into the Honda to avoid detection. Finley oozed money from every pore. The Longhorn tie clip had looked like genuine gold, and I figured Finley probably wouldn't wear one if it wasn't. The Lexus was a current year model, although I'd have to check the plates to make sure. Cars weren't my bag. But they meant something to Finley, I noticed. His car flashed off every bit of its luxury trim, from gold-embossed door handles to a wood grain dash.

On my way out of Magee, I added the confrontation with Finley to what I'd already gleaned about him. There was no doubt in my mind that Finley had been the man responsible for bribing Judge Schiedle in Birmingham. The picture on Schiedle's office wall offered enough circumstantial evidence, but the judge's connection to Henkel made it all clear.

Henkel, Schiedle, Finley.

The unholy triangle?

I needed more information.

I pulled over again, snatched the cell from my jacket pocket, and dialed a number. In a few minutes, David Novak answered from what must have been a pretty swank setup in downtown Tampa.

"How's it looking, David?"

"I'm only just starting to get into it, Jack," my cousin replied. His voice hushed considerably, and I immediately regretted calling him at work. "But if this is on the level, I think we may be looking at a securities fraud kind of event."

"That bad, huh?"

"Let me put it this way. I went back and pulled everything I could find on Finley. Jack, the man's a machine. He went to the University of Texas on his own bill, and there's no record of a loan in his credit report. The only time he ever borrowed any money was when he initially bought out the company that became PetroJet. He had three separate trust funds that matured when he turned eighteen, twenty-one, and twenty-five, and one of those was the base stock portfolio that he uses privately now. He's worth millions."

"How many millions?"

"More than you want to know about."

"Thanks a lot, asshole."

"Sorry."

"I've got another lead I want you to look at. Wolverton's LP Gas in Magee, Mississippi. Former owners were Terry Wolverton and Fred Acheson. Wolverton was a fiend for stocks and bonds, but he played himself out over a year ago and ended up having to sell out to PetroJet."

"You think Finley swindled him?"

"I'm pretty sure. I just bumped into him in Magee, and he treated Acheson like the guy had been sold into slavery. It was pathetic."

"I'll check it out. But I got to warn you, Jack. I'm skating the bounds of professional integrity here as it is."

"I know, David. And don't think I don't appreciate it. I just have to figure out the moves on a couple of other players before I know what to do for sure. Just keep putting that review together. Anything else?"

"One thing. I called a friend of mine to get a look at this Will Schiedle's financial records, and they're pretty screwy. But I don't think he has anything to do with the missing investment money."

I clicked my tongue against the side of my mouth. "But those QuickBooks records said otherwise."

"Those came from a private program, Jack. Not an accredited financial institution. I couldn't track down a bank account or any kind of transaction record Schiedle may have been linked to. If he did receive that money from Truman and Binnell, he put it somewhere else."

"So we still can't find the money?" I punched the dashboard. "Fuck! I thought we were onto something there."

"It may not be a dead end, Jack. If Schiedle did get those payments, maybe he funneled them elsewhere. Into something else."

"Something other than Finley's coffers? Where the hell else would he send it?"

"I can't say for sure. But if you ask me, this looks a lot like what Elliot Ness nailed Capone for in the thirties."

I made a rude noise. "Tax evasion? What the hell?"

"Think about it. The money gets started at Truman and Binnell. Schiedle is the primary launderer. He does something with those checks and hides it for Finley. After taking out his own cut, of course."

"Of course." I tapped my fingers on the steering wheel and looked at the Saint Christopher medallion hanging from the rear-view mirror. "Okay, David. Thanks. I've got something else to work with now. Listen... Is there anything I can do to..."

"Jack, hold it." The serious tone in his voice deepened. "Don't offer me anything, okay? It's just... It's not right."

"Not right?"

"That's right."

"You're sure?"

"Very sure."

"Can I ask why?"

There was a sigh in the cellular's earpiece.

"I'm not like them, Jack. I don't want a bribe."

"I wasn't offering you one."

"Well, whatever. Just... I don't need anything, okay?"

"Okay, David." I looked out the window, watching cars race down the highway. "All the same, thank you."

"Yeah, no problem. I'll call you later."

I flicked off the cell phone. One of my many failings stems from the fact that I don't know my family all that well. I certainly didn't know David. I felt bad about his interpretation of events, and it made me feel even worse that he thought such a thing of me. But wasn't that what it was about in the first place? I damn sure wasn't doing anything for free...

My reflection looked back at me in the rearview mirror. It told me that it could live with me if I could live with it.

Good enough.

The Honda swerved back onto 49 and double-timed it back to Hattiesburg.

12.

ON POINT AND OTHER DEVIATIONS

Wednesday was comics day.

I had neglected to pick up my stash the previous week, and by the time I arose that morning, I had the full-on DTs for some good four-color action. The most tragic part about living in Hattiesburg was that a good comic book store didn't exist. After Hub City and Dog Star went under, my only recourse was a dilapidated shack called The No-Zone. Thankfully, a new owner had taken over the store about a year ago, and with some minor improvements, it no longer smelled like the bottom of a toilet. One time I came into the place and there was a ferret scampering across the back issue bins. A goddamn ferret.

Say what you want to about quality entertainment, but comics are where it's at. I'd just as soon sit down with a stack of old Claremont *X-Men* than go see a movie. Granted, times had changed in the comics industry, and I had graduated from simple super-hero action to something new and different. While I still kept titles like *Justice League* and *Detective Comics* in my pull box, I got my jollies from hardcore books like Garth Ennis and Steve Dillon's *Preacher* and Frank Miller's *Sin City*.

On that particular day, there was plenty'a swag to keep me happy. I walked into The No-Zone and waved hi at the bearded, tattoo-covered owner. Damned if I could remember his name. Every time we talked, I concentrated on distancing myself from the smell of old Happy Meals and pot. He took good care of me, though, I'll give him that. He pulled every title I wanted and then some, constantly forcing me to try new comics out on a regular basis. I didn't pick up his recommendations that often, but at least he tried to keep me happy. After all, I was probably one of the few customers in the place that spent over a hundred bucks a month on something other than Pokemon cards.

"Hey, I've got a *Titans* back here if you're still interested," the No-Zoner said.

"Nah, I dropped that," I replied, flipping through my stack. "Having a hard time staying interested in stuff from the Big Two lately, y'know?"

"Yeah, I've been hearing that a lot, man." I snorted. The guy knew only two names in the comics world: Todd MacFarlane and Frank Miller. Miller I could forgive him for. If the guy put out anything regularly, he'd be a saint. *Sin City* had slowly fallen down the drain as its sporadic publishing schedule gave way to the sheer insanity fallen into by its creator. MacFarlane was another matter. The next time I found a piece of sperm fluff like *Spawn* in my box, me and the No-Zoner were gonna have words.

"Say, I found a better deal on that Batman snowglobe you were looking at."

"Oh, yeah?"

"Yeah. Some guy's selling a couple on eBay for thirty percent off MSRP."

"Word. Thanks for the tip." I started for a second. "Hey, is there a new *Planetary* yet?"

He made a weird face at me. "Are you waiting for *Planetary*?"

I blinked. "Yes. We're waiting for *Planetary*."

"Huh," he said. "No, no *Planetary* yet."

"Well, shit," I said.

I paid for my haul and beat a hasty retreat. I'd acquired a fancy for collectible comics art and memorabilia, particularly statues, no doubt spillover from Rick's similar obsession with swag like that. He'd given me a bust of Marv, a character from *Sin City*, for my birthday last year, and I'd slowly come to respect what Rick had seen in statue work. The aforementioned Batman snowglobe had almost put me in tears when I saw it in the order catalogue. If I could get a decent deal on it, the globe would join Marv and my one Warner Brothers maquette atop my entertainment center. The Superman maquette was the prize of my collection so far. Sold out from the manufacturer, it went for a cool $1000 on eBay, over $800 up from its original in-store price. I figured if I ever ran into money trouble, investing in statues and the like could get me out of the hole in a hurry or at least provide me some quick cash to fix problems. You could find a ton of those things selling at crazy prices on eBay, so investing early in good ones made sense.

The stack of comics landed on the passenger seat with a crinkly noise made by the bag. As much as I wanted to get home and begin devouring the week's reads, I had to get to the Payne Center at Southern quick. I was already twenty minutes late for my appointment with a sprained ankle and a busted knee.

"Hit it, boyo! *Hit it!*"

"Goddammit, Doc, I can't hit anything with you yelling at me all day!"

The racquetball caromed off the top right corner wall and double bounced under my legs, rolling to a stop in Old Doc Faller's hand. I coughed up a generous amount of nicotine revenge and bent over to lean on my racquet.

"Oh, come now, Jackie, you're not falling apart on me so quickly, are you?" Doc teased, tapping the ball with his racquet.

"One day," I huffed, "I'm going to exterminate your whole fucking presence in this building."

"Aye, the Black and Tans said the same thing, too, and look where it got good old England." The Doc took his position at forward. "Are you ready?"

I got back into position and twirled the racquet's safety rope around my wrist. "All right, Doc. Bring it."

Doc Faller liked to use this trick where he serves the ball down on an angle that hits perfectly where the floor meets the back wall. This causes the ball to gain a maximum of about two inches return fly off the floor before it bounces. The trick pissed me off because I hardly ever got to the ball in time to return, and when I did, it was so low to the ground that I couldn't get my raquet under it, leading to Sports Ridiculosity where one Jack Dooley bangs his raquet on the court floor and trips over himself into a pile of unsportsmanlike conduct. It took me a good year of weekly matches with the Doc before I could offer a better resistance.

I came in low and backhanded the ball across the court, sending it to the far-right corner where Doc had to run forward to catch. He delivered a snappy save that sent the ball all the way back to the reinforced glass wall. I let it bounce once then power-slammed it into the glass, propelling the ball at breakneck speed back toward the forward court.

Naturally, Doc caught it in mid-flight and took advantage of my position near the glass. He lightly tapped the racquetball, dispatching it rather quietly into a corner where it barely scraped the walls and came straight down to the court floor. By the time I made it forward, the ball had already bounced twice.

When the Doc pulled chocks on his racquetball game, he slipped into a frenzy of motion and speed that hardly anyone could keep up with. He had long told me that racquetball kept him young, having given up boxing years ago to preserve his lovely potato face and avoid the cauliflower ear. We matched up every other week or whenever I could drag my sore ass into the court for another beating, because Doc *always* won. I watched him play a tournament or two at Southern, but as former faculty, he couldn't compete officially for the university. Doc loved to get in there and chase that ball though, every day. People would challenge the old man to a racquetball duel, and he'd gladly accept, whipping that ass like a newborn, just enough to demonstrate his prowess to his oft-younger opponents. Dooleys generally cannot *athletics,* as has been proven to me over and over again by Doc's repeated ass-whuppins on the court. "Point and game," Doc Faller said, pirouetting his racquet and bowing as if he were a fencer.

"I almost got you that time." My breath came in ragged gulps, and I sank against the corner of the court's white walls, my racquet clattering to the floor. "Two more points, I woulda had you."

"Would have, could have, should have," Doc cackled, pushing his safety goggles up onto his sweaty forehead. "Jackie, I told you I'd make you a better player, not a better complainer."

"You *told* me this was more fun that just chasing the ball around the court by myself." I coughed and shook my head to clear the sweat from my eyes. "It ain't."

"Whatsamattah, Jack?" Doc swished his racquet through the air, continuing to perpetrate his swordsman's persona. "I'm supposed to be the old one here."

I ran a hand through my sweat-soaked hair. "Excuse me while I crawl out of my Depends." I got to my feet and trained my racquet on the Doc. "I'm gonna beat the shamrocks out of you one day, Doc."

"You're welcome to try."

He led me out of the court and to the three rows of bleacher-style benches opposite the courts. The Payne Center at Southern Miss towered over the rest of the campus like it had been transported back in time. The surrounding buildings on campus retained their old-world architecture, throwbacks to the university's early 20th century design. The science center vaguely possessed a modern feel in the sixties. The school's athletic building had been constructed in the early nineties, and its contents bordered on the revolutionary. Not to say that the place waxed futuristic, but the Payne Center did provide one of the coolest places to get in a good workout in Hattiesburg. Being an alumni, I got a discount on annual membership. That included everything from racquetball supplies to cheap massages from girls majoring in sports medicine. As I leaned back on the carpeted bleacher steps, something popped in my back. A massage would have been a blessing right then.

"What have you been up to lately, Jack?" Doc Faller asked, untying his shoe so he could shimmy out of the knee brace affixed to his left leg. "I've not heard from you lately."

"Working," I told him, pulling my own knee brace off. "Remember that bit for my uncle I told you about? It gets heavier every day I'm in it."

“I warned you not to go off like a blasted fool, snapper. This may be a decent line of work for you on first glance, but don’t forget that you’re a stranger here. Your home soil is far away from this land.”

“I know, I know.” I sighed, working the kinks out of my right arm. “Doc, I made Uncle Carter a promise that I’d see this thing through, and I’m going to. I’m trying to be as thorough as I can about it, but I can’t help thinking that I’m missing something.”

“Then slow down. Take a look at all your research for a while.” The Doc bounced his racquetball between his weathered hands. “You’ve not a deadline on this, I assume, so don’t be so hasty. Remember, there’s more to every situation you get yourself into than you can possibly be aware of. It’s the society of things.”

I frowned. “What do you mean?”

The Doc turned to me and scratched at his graying salt and pepper hair. “Let’s say this racquetball is someone you’re investigating. Now, if I throw this into the court, there are virtually a hundred different ways the ball can bounce around before stopping. It can ricochet off a wall, bounce a few times off the floor, or just get stuck in a corner and roll around.” The Doc touched his forehead as his green eyes met mine. “It’s the geometry of the game of that gives you an advantage in predicting where the ball is going to end up.”

I made a face. “How is that…?”

“*People* can be exactly the same way, snapper. You never know which way they’re going to bounce. There may something hidden in their social makeup that compels them to do something. If you show a convicted criminal someone in a policeman’s uniform, he’s going to tense up, get nervous. If you mention to a widow the details of a particularly grisly murder, maybe she’ll break down over the loss of her husband. It’s all in the science of things, lad.”

I considered Doc's words as I snapped off the racquet glove on my right hand. "I don't have much an intuition when it comes to people, Doc. I'm either too trusting or too wary. I just can't think in those terms."

The Doc bit his lip and pulled on a water bottle. "Then you're in for a rougher time than you may expect, snapper. I suppose I'll have to bring you down to the house soon and instruct you in the ways of the pugilist."

"Pugilist?" I narrowed my eyes. "Doc, you're a boxer?"

"How do you think I got myself to the States, lad?" he crowed in a disbelieving tone. "Golden glove champion for four years straight coming out of Belfast."

"You went to school on a boxing scholarship?" I cackled. "Who are you, Thomas Crown?"

"I resent that, lad. Crown was a dirty Scot."

"No, Pierce Brosnan was a dirty Scot. Steve McQueen was a tried and true American."

"And a randy American he was, at that. So whaddya say, snapper? Care to go a couple of rounds with the old Doc?"

I imagined an image of Doc Faller bouncing around a boxing ring, landing long-armed jabs on his opponent. "I suppose I can give it a try. Where's your ring?"

"Don't have much of a ring to speak of, lad. It's just a mat and a punching bag in the garage at home."

"Good enough for me. But if you break my nose, I'm gonna fucking sue."

The Doc pounded my back and chuckled. "Sold."

When we hit the locker rooms, Doc got assaulted by a bevy of students milling about the Payne Center. He signed a few copies of his book, *Sociopolitico*, for them, living up to his reputation as the undisputed master of the gab on campus. Even in semi-retirement, Doc Faller demonstrated a complete mastery of mirth in his former work environment. I could see him sizing up people as we walked by, making conclusions about their family history and love lives as if he possessed some divine insight into the human social engine. And he did, I supposed. For all of my desire to hurry up and leave Hattiesburg, I admitted that I would miss Doc Faller the most.

After showering and dressing, I met the Doc in the Payne Center's massive entry foyer, which contained a health food bar and several tables. I pondered grabbing a baked potato, but I knew I could just as easily whip a decent one up once I got home. Walking out onto the bright green lawn in front of the athletic center, I slid my sunglasses on and looked over to Doc, clad in his Hawaiian shirt.

"When do we start, Doc?" I asked.

"I've got nothing but time, snapper," the oldster said with a grin. "You come on out whenever you're ready."

"Hey, I forgot to tell you something." I hesitated momentarily. I think I've met someone."

"Really?" He peered at me over the top of his sunglasses. "Local girl?"

"Jackson. Met her at the last Jive-T's show." I shaded my eyes from the bright sun above us. "I think I'm kinda into her, Doc."

"Into her in a Crys-type way, or into her in a one-brief-moment way?"

I hedged. "Well, we've spent time together. I told her about Crys. She's really cool, Doc. Likes James Bond flicks and everything."

"What's her name, snapper?"

"Liz."

"Liz what?"

"Liz..." I frowned. "Oops."

"She doesn't have a last name?" The Doc laughed. "Or did you forget to ask?"

"Forgot to ask. Dammit, I hate when I do that. Now I'm gonna have to go all Seinfeld and steal a peek at her wallet while she's in the bathroom."

"Liz, eh?"

"Yeah." I quirked a sidelong glance at him. "What?"

"Nothing."

"C'mon, Doc. Give."

"Liz her real name?"

"Well... sure. I mean, why wouldn't it be?"

"Liz can be short for Elizabeth or Lizza or some other thing."

"Why does that matter?"

Doc Faller fixed me with a deadly serious glare. "It matters, Jack."

I shrugged off the feeling of uneasiness brought on by Doc's questioning. As we approached our cars—Doc's 1967 Cobra looked quite out of place next to the Little White Honda—I slapped him on the back.

"Thanks for the time, Doc," I said. "I mean it."

"Imparting my vast storehouse of accumulated wisdom and poise is incumbent upon we wise folk anyway, Jackie," the Doc said, offering me one of his wide-angle grins as he stowed his gym bag in the trunk. "Take it easy now, snapper. And call me if you need anything else."

"I'll drop by soon for the title bout," I said. "Say, should I go dig up some gloves?"

"Not yet, lad. You're going to be on the bag for a while as it is." He waggled his fingers at me as he climbed into the Cobra. "Be ready."

I watched the Doc swerve out of the lot and tear off into the street. Looking after him, I speculated about the looming boxing session I had agreed to. Doc didn't look like an ex-prizefighter, but with my experience with him in the racquetball court, I knew he could spring more than a few surprises. I whined momentarily, already seeing the bandages across my nose and eyebrows.

There was only one message on my machine once I got home, a reminder from Jeffie Nils that we needed to get in a decent rehearsal before the Ocean Springs show. Jeffie's got a pretty inflated sense of how 25 to Midnight should work, always dictating when we should practice and how we should go about booking jobs. The truth was, the band boasted some of the most talented musicians in the state, Jeffie included, and we really didn't need to rehearse unless it was to work up new material. I certainly performed better when I learned lyrics in the car, listening to the tapes. By the time we rendezvoused on stage, usually our individual interpretations of the songs mixed into something a lot more intriguing than anyone had heard from the original tune. That was the way I liked to work. Your best work always comes at the most unexpected times. I knew we'd smoke the crowd in Ocean Springs.

After cleaning up and pouring myself a glass of water, I settled in for comics day. Comics are like television and movies with me. As soon as I crack that cover, I'm in another place. I just go away and don't come back for a while. Especially when the comics are as good as *Preacher* or *Planetary*.

My Dad was unwittingly responsible for getting me into comics, and I'm sure he regrets that fact to this very day. I still had the battered, dog-eared copy of *Transformers* #3 he had bought me when I was five, and I'd since had to replace *Legion of Super-Heroes* #303 with a newer copy. Those two comics had been my introduction to the world of comics, and I had not stopped reading ever since. Fifteen boxes of bagged and boarded issues rested in my closet, testaments to the longevity of the medium. Little did my parents know at the time when they took me to the E-Z Mart and bought me those books, that they were giving me a leg up on my growth as a reader. Contrary to what most folks think about comics, they can be a hell of a great introduction for younger kids to reading. Duke didn't believe me whenever I told him that, but it was true. After all, I had no idea where New York was on the map until I read *Uncanny X-Men*.

As hard as I tried to concentrate on the latest adventures of the Legion of Super-Heroes (Giffen-era v.4 stuff, mind you), the case nagged at me. In truth, I wanted it to be over. The allure of the payday settled on me, and I couldn't stop thinking about Tex-Mex restaurants in the Stockyards and tall pours at The Flying Saucer in downtown Fort Worth. I had what Carter wanted. With the stock docket David was putting together for me and the background I'd compiled on Finley, I had enough evidence to at least satisfy Carter on a technical level.

What he wanted out of me from that point was more difficult to pinpoint, and I could only guess in oblique angles. I wasn't about to agree to waltz into court as a witness, although I would probably have to if Carter decided to go to the police or the SEC. Still, if Carter went to the police or the feds, his own little skirt on the edge of legality would come to light. Carter retained a snazzy lawyer in Hattiesburg, one of those suits that looks totally out of place in town but apparently slays it in the courtrooms on behalf of his clients. Maybe that guy was who Carter wanted me working with next.

This could be enough, I told myself. I could serve Finley on a platter and just walk away. I could tell Carter that I wasn't about to get involved in criminal acts, committing or abetting for that matter. My record was clean. I wanted to keep it that way. I could take the other twenty-five grand Carter owed me and start planning my return to Texas.

But I couldn't.

Something in me wouldn't let me. I imagined never coming back to Hattiesburg again, not being able to look anybody on my father's side of the family in the eye. Because I had failed them in some way? Maybe. I could count on one hand the times I had really let my Dad down, and most of those were stupid things that I paid for in life lessons that the old man forgave fast.

A good part of the guilt creeping up on me lie in the infrequent months I'd spent working with and for Carter and Duke. They had always given me crap jobs to start out when I'd first moved to Hattiesburg. Cleaning out old truck trailers filled with junk. Delivering drug test kits to labs. All kinds of little work that I eagerly ate up because I was so hungry for cash to spend on other stupid shit. Truth is though, I loved that shit. I.L.D.S., baby. Those were some good fuckin' times working for Carter and Duke. Learning how to read maps and navigate the boonies of the south. Drinking cold beer with rednecks who never finished high school and loved their jobs hauling gas on bobtails. I didn't want to admit it right then, but there was something man-shaping about that life, that work, that family. I finished every one of those shit tasks not because I wanted the money, but because I wanted Carter and my Dad to be proud of me.

If I walk away from Finley now, I'd be quitting on them.

I told myself that contrary to popular Gen X belief, I finish what I start, and I hate leaving a mess. Most of the time. So, there.

Relaxing into my easy chair, I read for a good thirty minutes before the phone rang. Still unsettled from the quandaries filling my gas tank, I gathered up the stack of comics in my lap to lunge for the portable.

"Yes?" I answered peevishly.

"Jack," my dad said from the earpiece. "You've got to get down to the hospital. Quick."

Something cold happened to my stomach.

"Dad? Dad, what is it?"

"It's Carter, Jack. There's been an explosion at the plant."

I shot through the door faster than the Flash, leaving my four-color world in a pile on the floor behind me.

13.

EMERGENCY RESPONSE

Evening had begun to fall by the time I reached Forrest General. Darting through rush hour traffic like a kamikaze pilot, I managed to keep my temper in check. I double parked in the hospital parking lot and raced up the stairs to the ICU wing. The hospital, a mismatched collection of add-on buildings and crisscrossing corridors, made for quite an obstacle in locating the right wing, but I finally found the appropriate area when I spotted Duke in the hall talking on his cell phone. Seeing me 'round the corner, he hung up and pivoted to meet me.

"Dad!" I said, catching him in a brief hug. "What the hell happened?"

"Still looking into it," Duke said, his voice surprisingly calm. "The fire department's on the scene at DPI, but first glance looks like a pressure valve exploded."

"And Carter was on the yard?" I craned my neck to look around. *Where were they keeping him?*

"Standing close to the storage tanks, yeah. He caught it in the back."

"Jesus *fuck*..."

"Jack, he's all right," Duke said, gripping my shoulder. "He's burned up pretty bad, but the doctors say it's not life threatening."

"Have you seen him?"

"Not yet. We're waiting for the doctor to come out of surgery."

"Surgery? What the hell does he need surgery for?"

My dad shook me to calm me down. "Jack! It's okay! He's just got some shards of debris embedded in his back and legs, that's all."

A door opened just behind Duke, and Dee Dooley, Carter's wife, walked out clutching a towel. Upon seeing her, I pushed past Duke and met her in an embrace.

"Aunt Dee," I said. "Are you okay?"

"Yes, yes, I'm fine; everything's fine," she said in her rapid fire New Orleans accent. "I just got the call. I was on my way to the coast. They called me while I was in the car. I didn't even..."

"Hey, easy there," I said, keeping a tight arm around her shoulders. "Duke said he's going to be all right. Who else is here?"

"Craig and a few other people. In the waiting room. Craig brought him in. He was the one that called." I saw the wily look in Dee's eyes. She was the last person in the world who needed to deal with something like this. Dee reveled in hers and Carter's lifestyle, always off to one party or another, always enjoying the best parts of high society. Before that moment, I'd never even considered how she might have handled a predicament like that one. And now, I was getting the worst kind of tutorial.

"The doctor ought to be out here," Duke said.

"Yes, yes, where is he?" Dee agreed. "He said he'd come out thirty minutes ago. Where is he?"

"Dad, are you sure it was a defective pressure valve?" I said, my senses coming back to me for a moment.

Duke looked at me square for a moment. "What do you mean?"

I looked over to where Dee was pacing in front of the ICU doors and wiped the back of my hand over my mouth. "Later, Dad."

The doctor chose that moment to sweep through the doors of the off-limits ICU area, a clipboard clenched tightly in one hand. Dee immediately zipped to his side, badgering him with all manner of questions, many of them repeated over and over.

"Mrs. Dooley, please be calm," the doctor said, touching her shoulder. "Your husband's out of surgery, and he's going to be all right."

Dee seemed to deflate at the physician's pronouncement. I folded my arms and cocked my head toward the lab-coated doctor, sizing him up. He couldn't have been two years older than me. Good for him.

"Can we see him?" Duke demanded instead of asked.

"Three at a time, yes," the doctor said. "He's still very weak from the painkillers we've prescribed, so do not expect him to recognize you. He looks fine, though, and he's going to make a complete recovery."

"Pull that out of your 'stock answer' bag?" I said. I don't like hospitals. I like doctors even less.

The doctor in question could see the animosity on my face and chose to ignore my question. Instead, he led us back into the ICU ward, instructing us to wash our hands at a maintenance station and tread quietly back to see Carter. Passing the rows of beds divided only by thin sheets and mountains of technical gear,

I suppressed an urge to vomit. The antiseptic stench of the ward combined with the foul odor of unwashed bodies and decaying tissue. I had my own issues about hospitals, and I had to fight through the nausea in order to follow Duke and Dee. It's not that I don't respect what physicians do, but rather why they do it. I've seen a man plagued by cancer, completely incurable, lie in a bed and listen to a doctor calmly tell him that all he can do is make the man more comfortable. Then the doctor goes and grabs a snack cake from a vending machine and starts bitching to his residents about how his salary should be this or that. Doctors think themselves gods in the operating room. I just think they're fucks.

Carter lay in a corner of the ICU, tubes and ampules connected to him at various points on his body. The explosion had sizzled a lot of his hair, leaving some scarring beneath the patches of hair that remained. His ears looked like they had been gnawed on by pit bulls and then coated in a thick steak sauce. Parts of Carter's beard bore more wounds, gray singed to black and pieces missing or burned into the skin itself, and a large bandage covered his forehead. I shuddered to think about what his back looked like. The one arm that rested above the covers was purple from ministration. I had expected worse, and I looked at Carter's doctor to pose the question.

"First and second degree burns over most of his back, legs and arms," the man said, having anticipated my inquiry. "Third degree scarring scattered about the burn area, but it wasn't as serious as we were led to believe. He's going to itch for months while the scarring heals."

"What about the debris you removed?"

"He caught a large piece in his right calf, and that's the only major concern I have right now. He may require some physical therapy if the muscles don't knit together properly. In any case, he's going to walk with a limp from now on."

"Carter? Carter, baby, it's me," Dee whispered as she leaned over him. Carter's eyes rolled back and forth between consciousness. His mouth parted slightly, and a slow hiss came out.

"Like I said," the doctor noted, "the drugs are going to keep him under for a while. He'll probably be lucid again in about twelve hours."

"Got lucky there, brother," my dad said, touching the outline of Carter's foot beneath the sheets.

"How many others were injured in the blast?" I thought to ask.

"Four more are in surgery now," the doctor replied, eyes on his clipboard. "They're in much worse shape having been closer to the blast. Seven others were treated at the scene, from what I'm told. Most of those are being brought in for full examinations. It's a lucky thing no one was killed."

I cast a glance over at Duke who had jounced out of his inspection of Carter to follow my line of inquiry. Our eyes met, and we left the area of family concern for business.

"Doctor, do you still have the debris you... removed from him?" Duke asked.

"Yes, it's in storage."

"I'm going to need to take a look at it. Keep it sealed and out of anybody else's hands, all right?"

The doctor offered my dad a skeptical glance. "On whose authority?"

"I work in emergency response for hazardous materials carriers," Duke said. "Just hang on to that stuff until someone from DOT comes by and asks for it. Oh, and make sure all the people coming in from the plant are drug tested as well."

The doctor nodded. "Urinalysis will be sufficient?"

"Yes." Duke touched Dee's shoulder. "Hey. Are you going to be okay here?"

"Yes, yes, I think so," Dee said, touching a blackened portion of Carter's beard.

Duke looked at me. "You ready to take a look at the plant?"

My face remained immobile. "Let's go."

Five hours had passed since the time of the explosion once we reached DPI. The plant was a mess. Wisps of black smoke drifted up into the night sky from behind the yard where the propane storage tanks rested. A multitude of flashing lights from police and emergency vehicles mixed together to create a dizzying kaleidoscope about the grounds. Duke's Cadillac crossed the threshold of police tape and skidded to a halt in the gravel pit just beyond the main office. As we exited the car, a police officer waved to us, his boots crunching on the pebbles as he moved in our direction.

"Gonna have to ask you move out of here, folks," he said. "No onlookers allowed."

"We're with the emergency response people," Duke said, and it wasn't quite a lie. DPI had its own emergency response team already on the scene, but our qualifications with DCS could get us past any scrutiny. We handed the officer our wallets, showing him the registered inspector cards.

"Okay, but get your hardhats and be careful. There's still a good amount of gas in the air."

"Have they moved in the foam trucks yet?" Duke asked, opening his trunk to retrieve the hardhats.

"Fire department just got finished spraying."

I plopped the ungainly yellow hat on my head and followed Duke into the roped-off section of the plant. The ground was stained black in a twenty-foot radius around what once was the primary storage vessel. Twisted and charred pipes dotted the landscape, protruding from other machinery on the yard or sticking right out of the ground where they had landed. We paused at the rim of the devastation, and Duke let out a long whistle.

"That's some accident," he said.

"Don't have to tell me," I told him.

We found a collection of people milling about the fire truck that had pulled up to the edge of the blast radius. Duke went straight up to a mountain of a man in a yellow fireman's jacket.

"Eddie!" Duke said. "What happened?"

"Duke!" Eddie grasped Duke's hand but did not smile. His face was smeared with grease and smoke stains. "Pressure valve went out. We think it's in tandem with a lit cigarette, too."

"A what?" I said, disbelieving. I had never seen anyone smoking on DPI's yard, and I personally had been chastised about it the first few times I had visited the plant.

"We found a collection of cigarette butts close to the broken valve," Eddie went on, indicating with his finger. "Apparently, some dumbass hasn't been listening to my safety seminars and decided he'd make a new smoking depot out next to the tanks."

"Are you kidding me?" Duke said, equally stunned. "Eddie, I know these guys aren't rocket scientists, but come the fuck on! They know better than to light up within fifty feet of a thirty-thousand gallon storage tank."

"You'd think so," Eddie spat, looking back at the still smoking tank. "You want to take a look?"

"You bet. By the way, Eddie, you know my son, Jack."

"Eddie Biltmore," the man said, grasping my hand. "You cleared for this?"

"Yes," was all I said, bullshit aside.

I silently congratulated myself on keeping a spare change of clothes in my trunk. Before leaving the hospital, I'd had to change out of my shorts and T-shirt into some more protective jeans, boots, and a work shirt. I didn't wear boots often, and I kept my only pair of ropers in the car in case I needed them. I certainly didn't need any pair of Reeboks catching on fire as I walked on the scorched ground.

The storage tank looked like it had split along the left side. Its shell listed off to one side, exposing the burnt interior where all the propane inside had gone up and laid waste to the surrounding area. I was surprised that much of the piping and delivery systems around the tank were still standing. We strode across the smoking ground to a patch where Eddie pointed.

"You got no idea how lucky we are," Eddie said. "The tank was only about half-full, so the explosion could have been a lot worse. Best guess is, the valve cracked, product leaked, caught fire from a nearby cigarette butt. Valve pops, cracks the tank, and lights up. First explosion took out the windows in the office, and then the fire started. By that time, most of the product was all used up so there wasn't much else left for a secondary explosion."

"That's why the other tanks and the piping are intact?" I asked.

"That's right," Duke chimed in, looking at one side of the cracked storage tank. "Shit, they got lucky."

"You keep saying that," I told Duke, wordlessly reminding him that his own brother lay in a hospital. Duke got the idea and nodded solemnly.

The heat wasn't nearly as bad as I'd thought, but I could still feel rivers of sweat trickling down my back. I'd be crusted with grime and soot by the time I returned home, but none of that entered my mind at that moment. Eddie took us closer to the damaged tank and pointed at a large hole near the rear piping area.

"See all those broken pipes? That's where it happened," he said. "You guys take a look-see. I gotta go coordinate with the fire people."

I stepped over a mass of white foam, the fire-retardant that the firemen pumped to cover hazardous materials spills. The hole near the piping had split the tank up and over, and I could imagine the seals on the tank breaking as the fissure widened. Duke brushed aside some more foam until he found the point Eddie had indicated.

"Look at this," he said, holding up a charred and contorted piece of piping.

"This is the valve?" I said, looking the piece over.

"Yep. See the striations here and here? It was definitely defective."

I looked over the metal and wiped pieces of grime away. "Or sabotaged."

Duke looked over his shoulder at me. "You think so?"

"I bet if we were to walk into DPI's office right now, we wouldn't find the SARA Title III inspection reports on the tanks, Dad," I said. "Those are supposed to be done annually, right? And filed with state and federal registrars?" SARA reports meant Superfund Amendments and Reorganization Act, an important DOT reg that required motor carriers and hazardous materials companies to conduct and record inspections of any hazmat storage or transportation equipment they owned. Most companies thought they were a joke and hardly ever made the inspections, and those that did cut corners with a bullshit couple of sentences on a piece of paper indicating that everythin's fine. Dooley Consulting Services actually put the time in to take photos of the sites and set up regular, evidence-based inspections with checklists, interviews, the whole shebang. Duke and I had documented these plenty of times for DPI.

"Yes, they are," Duke said, pursing his lips. "And I know Eddie Biltmore isn't a slouch when it comes to that kind of stuff. DPI's never had a problem with defective material before. It just doesn't get installed if it is." He frowned at me. "So someone may have stolen the reports and faked a defect?"

"No reports, no proof it wasn't defective."

I crawled over the twisted metal until I was closer to the hole in the side of the tank. Sweeping away some of the grit beneath me, I found the stash of cigarette butts. Most of them had been incinerated in the blast, but more than a few had been left behind, survivors of the doom that came to DPI. I picked one up and held it close to my eyes.

"Dad, these are all Pall-Mall butts," I said.

"So?" he replied, digging around the ground himself.

"That's a pretty off brand for a smoker. Not as common as Marlboros, for instance."

"You think they could have been planted?"

"Absolutely." I looked over my shoulder at the commotion on the yard. "Who smokes Pall-Malls around here?"

"Never paid that much attention," Duke said, and I could hear a tinge of regret in his voice.

I put a hand on his back. "This isn't your fault, Dad."

"He should have let me handle his safety work."

"Biltmore sounds like he's just as capable, Pops. I mean, he's not Yoda-class like you are..."

Duke grinned up at me and patted my back. "Thanks, Jack."

I gritted my teeth as a wave of heat passed over us. "If it's anybody's fault..." I couldn't complete the thought.

"You think this may have something to do with what you've been doing for Carter?" Duke asked, understanding blooming on his grime-covered face.

"God, I don't know."

"Jack, don't let this get to you until we've got all the facts. DOT'll be here by morning, I assume. That gives us a little time to check out those SARA Title IIIs."

"Agreed. Let's keep this under our hats for the time being," I said, scooping some of the cigarette butts into a plastic baggie I'd brought along. "I've gotta check this against my work."

"What do you want me to do?"

"Check out the paperwork and see if those reports aren't there. I'm going to go talk to the yard foreman and see who was on duty when the explosion happened."

"I think the foreman was one of the guys that got sent to the hospital."

I chewed on my lip. "Time cards. Where's their time clock?"

"Driver's ready room. What else?"

"DOT's going to fine the shit out of them, aren't they?"

"With no SARA Titles and these cigarette butts? It's going to be nasty."

I had to think quickly. If the accident was connected to PetroJet in any way, then I wasn't sure exactly how to prove that DPI hadn't been negligent in their safety work. If industrial espionage came up, then there was a fair chance that Carter could squeak by the federal inspectors and avoid getting fined. Fines for "accidents" like that one could cripple a company, reaching into the hundreds of thousands of dollars. And with Carter's present financial troubles, including the disappearance of his emergency stock fund, I knew that this could indeed be a damaging blow to Dooley Petroleum, Inc.

Against my better judgment, I swept the remains of the cigarette butts into the plastic baggie and made sure I had erased all traces of our probe into the ground. Duke didn't protest, and he rose to start his way back to the group of personnel clustered around the fire truck. I joined him as soon as I had finished sweeping the dirt into natural patterns.

"See if you can get Biltmore to get an analysis of that pressure valve, too," I told him. "If that thing was jacked up, too, maybe we can get a lead on who was dicking around with it."

"With a burning cigarette lying nearby, all someone would have to do is open the valve a hair," Duke said in a low voice. "Explosion could have caused the striations we saw what with the heat treatment. That'll go to a federal lab for analysis."

"Keep track of it if you can. I'm gonna go check out those time cards."

I stuck the baggie inside my shirt pocket to conceal from the authorities. I was going to need that evidence to find my suspected saboteur. And if my hunch was correct, I already had a pretty good picture of the son of bitch I was looking for.

The main offices had been vacated since the explosion. The concussion of the blast had shattered all the windows in the trailer building, littering the floors and desks with shards of glass and debris. The staff had probably already gone home or to the hospital. Despite the various personalities associated with DPI's people, there was a general fondness for Carter that no one could dispute. That made it all the better for me, because I didn't know if I could handle too many platitudes at the moment. I'd been fighting the anger ever since I'd left the hospital, and I tried to channel that into an ardor for the investigation. I was only half-successful.

The driver's ready room was vacant as well, leaving me to blessed silence as I made for the time clock. The room featured some dilapidated carpet and a few grime-soaked sofas on which the DPI drivers could kick back. Shelves of time schedules and delivery logs covered the walls, and an ancient, crusted coffee pot blazed with a low hum in the corner.

The time clock rested on the far wall with several slots below it for the individual drivers' time cards. I pulled all of them and sat down at a desk, grabbing my notepad to scribble down the names of the personnel who had been present at the time of the accident. I stopped looking as soon as I got to Al Henkel's card. He hadn't even bothered to clock out for the day.

It was all the motivation I needed.

I replaced the cards as I'd found them and went outside to check in with Duke. He and Eddie Biltmore were going over a reconstruction of the accident with a few of the firemen on the scene. The police officers who had formed the cordon around the plant took turns interviewing the remaining DPI personnel, taking statements for official record. I waited for one particular man I recognized to finish up with a cop.

"Hey, you got a minute?" I asked him as soon as he turned away from the officer.

"Yeah, sure," he said. "Hey, you're Jack Dooley, right? Carter's nephew?"

"Yeah, that's me."

"Gary Wayne, remember? Serviceman? You worked for me one summer at the truck shop."

"Oh, yeah." I accepted his handshake. "How're you holding up, Gary?"

"Fair to middlin'." Wayne huffed loudly and took off his cap. He wore grease-stained coveralls with the DPI logo on the breast. "Can you believe this mess?"

"Too well. I need to ask you something, Gary. Do you remember if Al Henkel was out on the yard before the explosion?"

"Al?" Wayne smacked his lips and looked up into the dark sky. "Yeah, I think I saw him around. His truck just got lined in for a tune up. So, yeah, he was here."

"Thanks, Gary."

I turned and left without another word.

"Hello?"

"Doc? It's Jack."

"Jackie. I'm watching the news, and I'm seeing something about your uncle's plant going up in flames. Jack, what's going on?"

"Tell you about it later. You still have that punching bag set up?"

"Sure do. When you coming by?"

"First thing in the morning."

I didn't sleep that night. I got home late, having left DPI and returned to the hospital to check in on Carter. According to what Dee had told me, he was going to be fine and had been moved to his own room. There was some consternation about the lasting effects of his injuries, but the doctor indicated that Carter wouldn't be majorly disfigured. He predicted that the mangling of Carter's ears could be fixed through plastic surgery, leaving only twisted skin from the actual burns. The waiting room had filled up with various family members in the interim, and I had to retreat before the handshakes and teary eyes overwhelmed me. I caught up to Duke on my way out, and we exchanged information on our probe into the accident. I told him not to worry about what I'd found.

When I came in to my apartment, I groaned upon seeing the comic books scattered on the floor, their spines bent this way and that, covers folded in that unnatural way that hits only comic collectors in the feels. In my hasty departure, I had damaged them a good bit, and even though I wasn't much a collector, I still got irritated when my comics got messed up. I gathered them up and tried to finish reading them. I couldn't.

I fixed myself a baked potato, ate half of it. I couldn't find anymore local news at that time of night about the accident so I channel surfed for a time, hoping to exhaust myself into sleep. Eventually, I moved to the sofa and entered a fitful on and off sleep. I saw illusions of fire and a mad laugh behind my eyelids. I saw handcuffs that may or may not have been on my own wrists. I saw too much blood saturated money.

I shrugged off sleep and counted the minutes on the clock until morning.

14.

CHILD EMPOWERMENT FANTASY

Six o'clock on the nose when I knocked on Doc's door.

"Early for you, Jack," the Doc said, seeing my face.

"Let's get started."

It lasted nearly all day.

Doc Faller watched as I went to work on the bag, attacking it with the hardest rapid-fire punches I could manage. After about twenty minutes, I recoiled with a heaving chest. Doc wagged his finger and showed me my first lesson of the day. I sucked at it.

He taught me how to throw my punches for more effect, turning the fist and hips in midflight to add more power to the blow. He put a mouthpiece in my mouth and made me breathe through my nose, pushing me even harder than my first round. I blew out chunks of snot and regurgitated spittle as I laid into the bag. I fell to my knees often, retching for breath.

The Doc let me drink some water and then set me to work again. After two hours, I managed to get a handle on my body's limit, pushing past it as hard as I could. Doc corrected my stance, balanced my attacks, showed me the best combinations of jabs and haymakers to take down an opponent. Soon, he had me doing push-ups, commanding me to deliver even though my arms felt like rubbery waste from a pencil eraser factory. I collapsed more than once, and Doc never let me stew longer than a few minutes. Soon he would have me back on the bag or back on the floor, exerting myself to no degree I thought possible.

We broke for lunch and shared a meal of grilled chicken and salad, and I sucked down water like it was the only thing keeping me alive. I wanted a cigarette, but Doc wouldn't let me, telling me I had to work past the urge in order to get over the effects of the cigarettes on my system. He told me that in one day he would show me everything I needed to know to be a powerhouse in the ring. Everything after that would be practice.

I had a few targets in mind for that practice.

Doc Faller dressed me up with some spare gloves and brought me to the padded mat that covered the floor of his garage. Almost immediately, he knocked me down with a couple savage blows to the gut and head. The pain was worse than anything I'd ever felt, and I wanted to vomit. But the Doc simply pulled me back to my feet and ordered me to repeat his moves. I sluggishly tried to imitate his attacks, sloughing off his lean body and bouncing off the mat. The Doc toed me in the side and told me to bow up. I did.

We sparred for the next two hours, and the Doc showed me how fragile the human body could be as he landed punch after punch on me. I knew I'd be sore in the morning, probably to such a degree that I wouldn't want to get up for days. I copied Doc's moves exactly, learning his defense as well as his attack. By the time the late afternoon arrived, I was a tangled mess of bruises and throbbing muscle. Doc told me that with practice, I could maybe get into the groove, but it would take more than a day's worth of practice. I told him I'd kick his ass next time, immediately regretting it when I saw Doc's malicious grin.

I returned home more worn down than I had ever been. I had played football for about two years in high school, and in Texas, that made for a worse punishment than boot camp. Two-a-days had constantly driven me over the edge, forcing me to abandon night life as I'd started sleeping for twelve hours at a time. But the workouts did me well. I'd started each year as a tackle and filled in for the primary two-technique whenever he needed a break. I'd never been in better shape than I was while playing football, and I masochistically missed the discipline. Perhaps I should have seen about training with Doc on a more regular basis before now.

Stumbling into my apartment, I showered quickly and devoured a turkey sandwich. Still reeling from the sleepless night before, my head hit the sofa pillow and didn't move for four hours. The comforting blackness of a dreamless sleep finally closed in on me and sucked me into itself.

I awoke at half past eight the following day and spent the next hour waking myself up. The battering I'd taken from Doc Faller had slightly begun to ache in all the wrong places, and I slammed down some aspirin with apple juice and a Pop Tart to get my energy back and diminish the soreness that was about to cripple me. I entered the shower again and stood under the machine gun head for thirty minutes, letting hot water seep into my pores and massage the tightening muscles. Once I'd dried off, my mind sharpened and cleared. Old Doc Faller prescribed some stretching exercises for after my schooling in the sweet science, and I dutifully, albeit painfully, undertook them to prevent inevitable cramps.

I called Duke at the hospital, hoping to get some kind of update on Carter's condition.

"He's awake," my dad told me. "Still pretty wacky, but awake. He's going to be fine."

"Small miracles," I said. "Anything on the SARA reports?"

"I checked the office before the DOT people got in this morning. Looks like someone pilfered them. I talked to Eddie Biltmore about it, and he almost went through the roof. He filed those things himself, and he knows they should have been in the safety file."

"Did you call the state registrar?"

"Yeah, I put in a copy request this morning. They have 'em on file somewhere, so he's covered on that end. They just have to get 'em out here so the DOT boys have something to look at. What are you up to?"

"About to get some answers. Call you tomorrow, okay? Tell Carter I love him."

"Will do, Jack."

I chose a pair of jeans and a long-sleeved shirt for the work to come that evening. Nothing fancy. Just enough to keep me warm without having to wear my jacket. I put on some canvas Nike tennis shoes with reinforced rubber soles and did some squats to test my muscles. Doc had been right. I was sore, but I felt great.

The phone rang just before I gathered my things to leave, and against my better judgment, I broke mindset and answered it. It was Liz.

"Hey, stranger, how've you been?"

"Could be better," I admitted, pacing the living area. "Some nasty shit's been happening down here this week."

"Really." A pause. "Anything you want to talk about?"

I sighed. "Not on the phone. Okay? It just... It doesn't feel right."

"It's okay. I was thinking maybe you might want to come up this weekend anyway."

The offer knocked me back into reality, and I cast a glance at the desk calendar next to my computer. "Well, I was about to ask you the same thing. You feel like a little trip to the coast this weekend?"

"The coast? What's down there? Besides the obvious, I mean."

"We have a two-night Friday and Saturday gig in Ocean Springs at The Sand Bar, and the girl down there put us up in the Fairmont just outside of Biloxi." I let a smile take over my features. "You feel like hanging with the band for the weekend?"

"Oooh, I get to play groupie girl?" She granted me a little laugh. "I'm on board. You have enough room?"

"We've got two rooms, but I can get us another one on my bill. I figure we could do the show Friday night, get up and misbehave all day Saturday, do the show again, and wake up Sunday for a little more wacky fun. You interested?"

"No, pop trash, I think I'm going to pass. Come on! What time should I be there?"

"I'm probably going to head down early with the gang and get set up, stake out the joint. You want to meet me at the bar at... three? Is that too early for you?"

"I was just looking for an excuse to take a half-day. Three it is. How do I get there?"

"Forty-nine south to I-10 west. Third exit should be Highway 67. Get off there, take a left toward the Gulf, and head down about four miles until you see a bridge over an inlet. The Sand Bar's on your left just next to the bridge."

"Close to Biloxi, isn't it?"

"We can be on casino row in ten minutes. You game?"

"I'm game." I heard a pen hurriedly scribbling down the directions. "I'll be there at or around three depending on how much I've got to tug the boss's toupee to let me out."

"Sounds perfect." I noticed that the aches from Doc's boxing session didn't feel as bad anymore. "Oh, and pack a nice dress."

"A nice one, eh? Hmmmm, what have you got up your sleeve, Rico Suave?"

"Show ya when we get there. All good?"

"All good." I heard the pitter patter repeats of some quick kisses in the earpiece. "See you Friday."

After I hung up, I had to sit for a moment and recollect my thoughts. I didn't want to admit it, but I needed Liz at that moment. I needed someone totally independent of all the crap I'd thrust myself into. I needed to unload the weight of what I was carrying.

I made a fist and got up.

I already had plans for part of that unloading.

The Little White Honda pulled into the first gas station I could find. I left him running while I took the short steps to the pay phone. The number I needed came to me from the notepad which

I promptly threw back in the car as soon as I'd dialed it. The phone rang three times before someone picked up.

"Y'ello?"

I hung up and climbed back into the car, gunning the engine.

Al Henkel was home.

A piece of gum made for all the equipment I would need that night. I popped it into my mouth four blocks from Henkel's apartment complex and started chewing. The lights from the complex's parking lot security cast a yellow glow on everything, and I left the car at another building across the way. Careful not to draw too much attention, I walked back across the lot to Henkel's building.

Lightly taking the steps one at a time, I listened to find out if anyone else on the second floor was awake. A television turned up way too loud spewed the latest exploits of the worst side of American society on what must have been Springer. I marked the apartment it was coming from. No light or sound emanated from the one across from Henkel's, and the unit next door was silent as well.

I pulled the gum from my mouth and stuck it over the peephole. I had that cool hitman movie, *The Professional*, to thank for that trick. I'd downloaded some deleted scenes from the flick a while back, and there had been a whole sequence where the hitman and his young girl protege went about capping a bunch of lowlifes for practice. The gum on the peephole made for one of their preparatory details.

I gave the door a few loud raps then moved aside to knock on the window. The assault would have annoyed even the most masterful of Tibetan monks, and I let the volume die somewhat to avoid attracting attention.

"Hang on, hang on, goddammit!" the muffled voice said within.

I heard the chain rattle on the door, and as soon as I saw the crack, I kicked. Putting all the force of my mass behind my leg, I struck the door with enough force to smack Henkel directly in the nose and break the safety chain off. I swept inside quickly thereafter and closed the door behind me.

Henkel had fallen to the floor and clutched his bleeding nose with a whimpering noise. As I turned around from bracing the door, I saw him clambering into the kitchen. Henkel kept a gun in his cookie jar, I remembered, so I leaned down and dragged him back into the small efficiency unit stomping on his stomach to keep him from struggling.

"You fuckin' cocksucker!" he wailed, struggling to get to his feet.

The jab flew as if it had come straight from Doc Faller's own arm. I had to put him down as quickly as possible to avoid causing a struggle that would bring attention. So the knuckle sandwich bit back, further splintering what must have already been a bruised nose. Henkel fell backwards onto the floor and writhed, hands covering his bloodied face.

"Stop talking," I said, squatting next to him and searching his pockets for any more weapons. Henkel tried to sit back up, and I drove the heel of my hand to the underside of his middle brow. Wailing like a small child, Henkel fell back down again.

"If you keep acting like a damn freak, I'm going to keep hitting you." I was surprised how cold and remote my voice seemed. "Answer time, Al. Did you set up the explosion at DPI yesterday?"

"Fuck, no!" he said, muffled by the hands on his face. "I didn..."

"Wrong." This time, I punched him in the jaw, feeling the click as his teeth jammed together. He coughed a cry of pain, and his lip split where his teeth had clamped. I grabbed the front of his musty sweatshirt.

"Start talking now, Al," I said. "Or in addition to getting a face-fucking tonight, your wife's gonna get a wake-up call about the hookers you've been banging in Birmingham."

"Okay, okay, fuckin' *stop*!" Henkel scrambled back on the cheap carpet, trying to slither away. I let him have the illusion of distance as he backed squarely up against the side of his couch. I remained in my squat position, ready to spring if I needed to.

"Talk," I commanded a second time.

"Okay, okay!" Henkel looked at the blood on his fingers and whined again. "Fuck, man, ya didn't haveta fuckin' hit me..."

"Want me to do it again?" I added a sadistically malicious grimace.

"No, okay! Okay, yeah. Now wait..."

"Al..."

"Listen, it's not my fault! I had to set it up to look like an accident."

I looked over at Henkel's desk and saw a pack of Pall-Malls sitting next to the ashtray. I picked them up and took one out, looking at the filter. "You left the cigarettes there."

"Yeah," he moaned. "Look, don't tell the cops, okay? I can work somethin' out. I can getcha money if ya want it."

"Why would I want money, Al?" I ran the Pall-Mall under my nose, sniffing the unlit tobacco. "You actually smoke these things? Jesus, they smell like shit."

"Look, whaddya want, okay?" Henkel said, moving himself into a sitting position. "Listen, I can get ya..."

I tossed the cigarette at Henkel. "You almost killed my uncle, you stupid country fuck."

"He wasn't supposed to be on the yard, okay! It was just supposed to look like an accident!"

"What kind of accident? Defective safety measures, something like that?"

"Yeah, yeah, man."

"What did you do with the SARA Title IIIs?"

Henkel paused, breathing shallowly as his eyes searched the room. I shook my head and sprang, launching a coiled haymaker right into his stomach. Henkel coughed hard and doubled over, making horrendous noises.

"SARA Titles, Al," I said.

"Burned..." he wheezed. "Burned 'em."

I threw the rest of the Pall-Malls at him, clenching my teeth. "You stupid ignorant fuck. Are you working for Bill Finley?"

Henkel kept wheezing, clutching his gut and rocking back and forth on the floor. I stood up and kicked him in the shins. "Tell me, goddammit! Are you working for Finley?"

"Stop, stop..." he panted. "Yes! Yes..."

I staggered back a few steps.

The truth.

They say that the truth is liberating, and I've never been much one to buy into sentimental metaphors. But right then, I felt it. The aches in my back and arms drained out of me to somewhere far away. My head swirled as if I had taken a heavy hit of pot. Rick had told me about the rush. He'd told me what he'd felt when he cracked his first mock investigation at Quantico. I hadn't paid much attention then, but his words came fluttering back to me. I'd seen the evidence. I'd made the connections. I'd worked the case.

And now I had it direct from the suspect.

A confession.

I began to rethink my skepticism of entering law enforcement. Then again, most cops frown on getting physical with suspects. Reasons.

A towel hung from under the cabinet in Henkel's kitchen, and I snatched it up to wipe down the places my fingers had graced. The desk, the door handle, the door itself. I left Henkel convulsing on the floor, and on my way out the door, I tossed the towel at him.

"Why don't you get cleaned up, Al?" I said, forcing the grin away. "You ought to start looking for a new job."

Limp Bizkit started in the player when I cranked the car.

I turned it up.

Loud.

I cruised Hattiesburg until nearly one in the morning, fighting sleep as I let the wind rush in through the open windows to tickle my face. Some things simply can't be matched, and the feeling of a late night drive through town with the windows down and the radio on is one of those things. My voice was still scratchy so I avoided practicing with the band tape as I drove, saving myself for the show tomorrow. But I wanted to. Hell, I felt like crooning.

Pressing Henkel for details on his relationship with Finley would have been pointless. As much as I wanted to sit down in front of him with a tape recorder, I knew that whatever he told me would be nothing compared to what I could divine from other sources. Besides, he probably didn't know anything anyway. He was just hired help. Do your job, collect a check. He probably didn't even know about the Judge Schiedle connection or how his money got laundered. The real payoff would have to come from Finley himself.

But that was the problem. Finley more than likely had an army of attorneys on station to protect himself from blame. Beyond the theft of gas from DPI and transferral thereof to PetroJet, there really wasn't much to go to the police with. Granted, David Novak would have a monster of an SEC case for me in a matter of time, but I weighed the probabilities of that action and found myself lacking for a satisfying conclusion. Finley could always put everything on that end straight to Truman and Binnell.

Schiedle? I asked myself. That's a quandary. The judge would probably bend over backwards to get immunity if he testified against Finley. But the unknowns on that front remained in Finley's hands. Did he have something on the judge? Was that why Schiedle had been laundering money for him? Or was it simply a collegiate relationship? Every time I came back to that angle, I fingered Schiedle for the first person to take a long trip across the Atlantic. Finley only had money to lose, maybe jail time if it ever went that far. But Schiedle would end up bum fluff for the sisters at Parchman the moment someone dropped a dime on him: he'd never make it through prison at his age.

Of course, I hadn't completely forgotten Schiedle's entire role in the larger scheme. From what David had told me, the judge wasn't just laundering money, he was making it disappear. I tried to find a correlation between that and the massive gains PetroJet's stocks had seen in the past few years. I couldn't nail it down. Something was missing.

I passed by the park square near the downtown thoroughfare. Well, it was a streetlight and a couple of lane dividers. Holding on the red, I examined the street in front of me, my eyes unfocusing as they often did when the old slush factory started churning. I didn't notice the light turn green.

Something clicked.

Could Finley be connected with the mob?

On the Mississippi coast, there are hushed whispers about organized crime, mostly because no one knows if they're actually working for a legit enterprise connected to one not so legit down south. Traditionally called the Dixie Mafia, these shadowy men who hide in plain sight coordinate everything from drugs to prostitution and racketeering on a bright neon Biloxi night. Duke had told me a little bit about it upon my first visit to the coast. Rumor had it, a group of Ivy League mobsters moved down south when the chaos of Capone's downfall back in the thirties drove them out. Word had it that these men set up shop in quiet, unassuming businesses, drawing little attention and saving up for a new score along what they saw as virgin Mississippi coast. Several years later, Orange Beach, Biloxi, and Pass Christian boasted gleaming new casinos and resorts. Initially given form as boats built on the water to escape a prohibitive anti-gambling clause in state law, the casinos became a tremendous source of income and jobs for coastal Mississippi. Soon, no one protested too loudly that some unsavory Yankees were playing fast and loose with the law to get their way.

In the past twenty years, the casinos had become *the* major tourist attraction around Mississippi's coast. They brought millions of dollars into the economy from both out-of-state visitors and local yokels who didn't know any better. The biggest indicator of the Mafia's influence on the coast came when several laws were struck down by the state legislature to allow the construction of the most ambitious project yet, the Beau Rivage Resort. The Beau Rivage was totally built on land, forgoing the usual "on the water" rule imposed on previous casinos like The Grand and Casino Magic. Steve Burns had won tickets to the grand opening of the casino through the Harry Connick, Jr. Fan Club and had gone primarily to see the big band jazz man perform. Steve had also told me that at that opening show, he'd seen more than a few pinstriped suits in the front row with dames boasting rings on their fingers that probably cost more than a modest Biloxi business.

If Finley had gone into business with the Dixie Mafia, then I had my lead to the missing money. Finley could easily funnel the cash through Schiedle to Biloxi where any number of "businessmen" would take Finley's investment, run it through the casinos or other trades on the coast, and finally pump it clean with a sizable return back into money that Truman and Binnell could hide in the stock market.

Was Finley shrewd enough to pull off something like that though? I asked myself. That leap of logic traversed a fair boundary of supposition, and even if it was true, there would be no way in hell to get proof. The Dixies *owned* the law down south. You don't just pull up state law like it was dead grass and toss it into the Gulf so there's room to build your new casino without some kind of guarantee that the authorities won't make a move against you.

Something kept popping behind my eyes, though, and suddenly, I had it. I crawled into the embryo of a thought and played chopsticks with the chromosomes. I dwelt inside the premature idea and nourished it into adolescence. I spent some extra time making sure it was sound by dressing up it nice and sending it to the wrong schools. When it came back, the idea glared at me and begged for attention.

I would be in Biloxi in the morning.

15.

COAST RATS

25 to Midnight convoyed down to Ocean Springs in my car, Steve's Ford Explorer, and Jeffie's pickup truck. Between the three of us, we could haul all the necessary sound equipment and lighting in addition to all of our instruments and PA hook-ups. Jeffie managed to swing a sweet deal with Lowery, the bassist for Duke's band, who loaned us his private sound system for a cool fifty bucks. It was only a twelve-channel board and a couple of heavy duty JBLs, and it did the trick. Steve snatched a few small Yamaha monitors from MS Music before we left as well. Chad from the Jive-T's could hook us up like that since he ran the combo department. I also picked up two light trees, some gels, and a separate power amp for the lighting system and its foot control pad, bartering with Chad

and promising him I'd return the new model in perfect shape. The light trees, forged in some new lightweight aircraft metal, folded up and fitted easily into Jeffie's truck. I kept the foot controls for the system in my trunk.

"Breaker-nine, breaker-nine," I said into my cell phone, grinning at the back of Steve's Explorer. "Come in, breaker-nine."

"Breaker-nine here, double-oh-fuckstick," Steve squawked back ahead of me. "Over, copy, roger, 10-4."

"Breaker-nine, we have intelligence that an escaped Russian asshole and some Southie fuckwit are hiding out in your vehicle. Do you confirm, breaker-nine?"

"Tell that *fuck* I'll *smack* 'im!" I heard Dave yell from the Explorer's passenger seat.

"Uh, double-oh-fuckstick, we have a problem," Steve replied.

"Well, you're on your own then," I catcalled, flashing my headlights. I switched off the cellular and watched as Steve wound his truck around the highway. Alexei leaned out of one window and flipped me off, having just learned the middle finger expression of American sweetness. I waved back and laughed.

I had been sore as hell when I'd woken that morning. Doc's boxing session had just about whipped my ass into permanent toilet grounding, and helping the gang load all our equipment up for the show didn't make me feel any better. Still, there simply weren't better times than cruising the road, putting on shows and screwing around with 25 to Midnight. Earlier in the year, we'd embarked on our first long haul, heading up to Georgia State in Atlanta to play a few fraternity and sorority parties. It had been even more of a pain in the ass then, hooking up a U-Haul to Steve's Explorer in order to get all our stuff up there. The voyage out had taken us thirteen hours due to Steve's ignorance of the fact that you just can't pull that much weight in first gear. Just outside of Atlanta, his transmission had exploded, and we'd spent three hours in various states of zombie-like sleep around a repair center in the middle of nowhere. Colder than all get-out, we'd managed to grab a two-hour nap and dinner at The Spaghetti Factory before playing two shows back to back. We ended up a worn-out, snapping turtle gang of a band by the time four in the morning rolled around, but the whole affair had been a joy. I would never forget the fun we had on the road.

And despite my current woes, I was very much looking forward to the shows at The Sand Bar. 25 to Midnight always had a way of taking my mind off whatever crapulous and sordid affair I happened to be in the middle of. Granted, we had our share of conflicts just like any other band. 'Lex constantly wanted to venture out into weird untried original material. Jeffie had an ego on him the size of Alcatraz. We could never get Steve to show up anywhere on time. Dave had trouble learning his parts on the keys. I frequently found myself playing peacemaker between my bandmates, but I only complained minimally. We were making a ton of money on the road for little effort. It's easy to do that when you lock yourself into a set way of playing music, and specifically for us, *pleasing the crowd*. Folks could care less about new bands and new sounds down south. They wanted Motown. They wanted eighties. They wanted a silly bastard in a floral silk shirt hopping around on stage and bringing girls up to sing with him. And we delivered. Every time.

We pulled into The Sand Bar at ten in the morning, meeting the bar's owner out back to off-load our equipment. We liked to set up as early as possible so we could troubleshoot any problems that might come up during sound check. The whole setup process took us a total of sixty minutes now that we had perfected it. By eleven, we were running through "Down Under" for sound check and putting the final tweaks on the show.

"Man, that is one *small* fuckin' stage," Dave whistled, stealing one of my cigarettes as we climbed off the tiny corner dais.

"What, you got a problem with rubbin' against me?" Steve jibed.

"Hey, you're on the other *side*, dickcheese! If *anybody*'s rubbin' against *me*, it's fuckin' *Dooley*."

"Don't get your dick hard, Dave," I said, polishing off a complimentary beer. "I've only got eyes for Steve."

Steve winked at me and made a kissy face. I patted his knee until he recoiled, causing Dave to slam the table with a fury. "You guys are fuckin' *nitwits*!"

"You got the set lists, Jack?" Jeffie asked.

"On my music stand. We all set?"

"Everything sounded fine. There's a little feedback in Dave's monitor, but he can just grin and bear it." Jeffie turned to our resident Bolshevik. "What do you think, Frippy Magoo?"

It took Alexei a moment to see that Jeffie was addressing him. "What is Frippy Magoo?"

"You," Jeffie said with a smirk.

"I thought I was Frippy Magoo," Steve protested.

"No, you're 'rocket-head,' remember?"

"Oh, yeah. Well, *fuck*."

"I think it sounded good, yes?" 'Lex said, regarding a stout glass of Scotch. A lot of people think that hard-drinking Russians is a stereotype. You hang around with 'Lex for a night, and I guarantee you'll change your mind. Stereotype or not, that guy could put away some hard liquor. "The 'Ants Marching' will be fun to play tonight."

"'Nuts Marching,'" Jeffie giggled.

"'I Want a New Nut,'" I joined in.

"'Tripping Nuts,'" Steve said.

"'Down Under,'" Dave said. We all paused. "'*My Nuts!*'" he finally added.

"I thought we should open with 'Billie Nuts' tonight," I said. "Seems to go over better to a new crowd than '25 to My Nuts.'"

"If we're looking at that kinda crowd tonight, let's sneak 'The Way' in there," Steve said.

"The *what*?" Dave poked.

"Oh. Um, 'The Nut.'" He narrowed his eyes. "'The Nuts?' Plural?"

"That's more like it."

"You want two bars on 'Nuts in a Bottle,' 'Lex?" I asked.

"Please, please," Alexei replied. "And another on... say, 'You Can Call Me Nuts?'"

We exploded into laughter, and Jeffie pounded Alexei on the back. "He got it! He finally got it!"

I slid my beer bottle across the table to clink against the other empties. "That's how you do it, 'Lex!"

"Yes, I learn," he replied with a big grin. "Chevis?"

"Hell, no. And it's *Chivas*, you communist bastard."

"Why do you say communist? I am green carded now!"

Dave looked behind Alexei down at his backside. "I dunno, 'Lex, *looks* like a *red* card t'me."

Steve put both his hands up, referee style. "Goal!"

We shared a round of laughter, and I stood up, grabbing my jacket from its resting place on top of my microphone stand. "What's the plan, gang? I've got to make an errand."

Jeffie looked at his watch. "Steve said something about a fight at The Grand."

"Yeah, Platinum Stan Felder's warming up against Fracas Frank tonight," Steve said. "That's what we're competing with, by the way."

"The fights? Get outta town!" I said. "Damn, that would have been cool to check out. What, they're doing a bout right now?"

"Middleweights at noon, and the heavies cowboy up tonight at six. I wanted to go check out what we could."

"And I want to do the... uh." Alexei frowned. "What is word?"

"Slots?" Jeffie supplied.

"Yes, yes, the slots and the shots."

"That's my boy," I tittered. "You guys enjoy. I'm gonna go grab some lunch and do my thing, then I gotta be back here to meet Liz at three. What time are we on?"

"Nine-oh-oh," Jeffie said. "But I bet we can squeeze Judy for some extra cash if she wants us on a little earlier."

"So seven at the earliest?"

"That's a roundup."

"Word. Okay, gang, I'll holler atcha then."

I left the jokers from 25 to Midnight and walked down the outside deck stairs to the sandy parking lot. The Sand Bar rested on a gorgeous piece of land next to a bridge where people liked to come and fish during the day. An odd place to put a bar, but a smart one if you thought about it. The joint was far enough away from the main strip that it held a modest clientele at night, which was somewhat hard to accomplish considering the location. Nightlife on the Gulf Coast could be some of the most fun times you ever imagined if you knew where to go. The tourist trade was so fickle, though, that club owners had a tough time of it if they didn't plan their activities well. I knew that Judy, The Sand Bar's owner, offered some of the best drink specials this side of the Mississippi on band nights. I was looking forward to the night ahead.

I jumped into the Little White Honda and cranked the windows down. A warm breeze flowed off the water, lightening the chill in the fall air. I took the highway south to the main strip along the Gulf Coast and headed east. Highway 90 ran through the most attractive areas of Biloxi, Ocean Springs, Pass Christian, and a number of other Gulf communities. Of course, the entire beachway had been replaced by multitudes of casinos, resorts, and other tourist traps. I passed about twenty seafood restaurants as I wove through lunchtime traffic. On my left, I could grab intermittent peeks at the ocean and what little beach remained between the resorts. To the right were the restaurants and clubs as well as a few private homes that had managed to defeat the encroaching bulldozer of progress. More than a few languid palm trees listed slowly left and right in the breeze, planted intentionally in the median of the street. I passed The Grand, Casino Magic, The Isle of Capri, and that magnificent monster known as The Beau Rivage.

About half a mile past The Rivage, I turned right into a parking lot that snaked around behind Ferrely's Fish. Set into the lot's rear, amongst a smattering of dying palm bushes, was a two-floor club called The Dead Ringer. Its once garish neon sign had fallen into disrepair and only blinked when it felt like it. The beige plaster covering the building had begun to decay a long time ago, and pieces of it littered the lot. A very cool Spanish-style roof topped the place, offering a couple of third floor windows to rooms where things went on that I didn't need to know about. I parked the car and went inside.

The guy at the bouncer's bar next to the door towered over me at a cool six-five. His reddish blond hair gave way to a severe face that could have been considered handsome in some circles. I just thought it looked modern Italian. He cast a neutral stare in my direction, a sports column from the newspaper folded on the stand in front of him.

"Can I get you a table?" the fellow said.

"How about a spot for me and Mr. Gaetano to talk up at the bar?" I said.

The carrot-top's eyes narrowed. "Do I know you, fella?"

I stuck out my hand. "Jack Dooley. I roadied for Duke Dooley's band, Kabana, a few years back."

"Dooley, Dooley, Dooley," the giant said, tapping the desk. "They played some of that Van Morrison stuff?"

"'Domino's' a must-have these days, or so I hear."

"Yeah, yeah. Hang on here for a minute, buddy. I'll be right back."

The giant took off to the upstairs dance club. I lounged against his desk, casting a look down at the paper he'd left. The page had been opened to the horse races at Louisiana Downs, Retama Park in San Antonio, Texas, and another racetrack in Arlington, Texas. I found a couple of horses circled in bright red pen. Going down the list at the Arlington race, I found a horse named Night-Night. A while back, my mother had married an old rancher from north Texas, and while he maintained a relatively okay job at a trucking company in Fort Worth, his passion lie in racehorses. Mason, apple of my Mom's eye, had bought a horse along with a couple of partners from his trucking firm. Mom had been sort of shocked when she saw the bill of sale of come in, but we both went with Mason to check out Night-Night's first race in Arlington. The horse had proven to be a son of a bitch that night, and I'd lost thirty dollars. But Mom called me a few months later and told me that Night-Night was getting up in the circuit. Apparently, she and Mason had taken home a cool two-grand from one race. I knew very little about horses myself, but every time I was in town, even though they had since split, I'd place a bet or two on Mason's horse. I could certainly understand the appeal. The racetracks in Texas were the closest thing they of the landlocked variety had to casinos.

The towering inferno came back downstairs a few minutes later, a wide grin set on his features. He patted me on the back and bumped up close against me. It took me a moment to realize that he was respectfully performing a hands-free frisk.

"Nick's up at the bar, Jack," the bouncer said. "Go on up."

I thanked the man and headed upstairs, passing my hands over my pockets to make sure the guy hadn't filched anything. Usually, the security in The Ringer wouldn't bat an eyelash at frisking someone who walked in and asked for their boss. Obviously, Nick had deigned otherwise for me.

I hoped that was a good sign.

The upstairs section of The Dead Ringer was laid out like a fancy club that one might have seen inside one of the casinos. Polished black marble floors held upright tables and chairs arrayed in front of the bandstand. The stage wasn't much of stage in the first place, though, merely a couple of long steps that led onto a narrow platform in front of three huge windows. Outside, one could see directly across the street to the beach and The Beau Rivage's red brick, lamp-lit splendor. A bar ran down the right side of the room, fully stocked and sporting a gentleman in a rather rice tuxedo shirt. However, his tie and cummerbund were loose and undone, and his sleeves were rolled up as he polished a couple of glasses. Some light jazz—Thelonius Monk, I believe—emanated from the house speakers. It was exactly as I remembered it.

"Jack Dooley! Come sit with me, *paisano*!"

Nick Gaetano possessed all the qualities one might suspect from an Italian mob lord and plenty more that no one would believe. A product of the migration of several Italian families from Chicago to the coast, Gaetano did not know how to blend in. He had a rakish pompadour of black hair atop his head and a thick moustache flecked with spots of gray. He wore comfortable and weathered blue jeans and a dark red shirt. I could see the bulge of a pack of cigars in the breast pocket that sported the image of a polo player on a horse. As I approached, he held out massive forearms bearing a couple of small tattoos, and his face's ridges and wrinkles curled up to accommodate a well-worn smile.

"It's been forever, Jack," Gaetano said, grasping my shoulders hard. "How're ya doin'?"

"Very well, Mister Gaetano," I said, bowing my head slightly in the proper amount of respect. "My band's in town gigging, and I thought I'd drop by and say hello."

"Jack. Jack! It's *Nick*. You know that, *paisano*." He bruised my already sore shoulders again and motioned me to the bar. "What can I getcha?"

"Crown and seven would be great," I said, sidling onto a stool next to him.

"*Tony*! Crown and seven for the boy here!" Gaetano turned to me, pulling a long brown cigar from his pocket. "Cigar?"

"No, thank you." I pulled my pack of Camels out of my jacket. "I've got my own."

"The hell." He swiped the cigarettes out of my hand and crushed them in his grip, tossing the mangled box and tobacco into a trash can behind the bar. "Here, you're smokin' this tonight."

"Okay." I took the cigar and let him light it for me. I really didn't get off on cigars all that much. I kept wanting to inhale, and that invariably led to an embarrassing coughing fit. The first time I'd tried one was back in high school, and the result had been a very green and vomitous Jack Dooley.

"So Mikey tells me you got something you wanna know?" Gaetano said once he'd lit his own stogie. "You mentioned you got a band now. Followin' in your dad's footsteps, are ya?"

"To some degree. The music style's a bit more contemporary, but the fun's the same. We're playing at The Sand Bar in Ocean Springs tonight and tomorrow night. You should come see us if you have the time."

"Dammit, I'd love to, Jack. I'm going to the fights tonight, though. Maybe tomorrow."

I grinned. "Who's your man tonight?"

"Platinum Stan, of course. Seven bouts undefeated, *paisano*. You watch the man. He's goin' places."

"I'll remember that," I said, thinking something else in the back of my mind. Knowing Gaetano, Felder's fights were probably thrown. In a coast culture full of unsavory deals, rigging a boxing match was nothing.

"You want a show at The Ringer, izzat it?" Gaetano fiddled in his pockets. "Lemme getcha a card and we can set somethin' up."

"That'd be great, Nick," I said, handing him a 25 to Midnight card. "But that's not why I'm here."

"Oh?" I could tell that he recognized the stillness on my face. Something twinkled in his eyes. Nick Gaetano was a man of business.

I intended to give him some.

"I'm looking into some industrial espionage for my uncle, Carter Dooley. Dooley Petroleum?"

"Yeah, yeah, I heard of him. What's the score?"

"So high that Uncle Carter ended up in a hospital a couple days ago when someone blew up one of the storage tanks on his yard."

I could tell I had Gaetano's attention. He stopped dragging on his cigar and let it hang limply from his fingers.

"No shit," he said quietly, pacing himself.

"No fucking shit." I tapped some ashes from the cigar into an ashtray. "So, naturally, I want the son of a bitch who did it wrapped up in a cardboard box with a nice little bow on top."

"You got a lead?"

"Sure do. Bill Finley. PetroJet Chemical."

I saw the flicker in Gaetano's eyes. Before he could respond, I said, "You know him."

Gaetano looked over his shoulder at the bartender. He saw that another customer was enjoying a lunchtime martini at a table. Gaetano jerked a thumb at the customer and said, "Tony."

The bartender set his glasses down and headed over to the bar patron. He bent over, spoke some hushed words, and he escorted the martini man downstairs. The man knew better than to protest, and I figured that the reason Tony's cummerbund was loose was because there was a gun in his waistline.

"All right," Gaetano said, sipping a glass of water. "Tell me what you know."

"Finley's been playing a different kinda game on the stock market for a while now," I said. "He uses phantom stocks from floundering companies to swindle them out of their business. Devalue their company and step in to buy them out. You heard of Terry Wolverton? Wolverton's LP Gas? I've got confirmation on that sellout."

Gaetano's face didn't change, and he nodded slightly. "I know of him. He spends a lot of money around here."

"That came from Finley's pocket. That in turn came from an investment scam involving brokers from Truman and Binnell and a judge in Birmingham named Will Schiedle."

Gaetano closed his eyes and shook his head. When he opened them again, I could feel the ice crystals shooting out. "You know a lot, Jack. For a college boy."

I sipped my Crown and seven and inclined my head. "I graduated a long time ago, Nick."

The club owner took another gulp from his water glass and dragged on the cigar for a moment. He seemed to be appraising me, looking me up and down, searching my eyes for some sense of deception.

In light of what had happened in the past week, I had nothing to show for him.

"Okay, Jack," he said, seeming to make up his mind. "I understand what family means, and your dad's a good friend of mine.

I've never met your uncle, but, trust me, I know where you're going with this."

"I think Finley's funneling his money to some of your... business associates," I said quickly. "Nick, listen. I'm not police, okay? I'm not a plant either. I wouldn't fuck you like that. You want to search me for a wire?"

Gaetano shook his head. "I believe you. But understand now, Jack Dooley... if you *are* fuckin' me, you're stepping into room with one big goddamn lock on it. *Capice*?"

I nodded. "I hear you."

He turned back to the bar and away from me. "Finley knows a couple of my... associates down here. A few of them are keen on the petroleum business, y'know? They think it's a plum market. Not enough power in Congress to make problems. Plenty of money to be made if you know how to do it."

"Go on," I said.

"You sound smart enough to know what I'm talking about, Jack." He pinned me with a hard glare. "You know what we do around here."

"I have an idea."

"Finley has an informal partnership with a couple people down here. They see a good opportunity to make an investment in his business by helping him out, you understand? All that cop shit you see on TV is bullshit. We don't gun down people in the streets and concoct wild schemes to fatten our wallets anymore. You ask any of my contemporaries, they'll be happy to show you. Legitimacy is a good thing."

I sipped on the drink again.

"Especially in the banking and the laundry business," he said.

I paused to find Gaetano staring at me again. "They're funneling his money, aren't they? Taking dirty shit, cleaning it up, and spitting it out clean into Finley's wallet."

"It's not hard to do if someone else is providing the money," Gaetano said. "There's almost no liability, from what I understand. Minimal risk, good payoff. Finley pays them a stipend off the money he scams from the brokers. I'd heard about a judge in Finley's stable, but I didn't know who or where until you just told me. He's the link?"

I nodded. "I checked his records. He's sitting on tons of dough that seems to disappear every so often. Your *associates*' doing?"

Gaetano nodded. "Easy enough. We've been known to employ a banker or two who can make checks vanish and magically reappear as solid bank notes, if you get my meaning."

"What do they have on him? Judges don't just turn like that for the sheer fun of it."

"Shit, he makes a pretty penny in the process. I'm sure Finley has him set up with his own stock options and a bleed from the money that comes in from the brokers. And then, of course, there's the idea that Schiedle's dealing *directly* with my associates."

I pursed my lips as the connection was made. "I see." I took a sip of my drink, wetting my dry mouth. "Nick... are you in on this?"

Gaetano turned on his stool and pinned me with another stare, this one on the verge of the malevolent. I held my hands in respect, lowering my eyes. "I need to know in case I decide to take action."

"What *kind* of action?" Gaetano pressed.

"Action that'll dry up the flow of money from Birmingham, if you get my drift."

Gaetano blew out some cigar smoke. "*Paisano*, you're treading on light—"

"Nick, my uncle is in the *hospital*," I growled, surprised by the fury in my voice. "His business is under attack, and Finley stole over seven-hundred-thousand dollars from him. And now he's not in the position to even get up and whine about it. He asked me to do it for him, and by God, I'm gonna have somebody's ass for breakfast."

Gaetano's chin bobbed up and down imperceptibly, and he drained the rest of his glass. "I'm not involved directly, but things are interconnected down here, Jack. Everyone rubs everybody else's shoulder. Is it big enough to cause some ripples? Yes. Will someone get pissed off enough and come for you? That, I can't say."

"Then I need you to do me a favor."

"Hah! I'm doing you a favor right now, *paisano*."

"I understand that, Nick. Listen... You know about *omerta*, right?"

Gaetano's eyes twinkled. "You have to ask *me* that?"

"Right." I shifted position on the stool. "This is no different, Nick. And I am showing you the respect and courtesy you deserve by coming to you first before I start making bad decisions with sharp objects."

He chuckled, amused. What seemed like an eternity passed between us. He stared into his glass and let his cigar burn down to a nub. Finally, just before I was about to beg him for an answer, Gaetano turned back to me.

"What is it you want?"

"Let them know that this is coming to an end, Nick," I said, my eyes as hard as his now. "Tell them to expect Finley's money to stop heading south any day now. He's a walking bullseye."

"You're going to... *remove* him?"

I shrugged. "Let's just say when I'm finished with him, he'll wish I had. Tell your friends to start pulling up roots, canceling accounts, the whole nine yards. They need to get back under the covers. There's about to be a nasty cockfight in Hattiesburg."

Gaetano nodded slowly. "*Omerta*, eh? Heh, you look like you might have some Italian in ya, Jack."

I grinned. "I won't dispute you."

"Good boy. All right, Jack. I'll do as you ask. But you gotta promise me something."

"Name it."

Gaetano looked past me to the stairs where Tony the bartender stood. I'd felt his presence on the back of my neck, but I wasn't terribly sure I should turn around and check. Something like that would seem almost rude to Gaetano. But the guy *had* appeared. I felt it. Nick needed the witness. The bookkeeper. The notetaker.

"I might need you to come down here sometime, do a little work for me," Nick said. "You'll find all my boys downstairs are compelling companions."

A brief flicker of sleet passed through my heart. I suspected that Nick Gaetano had plenty of ties to the Dixie Mafia, but I really didn't know *how* connected he was. Based on what I saw at The Ringer, I'm sure he had more than a modest side business going on some front. And generally, when people like Gaetano had those sorts of things going on, it created the need for people like Tony. I'm sure Gaetano had been telling the truth when he mentioned the overblown portrayal of the Mafia that one often saw on television and in movies. But I couldn't help but wonder... What could he possibly want *me* to do?

I decided to risk it.

"You have my number, Nick," I said, tapping the 25 to Midnight business card on the bar. "I'm only an hour away."

That seemed to be enough for him. "All right. Now, can I interest you in some lunch, *paisano*? We have a veal *pinoche* that I hear is superb."

I grinned and finished off my drink. "I could do for a little lunch."

"Tony! Set a table for Mister Dooley here. And bring up some of that Chianti from the back." Gaetano smiled and patted my arm. "We may have a new friend to entertain."

As Tony scuttled off to retrieve the wine and utensils, I let the flies in my stomach pass. Working off hearsay and rumors had paid off but not quite as smoothly as I'd hoped. I really didn't have any idea what Nick Gaetano was all about in Biloxi. But I knew one thing: He was not someone you called to cancel a gig with. I remembered that Duke had been quite solicitous toward the man back when Kabana gigged at The Dead Ringer. Gaetano had even gone as far as opening a sandwich café at four in the morning to provide some hot food for the band after a show well done. I'd only been a lowly roadie at the time, eking out cash by moving heavy speakers and taking cover money at the door. I remembered the way Gaetano had gone about his business. If you performed for him, he took good care of you.

Maybe that wasn't such a bad thing.

"Planning for a big time while you're down, *paisano*?" Gaetano asked as he showed me to a table. "Have you been to The Beau Rivage yet?"

"A couple of times," I said. "I have a girl friend of mine that's coming to spend the weekend with me. I've got a real hard-on for that baccarat bar."

"Ah, baccarat's a waste, Jack! If you're gonna gamble, gamble *right*." He patted my back and smiled again. "Third slot on the main concourse, second row. I hear it pays very well once it gets back from the machine shop. And if you're staying the night, ask Jimmy at the front desk for a room."

I grimaced, enticed by the prospect. "We'll have to check it out. Thank you, Nick."

I watched Gaetano shuffle off to hurry my meal, and I blinked a couple of times to settle my dizziness. What was I getting myself into?

Omerta, I thought, impressed that I'd remembered the word from *Detective Comics. Blood cries for blood.* Let's just pray it doesn't come out of *my* ass.

16.

COIN AND CUDDLE

The rest of the band hadn't returned to The Sand Bar at a quarter to three. I asked Judy if she had someplace I could change, and she ushered me into her office. I doffed my jeans and jacket for a white long-sleeve pullover with a single black stripe across the chest. A pair of maroon slacks went along with that as well as a full vest with a black back and a pattern of tiny gray and black checks that gave the vest a fuzzy gray tinge at long distance. I pulled on my canvas Nikes and a dark sports coat over that, ready to go to work for the night. In the bathroom, I brushed my teeth and cleaned my hair up somewhat. It probably would have been easier to do so at the hotel that Judy had set us up in, but I wasn't sure if the rest of the gang had checked in yet. Besides, Liz would be walking in at any moment.

When she did, heads turned. The Sand Bar wasn't exactly the locale for a well-dressed lady to set up shop in. Most of the patrons at that time of the day wore cut off khakis and loose shirts. With the river inlet just a few steps away from the deck, Judy got a fairly heavy amount of fisherman traffic during the day. Frank Vandy would have been so at home. When Liz swept in clad in her strapless black dress, it was obvious that more than a few men in the bar wondered if they shouldn't clean themselves up. Then their wives or girlfriends kicked their shins and they got right the hell back to their beers.

"Wow, you clean up good," I said, hands in my pockets as she approached the stage.

"That was supposed to be my line, Prince Charming," Liz said, offering me a wide smile. She had applied a generous amount of makeup, but it didn't hurt her at all. Her blonde hair was kept up in a tight wrap behind her head, and a few loose bangs hung over her green eyes. A simple pearl necklace adorned her neck. The dress shimmied and pulled in all the right places when she moved.

"Hey," was all I could muster as I came down to kiss her check.

"Hey, yourself," she said, touching my chest. "I like your jacket."

"Really? I thought it might be too gaudy."

"No, those shoes are too gaudy. Don't you own something a tad nicer?"

"Hey, these are genuine kicks! I come from the Huey Lewis and Al Giardello schools of proper dress."

"Huey Lewis I can see. But who's Al Giardello?"

"Yaphet Kotto? *Homicide: Life on the Street?*"

"Sorry. Never seen it."

"We absolutely *have* to do something about that. Drive down okay?"

She shifted her grip on the small gold sequined purse in her hands. "Good as can be. How'd sound check go?"

I winked. "Pavarotti's got nothing on us."

Liz grinned. "Do tell."

I stuck my arm out for her. She wrapped her hand around it, and we headed out the door. She looked expectantly at me.

"You take me to the nicest places," she quipped, nodding her head back at The Sand Bar.

"Just you wait," I said, leading her to my car.

When you walk into the main lobby of The Beau Rivage, the word "overwhelming" is something of a necessity for first-timers.

Enormous columns of marble held up a wide ceiling decorated in ornate frescoes. The floor reflected a white and green marbled sheen, hidden in places by lush fronds and ferns that dotted the floor in pots of earth sunken level with it. A huge—and obviously transplanted—palm tree grew up from real soil in the center of the lobby. To the rear, the magnificent scope of the place continued as the lobby emptied into a bazaar hallway, sporting several shopping outlets of reputable name and fashion. People of every walk of life and social standing rushed about. It was not uncommon to find folks in tuxedos walking next to someone in a T-shirt and cutoffs. Liz's mouth dropped open wide when we entered.

"Oh, my God!" she exclaimed. "*Look* at this place!"

"Is this nice enough?" I asked, clasping her hand.

"I think it'll do," she replied, squeezing back. "What's there to do?"

"What isn't there to do? Casino, shopping outlets, a couple of different restaurants. Hey, look... there's Tony Danza."

"What?!" Liz craned her neck, catching sight of the man I had pointed out. He was strolling along leisurely down the main concourse, probably on his way down to the casino proper. Liz pinched my arm. "Hey, he doesn't look too bad."

"Yeah, I guess *Who's the Boss?* didn't really do him in that bad. But hang on a sec; let's get checked in."

"Checked in?" Liz made a face as I pulled her toward the front desk. "*This* is where we're staying?"

"You bet." I shrugged as we walked, our footsteps echoing in the cavernous lobby. "If we stayed at Best Western with the rest of the band, I'd never live it down. I'm telling you, they'd be messing with us all night."

"At least promise to introduce me to them," she said, tugging on my arm. "You skipped out on that last time."

"Deal."

"I've never understood the draw of casinos, you know. There's just something about wasting your money on something that almost never pays off."

"Ahhh, that's the fun of it. Granted, you can't afford to do it too often..."

Liz gave my arm a squeeze. "Win me something tonight?"

I grinned. "This isn't a carnival fair, sweetheart."

Liz covered her mouth and giggled as we got up to the desk. A fresh-faced young lady assaulted us with her toothy smile. Before she could get a word of her prepared greeting out, I jumped right into it.

"Jimmy has our reservations, miss," I said.

Without another word, the young woman shut her mouth and darted down the length of the front desk. Liz tugged at my arm again and whispered at me as I tracked the woman's progress.

"Who's Jimmy?"

"I'm interested in finding that out myself."

A burly fellow with slicked back hair came out of one of the side doors to the front desk office. He sidled up to where Liz and I were standing and buttoned his coat. "Hello, I'm Jimmy. Can I help you?"

"Jack Dooley," I said. "I was told you had reservations for me?"

Realization dawned on Jimmy's face, and he immediately started tapping keys on the desk computer. "Mister Dooley, it's good to have you with us tonight. We have you all taken care of, sir. How long will you be staying?"

"Until Sunday." I looked at Liz questioningly. "If that's okay?"

"Not complaining," she peeped, eyes aflutter.

"Sunday it is, sir," Jimmy said, handing us our room keys. "You're in 908, Mr. Dooley. Can I send a bellman for your luggage?"

"Yes, that'd be great. And here's my car keys. If you wouldn't mind parking the car and sending our stuff up to the room, I think we're going to indulge ourselves at the casino."

"Excellent, excellent. Just let the concierge know if you should need anything else to make your stay more enjoyable, sir. Mister Gaetano sends his best wishes and hopes you'll have a good time with us. He also says that your stay is *en gratis*, sir."

"No kidding?" I was just as surprised as Liz. I'd expected Gaetano to get me a discount on what were usually two and three-hundred dollar a night rooms. He was doing me more than a few favors, and I made a mental note to think harder about that later. If I could.

I inclined my head respectfully to Jimmy. "Give Mr. Gaetano my thanks and good graces," I said. "Yes, sir," Jimmy replied, trying on a smile that didn't seem to fit him. "You enjoy yourselves, and if there's anything you need, just ring me at the front."

Liz managed to sputter out a brief thank you as I pulled her away down the concourse through the bazaar. She turned to offer me an open-mouthed stare.

"What was *that* all about?" she said.

"I'm not totally sure myself," I said, shrugging. "This guy I talked to today told me to ask about a room when we got in. I didn't know he was going to hook me up."

She gave me a skeptical look. "This guy a friend of yours?"

I shrugged again and blinked. "I guess he is now."

Liz's head turned as she looked through the windows at all of the expensive gifts shown off by the shops. Diamond rings, gold watches, necklaces of immaculate craftsmanship, signature golf clubs, rakish polos. She pulled me closer to her through the arm she had hooked around mine.

"Are you doing all this to impress me?" she said.

"The thought crossed my mind," I said, unable to help the grin. "Okay, I admit it. I wanted to do something really special since the last time we went out it was to a pancake and bacon barn at two in the morning."

"Aren't you a doll." She leaned over and kissed my cheek. "This is astounding, Jack. I've never been to the casinos before."

"Well, prepare to be amazed by my gambling prowess, fair lady, and steel yourself for a delightful night of good food, wine, and music."

"Oooh, are we going to play cards?"

"Honestly? I suck at cards. But I can throw a mean craps."

"Lead on."

The bazaar turned a half crescent and led into the main casino, a chamber of immense size and glittering finery. The walls were peppered with irreproachable tapestries and inlaid friezes of woven material with shiny golden outlines. Crystal chandeliers hung at equidistant points throughout the entire casino, hiding a lighting system that offered just the right glow down upon the card tables and slot machines. The floor was covered in a carpet design of equal pristinery, and we walked across it into the den of coins and dice.

We found a craps table that wasn't terribly crowded and muscled ourselves a position to watch as players threw dice and racked in chips. I left Liz for a moment to get some chips to play with, and when I returned, I found her yelling in delight as someone threw a few perfect numbers and won the pot. After a couple of side bets where we lost a good hundred, we got to the throwing position, and I let Liz toss the dice. We made out all right, winning back our losses and a little more in the process. She gave me a pouty lip when I said it was time to move on.

"Quit while you're ahead," I told her. "Never has a rule made more sense."

"I'm having fun!" she declared.

"Well, let's go have fun somewhere else."

Her smooth fingertips tickled the back of my neck. "If I didn't know you well enough, I'd say your mind was in the gutter instead of on the table."

I shuddered and grinned at her. "Gutter, table, wherever it's convenient."

We laughed and moved on through the casino. I had a fair amount of money with me, drawn from the account Carter had set up for me in Hattiesburg. Despite our awful streak of losses, I decided that it was worth it. Liz had the time of her life, raking in chips and giving them back. After a while, we strayed into the baccarat bar and found a seat on one of the sofas between a table and a piano where a jazz pianist played. I got us a bottle of sauvignon blanc from the bar and joined Liz on the sofa, letting her light a cigarette for me as we reclined.

"Are you a wine connoisseur?" she asked, sipping the wine I'd selected.

"Not really," I admitted. "I've got a sweet tooth for the white, though. My mother's got a mad-on for wine, and I guess that's where I picked it up."

"Yes, I like whites, too." She turned up her nose. "Reds are just too... *red*, I guess."

"I hear you."

"Jack, this is incredibly fun," she said, tapping some ashes from her cigarette. "What brought all this on?"

"I dunno. I guess I've always had a dream about high society, you know? Remember when we saw those Bond flicks? I used to *dream* about being James Bond when I was a kid. I thought it would be so cool to travel to all those exotic hotels and resorts he went to and spend money like it was nothing." I looked up at the pianist, smiling. "*One day*, I always told myself."

"I'm not exactly destitute, you know," Liz said. "And I'm certainly not going to let you get away with footing this bill by yourself. If you want to play some more, I can go get us some more chips."

"Nonsense. Will you just allow me live out my high roller fantasy and entertain a beautiful woman?"

She leaned over until her breath was on mine. "I'll allow you to do anything you want to me."

"I might have to take you up on that later, my dear," I said and kissed her.

"You smell good," she said.

"You think? Same stuff I've putting on for ten years."

"I like it. Most men drown themselves in good cologne, especially if they're smokers. It's sort of off-putting."

"I used to do that until my dad told me I smelled like ass. He gave me a bottle of his Old Spice and made me wear it for a month."

"Hah! Old Spice isn't bad either. That's one of my favorite memories of my father when I was little. He had the prickliest beard even after he shaved, but I always loved that Old Spice he put on." Liz closed her eyes and shrugged her shoulders in a pleasant memory.

"Your parents still around?" I asked.

"Yes," she said, briefly hiding behind a sip of wine. "My father has a business in Jackson. You know, the sordid tale of the company-driven man. He met my mother through that, and she works on his accounts from time to time. I've been doing a little work for him on the side, but I've barely got time what with paralegaling at the law firm."

"Family business is the best," I said, ignorant of the wistful look on my face.

Liz caught it and moved closer to me on the sofa. "You sound down about something, Jack. You sounded that way on the phone. And don't sass me now. I have a very comfortable shoulder to lean on."

I smiled and patted her leg. "How about later? I still owe you a completed dream date at The Beau Rivage."

She squeezed my hand. "Okay."

The afternoon really was a dream. My head swam with it as we moved in and out of the conglomeration of people spending and losing and winning. We even stood around a blackjack table and watched a couple of people ante up to the big dollars, moving thousands back and forth across the table with each hand. As evening approached, I decided that it was about time to call it quits for the day.

"Are you hungry?" I asked. "They've got an unbelievable restaurant upstairs with this cool fish tank aquarium thing going on."

"I could eat," Liz said. "What time do you go on at The Sand Bar?"

"I told the boys I'd be back around seven in case Judy wanted us to go on early. There's a boxing match at The Grand tonight that might eat into our crowd, so we probably want to get started early and keep as many people around as we can." I made a goofy face. "Given that we don't screw something up."

"Oh, please, master musician. Stumble around and make silly." She giggled.

"Hey, wait. I want to check something out."

We had moved to the end of the casino just in front of the entrance. I counted the slot machines in front of us until I found the one Gaetano had indicated. I pointed Liz toward it.

"Hang around that machine until that guy gets up. I'm going to cash these chips in and get some change."

"You want to play slots?" she said quizzically. "It looks like a drain on your pocket."

"Maybe. Just snag that machine, and I'll be right back."

I went to the cash office and traded in our chips, realizing that I was about three hundred dollars down. I asked the cashier for twenty dollars in quarters to hit the slots and said a silent prayer to Nick Gaetano. Losing money that I didn't have three weeks ago really didn't bother me that much, but I was caught up in the action. Casinos had that effect on me, and that's why I didn't gamble all that much.

But if I had an edge...

When I returned, Liz was sitting at the machine and already plugging in quarters from her gold sequined purse. I handed her the bucket of quarters I'd appropriated and sat down at the machine next to her.

"Just keep feeding," I said, reaching for the go button. "I got a tip about that machine."

"Really?" Liz said, watching the bars roll and go bust. "It looks like it might be a bum tip. Do people really get off on this?"

"Look at all the senior citizens sitting next to you, Liz. What else do you have to do when you get old?

"Live off your retirement fund instead of piss it away on slots?"

"*Touché.*"

We played for a good twenty minutes, watching as our quarter supply got lower and lower. We won a couple of decent payoffs here and there but nothing major enough to warrant the kind of craftiness I'd seen in Gaetano's eye. We were down to about seven quarters when Liz's machine started whooping and ringing.

"What'd I do? What'd I do?" she said, jumping up.

"You won!" I shouted. "Look!"

The machine was spitting out quarters like a monsoon. We scrambled to pick them all up as they started overflowing from the bin, and I had to flag down one of the attendants to get us some more buckets. Liz's eyes went wide as she read the payoff schedule on top of the machine.

"Jack, it's a *thousand*!" she screeched.

"Hot dog!" I yelled along with her.

Gaetano's tip hadn't been far off the mark. I assumed that one of his side businesses was slot machine repair. The casino had its own machine shop in the basement, and I could just picture Gaetano sending Jimmy or one of his other boys to fix the machine. I had no idea how, though, since it hadn't paid out to the guy that sat there before us. Maybe somebody up in security was looking out for us or the pit boss had recognized me. Or perhaps it was just programmed to spit out better payouts after a certain combination of losses. Math shit. Whatever the reason, I was ecstatic.

"You, my dear," I said, hefting one of the heavy buckets of quarters; "are about to have one of the most extravagant meals you've ever tasted."

The restaurant at which we ate had to have been the crowning achievement in modern architecture. I never got tired of eating there. The walls were totally made up of aquariums, from floor to ceiling. Even the dividers that sectioned off portions of the restaurant acted as large fish tanks, replete with blue tinged water and a bright collection of exotic fish. Most of the fish were probably imported, I figured, since the Gulf Coast really wasn't the cleanest place to harvest and showcase sea life.

Liz and I enjoyed a full five-course meal along with our bottle of wine. Lobster, French onion soup, baked potato, even a finishing dish of exquisite cheesecake. I tried not to gobble too much as I would eventually jostle my tummy around on stage, but I couldn't help it. It was some damn fine eating, and I'd been living off of Lean Cuisines and Special K for too long.

"Look at that one!" Liz decried, watching a bright orange spotted fish swim by the glass wall behind us. "That must be Jamaican. I went to Jamaica once and saw all kinds of fish like this when I was scuba diving."

"You scuba dive?" I said, picking at the remains of the lobster.

"Absolutely. It's a blast. It's just so... so serene when you're down there in clear blue water. And there's nothing but you and the coral reefs and the all the fish and sea life. It's incredible, Jack. You should try it sometime."

"I'll put it on my to-do list."

Liz reached across the table and touched my hand. Her grasp was electric, and I brushed my thumb across her fingers. I really didn't have anything else to say. There we were in a five-star restaurant, dining on delectable dishes, checking out the fish. Enjoying ourselves. It felt like I had been jerked out of my life and transported to the fifth dimension. Sitting there with Liz, I thought that if the fifth dimension was anything like that, I'd have to thank Mr. Mxysptlk as soon as possible.

"It's getting toward seven," she said.

I couldn't get out of her eyes. "I know," I said.

She smiled. "I wouldn't want you to be late."

"Me neither."

"Then we better go."

I sighed. "Do I have to?"

I felt her foot caress my shin underneath the table. "There's always later tonight."

We ended up drawing a bigger crowd than I'd anticipated. The fallout from everyone in the bar spilled outside onto the deck. Judy did ask for us to open a little earlier than expected, offering up free bar bills and an extra hundred a man. Who were we to argue?

We put everything into the show, showing off at every opportunity and refusing to give up the intensity. I felt the floor vibrate from the audience's dancing and jumping, and I got caught up in it, jumping around myself in total ignorance of the aches I still felt. Jeffie broke five drumsticks in the first set. That was a good sign.

Liz sat at the first table closest to us and didn't move away all night long. She swayed and applauded with everyone else, and I saw her turn down offers to dance from more than a few potential suitors. Steve thought it would be kind of me to pay her back for it, and as we closed the show with "Purple Rain," I moved out to her table and sung the ballad directly to her. As Steve took the biting guitar solo, I took her into my arms and slow danced her in front of the stage. Feeling her against me, against my sweat-sodden raiment, uncaring... Hard to summarize. I almost collapsed when the show was over.

We sat around for a good hour after the bar cleaned out. Not having to worry about breaking our equipment down, we enjoyed our open bar tabs. Liz got along wonderfully with the rest of the band. Dave gave his customary shriek of approval when he saw her, and Steve kept making carnal grunts as we talked. That was about as bad as it got. I promised Steve that I wouldn't let his own girlfriend get away with a smooth night when she came down for the Saturday show.

We packed up and left at about three-thirty in the morning. On our way out to the cars, Liz blocked my entry into the Little White Honda.

"Is this a game?" I said, my cheeks hurting from all the grinning I was doing.

"No," she said firmly. "Get your stuff and let's go. I'm so not letting you drive me to the hotel."

"It's the car, isn't it? You don't like the Little White Honda." I feigned heartbroken terror. "I shall kill myself now."

"No, silly." She lightly punched my shoulder. "I am going to drive you in *my* car, mister rock star. Go get your things. Hurry! Shoo!"

"Yes, ma'am!"

I grabbed my duffel and threw it in her trunk then got to relax in the comfy Camry. I had to admit after all my exertion, it felt good to simply melt away into the seat. Liz got in, started up the car and drove steadily back to The Beau Rivage.

"I'm thinking you're going to be too exhausted to do anything tomorrow," she said, looking over at me. "You want to stay in?"

"I could do that," I yawned. "I had a boxing lesson yesterday that just about tore me apart."

"Boxing? Maybe I should drive you over to The Grand then. Platinum Stan needs a new *contendah*!"

"Pass! Me need sleepy."

Her face was illuminated only by the slight glow of the dashboard instruments. I could see her eyes twinkling in the low light.

"We'll see about that," Liz said.

The shower felt like heaven, massaging the pins and needles out of my back. We'd found that Nick Gaetano had gotten us one of the best rooms in the hotel, a suite complete with a wet bar and a sunken jacuzzi. The near-panoramic view from the window gave us a perfect glimpse at the ocean and the roiling waves that came to meet the beach's sandy embrace. Liz bade me to clean up while she settled into the room.

Alcohol and performing could take its effect on me, and I'd had plenty to drink that day. The dizziness could either be attributed to the wine I'd drunk earlier or the vein-popping ardor that had consumed me on The Sand Bar stage. Either way, I had to lean my head against the tile and allow the pulsating shower head to knead the disorientation out of my body.

I felt something press against my back as I stood under the warm water. Hands started caressing the muscles between my shoulderblades. I started to turn my head but winced at the pain in my neck. A pair of lips touched the nape of my neck.

"Oh, *this* is happening," I said, making it sound like genuine surprise and irony all wrapped together, which it was.

"This isn't too uncomfortable for you, is it?" Liz said.

"No, no... I just hope..."

"Yes...?"

"I want you to be as happy as I am right now."

"I'm perfectly happy right now," she whispered into the rush of steam and water.

Her hands ministered to my body, and she pressed harder against me. She remained patient and smooth, never tiring or stopping. Eventually, I turned around to take her into my arms.

"I'm sorry if I wasn't any good."

"What are you talking about? Hush that."

"It's just... I don't have a whole lot of practice."

"Did you hear me complaining? Jack, sweetheart, just relax... You've got to learn not to take everything so seriously."

I turned around in her arms, shuffling the enticing satin sheets of the master bed. Her elfin nose and mouth were only a few inches from mine.

"Liz... how do I say what I'm feeling right now?" I whispered.

She put her mouth on my lips. "You don't have to say anything."

"What about 'thanks?'"

"I could say the same. Jack, I'm not just another Friday night pickup line. I'm not getting anything that I can't do for myself. I'm here with you because I want to be. Because I like you."

I felt her smile against my cheek. "I like you, too."

"See? That wasn't so hard."

"Well, now you say..."

"Dirty man."

"Clean up pretty good, though, don't I?"

"You're a cuddler," Liz teased, drawing patterns on my chest with her fingers.

"Worse things in the world to be," I said hoarsely. "Liz..."

"Shhhh..."

"Okay..."

17.

TRANSITORY

It couldn't have been more than ten or eleven when I finally opened my eyes, and even then it wasn't anything I wanted to do. Bright sunlight streamed into the room between the vertical blinds on the windows, bathing the silken sheets in a bright glow. I squinted my eyes and rubbed my forehead, working the cobwebs out. When I was able to attain vision once again, I noticed Liz was nowhere to be seen.

"You better be in the can," I said, half to myself.

"Did you say something?"

Liz's head popped around the corner of the bathroom. Her hair was slicked back and damp from a recent shower, and I could see the edge of a towel covering her top parts. I groaned and pushed myself up on elbows, casting a baleful eye around the room.

"Were you the one that opened those curtains?"

"Actually, there was a nice room service guy who came in and offered to do that," she said, sticking a toothbrush in her mouth. "I didn't have anything to tip him with, so I let him have his way with you. I didn't think you'd mind."

"So that's why I can't move my legs." I stuck my tongue out at her and edged to a sitting position on the end of the bed. I noticed a cart had been wheeled in near the TV bureau, bearing a couple of hot plates of breakfast. I sniffed the air and caught the scent of blackened bacon and scrambled eggs.

"Ohhh, munchies," I said.

"Figured you might be hungry, and I notice you have this thing about breakfast," Liz said, disappearing back into the bathroom. "I just charged it to the room. Is that okay?"

"Yeah, yeah, that's fine." I struggled into my Tasmanian Devil boxers and got to my feet, stretching the rest of the kinks and aches out of my back. Walking over to the breakfast cart, I poked around its contents and found all kinds of mid-morning goodies and a tall carafe of coffee. I poured myself a cup and set about searching the cart for the cream and sugar.

"Good morning, Oscar the Grouch," Liz said, appearing behind me and wrapping her arms around my middle. I felt her lips press against the back of my neck, and I closed my eyes.

"I'm not grouchy. I always sound like this when I wake up."

"It's a good thing you're not doing voiceovers for cartoons then, sweetie." She pinched my sides and patted by backside. "How's breakfast look?"

"Gutwrenching. My favorite."

"Good. Go brush your teeth, and I'll fix you up a plate."

"Brush my teeth? But I'm about to eat!"

"Well, fine then. See if you get a kiss from me then."

"Brushing my teeth now, madam."

After cleaning up in the bathroom and slogging a bit of soapy water over my face, I stumbled back to the bed and plopped back down. Liz brought the cart over and handed me a plate bearing scrambled eggs, bacon, some toast, and a slice of cantaloupe. Her own plate bore an omelette and fruit.

"Sleep okay?" she asked me.

"I don't remember a thing," I admitted, breaking the bacon strips into tiny crumbs across the golden landscape of eggs. "I was pretty tired."

"Could have fooled me, ace." Liz smiled and winked at me.

I took a sip of coffee. It reminded me of the specialty coffees Doc used to make in the morning to share with his students. I got a little maudlin then for a second, eyes focused on an invisible horizon just off the center of the window, jaw cracking softly as I ground breakfast between teeth.

Liz pointed her fork at me accusingly. "Something's been on your mind lately, and I can see through that stage man's charm of yours. What's up?"

I took a deep breath. I hadn't really planned on telling Liz about what I'd been doing for Carter lately, about everything I'd been through in the past week. But you just don't start a relationship with someone, expect it to last, and keep the important stuff out. Well, some people do. Those people are dumb shits. And none of them ever had a lady like Liz.

"It's a little complicated..." I started.

I told her everything.

"Jesus Christ, Jack," Liz finally said. "What kind of a fucked up world do you live in?"

"Exactly," I said. The remnants of the breakfast had been pushed to the far side of the room, and we had ended up curled up against one another in the soft sheets.

"So you think this Finley guy is responsible?"

"I'm positive. Henkel, the dickhead driver from DPI? He all but confirmed it."

"Wow." I could feel her taking a deep breath against my chest. "I didn't know you were a private eye."

"That's just it," I said, turning over to face her. "I'm not. I've never done anything like this before. I feel like I'm getting too many breaks. Like I've stumbled onto shit I shouldn't be hearing about. But when Carter got hurt..." My eyes flashed, and I felt the cold thing happen again. "Fuckin' hell, that's some serious shit."

"You're right about that," she said.

We lay there for a good twenty minutes, occasionally lacing fingertips, contemplating in silence. "What are you going to do?" Liz said.

I cast a glance at the window, seeing the telltale signs of clouds moving on out to sea.

"I don't know."

"The way I see it, you've got two choices. You take what evidence you have to the police and let them sort it out. Or you use it to blackmail Finley into giving it up."

We were walking on the beach, letting the waves roll up and touch our feet. It was a little later in the afternoon, and we had availed ourselves in a swim at The Beau Rivage pool then headed out for some sun. The breeze chilled my skin slightly, it being

October, but I had come out with a long sleeve T-shirt and cargo pants. I knew we wouldn't be staying out long in that kind of whether, but we had to get in a little beach time while we had the opportunity.

Liz hadn't said much else about my confession since our conversation in the hotel room. Instead of dwelling on it, we did The Sex again, this time with a heavier intensity that bothered me a bit. I was beginning to think that I had scared her off until we'd made it to the beach and she opened the subject up again.

"I'm tempted to go with the former," I admitted, hands jammed into my pockets. "I've got enough to quit all this and just bug out before something else bad happens. But lemme tell ya, I'm not the least bit calm after what happened to Uncle Carter. You don't just go burn up somebody's family and expect them to sit back and wank off all day."

Liz had changed into a comfy sweater thing that wrapped around her beachwear, the kind of covering that only a woman could pull off and that men could never describe properly. The material floated in the wind and couldn't have offered that much protection from the chill, but she didn't complain. In fact, she even seemed to enjoy the cold. She walked along the beach beside me, picking up sand dollars wherever she found them and skipping them into the ocean.

"Jack, whatever you decide to do, it's going to hurt someone," she said. "It sounds to me like your uncle would just as soon not have his name mentioned in all of this."

"Yeah, I'm sure he wouldn't. But then again, he's not exactly up and at 'em at the moment to do much else, is he?"

She stopped me and entwined her fingers in mine, wrapping my arms around her waist. Her green eyes demonstrated a hardness I'd not noticed before, and there was something odd about her look. If I'd known better, I wouldn't have chalked it up to lover's concern.

"It's dangerous, Jack," she said.

"Yeah, it is." I touched her cheek. "But I think I'm about done with being a behind-the-scenes kinda guy."

Liz smiled and leaned in to kiss me.

"Goddammit," she said when her cellular phone started beeping. "I should have turned it off."

"Ahhh, see who it is; it may be important," I said, tying my shoelaces. "I ought to call my pops anyway, see what's going on back in the 'Burg."

"We've got to be at the bar in an hour, Jack. I'll keep it short."

Liz opened the balcony door and walked out into the evening sky with her cell phone. Leaving her to have her conversation, I checked my appearance in the mirror and retrieved my own phone from my jacket pocket. I dialed a number.

"Hey, Pops," I said. "What's up?"

"Hey, man," Duke replied on the other end, sounding tired. "How's Biloxi?"

I spared a glance toward Liz out on the balcony. "You wouldn't believe. How's Uncle Carter?"

"Still zoning in and out on all those drugs. I'm up at the hospital right now with the rest of the family. You coming by later?"

"Probably tomorrow. The shows are going great so far."

"What about the other thing?"

I licked my lips. "Just about nipped, Pop. We'll talk when I get home. Just tell Carter not to worry."

"You got it. See ya later, Jack."

Seeing that Liz was still on her cell, I brushed my teeth and got finished cleaning up for the gig. When I exited the bathroom, she was standing in front of the balcony door, her eyes downcast. I recognized that look from things I had seen too often in the mirror.

"What's up?"

"It's my dad," she said. "He's being an asshole. Says he needs me to come back to Jackson tonight to check on Mom."

"What's wrong with your mom?"

Liz made stone solid face as she picked up her travel bag and started stuffing things inside it. "I guess I didn't tell you, did I? She's an alcoholic. She's having some problems."

"Oh." I compressed my lips into a thin line. "I'm sorry. I didn't—"

"Don't worry about it. It's just something I have to take care of." She cursed as she jammed her damp bathing suit into the bag. "Like always."

"Listen, if you need me to—"

"No!" She crossed the distance between us and put her arms around my hips. "You have a show to put on, mister. I don't need anything right now. I just... I have to go home and take care of some things."

I kissed her forehead and touched her cheek. "Sounds like you've got a little bit to unload yourself, sweetheart," I said. "Can I call you when I get home?"

"Yes, that would be fine." She squeezed me into a tight embrace and put her head against my shoulder. "I'm sorry, Jack. I had a great time. Honest. This was the most fun I've ever had on a date."

"I was hoping this could be more than a date."

She looked up at me, and I could see the tiniest sign of water under her eyes. Her mouth devoured mine. When she was finished, she put her head on my chest again and expanded her lungs in a deep sigh.

"I'll make this up to you somehow," Liz said. "I promise."

"You don't have to, Liz." I winked at her. "But a ride back to The Sand Bar would even things out a good bit."

That got a smile out of her, and she kissed me again.

"I'll get your bags," I said.

She didn't say much on our drive back to the bar, and I couldn't really blame her. I knew all about broken families and responsibility to one's parents. I felt a creeping sense of shame, having unburdened myself to Liz and not even considered asking more about her own problems. I promised myself that I'd rectify that error the very next time we met. It was only fair.

In the parking lot of The Sand Bar, we said goodbye and promised each other a phone call. It sounded almost like the end of a bad date, and I couldn't shake the feeling that something heavy had come down between us. But then again, we'd shared a lot in the past two days, and I supposed that couples had to make their own time when it came to coping with each other's pasts. I thought Liz had done a pretty good job so far with mine.

Our last kiss reminded me of the night before, the sweet tangerine scent of the body oil we'd bathed in and the softness of our bodies pressed against each other in silk. She held onto me for a moment longer before getting back into her car.

"I really am sorry, Jack," she said.

I nodded, out of excuses for her apologies. I just smiled and let her go.

I should have done that a long time beforehand.

I didn't have much energy left for the second show that night, but 25 to Midnight still pulled off a decent gig. The crowd wasn't quite as large as the previous night's, but we got by. By the end of the night, Judy cut our checks with a frenzy of well wishes and inquiries about our next availability. I told her we'd get back to her about coming back, and the rest of the band agreed. The Sand Bar would be a nice regular show if the pay kept steady.

One surprise that blindsided me was the appearance of Frank Vandy. We had just rounded out our second set with a little U2 when I saw this tubby guy hopping around like a Weeble Wobble near the tables to our right. As we bade the audience a brief break, I heard Vandy catcall and pound on his table, a very suspicious looking home-rolled cigarette perched in one corner of his mouth.

"Franky Frank!" I cackled, jumping off the stage and meeting my mentor's handslap in midair. "What are you doing out here? Thought you'd be giggin' on a Saturday night."

"Pat Murphy got the night off at Maleeny's," Frank replied, his reedy Pennsylvanian articulation cutting over the house music box. "Dave told me you guys were playing out here tonight. Besides I been meaning to come check this joint out."

"Good man. Got your sax? Wanna sit in?"

"Silly question, Schoolboy. I always wanna sit in!" He tapped the long cigarette over an ashtray and wiggled it in front of my eyes. "Want some?"

I raised a skeptical eyebrow then shrugged. What the hell. After all, you couldn't talk to Vandy in a public place and *not* have some pot. The guy worshipped the stuff. At least he wasn't dropping shrooms in public again; I'd seen that shit happen a time or two before, and damn if I didn't know how to deal with someone who thought the sky was bleeding all the time.

"Let's get some air," I told Frank, dragging him out to the deck. I grabbed a drink from the bar, and Frank refilled his vodka-tonic. We pushed through the anorexic crowd of barhops and found the deck. Jeffie and Steve were already engaged in a quick game of pool under the awning, so Vandy and I found a seat on the deck's wooden benches, which overlooked the inlet. I needed the coolness of the breeze wafting in on the chilly night. The attack of the sweat monsters had begun again.

"Not bad, Schoolboy; not bad at all," Frank said, passing me his joint. "You guys are really startin' to come together."

"Starting to?" I said, taking a swift inhale on the joint. "Aw, come on, Frank-*san*."

"Hey, like I told ya before. You move around a little bit up there, work for the crowd, you got 'em. You like James fuckin' Brown up there."

"*Hah!*" I shrieked in my best James Brown impression. "Too hot for the hottub!"

"Gimme that," Frank chuckled, taking his joint back. "No, really, I dig what you guys are into. That 'Let's Get it On' was tight! You've gotta come sit in with Pat Murphy sometime and sing that. They'd love it!"

"Thanks, Frank. 'Preciate the high praise."

"So what else you been up to around here?" Frank handed me the joint again. "I haven't seen you 'round the shop lately. Still on that job for your uncle?"

"Yeah," I said, deflating even as I inhaled. "You heard about that DPI explosion?"

"Someone at the store told me, yeah." Frank's wizened eyes blinked and expanded. "Shit, man, that's some nasty business."

"You said it. Anyway, I'm almost through with it. Couple more calls, and I think I can hang up my spurs. Here."

"Thanks. Good shit, eh?"

"You grow it?"

"Nah, I only do shrooms anymore. This stuff's too good to duplicate." Frank took another hit. Again with the goddamn shrooms. "Where ya staying?"

"The guys have rooms at a Best Western down the street, but I'm staying at The Beau Rivage. Had a girlfriend come down yesterday and part of today to fool around."

"Ohhhhh, izzatafactnow?" Frank elbowed me in the ribs. "Anyone I know?"

"Nuh-uh, she's from Jackson, but I met her at the Alley a couple weeks ago." I couldn't help the smile. "She's good fun."

"Think so?"

"Yeah. Maybe. I dunno. We'll see."

Frank made a sputtering noise as the burn went out on his joint. "Fuck. Where's *da kine*?"

"The what?" I said, frowning.

"*Da kine*! You know..." Frank made a motion like he was lighting a cigarette.

"Oh!" I flipped out my Zippo to relight the joint.

"Many thanks," Frank said, holding his breath to contain the pot smoke. "So you think all this junk's going to wrap up fine, hey? And you and the girl?"

"Liz?" I shrugged, taking the joint from his hand. "I hope so. The past week's been an ass-kicker, baby. I need some down time. I'm thinking about taking a vacation down in New Orleans. Y'know, Uncle Carter's got that condo in the Quarter."

"You seem a little strung out, Jack-*san*. Take it easy for a bit." He winked at me. "Take your filly with you."

"Yeah..."

We finished the joint and sat for a while, looking out on the inlet and the reflections of the stars above. As soon as Vandy finished his drink, he threw the empty glass down, and slapped me on the back.

"I better get my sax," he said. "What am I playin'?"

"We still got 'Who Can it Be Now?' and 'Super Freak' coming up," I said with a smirk.

"Whack pack! Be right back!"

I watched Frank trundle off to retrieve his baby and snickered. He really was a funky old dude. If I'd had the calling he did, I'd be working for him in his own shop over in Pass Christian. There would never be any replacement for my own Dad, but sometimes I thought about Frank and wished I'd met him earlier in my life.

True to form, Vandy tore the roof off The Sand Bar. Our final set featured some of our best tunes, and Frank's welcome addition only made us sound better. He and Dave dueled for a while on "Jungle Love" – *oh-wee-oh-wee-OH!* – but Frank eventually had to give it up when Dave smoked him on "Super Freak." We closed out the show with our rendition of "Message in a Bottle," and, as expected, Frank played it with his customary panty-dropping fervor. Once the show closed out, Vandy bade us goodbye, thanked us for the sit-in, and headed off back to Pass Christian in his doddering old Chevy pickup truck.

While we were breaking down our equipment and getting ready to call it a night, Jeffie cast a suspicious eye around the bar. "Hey, Jack. Where's your girl Liz at?"

"Had to go home," I snorted, rolling microphone cords. "Something about her mom being an alcoholic. I think she had an episode."

"Liz did?"

"No, dumbass; her mother."

"You know what this sounds like to me, huh?" Steve called from where he was wrapping up his amplifier. "Remember that other girl? From our first show?"

"Too well." I warned him with a look.

"I'm just sayin' is all."

"You *do* have a knack of gettin' *all* the ladies with the *hang-ups*, man," Dave added, brandishing his soprano sax at me.

"Will you guys cut me a break? Fuck, you sound like a buncha goddamn Dr. Laura clones."

"Hey, I was just asking," Jeffie said.

"Whatever," Steve said. "I'm tired. Let's get outta here."

I threw the last mic cord into its bag and reached for my jacket. "I'm with ya on that one, Steve-O."

The room at The Beau Rivage seemed a lot bigger than night. Big enough to let my mind gnaw at me again, to pry into places I had tried to lock away. Big enough to absorb the distractions of the past few days and remind me of the emotions hiding in between the folds of gray matter, underneath red and pink tissue, inside plaque-coated veins.

Crys.

Dammit.

18.

THE ONE STAR GOODNIGHT

"All right, brother," I said into my cell phone, driving on a two-lane highway with one hand. "Tell me I'm crazy."

"You're *fucking* crazy, Jack," Rick Sears chided me. "If you ask me, it sounds like you've got everything you need to put this guy down. Right? Checklist. Evidence?"

"Of?" I replied.

"Involvement in SEC fraud."

"Sketchy at best. Good enough to warrant an audit, but Finley's probably got enough attorney action going on to protect him from jail time. Best case? Company goes belly up, forced to sell off to cover the SEC fine."

"All right." I could hear Rick scrawling notes on the other end of the line, furiously writing in his incomprehensible squiggles of poor penmanship on one of a hundred dime store pocket flip notebooks that he always kept handy. "Industrial espionage?"

"Henkel *might* testify against him, but that's really shaky. Finley could have all sorts of dirt on him I don't know about, and if that's the case, then Henkel could be immune to subpoena. Same thing on Schiedle. You could set the feds on their ass, but there's no guarantee the fucker'll get an indictment. And *that's* unacceptable."

"What about the explosion at DPI?"

"Duke can prove it was intentionally set, but we're still sitting on that right now. Even if we turn it over to the cops, there's no direct link to Finley. He could set Henkel up to take the fall what with the cigarette butts we found on-scene."

"And what about these Dixie Mafia connections?"

"That's way beyond my mortal ken, bunk. I don't even wanna go there."

"Hmmm. You could be right then. I don't know, man. You know how I feel about the local law enforcement in your area."

"I hear that." I chuckled. Rick had had run-ins with more than a couple cops during his visits to Hattiesburg, and he'd been as impressed with them as he was with Firestone tires. "I want this phucko, Rick. But I'm just not sure how to do it."

"Tell you what," Rick said. "Let me talk to a few people up here and get a feel for a federal case. We could look up the regional U.S. attorney for your county and think about a special prosecution. It looks to me like that would be the only way of ensuring some kind of justice on this thing. I'll check on particulars and get back to you, okay? Just don't go off and do something stupid."

"Ahhh, I'm getting kinda burned out on the whole thing anyway, Rick. I had too much fun in Biloxi this weekend."

"This Liz lady sounds pretty hip. When am I going to get to meet her?"

"Whenever you and Nia find the time to come see me. I'll call you later, all right?"

"Whatever you need, whenever you need it, brother," Rick said, all business.

"Be easy, brother."

I hung up the cell just as the highway widened to four lanes and Hattiesburg loomed on the horizon.

My first stop immediately upon entering town was Forrest General. I got directions from Duke on how to find Carter's stateroom and braced myself for the smattering of family bullshit I'd have to go through just to see my uncle. Thankfully, no one was around when I got there, excepting only Aunt Dee who hadn't left Carter's side since the accident.

"I need a break anyway," she told me once I'd gotten into the room. "I've been sitting up here so long eating hospital food that I think I'll go batty. Be back in a bit, Jack."

She kissed her husband, and Carter made a lascivious comment to her that elicited a giggle. I was glad to see that he wasn't totally run down by the experience, and I offered Dee a genuine smile as she left. She hugged me in her Dee way – lightly but meaning it – and went off.

"Jack," Carter said, and I could hear the gravel on his vocal cords. "Where you been, boy?"

"Working," I said, seating myself in the chair next to Carter's bed and grasping his hand. He squeezed back tightly. "How are you feeling, Uncle C?"

"Better," he admitted. And he looked it, too. The burn marks on his face had colored up again, and most of the swelling had gone down. I almost didn't recognize him because someone had shaved his beard off, adding a whole new dimension of vigor to his appearance. For all intents and purposes, Carter Dooley looked ready to get back to work. His ears still looked pretty mangled, but I could tell that someone had already looked into doing some work on them. There were minuscule pinpoints of pen marks where a plastic surgeon must have been examining Carter.

"Dee won't let me talk on the phone," he said. "I'm going crazy."

"I don't blame you, bullshitter," I chuckled. "But you need the rest. Good drugs?"

"The best. But I can't remember who keeps coming in and out of this room. *That's* driving me crazy, too."

I patted his hand and sat back in the chair. "Okay, Carter. I've done what you wanted. I'm reasonably convinced that Bill Finley's the one who's been fucking you. Henkel's on his payroll, and he's the one who rigged the explosion at DPI."

I saw Carter's chest deflate heavily. "Yeah, your dad told me something to that effect. You're positive?"

"Pretty much. But look, this isn't just a simple case of one asshole buttfucking another. From what I can tell, Finley's got connections to the Dixie Mafia and a whole lot more trouble than I think we want to deal with."

Carter nodded, his eyes becoming glassy and opening and closing at irregular intervals. "So what do we do?"

"That's up to you." I looked out of the window, watching cars move to and fro in the parking lot below. "If you want my opinion, though, go to the feds. I'm getting some more information on what it might take to make a federal case that'll stick against this guy. Anyone who puts bombs on propane tanks isn't somebody you want to go see in person and demand an explanation."

"The hell I don't," Carter coughed. "That sonofabitch. I'll sue his fucking lungs for partaking in the air I breathe."

I held up my hands. "Whatever. Just think about this for a while, okay? Hold off anything until you get off the drugs and can think clearly. This cat's bad news, and you can't afford another protracted hospital stay."

"I guess..."

I could see that Carter was slipping back into unconsciousness. There would be plenty of time to talk to him later, I knew. But I wanted to be sure he understood. I wanted to be sure he comprehended. The depths of the wrongs inflicted upon him were things no average citizen should be expected to rationally handle. Carter had the propensity for rash action, and even though it wasn't part of the deal, I wanted to be sure that he *stayed* okay.

Family, I thought.

"Want the rest of your money?" he said, drifting out of sleep for a brief moment.

I squeezed his hand again. "It can wait, Uncle Carter."

He started snoring.

I stayed with him until the sun went down.

I met Duke at The Hog around seven. I briefly considered just heading home and going to sleep, but I knew I'd never be able to as keyed up as I was. Thankfully, Pops gave me an alternative when he called Carter's room in the hospital and found me on the other end of the line. En route, I suddenly remembered that I hadn't heard back from Liz since she left Biloxi. I tried to ring her, but she didn't pick up. I told her voicemail that I enjoyed myself in Biloxi and hoped she did, too. I told her that I hoped her mother was all right and that she could call me at anytime if she needed to talk. And that I was ready to drive to Jackson at a moment's notice.

I would have said more, but I have this thing about telephones and answering machines. If you do all your heavy emotions over a wire, then what does it really mean? Nothing? Everything? It just upset me for some reason, and I couldn't pin it down. Regardless, I figured I'd have plenty of time to tell Liz what she needed to hear soon enough.

Duke was already tugging on a Crown and seven when I arrived, and he had one waiting for me at the bar. I patted him on the back, sat down and went for the cigarettes.

"You ready to hear it all?" I asked.

"I think so," he said.

And so I told him.

I told him about my first interview with Al Henkel at DPI. About the research that David Novak, Deckhead, and Rick Sears had done for me. About my first meeting with Bill Finley in Magee. About my trip to Birmingham to meet Judge Will Schiedle. About Nick Gaetano's connection-making at The Dead Ringer. About the beat-down I'd served upon Henkel for planting the bomb on the DPI tank. When I was finished, my father looked paler than I'd ever seen him. By that time, we'd already been through four drinks each.

"Oh, my God," he exhaled, borrowing one of my cigarettes. "This is a hell of a mess."

"You said it," I replied, lighting it for him.

"Did you tell Carter?"

I nodded. "As much as he could handle in his condition. He needs to be thinking sharply when he gets the full story. This isn't exactly a customary deal with a hard-nosed propane dealer."

"Isn't that the truth," Duke breathed. He looked at me. "What do you think?"

"I think..." I paused for a moment. "I think I'm done with this for the time being, Dad. When I get home, I'm going to get a good night's sleep, wake up, and write all this down in a formal statement of some kind. After that..." I shrugged. "That's up to Carter."

"Jack," my Dad said; "this is pretty... *heavy*, son. I mean, you've really dug hard into this thing."

I looked at him. "He's my uncle, Dad. Your brother. It wasn't so hardcore in the beginning, but when that explosion happened at the plant..." I shook my head. "Dammit, it's not fair."

"You're right about that." Duke rubbed his eyes, and I could see that he felt his age at that moment. "I don't know what to say."

"That's a first." I grinned at him.

"No shit," he said, grinning back. "We should have a pow-wow about this. Soon. All of us."

"I agree. But let's keep it on the down-low until Carter gets out of the hospital. We don't need word of this getting back to Finley before we can decide what to do. If he finds out we suspect what's going on, his asshole could pucker up to the head of a pin and we'll never bring him down for it."

Duke nodded slowly, throwing back the rest of his drink. "How was the show?"

I blinked. "Great. Vandy sat in with us last night. And Liz came down."

"Really? What do you think about her?"

I stubbed out my cigarette. "I think it's about time something went right around this family."

Duke chuckled, and I realized then that I hadn't seen him do that in a while. My Pops is an ebullient kinda guy. Always quick with the wit and never a stranger did he meet. I patted his back.

"I love you, Dad."
"I love you, too, son."

The buzz that floated inside my skull had as much to do with the Crown as it did with my fatigue. I hadn't slept all that great the night before, even in the big, silky bed at The Beau Rivage. Too many neurons were firing off in my brain, and it had taken its toll. I needed about a day to recover my senses and veg out in front of the TV.

It was dark and late when I pulled up to my apartment complex, and I only had the wherewithal to grab my duffel. I left all my equipment and other leftovers from the Biloxi trip in the Little White Honda. Trudging up the stairs, I fumbled for my keys and got a very mellow vision of a comfy sofa, some apple juice, and a DVD. Ridley Scott's commentary on the *Alien* disc would do the trick, I thought. He'd put me to sleep in no time.

I didn't even think twice when I stuck my key in the door. It felt unlocked, and I would have paused to consider this before opening the door under normal circumstances. But I was so worn out that I just walked right in and never noticed the chipped wood and splintered plaster around the doorjamb.

Something heavy and cold struck me in the temple as my arm went out to get the light switch. The pain was incredible, totally piercing my skull in a lightning bolt that made my worst migraine seem like a too-tight baseball cap. As I dropped my bag and stumbled, two pairs of hands grabbed me by my clothes and manhandled me into the apartment. I faintly heard the slam of the door.

Knuckles crashed into my face, spontaneously evolving the lightning bolt into a thunderstorm. I felt my jaw pop as the blows continued to come down, and my legs went limp. But I didn't fall.

Someone was holding me up, presenting me unto the raging storm that tore across my face. Why would anyone do that...?

The punch to my gut sucked the wind out of me, and I lurched over with the force of the worst retch I'd ever felt. I coughed and choked, tasting bile and remnants of liquor in the back of my throat, and the taste made me gag again. I cried out as something jerked me by the hair, my head coming up to receive another slam square in the nose. There was another pop, and I felt a warm stream pour down my mouth and chin. I couldn't see for the tears that welled up in my eyes.

Whoever was holding me upright let me go, and I crumpled into a pile on the floor. It was at that point that I noticed that something was wrong with the interior decor of my apartment. Cracked and splintered CD cases crunched under my already bruised face, and I saw a pile of books nearby that had fallen from my bookshelves. I didn't have time to ruminate on this because that's when the kicking started.

My back and kidneys went first, and I shrieked as I felt the lance of agony shoot through them. Even as I cried out, I gagged again when tough boots dug into my stomach and chest. I would have vomited if my stomach could have handled the strain, but the rapid deliverance of kicks kept it from getting any kind of equilibrium. The hard thing that had hit my temple came down on my hands and arms, and I felt a crack so egregious from my fingers that my vision went stock red for a moment.

I doubled over into a fetal position, jamming my gnarled hand into my crotch, as if by spiriting it away from the torment I could somehow rejuvenate it and end the pain. But the torrent of kicks and blows continued all about me until finally, mercifully, I heard a voice over the din of my own sobs.

"Wait, wait, wait, *wait*! Don't kill the little shit!"

The assault stopped, but the pain only intensified. In the quiet stillness around me, I could finally hear the sounds I was making, and they sounded like nothing any human could ever muster let alone be forced to listen to. Tears poured out of my eyes, mixing with blood to sting at open wounds and lacerations. It felt... No. I've never felt anything like it. Nothing so terrible, so agonizing. And the noises made it only worse; the whiny, pathetic little screams and moans that I could not control, could not stuff deep down inside me.

"All right, that's enough," another voice said, a female one.

"He said to make sure he understood," the first voice said. I recognized them. Both of them.

"Albert, *that's enough*. This doesn't have to be too... *hard*. He'll get the point."

"Goddamn right about that..."

A hand jerked my head up by the hair, arching my neck at an unusual angle and sending another sliver of pain down my spine to mix with what was already festering inside me. My vision started to clear, and I could vaguely make out dark blobs standing above me. A light was on behind them, the kitchen light, I think. Then one of the blobs moved closer to me, and I could see who it was.

"Hey, kiddo," Al Henkel cackled. "How're ya feelin'?"

I tried to say something, but it came out as a high-pitched groan and a river of blood.

"Heh, heh, heh," Henkel chortled, his face a death mask in the ghostly non-light around us. "Feels bad, don't it? Why, I never thought I'd hear a man whimper like that, like some kinda stuck pig. Heh!"

I saw the backhand coming and couldn't do anything to stop it. The blow drove another bolt of torture through my sinuses, and I expelled a fair amount of blood from my nose and mouth. Whoever held onto my head let me go, and I crashed back onto the carpet, writhing onto my back, trying to find some sense of being in all the agony. Looking up, I counted four blobs plus Henkel, and maybe another one further back near the kitchen light. It was all I could to hold onto that number, to reassure myself that I wasn't going insane.

"Boy, you done fucked with the wrong people this time," Henkel went on. "And the bitch of it is, ya don't even know *how* ya got fucked!"

Crooked redneck laughter filled the four walls of the apartment. As my vision started to clear, I could see that they had wrecked the place. Furniture was overturned. The television had a hole in it. All kinds of knickknacks and trappings were strewn broken on the floor. Henkel nudged the side of my face with his foot.

"See, look up here now, boy," he managed around his snickers. "Look up here."

I looked to where Henkel indicated, trying to get my eyes to stop crossing and see straight. When the vision finally coalesced, the pain only got worse. I could cleanly make out who the sixth person was in the kitchen entrance. The female voice I had heard before.

"*Liz...*"

"I'm sorry it had to come to this, Jack," Liz said, arms folded, leaning against the opening to the kitchen. "But Daddy said it had to be this way."

I tried rolling onto my side, reaching out a mangled hand toward her. "*Liz...* what...?"

"It's Elizabeth, Jack," she said, keeping just out of reach of my hand. "Elizabeth Finley. I guess this is what it comes to when somebody never thinks to ask what his date's last name is."

I felt the torment begin anew inside me, and I tried to bite back the wail that came, leading to what sounded like a dying animal instead of anything remotely human. Tears started dripping down my cheeks again, and I lost sight of everything.

"Why?" was all I could manage.

"Because Daddy said so, Jack," Liz—*Elizabeth*—replied, nothing in her voice. None of the sweetness, none of the charm. Nothing at all. Just plain, cold, matter-of-fact. That was it.

"I'm sorry, Jack," she repeated.

"No..." I began, but another kick to my gut silenced me immediately.

"Now you listen to me, motherfucker," Henkel's voice returned. He seemed very close to one of my ears, but there was no way to tell for sure. The ringing wouldn't relent to allow me time to focus.

"You gonna give up this bullshit you're doin'," Henkel continued. "You gonna forget all about your uncle's business and Mister Finely's business and my business and your girlfriend's business. You just shut up and stay low, and me and my buddies won't have to come back and see you."

As if to emphasize his point, another blow landed in my solar plexus. My breath fled me in an instant, and I clawed at the air trying to recapture it. It did no good because my arms just got kicked for the effort.

"You understand me, boy?" Henkel shouted. "Do ya? Answer me, goddammit!"

Another kick. And another. And again.

I didn't even think about how pathetic I sounded. I just said it.

"Yes... Yes, yes, yes... *please...*"

"That's more like it," Henkel said. "Guys, make him understand how serious Mister Finley is."

The hands grabbed me again, and I couldn't even protest as I was lifted into the air. My head swam, and I felt the nausea bubble up inside me. Before I could acknowledge it, though, I was flying.

It seemed as if I had been dropped into a zero-gee freefall. But only for a split second.

Then my head crashed through the glass balcony door.

The blackness started to overtake me at that point, and I surrendered to it. As my perceptions started to wink out one by one, I heard them shuffle around behind me, a lone voice bidding me goodnight.

"I'm sorry, Jack," she said again. "Honestly. It's nothing personal. I did have a good time in Biloxi."

And then that was it. The last thing I remember is looking up from the balcony and seeing one star in the night sky peeking out from the clouds above.

It bade me goodnight, and I went away.

19.

AWAY

There was no way to tell how long I'd been out. All the clocks in the apartment had been smashed. I knew there was glass sticking out of me, but it hurt too much to try and find all the shards. So I didn't. As it was, I think it took me seventeen years to get on all fours.

The moonlight poured in from the broken balcony door, bathing the wrecking ground that was my domicile in a baleful blue glow. I crawled off the balcony and into the living area, my hands stinging as they slid across broken glass.

As I looked around, I realized that I was in Hell.

My desk and entertainment center had been turned over, their contents strewn all over the floor. The television was in three pieces and sat upon a pile of broken DVDs and splintered cases. The sofa had been sliced open, and interior pillow stuffing joined the rest of the refuse on the floor. My computer looked like it had been taken apart with a band saw. I saw bits and pieces of shredded comic books all over the place, and upon seeing this, I couldn't help the sobs that started racking my chest.

As I crawled through the mess, my hand folded atop something that opened another gash. I looked down to see the headless, legless form of my Superman maquette, the red and yellow shield on his chest tarnished and cut. Sobs turned into nausea again, and I threw up on the floor. The retches, the taste of bile, started me shuddering, and I collapsed into a quivering pile on the floor.

I think I blacked out again, but I can't be sure. The next thing I knew, I was falling down the stairs outside my apartment. The pain was so intense that I almost prayed that I broke my neck on the way down.

No such luck.

I found myself in my car, seeing a dark streak of crimson trailing my hand on the white paint of the Honda's hood. I couldn't get the door open, and I realized that I was still carrying the remains of my headless Superman statue. Somehow I found my keys, mercifully intact in my jacket pocket. The door opened. I found a position behind the wheel. The engine started.

I went away again at some point during those events. Somehow, I found the perspicacity to drive. I don't remember how or why, but I thought I had a destination in mind. Every time I moved the wheel, images of what had happened to me came back. I saw Carter and Duke and Doc Faller and Jeffie and Steve... everybody I knew in worse shape than I was.

The despair almost killed me right there.

I still had one place I thought I could make it to. Somewhere I was long overdue to return. It was no small miracle that a policeman didn't pull me over for all the weaving and winding I was doing with the car. The DUI Task Force would have had a field day with me even though I wasn't drunk. I even woke up again on the side of the road, the Honda mysteriously idle in a ditch. It took me an eternity to get it out again and back on the road.

The route I took was hard enough to navigate as it was, never mind my current state. I wove through huge clusters of overhanging trees, taking a desolate road through the south part of Hattiesburg and into a suburb town called Oak Grove. I strayed away from streetlights and other signs of civilization, and I soon found myself enveloped in total darkness. It was only then that I found the foresight to turn on my headlights.

I don't know how I found the duplex subdivision, but I did. The car parked at a rakish angle in the second drive to the left, narrowly missing a clip against an Oldsmobile. I was still gripping the maquette as I fell out of the Honda. I felt glass dig deeper into my hands as I collapsed onto the hard, cold concrete. The pain raging through me blinded me to the further scrapes and lacerations I received as I dragged myself to the door. 34-B, I saw in gold above the doorknocker.

The doorbell rang again and again as I drove my thumb into it. I had to switch from finger to thumb when I hit the button the first time, suddenly aware by metacarpal agony that my fingers must be broken. I leaned my head against the doorjamb, my breathing ragged and irregular. Why didn't she *answer...*?

The door creaked open an inch. Darkness flowed from the crack. I moaned and fell against the door, sliding down to the welcome mat outside.

"Help..."

The door swung open and she came out as lithely as a cheetah. I felt her hands through the shredded sleeves of my jacket. When she took my face in her hands and propped my head up, a spike of heat seared through the iciness that gripped my body.

"Jack!" she said. "Oh my God, what *happened*?"

"Crys..." was the last thing I managed before giving up entirely.

"Jack? Jack! Stay awake, Jack! Jack, talk to me."

Something reasonably soft rebounded against my head repeatedly. As I swam out of unconsciousness, I discovered that I was lying face down in the backseat of a car. Dark interior. Plush seats. Very comfortable, all things considered.

"Jack! Dammit..."

My body jerked as the car slowed and stopped. I tried to look up and immediately regretted it as the pain shot down my neck and into my back. Through the wetness in my eyes, I saw Crys leaning over her seat and shaking me.

"Jack, wake up!" she crowed, jostling me. "Oh God.... Does that hurt?"

"Yesssss..." I managed around the bubbles of blood in my mouth.

"Just hold on, Jack. I'm taking you to the hospital."

"No!"

I managed to grip her elbow before she turned back around in her seat. Crys' brow furrowed in that way that it did. A brief flicker happened to my heart.

"No hospital," I said firmly.

"Jack, you have broken bones," Crys said, touching my hand. "You're cut up like you've been in a knife fight. You need to see a doctor."

"You're a... nurse..."

The squeeze of her hand on mine hurt, but I didn't mind. "I'm just a nurse in school, Jack..."

"Crys, please..." Her face started to blur as the tears came again. "I need... your help..."

Silence. I couldn't see at all.

"Okay, Jack. Okay. Where do you want me to take you?"

"New Orleans... The Provincial... Chartres and Ursuline..."

"New *Orleans*? Jack—"

"Have to get... away..."

And I was gone again.

The next several hours were nothing but a jumble of half-coherent images and spikes in my pain meter. I remember the bright lights of a 24-hour gas station where Crys sat me up in the backseat of her car and treated some of my wounds. Every so often, my eyes would open, and I could see the interstate rushing by beyond my window. I felt sticky at one point, and I figured I'd pissed myself or worse. The humiliation was so bad that I welcomed the blackness.

I don't think Crys said much during the trip to New Orleans. I handed her my wallet at one point, concerned that she may not have any money, and Crys took it without a word. A bump in the road knocked my head savagely against the window, and I think she pulled over to check on me.

She shook me awake again once we reached New Orleans. It was still dark outside, and I had no sense of time at all. I tried to sit up to see where we were or look at the dashboard clock, but it was no use. Even as I craned my head around, my eyes wouldn't focus on anything. It occurred to me to look at my watch, and when I did, I saw that the crystal face was cracked and dented.

Broken.

Just like everything else.

"Where are we going again?" Crys asked.

"Chartres Street," I said, dazed. "Go to the French Quarter... Corner of Ursuline and Chartres Street..."

When I came to again, the car was still and Crys was pulling me out of the backseat.

"What do I do, Jack?" she asked. "Where are we?"

"Help me up," I said, grabbing her shoulder. "Find a porter."

Crys got my arm around her shoulder and, with difficulty, got me to a semi-standing position. Almost as soon as she'd done this, a man in a white uniform was upon us.

"Can I help y'all— Gawdamighty! Mistah, you lookin' like Hell itself!"

"Dooley," I said, struggling to keep the man in focus. "Carter Dooley's condo. I'm his nephew... Crys..."

Crys fumbled with her jeans and pulled out my wallet. The porter helped prop me up against the car. She dug out my driver's license and a credit card, handing them over to the porter.

"We need to get upstairs quickly," she said. "Can you help me get him up there?"

"Well, hol' on jus' one second, miss," the porter said, inspecting my ID. "I never met this gen'leman befo'..."

"Etienne," I said, shaking my head to clear my vision. "Where's Etienne?"

"Etienne?" the porter said. "Well, hol' up one second. He inside."

I slumped against the car again, and Crys reached over to steady me. She touched my forehead, and bolt of pain streaked through my head. She must have sensed it because I heard her sharp intake of breath echo my own.

"ATM card..." I said, fumbling at my wallet. "Take it... Get some cash... Access code's fifty-two-fifty-two... Use cash for everything..."

"All right, Jack," Crys said, holding me even as I started sliding down the car again. "Just be still. You're going to be fine."

"Sorry..." I wheezed. "Sorry I made you..."

"Jack, hush." A finger touched my split lips. "It's okay."

"Mistah Jacques! Oh my Gawd!" I heard another voice say as footsteps echoed on the cobblestone drive.

"Etienne?" I croaked.

"It me, Mistah Jacques," the deeply accented voice said, and I felt another set of hands help steady me. "Say, you no look too good. You get in trouble down in de Quarter, *hien*?"

"Etienne, I need to get into Carter's condo," I said.

"Whatever you say den, Mistah Jacques. Mistah Cartah say you alway' welcome here." I heard a loud whistle. "Remy! Get dis man car and take it 'round back, *hien*? And send a body de key to 202!"

"Excuse me," Crys said. "Is there an ATM machine around here?"

"Dere one in de lobby, *chere*," Etienne replied. "But you no need worry 'bout money, *hien*? Dooleys alway' come down here un'nounced."

I felt my feet scraping against cobblestones and steps as Crys and Etienne dragged me through The Provincial's pavilion. I heard a fountain just before they helped me up a steep flight of stairs, and my head lolled about limply. Etienne opened the door somewhere, and I felt Crys drag me inside.

"Dere you go, Mistah Jacques," I heard Etienne say as Crys dragged me further into the dark condominium. "You jus' call Etienne you need somethin'. Dat go for you too, miss, *hien*?"

"Thank you," Crys said, shutting the door as soon as Etienne had handed over the key.

She put me down on a sofa, and my head kept swimming. I felt her fingers caress my bruised, swollen face in the darkness. A sliver of light peeked into the condo from the shuttered doors to the outside terrace, and it illuminated the blue in Crys' eyes. I looked up at her.

"I'm sorry..." I said.

"Shhhh," she said. "It's okay, Jack. We're safe in New Orleans now."

"Not for this... Sorry for... for before." I tried to make my eyes stop dancing in their sockets, and failed. "Sorry I hurt you..."

I got one good glimpse of her perfect, smooth face and the sad smile that accompanied it before I faded off again.

20.

REHAB

Time passed.

No way of telling how much.

Crys disappeared while I slept. When I awoke, I found that she had appropriated a sack full of first aid and medical supplies. She stripped me out of my torn, bloodied clothes and tended to my injuries. The alcohol stung when it touched the cuts and lacerations, but I was still so out of it that the pain barely registered. Once, I passed out in her arms at the sight of her using a small pair of tweezers to pull out bits of glass from my hands.

The worst came when she set my broken bones. I must have had more than I figured. My fingers cracked at odd angles, my ribs tightened in a way that labored my breathing. Something wet and painful kept happening to my forearm. Every time she tended to something, I woke up for the pain and passed out again.

This must have gone on for quite a while.

"I can't see," I said during one of my lucid moments.

"It's okay," Crys said near my ear. "I had to put something over your eyes. You had some broken blood vessels in there."

"Oh..."

"How does that feel?" she asked me.

My arm? "Hurts?"

"I think you have a hairline fracture on this forearm. It's not too bad, but I'm going to set it anyway, okay?"

"Okay."

"How does your head feel?"

I tried to sniff, but the inhalation went straight to my brain and made me nauseous. "Going to be sick..."

Crys pushed me back down, not allowing me to get up. "I'll get you a pan."

"Jack, you have to eat something. It's been two days."

I avoided the spoon that hovered near my lips. "Don't wanna be sick again..."

"I think you can keep this down," Crys assured me. "It's clam chowder. Here, now. Open up."

"Mmmmm..."

I thought I was feeling better at one point. Crys took the bandages off my eyes, and I could see much better. I knew I was lying in a bed, which must have been an effort on Crys' part. She had to have dragged me upstairs all by herself.

When I moved, a wash of heat came over me, and I broke out into a very cold sweat.

"Oh my God," Crys said, coming to my side and putting the back of her hand against my head. "Jack, you're hot. You must have a fever. Dammit..."

"Sorry..."

"No, no, it's my fault." I saw her unwrapping a thermometer from its packaging. "I should have checked earlier. One of your wounds must have gotten infected. Here, put this under your tongue."

I let her take my temperature. When she looked at the thermometer, her eyes got very wide.

"Okay, Jack," she said, pulling me up. "We have to get you into the tub."

The retches came back with greater force than before. Crys held my head over a saucepan she must have found in the downstairs kitchen.

"It's going to be okay, Jack," she said, petting my sweat-soaked and matted hair.

"I'm sick," I said.

"Yeah. Do you feel like you're going to do it again?"

"Maybe."

"Okay. Here. Swallow these. They're aspirin. I'm going downstairs and getting you some food."

"Can't keep it down."

"That's okay. It's better than tasting vomit, right?"

"Yeah..."

"C-c-cold..."

"Okay, okay..." I felt her climb into the bed with me. Her arms encircled me and she lay my head against her chest. She pulled the blanket further up to cover us. My teeth chattered incessantly, aggravating my bruised jaw. And I couldn't stop sweating.

"Shhhh," she whispered into my ear. "I'm here, Jack."

"C-C-Cryssss?"

"Yes, Jack?"

"Th-thank y-y-y-you..."

"You're welcome, Jack."

I fell fast asleep, counting the even, rhythmic beats of her heart.

"Hold still now," she said, wiping the remainder of the shaving cream off her fingers and holding up the razor. "I'm just going to go real slow. Tell me if I hurt you."

"All right," I said. My eyes were swollen shut with sleep dust. The warm water woke me up, and the softness of the cream prickled at what must have been a nasty growth of beard.

"There we go," Crys said as the razor glided softly against my cheek. "You're going to look like a million bucks, Jack."

"Wish I could feel that way."

"You will, Jack. Don't worry." I felt her tug at the tuft of hair beneath my bottom lip. "Do you want me to keep your imperial?"

"No," I said. "Get rid of it."

One night, I heard something outside the shutters in the bedroom. I peered to see Crys standing at the open window overlooking The Provincial's common balcony, looking out into the New Orleans night. A golden glow from the gaslamps below bathed her face and glistened over the highlights in her hair.

"What's going on?" I managed.

"Oh, you're awake." She turned from the window and sat at the edge of the bed. "Is it bothering you? I can shut the window."

"No, it's okay," I said. I heard horns and drums and scores of people cheering outside. "What is it?"

Crys smiled and reached behind her. She brought up a small muffin with blueberries and almonds in it, a single candle stuck in the center. I frowned, watching her edge toward me, lighting another candle and placing it on the nightstand to illuminate the room.

"It's Halloween, Jack," she said, putting the muffin on my chest. "Happy Birthday."

I felt a smile creep onto my face, and with some effort I inched myself up against the pillows. Crys smiled back, her eyes clear. Perfect in the midnight glow from the Quarter. She gathered her hands in her lap and looked at the muffin.

"I didn't forget," said Crys.

"I won't either," I replied.

It took a little mustering, but I managed to blow the candle out with one breath.

The scent of freshly spiced crawfish wafted into the bedroom one morning, carried on a Big Muddy airflow with just a hint of baked bread. I was awake in an instant, my mouth watering. My stomach growled uncontrollably, and I figured the Dooley GI tract was just about fed up with the nominally liquid diet I'd been on.

Experimentally, I tried to swing my legs off the side of the bed. A deep ache wrapped around my midsection, and I noticed the tightly wound bandages wrapped around my ribs and back. The discomfort was plenty to keep me prostrate, but I felt I needed to get up and move under my own power. I placed my feet squarely on the dark carpeted floor and pushed myself up. My legs seemed to work fine, but my knees seemed a tad swollen. I was plenty used to that, though, since I had lived with inflamed kneecaps left over from days playing high school football and playing it badly.

I saw that I was naked, and I searched the room for some clothes. In one of the boudoirs set against the wall, I found a robe sewn of very thin material. Stretching into it sent rivers of pain along my shoulders and sides, but I managed it. I did have trouble with the belt, though; three of the fingers on my left hand were bound in gauze tape and metal straightener. My right hand didn't feel much better, but at least all the digits worked. There was a makeshift splint wrapped around my right forearm from the wrist to the elbow. I couldn't move the right hand at all, but the fingers definitely moved. It was getting around the patches of gauze and Band-Aids that was the trouble.

Stumbling through the bedroom, I found a clock that told me it was half past three in the afternoon. I had a sudden urge to relieve myself, so I waddled into the bathroom, flipping on the light. It was the worst thing I could have done, because I caught the ghost of myself in the mirror.

My body was covered in bandages. In addition to the reinforced wrap around my middle, several smaller pieces of gauze had been taped over cuts and abrasions. There was a nasty scar down the right side of my temple, ending in a blue-black bruise that spread to my black eye. The right eye bore a giant burst blood vessel under the retina, looking like some pernicious cataract. Another purple mark indicated the spot on my jaw where I had been hit, and I worked my mouth to see if any permanent damage had been done. My jaw popped every time I moved it, which was more annoying than anything else. A sealant cover was taped across my nose, and I flexed my nostrils to see if it was broken. It didn't feel too bad, just sore. I wasn't about to poke and prod it though just to satisfy my curiosity. There was another, larger bandage across my forehead, and my bottom lip bore the marks of having been recently split.

I sighed at the reflection and went to the bathroom, saying a silent prayer to all the Catholic saints that my boys were in decent shape. When I opened the robe, it looked like I had lost a little weight, and it prompted me to wonder exactly how long I'd been out.

Creeping back into the bedroom, I gripped the bannister and carefully made my way downstairs. The condominium was fully furnished and well-kept. In addition to the bed upstairs, there was a designer sofa and chair set downstairs. The coffee table and entertainment center matched the wood veneer of the bookshelf that stood in the corner next to the shuttered balcony doors. A fairly hi-tech television, VCR, and stereo rested inside the entertainment center, and a row of old homemade videotapes lined the center's top. A large, Oriental rug covered most of the carpet in the living area downstairs, and the stairs emptied onto old-fashioned New Orleans cobble style tile in front of the entry foyer and kitchen.

I saw that Crys had left my cell phone, keys and wallet in a basket on the kitchen counter. Rifling around through the basket, I found half a pack of Camels and my Zippo. What was left of my ripped clothes hung on the high stools in front of the counter. I made a face when I saw all the holes and tears in my leather jacket.

I had really liked that jacket.

My cell looked none the worse for wear, which surprised me. I'd have to reevaluate the make and model, which I'd initially written off as cheap when I'd bought it.

Inside the fridge, I found plenty of fruit juice, some milk, a few cold dishes, and beer that Carter and Dee always kept stocked. The cabinets above sported several cans of soup and vegetables as well as a few fruit meals and some pasta. The freezer was stocked with lots of frozen meat and a hefty tub of mint chocolate chip ice cream.

I walked across the living room and opened the folding doors that led out onto the wooden balcony that circled the perimeter of The Provincial. A wrought iron table and chairs sat off to the side of the door, and I saw a few other such decorations in front of the doors to the other units on that floor. The weather outside must have been in the fifties, the fall chill dampened somewhat by the breeze coming in off the warm waters of the Mississippi River. Across Chartres Street, I could see over the off-white walls of the rectory museum, and its courtyard remained a darkened green even in the fall weather. I looked left and right and saw the usual progression of people shuffling through the French Quarter. A horse-drawn carriage clip-clopped along with a trio of tourists in its berth, a wizened old Cajun tour guide spouting off local lore and legend.

As I went back inside to escape the chill, I heard the door to the main entry foyer open. Turning around, I saw Crys walk in carrying a bundle of bags. She strode into the living area to deposit them on the sofa and caught sight of me standing at the balcony door.

"Jack, you're up," she said, a slow smile breaking out across her face.

"Yeah, I smelled spicy food," I said, running a hand through my shaggy hair. "I think someone's grilling crawfish a couple blocks down the way."

"I had to go shopping," Crys said, setting the bags down. "You and I both needed some clothes, so I went over to the Riverside Mall and picked out some things. I hope I got your sizes right. And I hope you don't mind; I had to use your ATM card to get some more cash."

"There's plenty in there," I said, taking a few steps over to her. A sliver of pain slid up my side, and I winced slightly.

"Easy there, cowboy," she said, coming over to me. "Let me check your bandages. Are you feeling better?"

"Very much so." I grunted as she touched the bandages on my face. "You do a pretty good job for a nurse in training."

"Lucky for you, the injuries weren't as bad as they looked." She opened up my robe and checked the wrap around my ribs. She seemed completely oblivious to the fact that I was completely naked underneath. "How does your midsection feel?"

"Sore as hell," I said. "I don't want to breathe too hard or I think something might bust."

"You had a broken rib in there," she told me, feeling along my sides. "I was worried it might have punctured a lung or caused some other internal bleeding, but the bruise patterns settled after the first day. Lucky man, you."

Crys wrapped the robe around me again and tied the belt. She looked up at me when she finished. She looked great. Better than ever. Her thin body gave way to an unusually heart-shaped face with full cheeks. Her blonde hair was cut short just below the ears and swayed with her when she moved. She stood about an inch or two shorter than I. She wore a long sleeve white shirt with the sleeves rolled up and a pair of jeans, some flats. Something sad was happening in her big, baleful blue eyes.

I embraced her lightly, afraid at first that I might hurt myself and then worried that she might not accept me. But Crys' arms snaked around my back, and I could feel the familiar rubbing motion her hands made. She pressed the side of her head against mine, and this time I did get hurt. A sudden burst of something welled up inside of me. I fought down the urge to cry out, but tears came freely. It wasn't a pain in any way related to my injuries, but it hurt just as bad.

"Crys, I'm so sorry," I gasped over her shoulder. "I didn't want to hurt you. I didn't mean to go. I'm sorry I failed you. I'm sorry, I'm sorry..."

"Shhhhh," she said, rubbing the back of my neck. "It's okay, Jack. I know. And I forgive you, all right?" Crys disengaged so she could look me in the eyes, and she put a hand on my cheek to wipe away the tears.

"You don't have anything to be sorry for anymore," she said quietly.

I couldn't keep it in anymore. Something had broken open, and there was no shutting it. I collapsed onto the sofa, weeping like a child. Crys came with me, snuggling against me and taking my hand in hers.

"You had no reason to help me like this," I bit out. "You could have just turned me away."

"I would never do that to you, Jack," Crys whispered. "No matter what's happened."

"But how can—"

She put a finger to my lips. "Hush. You're still healing. We can always talk about it later."

I nodded and buried my head in her chest, unable to stop crying.

Feeling well enough—and starved enough—to eat a full meal, Crys broke open the freezer and cooked me a steak on the stovetop. She also heated up some green beans and microwaved a potato. I offered to help, but she wouldn't hear of it. She fixed me a glass of apple juice and had me sit down at the dinner table. When she finally served the evening meal, I wolfed it down like a slovenly slob-thing, so hungry that I didn't bother minding my manners.

"No surprise you're so hungry, cowboy," Crys said across the table. "You've been out for over two weeks."

I stopped in the process of dipping my fork into the sour cream and cheese-laden potato. I was having a hell of a time of it what with the splint on my arm. "Two *weeks*? God, what the hell happened to me?"

"Well, your head was pretty banged up in the first place," she said, spearing a green bean. "I was worried that you may have had a concussion, but it turned out all right after a while. Then you got sick. I guess I didn't clean up those cuts as well as I should have because one of them got infected. You were running a fever of a hundred and four."

"Really?" I shook my head, blinking a couple of times. "I don't remember too much."

"You shouldn't. You were really sick, Jack. I had to go down to the clinic and get some antibiotics after the first couple of days."

"Jesus." Two *weeks?!* "What day is it?"

"Tuesday the fifteenth. Thanksgiving's in a couple of days."

I made a face. "Oh, hell, I've probably ruined your school schedule! Fuck!"

Crys grinned and giggled in that way. "Don't worry about it, cowboy. I sat out the semester. Mom got a little sick earlier this year, so I took the semester off to make sure she was all right."

"Babs is ill? What's wrong? It's not her emphysema, is it?"

"Yep. I finally convinced her to quit smoking, which is something the two of us ought to do, mister chimney-mouth."

"Did a lot of coughing, did I?"

"It was awful. I thought you were going to go into shock."

I inhaled sharply and chewed on a piece of steak. "What else did I miss while I was out?"

"Your cellular rang a bunch. I wasn't sure you wanted me to answer it or not, so I just let it sit. Do you have voice mail?"

"Nope, but there's a caller ID record I can track back on. And thanks, by the way. I'm not keen on letting anyone know where I am just yet. Anybody else call? Come by?"

"Your uncle called once," she said, wiping her mouth with a napkin. "Apparently, Etienne called him and let him know you were holed up here. I talked to him; told him you probably wanted to be left alone for a little while."

"Thanks," I said. "Was he out of the hospital when he called?"

"I think so. What was he in the hospital for?"

"Long story," I said, grimacing. "Not in the least bit as long as why I pulled the stage 3 terminator act on your doorstep."

Crys looked at her plate. "Are you going to tell me about it?"

I nodded. "Yeah. But not just yet, okay? I need to get my wits about me again."

"Fair enough."

"Have you been okay through all this?"

"Sure. Etienne pointed out a few places I needed to go so I could get first aid stuff and supplies. The clinic, the Vertie Mart, the mall. I got a little tired of wearing the same clothes every day, and I figured you wouldn't mind if I went out and got us some new threads."

"Don't mind at all. As a matter of fact, I'm going to owe you pretty big for all this when it's over."

"Jack, you don't—"

"Crys, please." I looked at her in awe. "You came down here with me after I've neglected to talk to you for months. With nothing to go on. You just packed up and went. Do you think I'm going to let you get away with all this for nothing?"

She shrugged, sipping her juice. "You looked like you needed help. Besides... you were there for me once. More than once, actually."

I looked back down at my plate. "I could have stayed. Could have not chickened out and ran off when you told me you wanted to stop seeing me."

"I never said I wanted to stop seeing you," Crys said, her voice even and firm. "I had problems, Jack. You know that. With all the drugs and the shit at home, I just felt... *smothered.* I never meant to run you off."

Smothered, I thought to myself. *Flashback, Jack.*

"But you did," I replied, unable to meet her eyes. "After all that time I'd spent holding you while you cried, waking up in the middle of the night to come get you when your parents were fighting... Hell, picking you up from a bar when you were too drunk to know where you were. Crys, I tried to give you everything... and you made it sound like it didn't matter."

I held up my hands. "Not that I'm not to blame. I... I got angry. It doesn't sound like the smartest thing I could say, but I was pissed. Rejected. After all that I went through for you. I felt..."

"Used?" she finished for me.

This time I met her eyes. "Yeah. That's about right."

I coughed. Silence hung between us.

"Jack, can I tell you something?" she said after a moment.

"Sure."

"I was glad you left. I was glad you got mad and wouldn't return my calls."

I lowered my head, suspecting the truth of it. I thought I knew what was coming.

I didn't.

"I couldn't have checked into rehab without that anger," Crys told me.

I looked back up.

"You went into rehab?"

She nodded, making one of her customary faces like nothing in the world could surprise her. "Yep. About a month after we split up."

I frowned. "And what I did... was good for you?"

Crys reached across the table and touched my hand. "Jack, you saw how screwed up I was. Did you know that just about every time we had one of those talks and you convinced me to stop taking those pills... I went and took some when you were gone? I'm an addict, Jack. Just like my dumbass Mom and Dad. And let me tell *you*, I caught some shit from my mother when she found out you walked."

I grinned a small grin. "She did kind of like me."

"She *adored* you," Crys giggled. "We had the biggest fight when she found out, and I kept calling her a bitch and all this other horrible stuff. Spent the night in the car, I did. I got madder than hell, let me tell you. The very next day, I went out to the counseling clinic at Southern."

I took a sip of apple juice, eyes totally intent on hers now. "How long did it last?"

"About two months. The first month, I stayed there. Liked to have had a breakdown. All those creepy people and their jacked up stories. I had to listen to the worst stuff while I was in there. This one lady had a heroin problem, and she wouldn't stop scratching at her arms while she talked. I mean, she just kept scratching and scratching. I thought she would tear her skin off. I almost did it for her, too."

Crys shook her head. She got up and grabbed something off the kitchen counter. When she returned to the table, she tossed me my cigarettes and lighter and produced a pack of her own. We lit up, sharing the Zippo flame. I chuckled at her as I watched her inhale.

"Smoke?"

"Yes, thank you," she said. "Anyway, it was tough. But I got through it. All I talked about was you and Mom and Dad. And every time I did, I got pissed off. I turned into your worst nightmare, Jack."

"Hey, I was around for one or two of your DTs sessions."

"Okay, I'll give you that." Crys blew out a stream of smoke and tapped out an ash. "But the point is, I turned into Number One Bitch Queen of the Universe. After it was all over, I was glad you weren't around to see it."

"It's not something to be ashamed of," I said. "Everybody has to go through it if they're in rehab."

"Even still." She pointed at me with her cigarette and pinned me with a dark glare. "I was glad you weren't there. Because when I got out, I *did* have that breakdown when I realized what I'd put you through. When I understood that I *was* using you, just like any other dope in the house."

I scowled playfully. "Well, if you're going to be mean about it..."

She winked at me in *that way.* "God... It's been a long time since I heard that razor keen wit of yours."

"I wouldn't call anything about me keen anymore," I said, dragging on the cigarette. "But regardless... I think I still owe you an apology for the way I handled things."

"As do I. But you've got to understand something, Jack. I'm a fucking addict." Crys looked over at the balcony doors. "I get addicted to things. And the only way to stop it is to be strong. As there's no guarantee if I'll *be* strong when the time comes."

I tapped out some ashes. "I can live with that."

She looked over at me. "You can?"

"After the month I've had... that's a piece of cake."

"He said, broaching the pregnant subject..."

I stubbed out the cigarette, feeling the coughs coming back, the irritation of laying off the bad habit for so long that I might have given it up if I hadn't been a weak-willed little girl. But as I was learning, addiction was something people could live with.

"Let's clean up," I said.

We found a worn out copy of *True Romance* in Carter and Dee's video stash and decided to curl up and check it out. It had been a long time since I'd seen the movie, and when the part came with Patricia Arquette and Christian Slater confront each other over Slater's murder of Arquette's former pimp (ably portrayed by such a young Gary Oldman), Crys and I smiled at each other.

I leaned against her on the sofa, and she ran her fingernails along my scalp, creating a dizzying trail of goosebumps all the way down my neck and back. We swapped smokes, sipped apple juice, and watched a good flick about an odd couple. The irony wasn't lost on us.

"You told me you loved me one time," I said, right after Alabama wrote Clarence the *"You're So Cool!"* note. "Did you mean it?"

"At the time?" Crys replied, pulling at each hair on the back of my head. "No."

"Oh." I settled back against her chest. "Okay."

Her lips touched the top of my head. "But I came to after a while."

And that's how we went to sleep on November 15th.

21.

GET BACK, JACK

Crys had bought me a great pair of khakis and a couple of shirts. We got dressed as soon as we arose, and I took her for a walk through the French Quarter. We ended up at the Café du Monde for a delicious repast of beignets and coffee. The powdered sugar did me good, and a lot of my energy came back in the hours we spent at the outdoor diner. *Diner* doesn't actually describe Café du Monde well. It really kinda defies description. People ganged up around the small tables to share plates of beignets. The smell of fried dough wafted through the air. Young men and women in greasy white uniforms darted around busing tables and delivering orders. A grizzled old man tooted away on a saxophone nearby, and I threw him a couple of tens from the roll of cash I'd liberated from the account Carter had set up for me. By that time, there was no putting it off any longer.

"All right," Crys said, dusting the powder off her fingers. "I'm ready to hear it."

"It?" I said, reaching for my cigarettes.

She nodded solemnly. "Why were you all beat up when you came to my door?"

I lit up, sat back, and got to it.

"A little while ago, Carter, my uncle, asked me if I'd look into a problem he was having with his propane business. Apparently, someone was lifting about seven-hundred grand in stocks from his assets, and he was losing profits on sales for some undisclosed reason. I agreed to look into it."I find this driver of his named Henkel who smells shady. He's got a bad accident record, and I finger him for the loss of product around DPI. I check him out, find out he's got ties to another propane supplier out of Jackson: Bill Finley at PetroJet Chemical. I keep sniffing around Henkel and draw a lead to a judge in Birmingham who turns out to be on Finley's payroll. Looks like the judge is laundering dough for Finley. I get someone to do some outside research on Finley's investment corporation, and I think I've got the stock problem in the bag. My sources tell me that Finley could be ripping off Carter's DPI stocks through some underhanded trading, converting the profits to cash, running it through the judge and into someone else's hands.

"I go visit one of Finley's acquisitions in Magee. The guy in charge there describes a situation that led to the downfall of his business and the eventual buy-out by PetroJet. A situation that smells a lot like what's going down at DPI. Also, it turns out Henkel is dropping off stolen propane from DPI at the Magee location. I didn't find any proof about it, but I suspect Henkel's stolen delivery loads were covered up in DPI's records as accidents. Carter thinks maybe DPI had a few more accidents than he remembered, and

Henkel's snow job smelled right for the con. I figure I got this bitch in the bag, right?

"Then a propane tank at the DPI yard explodes, and Carter goes to the hospital. Dad and I look into the accident and find evidence that the explosion could have been engineered. I get mad, break into Henkel's apartment, beat the shit out of him, and find out he's the one who enabled the explosion.

"I make a leap of logic and head down to Biloxi to sniff around a destination for all the money the Alabama judge is moving for Finley. Where's it going to? The Dixie Mafia. Apparently, Finley's got friends in high places down there. For a small percentage, they launder the stolen cash from the DPI stock, reinvest it, garner *more* profit, and send it to Finley all nice and tidy."

I paused for a moment, finding that I'd smoked a whole cigarette in the time it took me to run through it. I lit another one. Crys just watched and listened in silence across the table.

"While all this is going on... I've met someone. Met her at a gig at the Alley. Sound familiar?"

Crys grinned a small grin, looking away for a moment, averting eyes that conveyed perpetual mischief. "You don't have much luck with chicks from the Alley, Jack."

"So it seems. Anyway, her name's Liz. Well. Was. *Is*, I guess. I like this girl, okay? She's great. Well, she comes down to Biloxi for a show we're playing down there, and we have the time of our lives. And what do I do? I open my big fat fucking mouth and tell her everything I'm telling you. Next thing I know, she's out of Biloxi and supposedly heading back to Jackson.

"I think everything's cool, right? I've got Finley by the balls with enough evidence to warrant a phone call to the feds. I'm digging this Liz chick. And Uncle Carter's getting better in the hospital. Good to go, right?"

My hand started to shake. I put the cigarette down and put my hands in my lap. The images I'd shut out of my brain came back to me. As I walked through the situation, I drew piece upon piece from each part of the path. As I went further, I felt my blood pressure rising with each new word.

"I get back to my apartment and Henkel's there waiting for me with five guys. Guess who else is there?"

Crys closed her eyes. "Liz."

"*Elizabeth Finley.* They warn me off the case, work me over, and put my head through my own fucking balcony door." I rubbed a hand lightly over my skull, feeling the indentation. "Surprised that didn't kill me."

"Me too," Crys said. "You must have hit right on that crack in your balcony door. Otherwise..."

I blinked a couple of times, remembering... Needing to remember why and how Crys knows too. It took a moment to order all the memories, to see the times Crys had been in the apartment back when I had just moved in. "When I wake up, my place is trashed, I'm trashed. Everything's trashed."

"I guess that explains that broken Superman thing you had with you," Crys said.

I flinched. "Do you still have it?"

She nodded. "It's in the car."

I looked down and put the heels of my hands against my brow. "It was right in front of me all the time, and I didn't see it. Every little clue she could possibly give me, and I couldn't get my head out of the fucking clouds and wake up." I looked up at Crys, my eyes clearing. "I've been...deluding myself. Not seeing reality for what it is. Seeing what I wanted to see."

I straightened as something else clicked. I remembered Doc Faller's warning about Liz's name, his intense grilling when I couldn't produce her last name. The connection was so striking that I didn't have time for anymore self-loathing. "Elizabeth Finley. Betsy Jones. They're probably the same people."

"Who's Betsy Jones?" Crys asked.

"The person who was signing Henkel's checks in Magee." I sat back in the chair and rubbed the aching bridge of my nose. "It was right fuckin' there... And you know what the crime of it is? I still didn't want to believe it when I got to your house. All the way there, all I could think of was that there must have been some kind of mistake."

I couldn't go on. I leaned over and felt the wave of nausea overtake me. My whole body had begun to shake. The enormity of what I'd become embroiled in sank into my every pore. And from the very beginning, I'd ignored the one thing that could have saved me the grief.

"Don't underestimate them, snapper."

Doc Faller had been right. I *had* underestimated them. All of them. From Finley to Henkel to Liz. It was just one long string of fuck-ups courtesy of the biggest patsy ever to blow in from west of the Sabine River.

"They broke me, Crys," I bit out, tasting bile. "And it didn't even take 'em long. They just laid into me and fucked me up and I cried like a baby. And the whole way home, I bet they laughed their asses off about it. Knowing that there was nothing I could do to fix everything that had gone wrong."

There was silence for a while. The sax melody drifted in and out of the café, at times drowned out by the din of the people on the street. I didn't even want to look up at Crys. The shame had finally taken me, and it was ten times worse than what she'd described about the rehab clinic.

I fucked up.

"Jack... Did you fuck her?"

Our eyes met again. Mine were brimming. "Yes."

"Was it good?"

I looked away. "Yeah."

Crys continued looking at me. "Well, that's okay."

My eyebrows steepled. "What?"

"Jack." She reached across the table for my hand. "It was just sex."

"She played me, Crys. She played me like a rigged slot machine, and I never saw it coming."

"*Jack.*"

Hey eyes were perfect blue.

"It was just sex."

It started to seep into me.

Crys just kept peering at me.

"What do you want to do now?" she asked.

I quit shaking.

"Commit a crime," I said.

I felt an ache in my gut that spread from my chest all the way around to the base of my spine. I told Crys about it.

"You may have bruised those ribs again," she said.

"I didn't hurt you, did I?"

"Does it matter?"

Silence. But we were both good with it. We both knew the answer to that.

Time passed. "I'm mad," I said.

"Good."

"Crys..."

"Hush. It's all about anger management, right?"

"And I needed you to show me that?"

"I can't answer that."

"It's a dark place in which you live, Crys."

"Don't worry. I'll show you around."

On my way out of The Provincial, my cell phone started ringing. I stopped outside the lobby area, which featured a long driveway surrounded by the moss- and ivy-covered brick walls of Stella, the restaurant attached to the hotel. I had checked the cell's call logs earlier and posited that Rick had called me three times, Duke four, and Doc Faller once. I checked the caller ID on the latest call and recognized it as a Florida area code. Standing in the hotel driveway, I pressed the answer key.

"Speak to me."

"Jack? It's David."

"Heya, cousin. What've you got?"

"I'm done with your report," the well-to-do fellow on the other end of the line said. "You've got a case here, Jack. We could call SEC, we could call FBI fraud. I'm reasonably confident there's enough behind this that investigating personnel can secure an indictment."

"Burn it."

"What?"

"Burn it. Write me a two-page summary and delete all references to DPI and Carter Dooley. Then take your report and find a flame to feed it to."

"Jack, I've been working nearly a month on this!" The frustration in David's voice was evident. "I've kept this as low key as you asked for, and now you want me to destroy it? Jack, what gives?"

"Don't worry about it, David." I opened a door and entered The Provincial's lobby proper. Etienne saw me from behind the counter and offered me a wide, toothy grin. "Just write me up a short summary with all the particulars and no mention of DPI. Then fax it to me at... Hang on."

I flagged Etienne's attention. "Write down your fax number for me, kaz."

"Will do," the Cajun replied.

"David?"

"I'm here, Jack. Jack, this is more than a little bit frustrating."

"David, trust me. You won't want anything like this on your person in a few days." I read of the fax number. "Send that to me, then destroy everything else. I mean it, David. Wipe your hard drive, burn your notes, *everything*."

"All right, all right," David said. "Jack—"

"Listen, David, I'll make this up to you. I promise. I've gotta go."

I hung up and jammed the cell back into my pocket. "Etienne, a couple of faxes are going to be coming in on your machine in about five minutes and few hours after that. *Don't* read them. Just put 'em in an envelope and send it on up to the condo."

"Whatever you say, Mistah Jacques."

I took the scrap paper that Etienne had written The Provincial's fax number on and proceeded on my way out. The combination hotel/condominium complex had been built in a courtyard style with most of the units occupying the outer walls. The inner area was covered in cobblestone and devoted to a tightly packed parking lot, a bar, and a small patio with a fountain. I walked out of the gates onto Ursuline Street and headed east. In a few blocks, I'd made it to the Vertie Mart where I found a pay phone on the corner.

It took a fair amount of persuasion and a twenty-dollar tip to get the sack of quarters out of the ganja-smoking fellow behind the counter. After the bargain, I returned to the pay phone and started slotting coins. I dialed the number from memory, even though it took me a minute or two to remember that memory. The Fort Worth area code was the only easy part.

"Jetfire Gym," a female voice answered.

"Special order for the Deck," I said.

"I'm sorry, who?"

"Pussy, it's the Saint. I need to talk to Deckhead."

"The Saint?" A pause. "Well, hey there, mudspitter! What's the crack?"

"No sense in not taking precautions," I said. I read the phone number for the payphone off the weathered inscription above the keypad. "Tell him to reroute and call back. And I mean *now*, Puss."

"Gotcha. Love ya, Saint."

The line went dead. I milled about next to the phone and had myself a smoke. I only had to fend off two people who wanted to use the phone, and I saw both pairs of eyes stray to the bruises on my face and the bandages. Ten minutes later, the phone rang.

"It's the Saint," I said into the receiver.

"The Jack Attack in effect!" a singsong voice greeted me. "I've been emailing you for weeks, succotash. Where you been?"

"My comp met with a rather unseemly accident," I said, lighting a cigarette. "Whataboutcha, Deckhead?"

"*De nada*, podna. The Deck's been kinda keepin' it on the down-low lately, eh? Too much pussycat around hee-yah to ignore."

I heard a sharp shriek in the background and some laughter, and I had to smile. Pussy Control and Deckhead had been an off and on pair for as long as I could remember. More than likely, the two were engaged in some half-naked affair behind the coffee counter at the Jetfire Gym right then.

"Hey, keep it in your keys, Deck," I said. "Are we secure?"

"What? Yeah, you bet, succotash," Deckhead's lilting Hispanic accent sang back. "You know the Deck. What's the score, Saint Jack?"

"I need you to get me some info on someone. Everything you can dig up on an Elizabeth Finley AKA Betsy Jones. Try every permutation of the first name, too."

"Right, right, got it. You got a hard-on for this chick or what, *jefe*?"

"Try a mad-on."

"Heard that tone before, Jack Attack."

"You know it." I gave him the fax number at The Provincial. "I'm staying way down south right now. Got jammed and needed to recoup for a bit."

"Jack, what the hell you up to down there?"

I looked around the phone booth, saw no one watching me and turned back to hide my visage against the wall of the Vertie Mart.

"Revenge," I said. "Something else I want you to do for me, Deck. It's major. I mean, super major."

I heard Deck snort on the other end of the line. "Is it super happy fun stuff?"

"Could be. Remember the Straylight Run?"

Deck breathed for a moment. "Now you're getting all literary on me, Jack Pack. I'm listening. What is it exactly you want me to do?"

I flicked the cigarette butt into the gutter, turned back to the phone, and told him.

While I really got a kick out of the threads Crys had picked up for me, I was jonesing for my leather jacket. The beating Henkel and his crew had perpetrated on me had also ruined the jacket. One of the sleeves had come unsewn and there were hundreds of rips, tears and shreds. Added to that, the leather was totally smeared in blood, vomit, and snot, and I knew the cleaning bill would be more expensive than a new jacket. So after I got off the phone with Deckhead, I walked the six blocks down the wharf to the Riverside Mall.

I spent a cool thousand shopping around in the mall, picking out a light beige jacket and matching pants as well as a new pair of shoes. A leather dealer who had set up shop on the third floor of the mall fitted me for a new jacket. The lady had a pretty swank livery of Italian brown that caught my eye, and I decided to go with that instead of the black that would remind me of my old jacket. She told me it would be about an hour to finish the alterations so I walked around the mall a little, got a snow cone, and found a cool women's clothier called Trashy Diva. Walking around inside, I spotted a low-cut black dress with lacy skintight sleeves and got an idea. Guessing Crys' sizes based on a similar sized saleswoman, I found the appropriate dress and bought that, too.

There was still about twenty minutes to kill before my jacket would be finished, so I went into the daiquiri bar on the second floor and ordered a bloody. I talked the bartender into letting me use the bar phone with a fiver, and I got the necessary number off my cell phone's call logs.

"Hello?" someone answered.

"Anybody been trying to find me, Ricky baby boy?"

"Jack! For fuck's sake, brother, where the *hell* have you been?!" The otherwise level-headed Rick Sears wasn't one to toss around profanity unless the situation called for it. The Bureau frowned on such displays of character that they culturally and institutionally found flawed and indicative of anything less than model upstanding citizenry. I chastised myself for not having called him sooner.

"I've been trying to call you for weeks, man," Rick sputtered. "Your apartment phone's disconnected, you won't answer your cell. Hell, I called your Dad to see what he knew, and he was just as miffed. What the hell is going on, Jack?"

"Rick..." The bloody mary swirled in scarlet in front of me. "I'm in trouble. I need your help."

"Trouble?" Rick paused. "What kind of trouble?"

"This case I've been working, Rick. It's fucked me up. I'm hiding out down in New Orleans, and I need your help."

"Hiding out? Jack, what did you do?"

"I'll fill you in when you get down here."

"Down there? Jack, it's not like I've got stuff going on at the fucking *Federal Bureau of Investigation*! For fuck's sake! Is it serious?"

"More than you can know." I went for a smoke, not envying the feelings that would come from this. "Rick, listen, I know this is sudden. But I need your help, brother. I'm fucking out in the dark on this one, and I'm hip deep in sheep dip."

I heard him exhale heavily. "What do you need, Jack?"

"Look. Thanksgiving's coming up, right? You got any time off?"

"Yeah, a week. But Nia and I were planning on flying out to see her family in Houston."

"Fly out to Houston with Nia then grab a connecting flight to New Orleans. Call me at The Provincial Hotel on Chartres Street when you know your flight, and I'll make arrangements to come get you."

"Jack, wait a minute, slow down! What the hell is *going on*? Your Dad's worried sick about you, and no one in Hattiesburg seems to know where you are."

I bit down on the butt of a cigarette. "There's a reason for that."

Rick smacked his lips. "How bad is it, Jack?"

My reflection looked back at me from the mirror behind the bar. "Rick... it almost killed me."

I could hear him churning it over in his mind, going through his obligations to his wife and career. Weighing those obligations to our bond, one born in shared Texanhood. I never thought about what either of us would do if we had to choose, and I felt worse than I did after the beating for shoving the choice down Rick's throat right then.

"We're flying out on the Saturday before Thanksgiving," he finally said. "That's... day after tomorrow. I'll be in New Orleans that night. What's the name of that hotel?"

"The Provincial," I said, feeling the breath come too easy. "Rick, listen. I wouldn't ask if I didn't need it."

"I know. What else do you need?"

I got out my shopping list.

22.

IT ONLY HURTS ONCE

When I opened the door to the condo at a quarter to six, Crys was inside making noise. I couldn't identify the ruckus at first, but as soon as I'd disgorged the bags full of clothes and knickknacks, I saw that she was rearranging the kitchen. I poked my head around the foyer's bookshelves and peered at her.

"What are you doing?"

"Hey, cowboy, you're back," Crys said, struggling with positioning one of the counter stools in front of the kitchen sink. She wiped her hands off and picked up a large tan bottle from the counter. "I got your hair dye."

"Dye or bleach?" I said, walking in and inspecting the bottle.

"I think it's a hybrid. The lady at Walgreen's recommended this stuff for fast action."

Crys leaned over and delivered a wet kiss to my check. I smiled. "Miss me?"

"Like the clap. Here. Etienne brought this up a few hours ago."

She handed me a manilla envelope marked with my name. A note scribbled on the back in broken, Creole-peppered English told me that the faxes had come in on time and occupied a fairly heavy amount of paper. I tossed the envelope onto the counter and turned to move my bags into the living room.

"Feelin' that jacket," Crys said, touching the lapel of the smooth leather. "Where'd you get it?"

"Leather vendor at Riverside." I pulled the suit out of the Banana Republic bag and lay it across the back of an easy chair. "I got you something, too."

Crys had just lit a cigarette and was pouring herself a glass of apple juice. "Pray tell."

I held up the black dress. "I hope I got your size right."

She came around into the living room and held the dress out, inspecting the plunging neckline and lacy design of the arms. A glimmer of a smirk appeared at the corner of her mouth.

"What brought this on?" she asked.

"I've never seen you in a dress before," I said, shrugging. "And I figured we could do that dinner date that never seemed to come around last year."

She sidled up to me, laying the dress on the sofa. "I guess we never did actually go out on a real date, did we?"

I shook my head. "Unless you count watching The Sci-Fi Channel every night for a week and going to 25 to Midnight rehearsals."

Crys snipped another quick kiss on my lips. "This isn't you doing the *owe-me* thing, is it?"

"Perish the thought."

She winked. "In that case, get out of those clothes, cowboy. We've got a dye job to do."

I slipped out of my shirt and jacket and took a seat on the stool that Crys had prepared. She turned on the faucet to the kitchen sink and started mixing the ingredients for the coloring work. I winced as I tried to lean backwards. The pain in my stomach had lessened to some degree, but I wasn't exactly executing Army-standard sit-ups every day. Crys touched the bandage wrap around my middle.

"Those ribs still giving you problems?"

"Nff... Just a little."

She retrieved a pillow from the sofa and lay it under the small of my back. "Try it now."

With effort, I managed to lean back and rest my head on the edge of the sink. My teeth clenched even as Crys held my sides. Pinpricks of sweat and cold-fire exploded in waves across my skin.

"I notice you're in a unique position to break my neck right now," I said, watching her stir the coloring mixture.

She inched the large bandage around my forehead up and off, her cool fingers playing across my scalp to make sure the lacerations were sufficiently healed. Then she ran water through my black hair, matting it down and brushing it out of my face. Her fingers felt cold on my skin in contrast to the warm water rushing over me. A long breath escaped my lungs, and I closed my eyes.

"I already did that," she said. "I'm trying to mend the bones."

The color job took about an hour, and Crys insisted on trimming my hair while the dye took. My jet black locks had gotten more than a little shaggy in my down time, and I put up minimal resistance. She also added a spot of coloring to my eyebrows, arguing that I was way too dark complected to go for the copper top look. When she was finished, Crys took me upstairs and held a hair dryer to my head to complete the transformation.

In the mirror, I saw a much different person. I had taken off the Band-Aids and bandages on my face, revealing scarred—but healing—skin. The purple glow of the bruises on my jaw and face had begun to diminish. My hair surprised me the most. I'd never gone through with a dye job before despite having noodled it over a time or two, mostly in various stages of drunken protest to someone that I could pull it off like Bruce Willis did in *The Fifth Element*. Crys had chosen a wax platinum tint that tapered into silky white where strands of hair stood out from the mass. Given my natural swarthy complexion – inherited from my mother's side – I wasn't prepared for the shift in shade. The lightened eyebrows helped sell the transformation. The recolored hair felt a little different from the usual texture to which I had become accustomed. Almost like thick straw.

"You look like a rock star," Crys said, shutting down the hair dryer.

"Two weeks too late," I said.

"Will you brush my hair tonight?"

"Yes, I will."

Maximo's was wedged into the thickest part of the French Market down in the Quarter. Sitting square in between Decatur Street and the market walk that bordered on the river, the restaurant offered up a fair bit of class and spitshine. Jimmy Buffet's Margaritaville was only a couple blocks away as was the Café du Monde, the entrance to the riverside park, and the Jax Brewery. Having been renovated time and again over the years, Maximo's had evolved from a simple 18th century brick affair into a muted, whitewashed eatery with an outside patio surrounded by four massive Greco-Roman columns. It was a gorgeous building that seemed sort of out of place for that part of town, but once you peeped the Hawaiian shirts and brand new Panama Jack hats adorning tourists inside, you could see how Maximo's catered to the Quarter blend. Crys and I didn't complain. Gourmets from all over sought this place out, and it occupied a great little Italian niche between classic New Orleans restos like Galatoire's and more pedestrian joints like The Royal House Oyster Bar.

Maximo's offered a delightful five-course meal as part of its executive package for foodies, critics, and uppercrust hoi polloi. We declined the full meal deal, settling for salads, a marinated portabello mushroom appetizer, crawfish etouffee, and a bottle of Chardonnay. The weather this time of year remained a tad on the chilly side, but not overly uncomfortable, so we chose a table on the restaurant's sidewalk patio near the door.

Crys had picked up makeup and other amenities during one of her shopping trips. I'd once told her that she didn't need any, and she never wore much. Just a soft ruby stain on her lips, traces of gold eye shadow, and a touch of perfume on her skin, of which my idiot olfactory sense could barely detect. The black dress had fit, wrapping around her slender thighs and middle and showing off just a sliver of pale leg. She'd gone simple for her hair, choosing to slick the blonde locks back and brushing out only a strand or two to fall sideways across her face. The sheen of her styling gel darkened the blonde to an almost chestnut degree, and when her blue orbs blinked, she looked like Charlize Theron. I told her as much, and she tossed a roll at me.

"Bitch," said Crys. "I'd die for Charlize Theron's tits."

"So would I," I quipped, sipping the wine.

She gave me a pinched expression. "My mother would disown me if she saw me in this thing without a necklace."

"I didn't even think to look for one."

"And I wouldn't have worn it anyway. Cowboy. You look like Don Johnson."

I flourished the lapels of my suit coat. "You like?"

"You have the fashion sense of a vice cop, Jack. What, no shoulder holster?"

"Couldn't find one that fit. I don't think I could stretch the right way to even get into one without passing out too."

Crys set her napkin back down in her lap and pushed her plate away. "Pa-*kow*. That was something."

"Maximo's is the bomb, babe." I held up my lighter when she went for a cigarette.

"All things considered, I suppose this makes for a decent first date," she said, inhaling a breath of smoke and looking around at the restaurant, the people on the sidewalk, the ambulations and the ululations of the Quarter as one phase wound down and another revved up.

"Sure beats beer at The Hog," I said, striking up a cigarette of my own.

"What else did you do today?"

"Made a couple of calls. Got some help coming down this weekend." I regarded her over the wisps of smoke that floated ethereally around us. "Listen, Crys, you don't have to stay. I know you've got better things to do—"

"Would you cut the knight in shining armor routine, Jack?" she replied. "I'm in this for long haul."

My eyes narrowed. "Why?"

"Huh?"

"Why? I mean, I'm grateful—not to mention a little surprised—for the taking care of the me. But I'm okay now. And I'm about to start a four alarm fire that they'll smell in El Paso."

"I heard you. You told me what's going on. I'm not bugging out now, though." Now her eyes narrowed, and I recognized the twinge of something there.

The chair felt suddenly heavy against me. "So what, you're addicted again? Is that it?"

"Is there a problem with that?"

"I don't know."

"Well, even if that was the case, I still have other reasons." Crys made a bemused face, and for a moment, I couldn't figure out what we were talking about. A second or two passed, and I realized it didn't matter. Not anymore.

I appraised her with a neutral glance. "It's dangerous."

She didn't look away. "I'm well aware of that."

"Okay," I said, making the decision. "You want in, you got it. But understand something: You do what I say when I say it, Crys. There's no room for fuck-ups here."

A smoke ring escaped the heart-shaped visage of her lips. "Lay it on me, baby."

"You remember me telling you about a friend of mine named Rick Sears? Special agent at the FBI?"

"Yes. You two grew up in together in Texas, right?"

"Right. He's flying in Saturday night. We're going to sit down and work out a plan for the next week. We'll probably be heading back to Hattiesburg Monday or Tuesday."

"What's in the envelope that Etienne brought up?"

"Information about Liz." My jaw clenched, and a ghost of the pain from before hit me. "Or Elizabeth, if you will."

Crys swirled the wine around in her glass. "Do you have a plan yet?"

My eyes twinkled, still dark despite the color change around them.

"I'm working on it."

We took a walk through the Quarter after dinner, weaving past fall passersby, of which there were few, and spending some time in Jackson Square. I thought about taking in a show at the IMAX or going on a tour through the Aquarium, but both complexes were closed by the time we got there. Instead, we walked along the sidewalks that ran parallel to the Mississippi River. We talked a little more, and Crys asked me a lot about New Orleans. She'd never been before despite Hattiesburg's proximity. I decided to do it properly, and we flagged down one of the tour guides on horse and carriage.

The carriage driver turned out to be one of the less talkative fellows, for which I was grateful. Instead of going on about the history of the Quarter and relating tantalizing little anecdotes about famous people of New Orleans, the driver simply sang a fragmented, Creole tune. His voice scratched out the jagged melody and did not intrude too much.

I told Crys what I knew of New Orleans as the carriage bounced over the rickety streets. Truth told, I didn't know much. The statue of Andrew Jackson in the Jackson Square courtyard prompted some memory of a couple war stories one of my college professors had told me. I regaled Crys with the legend of Jackson riding into the Florida territory and wresting control away from the Spanish. The enormous buildings that surrounded the Square had once berthed Jackson's men, an army that distinguished itself further at the Battle of New Orleans.

Crys asked me about Duke's childhood in New Orleans, and I told her a little of what I knew. Duke and Carter had been hellions in their day, or so I was told. Both had snuck out of their house uptown more than a few times to steal away to the Marigny via streetcar and sneak a peek inside brothels and music clubs. Carter, the older of the two, had once stranded Duke in the French Market, leaving him lost in the crowds. Duke, the wilier of the two, had taken his revenge by setting a pack of live crawfish loose in Carter's beloved '57 Chevy, stinking the exquisitely cared-for leather seats past recovery. It must have been a hell of a time.

The carriage driver dropped us back off at The Provincial, and we went upstairs. I fixed us a couple of drinks while Crys went to change out of her dress.

She indicated that she wanted to take a shower, so I settled down on the sofa and grabbed the envelope full of faxes that Etienne had delivered earlier that day.

David Novak's transmissions were the first I read. Skimming over the information, I detected a distinct slant in the securities analysis, as if David had been forced to make a conclusion without all the facts. A tinge of guilt struck at me as I read, and I couldn't help but damn myself for ever having involved David in the first place. Of everyone with whom I'd worked in this sordidry, David's ethics stood out to me. I should have been thinking about what I was about to do to Rick's ethics, but something about David Novak's high-end life clipping through wealth the *right* way reminded me that I could still regret.

Regardless, the report stated evidence of illegal trading practices at the firm of Truman and Binnell, specifically in connection to one of their clients, Bill Finley of PetroJet Chemical. I would rewrite the report later, including some more facts and pointers to the intended recipients so that the entire picture could be made clear. I wasn't going to volunteer too much information. The recipients would have to do a little legwork of their own. I made a mental note to grab a legal pad the next time I was at The Vertie Mart.

Deckhead's fax included nearly twenty pages of research. In addition to copies of driver's licenses, a birth certificate, and school enrollments, there was a complete set of photographs that must have originated from a newspaper room somewhere. Deckhead knew how to get his research, but it surprised me how thorough everything was. It appeared that Deck had more resources than even he let on. Some of those might even be Pussy's contribution to the Jetfire Gym as she had come into her own *on* her own quite a while before Deckhead. Word around the campfire back in The Fort was that Pussy so consistently hack-embarrassed Deck on jobs these days that all their peers preferred to work with her.

The woman I knew as Liz had been born Elizabeth Pauline Finley, only daughter to one William Thomas Finley and Mary Patricia Jones Finley. The birth certificate named a hospital in Gulfport. Her education records began with a preschool enrollment at the age of three and continued all the way up to her college graduation. Checking out the transcripts, I saw that she had done a year of undergrad work at Old Miss and then transferred to—

I blinked and read it again.

She had gone to Southern Mississippi for three semesters.

I tried to find more information on Liz—*Elizabeth's*—tenure at Southern, but Deckhead's dossier yielded little. She had participated in an internship through the university with a local law firm and the District Attorney's Office of Hattiesburg. Apparently, at the conclusion of the internship, she had transferred back to Old Miss and finished her college education with a double major in pre-law and accounting. I couldn't believe what I was seeing.

Elizabeth Finley had been in school at Southern at roughly the same time that I was.

I wondered if anyone remembered her.

Deckhead had dug up a copy of Elizabeth's resume, and in going through it, I found a reference that she had joined the Delta Chi Psi sorority at Old Miss. While I couldn't find any mention of a transfer of membership from Old Miss to the Southern Miss chapter, I made an educated guess that someone at Delta Chi knew her. It bothered me to some degree that even this slight fact had escaped my attention, and it furthered served to illustrate just how much sheepskin had been pulled over my eyes. Or how purposely blind I had stricken myself.The meat of the fax delved into bank records and Social Security information that Deckhead had hacked. Elizabeth Finley had an account at the Jackson division of SouthBank, and the transaction records showed numerous but irregular increases in the past several years. I had to blink a few times. She was operating on a balance of at least fifty thousand dollars at any one time, high for our little corner of the country. There were a couple of loan schedules drawn up for a car and college tuition. The real kicker, the reason I'd asked to Deck to get this for me in the first place, turned up on the very last page.

There was a separate bank account for a Betsy F. Jones in Magee, Mississippi, at the same bank. The address listed on the account didn't match Elizabeth Finley's account in Jackson, but Deckhead – or likelier the far more accurate Pussy Control – had done his homework. Several deposits had come from a single line address mailer that corresponded to a number of different banks in the south Mississippi area. One of those banks, I recognized, was the SouthBank branch in Magee. That particular branch was right down the street from what had once been Wolverton's LP Gas.

Betsy F. Jones...

I closed my eyes to let the data stew. Gather strength. Be reborn.

The name on Henkel's checks. The checks Henkel had been picking up for his deliveries from DPI. *Jones* was her mother's maiden name. How many times had she mentioned working for her father?

Elizabeth Finley synchronized the Magee operation with Henkel.

The confirmation washed over me with enough force to make me set down the faxes. I got to my feet and struck up a cigarette, my free hand straying to the half-drained glass of Crown and seven. I'd suspected it ever since I'd woken up in New Orleans. Corners of the entire investigation started making sense. Finley had been using his own daughter to run the disparate pieces of his enterprise against DPI.

It had been right in front of me.

I should have picked up on it, at the very least *questioned* it, the night I met her. Betsy Jones. Elizabeth Finley. The connection was so glaring that I felt ashamed to admit it, and I reflexively thought of excuses to pardon my ignorance. But I couldn't come up with any.

After pacing the condominium living room for a while, I shrugged off these last realizations, these signposts for the blind and the weak and the willing. Deckhead's work not only gave me the confirmation I needed but also proved just how gullible I'd been. How careless. How much of a sucker. Finding myself on the balcony, I looked out over the New Orleans night and inhaled the draught of scents created by New Orleans' myriad of things both delicious and detestable.

Don't underestimate them, snapper.

Crys appeared at the door to the balcony a few minutes later, wearing only a long button-up shirt. She held a hairbrush in one hand.

"Will you?" she said.

I took off my suit jacket and sat down in one of the garden chairs. Crys straddled one of my legs and settled back against me. I took the brush and began running it through her hair, using slow, deep strokes from forehead to the ends of her hair. I wrapped strands of her hair around the brush and pulled it back, letting the loose tresses uncurl and pull slightly at her scalp. The soothing motion of the task ameliorated the aggravation I'd begun to feel after reading the faxes, and soon, I had settled into a rhythmic, relaxing pattern.

I set the brush down to massage her scalp with my fingers. I could see that her eyes were closed. Mine took in the spectacle of the French Quarter night below us. Her shirt had drifted up across her thighs, and I could see the smooth, pale tint of the moonlight against her skin.

"Are you feeling better?" I asked.

"Are you?" she replied.

My breath drifted across her neck and chest, eliciting a brief patch of goosebumps. Her back arched against me.

"Yeah," I said. "I guess I'm feeling better."

We switched places in the chair, and I knelt in front of her. Her fingers slid into my hair, ruffling it unkempt. A new scent added itself to the mélange of the night. I bowed my head. To pray.

23.

PARTNERS

Rick's flight landed at nine-thirty Saturday night. I borrowed Crys' car to pick him up, and I told Rick over the phone to wait at the arrival strip running in front of the main terminal. New Orleans International is a twisted mess of concrete and chrome, a throwback to sixties architecture that allowed for lots of show and little utility. Designed for impression and not necessarily functionality. I figured it would be the easiest way to get in and out, and besides, Rick probably wouldn't recognize me anyway.

I drove through the passenger pickup driveway twice, craning my neck over the headrest to get a glimpse at the smattering of people on the pickup aisle. People in business suits. People in teenager clothes. People looking like tourists. People full of shit. People hugging other people. People looking shifty. People looking tired. People looking lost. On the third swing through, I saw him.

Rick Sears stands at about six-foot-six, towering over any would-be asshole that felt like giving him shit. Reed thin in a nondescript gray jacket and black slacks, Rick went out of his way to conceal a tightly coiled mass of muscle and nerve. Neither of us had been terribly athletic in our youth, but Rick's time meeting the Bureau's physical requirements had bulked up his lean frame, and I could tell from the way his confident Alex Toth jawline moved as he scanned the area. He kept his hair closely cropped in fear of allowing a monster afro-beast loose that we both knew lurked in his genes. A couple of gray streaks were visible right where the cut faded into cocoa temples and neck, an evolution of the premature gray Rick had sprouted in high school. He covered his eyes with a pair of wire-rim glasses, so wiry in fact that they appeared to simply balance on the bridge of his nose. Under his jacket he wore a solid black, unbranded polo shirt. The soft pallor of his palms contrasted against dark and taut skin on hands and fingers, the right gripping a small duffel bag, the left open and loose at his side. Friends and family back in Texas used to call us twins as a joke.

I parked the Oldsmobile on the sidewalk and got out, striding up to where Rick stood. It took him a while, and sure enough, he didn't recognize me until I was almost on top of him.

"Jack," he said, and I could hear the confused wholesomeness in his voice. "You changed your hair."

"But remember, you're still the albino," I joked, running a hand through my newly platinum locks. "How are you, brother?"

Rick dropped his bag. "How are *you*?"

We hugged each other hard, both of us pounding each other on the back. When we disengaged, he and I both could see the effects of the years on each other's faces, around the eyes especially.

I registered the golden wedding band around his left ring finger, and I wished I had a god to whom I could pray for Rick's blessing.

"Get in the car," I said, picking up his bag. "I'll fill you in. If you're smart, you'll tell me to turn the hell around and put you back on a plane to Houston."

"You know me better than that," Rick said, opening the passenger door.

I drove around New Orleans for an hour, laying it all out for my brother. As I talked, Rick remained completely placid, only moving to inspect the interior of the car. At one point, he looked in the backseat and found the broken Superman maquette that I had inadvertently clutched along with me to Crys' house in Hattiesburg. I kept talking, and he turned around in his seat, holding the mangled statue and running his fingers over it.

Before too long, I had looped the interstate a couple times, avoiding exiting into the cramped neighborhoods and tight streets of the Central Business District, the Quarter, and the Marigny. My voice was hoarse from speaking nonstop, not at all helped by the half pack of cigarettes I'd smoked. A light drizzle had begun to fall, and I found with some frustration that Crys' car sported those awful windshield wipers that just smear the rain across the window instead of making it easier to see. Eventually, I looped back to the CBD and exited onto Canal, heading back toward the river. I braked at a light and looked over at Rick.

"So..."

"So?" Rick said, looking straight ahead.

"So what do you think?"

Rick looked outside the car, watching the rain pick up as it distorted the images of headlights on the street. He held the

Superman statue in one hand, and his other hand remained motionless on his leg.

"I think it's a cruel fuckin' thing that's been done to this maquette, Jack."

When our eyes met, our expressions were the same.

"Let's go get something to eat," he told me.

"You know what really irks me?" Rick said through a mouthful of jambalaya.

"The fact that you use the word '*irk?*'" I replied, scraping the sides of my own bowl with the spoon.

Rick stared at me. "Irk's a good word."

"Irk sounds like you had a heart attack halfway through an episode of *Family Matters*."

"Okay. You know what *irritates* me?"

"What's that?"

"People who don't give you the courtesy wave."

"The what?"

"The courtesy wave. We must have driven in circles for twenty miles and the streets are really tight and there's a shit-ton of cars on the interstate. Every once in a while, some sonofabitch wants into the lane. So you back off on the gas a bit, open up a space and let him in. He's *supposed* to give you the courtesy wave."

The spoon clattered inside my empty bowl. "I never give the courtesy wave."

Rick brandished his own spoon at me. "That's why you're an asshole."

"I thought I was an asshole because I dragged you down here from your Thanksgiving holiday."

He left his unfinished bowl of jambalaya and stretched back in his chair. "There's that, too."

I frowned. "Isn't this a bit? From someone's standup routine?"

Rick pinned me with his iron ore stare. "What, you don't think I can be funny on my own? You got a problem, boy?"

We had driven into the Quarter and left the car at The Provincial, walking three blocks down to a tiny diner wedged between a law office and a brownstone that supported too many people for its size. The diner's name had been weathered away from the wooden sign over the door, a testament to its age. Everyone I knew in the neighborhood just called it Max's in honor of the owner. Max, a wrinkly old guy missing more than a few teeth and all of his genetic southern manners, yelled at everyone who called the diner "Max's" but never supplied anyone with the correct title. That's just how it is.

The eatery ran narrowly back through the complex that housed it in the tradition of the tight New Orleans buildings that dated back to the nineteenth century. There was enough room for maybe five tables and the kitchen counter at the back. The decor spoke of dilapidated wooden walls that had never been cleaned let alone properly nailed together. A thick musk of gumbo, spice, and cigarette smoke permeated every corner. In another ten years, the place would be gone, acquired by a faceless development corporation and remodeled into a shoe store with all the latest brands.

"So, you know how I am about Nia's family," Rick said, returning to a larger issue. "I put in the requisite number of appearances on major holidays and that's it."

"I heard that. Cheers." We clinked water glasses. "Well, if you're not going to give me anymore ball-busting..."

"Twenty-five to life for securities fraud, extortion, bribery of an elected official, and attempted murder," Rick said, like reading it from a court document or a really derivative *Law and Order* script.

"Maybe he gets it lessened to time served and a slap on the wrist if he drops the dime on your friends on the Gulf Coast. But that's setting himself up for worse than anything the state's attorney can hang on him."

I reached for my cigarettes. "It's not enough, Rick."

"Jack, it's a square deal." He fixed me with his eyes. "And it's provable with your testimony and the evidence we've gathered so far."

"It's not *enough*. Plus, who knows how many other judges this fucker knows, right? Schiedle ain't the only one, I goddamn guarantee. Rick, my uncle is in the goddamn hospital with a piece of propane tank shell in his ass. His company's bank account is missing about seven-hundred grand, and the thief sent his daughter after *me* to make sure the Dooley name stayed off a police report." I pointed to the scar along the side of my face. "Do you see this, Rick? *Do you*? Finley's gonna get his wish. I'm not going to the cops. But I *am* gonna show him my rendition of Ray Liotta's pistol-whipping scene from *Goodfellas*."

Rick watched me silently for a moment, evaluating my mood as I lit a cigarette. After a while, he said, "You could go to jail, Jack. Do real time. No bullshittin'."

I looked back at him, nothing left but fire in my eyes.

"Then help me make sure I don't."

Crys was watching the television when we returned to the condominium. When we walked in, she jumped to her feet and pulled her bathrobe closed, suddenly aware that we had company. I noticed that the robe had come from Aunt Dee's closet upstairs and featured a weird tribal pattern that reminded me of Bali for some reason. She offered up a muted smile when she saw Rick.

"Crys, Rick Sears," I said, tossing Rick's bag on the floor.

"I've heard a lot about you," she said, taking Rick's hand.

"Same," Rick replied, nodding once. "I guess I should thank you for making sure the Great Pumpkin here didn't get smooshed."

Crys cast a glance my way. I winked back.

"He's worth more than that," she told Rick.

"Rick, Crys is on this with me," I said, shrugging out of my jacket. "She knows what you know."

"In that case, I guess I can't persuade you to team up with me and talk this stupid son of a bitch down, hmm?" Rick asked, raising an eyebrow.

Crys crossed her arms a hair above her waist and sighed. "He needs this."

Rick looked at Crys, sizing her up while parking his hands on his hips and exhaling a deep breath. Then he looked back at me. "Yeah, I guess he does."

"Get some sleep," I told him, pulling a blanket out of the kitchen closet. "The couch is pretty comfy."

Rick chuckled. "Any more comfy than your floor?"

I matched the chuckle with one of my own. "You wouldn't want to see my floor right now, brother."

When I roused into consciousness the next morning, I found that the med-tape had peeled off the splint on my fingers and they ached like crazy. Wincing, I stumbled into the bathroom and re-wrapped them, testing their strength and finding that the fingers were still pretty stiff. I'd have to ask Crys how I was supposed to handle using broken digits in the future. These cracked bones were firsts for me. And I'd need them working pretty soon.

After I got dressed, I saw that the bed was empty. Crys must have stolen out before I'd woken. With a great yawn, I started creeping down the stairs. About halfway down the first flight from the top, I heard their voices.

"So," I heard Rick say. "About *us*. See, we grew up reading comics. A lotta comics. Probably too much comics. *X-Men*, *Daredevil*, *Justice League*, stuff like that."

"I've seen his room," Crys replied. "He's got…a few."

"So do I. Anyway, we read these things all the time. Still do. Thing is... a lot of who we are comes from comics."

"I don't understand."

"On some weird fundamental level, comics is where we built our foundation for who we are and what we're all about," Rick said. "It's pretty easy to draw a line from the customary super-hero mandate of justice to a career in the FBI, y'see? As clichéd as that might sound."

I heard something scrape across a hard surface. I stayed where I was.

"He bought this Superman maquette after I got mine. Warner Brothers store. They're cool. Well, this one used to be. They got ones for Batman, Robin, The Joker. Anyway, there's this dynamic that the two of us have. We read different stuff and the same stuff. I've always been into Superman. He's always been something of a Batman fanatic. Don't get me wrong: we like both characters, but there's always been a separate predilection toward one of them for each of us."

There was a hesitation. I couldn't tell by whom.

"Superman and Batman are the two most recognizable super-heroes in comics," Rick said. "But both of them, as characters, come from fundamentally different backgrounds. Each of them represents something completely different than the other."

"But they're still comrades, right?" Crys interrupted.

"To some degree. Superman is all about icons. The embodied form of upholding *the good*, right?"

"Truth, justice, the American way. Yeah, I saw the movie."

"Batman's darker. He embraces shadows and works obsessively and methodically toward *justice*. He's all about *fear*."

"Rick, I know Jack knows about fear." There was something a little hard in Crys' voice. "Especially now."

"That's what I'm trying to say," Rick replied, and now his own voice was a mite more intense. "If you know anything about Superman and Batman in comics, you'd know that even though both of them are friends and comrades... there's still a conflict between them. In more than one case... they've come to blows over it."

My heart skipped a beat. I knew where this was going.

"Depending on the era of comics you're into, Superman and Batman are either tight pals or complete assholes to each other. For some of the right reasons, but usually a lot of wrong ones cooked up by lazy writers who get bored easily." A pause. "I don't know why I'm telling you this. I guess it's...illustrative of our relationship. I mean...I'm not saying I'm Superman and he's Batman... nor are we either of us paragons of all that is and should be good." I could almost hear him shrug.

What surprised me about the exchange was what Crys said next.

"While we were going out," she said; "I used to spend the night at Jack's place to get away from my parents. Sometimes, things were so rough that he let me stay over all day while he went to work. Isn't that something? Would you trust a junkie enough to leave her inside your fortress of solitude all day alone?"

I heard Rick laugh. "Jack said you're not a junkie. Just that you had some... problems."

"I did. I do. Anyway, one time when I was at his apartment, I went through that massive stack of comic book... *books*. What are they called?"

"Trade paperbacks?"

"That's them. He had this real nice leatherbound one about Batman. I think it was a collection of this one artist's work."

"*The Complete Frank Miller Batman*," Rick supplied. "The one with *Dark Knight Returns* and *Year One*."

"That's it! That was the one. I didn't have anything else to do, so I took it off the shelf and started thumbing through it. After a while, I thought it was pretty cool, so I decided to read one of the stories. Before I knew it, I'd read the whole thing."

"Frank Miller's the man. Well...he used to be. You should check out his crime stuff."

"I might have to. The story I read had a Superman-Batman scene in it. The one where they beat each other half to death and Batman fakes his death."

I made a face. Crys read *The Dark Knight Returns*? And didn't tell me? Well...why would she?

"As I recall," Crys went on; "Superman found out that Batman was still alive."

"He heard his heartbeat in the grave," Rick confirmed, and I could detect a new note of respect in his voice...or perhaps that inner Rick voice that always said, *Where is this going?*

"But he didn't do anything about it," Crys said. "Even after all they had fought over, Superman let Batman go. Let him survive. He could have fried him with that heat vision or given him up to the shitty government he was serving, but he didn't do *anything*. He let his friend go."

"There wasn't anything left to fight about."

"Exactly."

A long silence followed the exchange. I could hear someone pouring a couple of glasses of liquid. Juice, probably, since we didn't have any milk around for Rick.

"Clark knew that Bruce still had a lot to do," Rick said. "The world in which they lived had changed. And Bruce thought it was too much for the worse. He was going to build an army and change it back."

"So you tell me," Crys said. "Just how different are they?"

Sipping sounds. Then Rick again: "You know...Miller lost his mind and wrote a couple sequels to *Dark Knight* that basically confirmed a longstanding theory that Superman and Batman both are psychopaths?"

With that, I decided to head downstairs. The last thing I wanted was for the two most important people in my life at that moment to start snapping each other's heads off. And under the stupidest possible subject for discussion, too.

"I see the two of you have met," I said, clomping down the stairs.

"Morning, cowboy," Crys said, rising from a stool at the kitchen counter to deliver a peck on my cheek. Rick was seated on the other side of the counter, snacking on some crackers and cheese.

"Your girlfriend's got a hell of a way of reasoning with people, Jack," he said.

I offered Crys a smile. She winked back at me.

"I could have told you that," I said. "What's first?"

The three of us cased a few blocks in the Seventh Ward for over two hours before we found it. The street had long since gone to shit, and the leafy, drooping branches of the trees in the median cast a protective shield over the sin in the neighborhood. We were right off Ursulines northwest of the interstate, walking concentrically between Treme-Lafitte and the Seventh. Rick identified four different pushers in our sweep and twice as many assorted hangers-on, bangers, and general public refuse for each dealer. We convened a block away from the supposed house and compared notes. We were pretty sure we had the right place.

Earlier in the day, Rick had taken some directions from me and disappeared into New Orleans. He'd returned three hours later with a few names and some more directions. After filling us in, he'd wanted to take only me to the intended destination, but Crys had immediately objected. Neither of us had the strength to protest, and it wouldn't have done us any good anyway. Crys was like that. He had untucked his shirt and put his service weapon in the waistband of his pants, covering the extruding handle with the back of his shirt and his jacket. An FBI agent never left his weapon. I wasn't sure if he was still carrying his badge though.

"Keep your hands visible at all times," Rick warned us. "Just so they don't get jumpy."

"And if they do get jumpy?" Crys intoned.

"Hey, you two are one behind me in the ass-kicking department," I said. "Bow up and let's go."

"You're the one with the gun though," I said.

"Not for long."

We crossed over the pavement toward the run-down house with holes in its screen door and chipped white paint. A group of men, older, hung out on the front stoop of the home, all wearing various signs of *dat thug life* on the New Orleanian street. Sweatshirts, oversized jackets, with football team logos, lots of gold and flashy jewelry. A kid with what looked like a Dr. Seuss styled sock on his head caught sight of us and nodded his head at another kid in a football jacket. The kid in the jacket nodded back, and Dr. Seuss got up to intercept us at the curb.

"Yo, bros, there somethin' you be wantin'?" the kid said holding up a triple ringed hand.

"Depends on your selection," Rick said, relaxing his typically formal way of speaking and letting his roots creep into his speech, matching the color of his skin. "This *is* Luco's, right?"

The kid eyed the three of us for a moment. Behind him, three others on the stoop had stopped playing a game of dice and looked up to see the potential new stains on the sidewalk.

"Whatchoo want for Luco, blood?" Dr. Seuss asked.

Rick cast a slow gaze left and right down the street, making to look as if he was checking out for heat. Then he looked back to Dr. Seuss and made his hand into the shape of a pistol, keeping it tucked against his stomach surreptitiously. He clicked his thumb a couple of times before saying, "You follow?"

Dr. Seuss' eyebrows climbed up into his hat, and he disengaged his scrutiny on us. He reached for his sweatshirt and held it up, revealing a black handgun stuffed in the waistline of his sagging jeans. "This whatchoo lookin' for, son?"

"You got a Smith and Wesson, .35 or better?"

"Yo, you think dis a shoppin' mall, muthafucka?" Dr. Seuss dropped his hand and cracked us a toothy grin. "How I know you not five-oh?"

Rick looked back at me, and I put my hand in my jacket pocket. Almost immediately, the three other guys behind Dr. Seuss stood up to get his back, their hands straying under their shirts to where similar handguns must have been stashed. Rick held his open palms up in front of the bangers.

"We got cash," he said.

"I betchoo do," Dr. Seuss said. "From some muthafuckin' cop shop."

"When was the last time you saw a cop down here?" I said, keeping my hand in my pocket. "That wasn't on a horse?"

Dr. Seuss eyefucked me for a moment then looked behind him at the kid in the jacket on the stoop. After a moment or two, the kid on the stoop nodded his head and rose to go inside the house. Dr. Seuss looked back at Rick and then at me and finally stepped aside.

"Why donchoo come inside?" he said.

I traded a look with Rick, but he didn't show anything other than the granite visage he'd worn since we crossed the street. Crys remained just as stolid, looking only at Dr. Seuss. The guys in front of us parted to allow us access to the house, and Dr. Seuss led us inside. Rick returned the eyefucking to the other bangers as he passed them.

The interior of the house was just as wrecked as the outside. Boards on the floor cracked and sagged, and what little furniture littered the rooms bore stains and holes. A TV blared from one corner, competing with the droning trap boom emanating from a sound system somewhere else in the house. A thick haze of secondhand smoke coated the air. Dr. Seuss led us through the entry foyer past the kitchen where I caught a brief glimpse of someone cutting a pile of white powder on the table. I looked back at Crys. Her face betrayed nothing.

At the back of the house, Dr. Seuss brought us into a room that must have been a library at one point. Bookshelves full of dulled, wet *National Geographic* magazines sagged on one wall. A desk had been shoved into one corner opposite the black spray-painted window. Several different pistols and weapons had been laid out on the desk. The kid in the jacket stood just to the side of the desk.

"If you five-oh, then K-Spot gonna cap yo' ass before you out the *do'*, boy" the kid said, nodding behind us to where Dr. Seuss stood in the doorway. "Might as well go down a big man if I's gonna go down at all."

"It's cool, yo," Rick said, already looking over the pieces on the desk. "What's your fee?"

The jacket kid—who I assumed to be Luco—shrugged underneath the black mass of neon letters and down stuffing. "Whatcha see you like, tall nigga?"

Rick let the jibe slide off him as he inspected the weapons, giving off the calm vibe of a man born into and perfectly comfortable in that environment, which was mostly an act given his upbringing as an adopted black son of a white East Texas couple. His real name was Derick, but I'd known him as Rick since first grade, and he'd never used Derick as far as I knew ever except on official forms requiring his identity. Derick had been the name his birth mother had given him, the only thing with which she had left him. Rick's adoptive parents, a garrulous sales executive for Keebler and a substitute teacher in Longview, Texas, had kept the name instead of changing it as many other adoptive families did in those instances, but they had also taken to calling him Rick, perhaps claiming their own little familial spin while honoring where their baby boy came from. Mixed race adoptions never even crossed the cultural divide into communal whispers of "bravery" or "that poor family" in the East Texas circles of big-haired ladies and loose-lipped grannies: it was easier to just ignore it. As a result, Rick grew up as white as privilege would allow, and he paid for it with exclusion from his natural race. Even I missed out on the cultural cost of Rick's transracial upbringing, and I was his best friend. It took him many years to reconnect with his African-American heritage, several of those acting on one side of the law enforcement divide between the peace officer and the suspected criminal. The side that didn't usually favor black Americans. In addition to the myriad of pop culture influences on both Rick and I that contributed to launching his FBI career, Rick found solace in the promise of being a black FBI agent, the pinnacle of law enforcement service where race did not—or should not—contribute to the Rodney King effects that just seem to keep bubbling up in the good old U.S. of A.

Rick picked up a snubnosed .357 of the same type and model that he had described to me earlier that day. Opening the chamber, he checked the breeches to make sure there weren't any scores or other damage. The grip looked worn down, the brown fiber showing signs of prior use or at least proximity to handling of some sort. The black metal finish of the barrel and the cylinder was caked with a fine layer of grime. Rick held it up, examining the indentation of the model and make then examining the cylinder.

"How much?"

"Cost you nine hundred large, my man," Luco said. "But they so many bettah other ones down there. Cost you a bit mo'."

"Little steep," I intoned. Rick looked back at me with a glare that told me to shut up. I did.

"Yo, this ain't no negotiation you dealin' wit' me," Luco said, crossing his arms and flashing a wide grin that shone plenty of jewel-encrusted teeth. "So hand over the cheddah or get the fuck out my house."

At Rick's glance, I reached into my pocket and pulled out the cash. I counted off nine one-hundred dollar bills and put them on the desk beside the other guns. Luco nodded to Dr. Seuss who came over and recounted the money, holding two bills up to the dim light in the room to check for counterfeiture. Seemingly satisfied, K-Spot turned back to his boss.

"They's cool," he said.

"'Preciate ya," Rick said, putting the gun in his jacket pocket and making a gesture with his hands that I couldn't decipher but one that seemed to put Luco at ease.

"Yo, I gots more than just pieces for sale, boy," Luco said, holding out his hands. "Any of your friends there have a nose for some candy?"

"No," I said, a little too forcefully. I ignored the look Rick gave me and saw Crys staring at the floor. Luco seemed to take all this in stride.

"Don't say I din' offer," Luco said. "Come back and see me you need anythin' else."

"I'll do that," Rick said with a look no less malevolent than Luco's own but also measured and fortified with steel.

Dr. Seuss showed us out, and we walked away from the house at a leisurely pace. At Rick's insistence, we moved across three blocks and headed down a connecting street opposite from the way we had come. He stopped to tie his shoe at one point, and I caught the sight of one of the boys on Luco's stoop hanging back a few blocks away.

"They're just making sure we aren't police," Rick told me, standing up. "Vice probably makes deals like that to sell undercovers. Let's walk another couple of blocks before we head back to the condo."

"Did you get what we needed?" I asked.

Rick nodded. "The gun's still got its serial number, but we can work with that. Just to be safe, I'd like to get another one. It's pretty new and I'm not up on all the sales tracking methods Smith and Wesson embeds in these things these days. I'm a SigSauer man."

"Let's wait until we get to Hattiesburg," I said. "I might be able to get you another one. But if I can't, can we make this one work?"

Rick nodded solemnly. "It'll do."

Back at the condo, Rick set about disassembling and cleaning the gun. I sent Crys back down to the ATM to get some more cash out of Carter's account and settled in to watch Rick work. He set a towel over the coffee table and started picking the weapon apart, kneeling in front of the table and moving at a slow, measured pace, eyes affixed to his hands and fingers as they worked in a shimmer. He didn't offer any instruction or explanation during the process, tuning everything else out, so I grabbed the remainder of the fax papers I hadn't finished reading. The rest of Deckhead's probe into Elizabeth Finley's past only served to further confirm what I already knew about her and didn't offer up any new information save for one interesting note.

The last page featured a table depicting a couple of numbers and the locations of five different bank accounts in the Caymans, Switzerland, and Jamaica. Included with each of these were identification numbers, pin codes, and contact points for the banks themselves. A familiar chicken scratch scrawl covered the bottom of the page and read, "Just give me the signal. DH."

"What do you have there?" Rick asked me.

"Info on Finley and the last stage of the plan," I said. "I had Deckhead open up some phantom accounts offshore and spruce them up with a little of the dough he and Pussy Control have on hand in Fort Worth."

"*That...*" Rick intoned, a little more darkly and incisively than I was prepared to expect; "I don't know anything about."

"Deckhead's good, Rick," I said, seeing his uneasiness all of a sudden. "He'll set this thing up so only one person will be singing solo when the rest of the choir falls down."

"Okay." Rick put the last component of the dismantled .357 down on the towel. He reached for his bag and dug out a small box that looked like a camera case. Clicking open the case, he removed a false bottom that bore half a model of a real camera and withdrew another .357 from the compartment below. This little bit of subterfuge must have come from a counterintelligence connection back up in Virginia at the Bureau, or perhaps even DEA or ATF depending on who Rick knew...but I was too polite to ask. The box was magnetically rigged to hide a gun inside and not trigger alarms at airport security, sort of like a contained reflector for X-rays and metal detectors. Because I knew how thorough he was, Rick probably still had a permit or a waiver or something in his back pocket to flash in case security flagged him, and I also knew that his FBI badge would waive him through virtually any checkpoint. *Always be prepared...*

He started tearing down the second .357, laying pieces identical to the one we'd bought from Luco side by side on the towel. After a while, he had both of them apart and started studying each component.

"Where'd you get the piece?" I asked.

"Evidence locker," he told me. "More of a training item than anything else. Nobody'll miss it. That's why I need the third gun."

"I see."

Rick held up one piece of his appropriated .357. "See? No serial number. No manufacturer's plate. Somebody put this one together, too, so if I get the third gun, anyone who tries to find the final product will be chasing four unknown, unregistered, and untrackable weapons. Granted, that's if the final product's ever found in the endgame."

"It'll be around," I assured him. "Trust me."

It took Rick thirty minutes to piece the .357 back together, using parts from both guns to complete the model. When it was finished, it looked like a mixed bag. It was obvious that pieces of Luco's weapon differed from Rick's .357 because of normal wear and tear. Rick had even mismatched the grips. He sat back on the floor, took a small file from his bag and started shaving the grips down to match.

"You ever shoot one of these before?" he said, eyes intent on his work.

"No," I said. "Will you give me a lesson?"

Rick looked back up at me, halting his filing for a moment.

"You bet, Bruce."

I smirked.

"Thanks, Clark."

24.

THEY CALL IT HUB CITY

We left The Provincial at nine o'clock Monday morning. I gave Etienne a couple of yards and thanked him for his help. He indicated that he didn't know what I was talking about since Mr. Dooley's condominium had been vacant for the past several weeks.

"I forgot, how long is this trip?" Rick asked from the backseat.

"'Bout two hours if we keep it under the limit," I replied, cracking the window to let out the smoke from my cigarette. "You comfortable back there?"

"You bet. This is a nice car, Crys."

Crys looked at Rick through the rearview. "Don't bullshit me. It sucks ass."

"Oldsmobiles are great cars. My wife has one. Not this particular model, but she has one."

"Duke drove a Ninety-Eight for a while," I said.

"The brakes squeal if I hit them too hard," Crys said. "I've replaced the alternator twice in the last three years. I think the last nimrod to change the oil screwed in the pan cap wrong and stripped the thread. And it makes a weird noise when I go in reverse."

"I think they all make a weird noise when they go in reverse," Rick replied.

Crys shrugged her shoulders, settling back in the driver's seat. "I have to get by with what I have."

Rick leaned forward so she could see his face. He was staring at me.

"What you have is as good as it's ever going to get," he said.

Crys looked back at him. "I think you're absolutely right."

We were all quiet for a long time, and for some reason I couldn't meet either of their eyes. I fiddled with the radio to get some music on, and I managed to snag the tail end of a Sheryl Crow song. It was "The Difficult Kind."

After a while Crys asked, "What do you want to be when you grow up?"

I looked back at Rick; neither of us could figure out which one of us she was talking to.

"I'm going to be a badass FBI agent," Rick said.

"You already are," I said.

"I didn't ask what you were *going* to be," Crys said, eyes on the road. "What do you *want* to be?"

Rick crossed his arms and looked out the window, watching I-10 rush by beside him. It took him a moment, but he answered Crys' inquiry crisply.

"I want to help people that need it most," he said.

"What kind of people?" Crys said.

Rick's eyebrows pinched together. "Single mothers."

"Were your parents divorced?"

"No. No, they weren't actually. But I was adopted. My parents are great people. I mean, the best. I don't know who my birth parents are." Rick shrugged. "I don't really care. But I remember Jack's mom growing up. She had it pretty rough raising him and his sister by herself. She did a pretty good job, though."

"Amen," I said.

"So what does that mean?" Crys pressed. "You want to be a social worker?"

"Not necessarily." Rick stopped for a moment, looking at his hands. "There's this author I'm pretty fond of. Andrew Vachss. I started reading his books when I was in high school, and that was a weird time in and of itself. I had a pretty hard time in school. I mean, I was fucked up."

"We all were," I said.

"Yeah, but you weren't one of only six black kids in a class of forty. I read this Andrew Vachss book, and it's all about this guy who was abused as a child and then raised by the state. Orphanages, foster homes, that kind of thing. Naturally – pause for dramatic effect – the guy gets into trouble. He goes through juvie and then on into prison. It's like a cycle. And the things Vachss describes in this book are... *awful*. It's a whole secret world that no one knows anything about because no one in The World wants to talk about it. And I thought, how close was I to a life like that?"

He shifted uncomfortably in his seat. "I believe in the law. I may not agree with its outcomes all the time, but I believe in it. Every kid should have parents like mine."

"Yes, they should," Crys said. I turned and saw her looking blankly through the windshield. There was a trickle of a tear in her eye. When she looked up again, Rick met her eyes in the rearview mirror. Something flickered in the reflective glass that I couldn't identify, and maybe I shouldn't have. Behind his glasses, Rick's eyes were large and bright.

"Why join the FBI then?" Crys asked.

Rick hesitated. "Because who didn't want to follow in Agent Cooper's footsteps after *Twin Peaks?"*

They exchanged glances again, and I saw the same thing pass between them. I thought I was the only who would understand that comment, but Crys didn't ask for elaboration. She just drove on without saying a word.

"What about you, Crys?" I said after the silence in the car had become too much.

"I want to be a physical therapist," she said without hesitation.

"For what kind of patients?" Rick prompted.

"Did you ever see that movie *Regarding Henry*? With Harrison Ford and he gets shot in the head? Can't remember anything, has to be rehabilitated?"

"Oh, yeah. Great movie."

"Really great movie," I added.

"That was the only movie I ever cried at. I thought it was because it was Harrison Ford, right? Y'know, who wants to see Harrison Ford all messed up like that? It's awful. I got to thinking about it, though, and I guess I needed something to latch onto in the therapy field. Something that wasn't about addiction."

"Jack told me that you'd had some rough times with that," Rick said.

"And I never want to be around it again," Crys said. "You'd think after all that time in rehab, you'd want to keep going back. Help the other people you met there. But I *hate them.* I hate addicts. I hate my parents for being addicts. And I hate that I'm one of them. And I never want to have anything to do with that again."

"Good thing you haven't seen *Go*," I said.

"Good movie, too," Rick said.

"Great fuckin' movie."

"I saw *Trainspotting*, though," Crys added with a sliver of a smile. "And I almost had a terminal gag attack when that baby started crawling on the ceiling."

"That was fucked up," I admitted.

"Yes, that would give *anyone* the DTs," Rick said.

"Okay, your turn, cowboy," Crys said, running the back of her hand under her eye.

"I don't like the question," I said, flicking my cigarette out of the window.

"Come on, it's a simple question."

"Bullshit. First, we're all already grown up. And second, when the hell has what I wanted ever counted for shit?"

"Hey, I answered the question," Rick said.

"Come on, give, Jack," Crys said.

"All right, all right." I exhaled heavily and went back to looking out the window. "I want to write…something."

"Really?" Rick said.

"Hey, I didn't major in English just to learn how to find my way around the library."

"He used to be a pretty good writer," Rick explained to Crys. "I read some of his creative writing assignments from high school. They were on point."

"You never let me read any of that," Crys said, smirking at me.

"Yeah, but that stuff wasn't comics," I said.

"What's the difference? You want to write comics?"

"On one side, you've got literature, okay? Prose. On the other side, you've got screenplays. For movies. Comics is the best of both worlds. Dialogue driven with artwork to provide the backdrop. You've got no budget to worry about; no directors, no producers, and no actors giving you shit about rewrites. It's just you and what you want on the panels."

"Unless you're Todd MacFarlane," Rick said.

"Well, there are exceptions and better ones than that fuckin' asshole. But think about it. It's the perfect storytelling medium."

"If you're working with a good artist," Crys said.

"Which is why I'm not writing comic books right now."

"Have you ever submitted anything?" Rick asked.

"Not in a long time. I got a rejection letter from Neal Pozner at DC Comics when I was thirteen for this springboard about Booster Gold and Blue Beetle, though."

"Who?" Crys said, making a confused face.

"Booster Gold and Blue Beetle," I said. "Only the funniest super-hero tag team *ever* in DC Comics."

"You could do it," Rick said. He mimed taking a drink from a cocktail glass. "'Yeah, I could be a comic book writer... *gulp-gulp-gulp*...'"

"Fuck you, Glengarry." I started fiddling with the bandage wrap on my fingers. "You've heard the stories, Rick. Breaking into that field is fuckin' hard. And there's always twenty guys behind you ready to take your gig if you don't produce."

I fidgeted in my seat. "Shit. Let's just drop it."

We rode along in silence for a while. In a perfect world...

"So who would you write about if you got the chance?" Crys asked me after a while.

I could feel Rick's eyes on the back of my head.

"I'll always have eyes for Beetle and Booster," I said. "But who could say no to Batman and Superman?"

As soon as I saw we passed the South Hattiesburg exit off of I-59, I called Doc Faller.

"Hello?"

"Doc, are you home?"

"Snapper? Jackie, m'boyo, where have you been hiding?" I had to hold the cell phone away from my ear as Doc's brogue cut through my eardrum. "I tried calling you at home all week. Have you already given up the boxing, lad?"

"I had to go out of town for a while, Doc," I told him. "Listen, I need a favor. Would you mind putting up a couple of houseguests for the next few days?"

"Lucky for you I don't have any Thanksgiving plans," the Doc replied. "Who and how many?"

"A couple friends of mine. *Close* friends, Doc. The kind that need to be quiet and unseen for a while."

"I see. This have anything to do with—"

"How about we talk about it when I get to your place?"

"Deal. See you in...?"

I saw the Hardy Street exit coming up. "Ten minutes."

Once Doc had hung up, I called John Lewis and told him to meet me at the House.

When Doc opened the door, I didn't expect the abject look of irritation on his face. I should have, though, given my insistence and the quick speed at which I was going through favors these days. Upon seeing Crys, his demeanor lightened somewhat.

"Snapper, I had to chase out a mighty fine piece of tail for you," the Doc said.

"Like you couldn't get it back," I said, feeling the smile genuinely.

Doc Faller showed Rick and Crys into his home, and I brought up the rear. Doc's Canebrake house displayed the usual air of affluence with its brightly shined tile floor and art on the walls. Once we got inside, Doc held out his hand to Rick.

"Doc, this is Rick Sears, my much better half," I said.

"Doc Faller, Rick. A pleasure."

"We're really not gay," Rick said.

"And this is Crys Smith," I said, putting an arm around Crys' shoulders.

Doc took Crys' hand and bowed to kiss it. "My, my, m'lady, what are you doing hanging out with a ruffian like Jack?"

Crys smiled at him. "He knows how to push all the right… *buttons.*"

Doc did a double take, looking from me to Crys to Rick. Rick rolled his eyes and turned away to look at a portrait on the wall. Crys smiled pleasantly back at the Doc.

"Maybe I should ask him on a date sometime," Doc said.

"I ain't cheap," I snickered.

"Now that these lovely formalities are concluded," the Doc said, leading us into the den; "snapper, what the hell happened to your hair?"

I shook my locks at him. "Needed a change, Doc. Let's talk."

"Well said. Can I offer anyone a drink?"

"Crown and seven," Crys said pointing to herself and then at me.

"Milk, please," Rick said.

Doc Faller went to the den's walk-in bar and started pouring the drinks. "So what brings you triad to the doctor? Run out of room at the apartment, snapper?"

"Ran *out* of apartment, Doc," I said, seating myself beside Crys on an Oriental-style sofa. "Long story."

Doc handed each of us our drinks. He gave Rick a strange look when he handed over the glass of milk. "Does this have anything to do with why you were taking boxing lessons? *One* boxing lesson to be exact?"

"Muchly. How are you at covering alibis, Doc?"

The Doc sipped a Long Island iced tea and smirked at me. "Jesus wept."

"So the question is, are you willing to help Jack?" Crys said, sipping her own drink.

He eyed both of us for a moment. "How much trouble are you in, young lady?"

"She and Rick are clean, Doc," I said, peering over the lip of my glass. "But it's about to get pretty dirty in the 'Burg."

"Far be it for me to ever run from a fight, snapper." Doc leaned up against the bar, clad in some plaid pajama pants and a sweater. "But don't you think I should know the details instead of fencing with you all morning?"

"I'll tell you what you need to know, Doc. Don't ask me for anymore." I sighed slightly. "Remember what you told me a while ago? About the people that live here."

Doc's weathered old trickster's face betrayed none of the wisdom contained in his potato-headed skull. "Don't underestimate them, Jack."

"Right." My fingers tapped the drink glass. "I did."

Doc Faller seemed to consider this for a moment, swirling his drink around in its glass and evaluating the faces of Crys, Rick, and myself. I'd told them only the briefest bit about the Doc, about how his mind worked in ways that we mortals could never fathom. But even when I knew this about him, I still saw Doc with his boxing gloves on. He'd fought the censure board at Southern. He'd fought his way out of Ireland and to the United States. I prayed he would fight for me.

"All right, snapper," he said at last. "What do you need?"

"How do you feel about throwing a party, Doc?" I said, letting the smile come.

I got moving pretty quickly after we'd set things up with Doc. He agreed to drive Crys back to her house so she could pick up the Little White Honda. Rick and I took Crys' car and headed into town. The rain had traveled up with us from New Orleans, and a light drizzle blanketed the whole town. When we got to the intersection at Hardy and Westlake, my eyes strayed through the windshield wipers down the street that led to my apartment complex.

"Do you want to get something from your place?" Rick asked me.

"No," I replied. "I don't know what's left."

We turned off the main drag and wound through the back streets off Hardy to the campus grounds of Southern Miss. Student housing was scattered all over the place since the need for more dorms increased every year with higher enrollment. In addition to the dorms (whose styles you could identify by the decade in which they were built), masses of apartments sat just off the grounds, leased mostly to students and grad students. After turning off the apartment maze, I drove down what was affectionately called Frat Row.

The second house on the left bore the Greek letters Sigma Tau Delta in large golden polish above the columned front porch. I pulled into a parking space in front of the House and left the keys in the ignition.

"I shouldn't be too long," I told Rick.

"I'll be here," he replied.

The rain didn't bother me too much as I walked between the two golden lions that guarded either side of the front walkway. I was tempted to rub a palm over the right lion's head as I'd done so many times during my tenure as a "D." A sign of reverence, not luck, or so I was told. Maybe I should have.

Upon opening the front door, I walked into the entry foyer of the main floor. To my left stood the closed doors of the chapter room, a stuffy, cramped little place where the entire brotherhood conducted its meetings every Sunday night. I was surprised to find that an iron gate had been installed to the living room on my right. I peered through the bars to see an unusually clean fireplace setting, sofas, and bookshelves. The fireplace room had been the site of more than a few late night poker tournaments, and I supposed that the alumni had gotten sick of coming in and seeing it trashed every Sunday morning.

Passing straight on through the foyer, I turned left at the corridor that ran the length of the building. Two doors down, I heard laughter and conversation from the open door at the very end of the hall. I stepped inside the doorway and knocked slightly on the frame.

"Anybody know where I can find a buncha rednecked young Republicans with daddy issues and unexpressed glandular conditions?"

"Heathen on the premises!" a guy in a cut-off sweatshirt and Umbros cackled. He threw a Nerf football at me from his place on a couch in the corner of the dorm room. "Bar the fuckin' doors!"

I caught the football and stepped fully into the room. Scott Dole had been initiated into the fraternity a full year before me, but we had graduated during the same semester. By that time, I had already left Sigma Tau and Scott was on his way to graduate studies at Southern in the law department. I had heard that he'd been elected as the fraternity's new graduate academic resident, but I'd fully expected a go-getter like him to have left the the booze and the broads for a bigger law school or even direct practice with his family's firm in Hattiesburg.

"Bar those doors, I'll break 'em down" I said, seeing two others in the room with Dole. I tossed the ball to the man leaning against the bunks and smirked. "Miss me, Johnny?"

John Lewis missed the Nerf, and it hit him in the crotch. He stumbled for a moment then righted himself. "Jack, you are, uh, a sonofabitch."

"Nerf football! Not for use with Crotchbat!"

"Doo-dis! God-*daaaaaaamn*, what the fuck happened to your hair?" Barry Bryce exited the cubbyhole under his bunk and came over to offer me a high five. I met it, declined the brotherhood handshake that he offered, and winked at him.

"To much jerking off'll do this to you, boys. Be warned. Came by to grab some info, Bryce," I said, clapping his shoulder. "What are you fellas up to?"

"The *fuck*!" Dole said, pointing to a stack of papers on his coffee table. "Stupid pledges!"

"They don't know shit, Doo-dis," Bryce agreed. "There's not even one of 'em that's got the brains of a damn dog."

"Well, not everyone can be first badge of the class, boys," I said.

"Yeah, and, uh, cut out on us a year later," Lewis said. "Why'd you tell me to meet you here?"

"I need to ask you fellas if you remember a girl."

"Don't ask Dolemite," Bryce said, picking up the football and tossing it back to Dole. "He's getting hitched!"

"Dolemite, you getting married?" I said.

Dole shrugged, tossing the football up and down on the sofa. "Dunno. She wants to. I'm thinking about it."

"Shit, you two have, uh, been seeing each other since freshman year," Lewis said.

"Remind me to show you my dad's two divorce decrees," I cackled.

"So who's this girl, Doo-dis?" Bryce asked, plopping down on the couch and cracking open a can of Miller Lite. Normally, cases of Milwaukee's Best – nicknamed *"The Beast"* for its horribleness – would have been evident in the House, Miller Lite costing a full two dollars more per case for a college-inappropriate total of eleven-fifty-two for 24 cans of beer. Bryce must have gotten an early Christmas present from his dad.

"Her name's Elizabeth Finley. May have gone by Betsy or Liz while she was here. I think she was a Delta Chi Psi."

"Lot of Delta Chis, Doo-dis," Dole said. "Finley?"

"Up from around Jackson," I prompted. "Only stayed about three semesters while she was on a work internship with some law firm in town."

"Blonde hair?" Bryce said. "Great tits?"

"They *all* have great, uh, tits, Bryce," Lewis said. "Jack, I may remember her. I think I had basic accounting with a Betsy Finley."

"Hey, that's her!" Bryce said, sloshing his soda around. "Betsy Finley! The *Beast*!"

"The Beast?" I said.

"Yeah, that's what Mudflap called her. Remember that week when he broke up with Stace? Well, he went and got a little somethin'-somethin' for the kids on The Beast's field. Muddy called her that coz she fucked like one."

My eyes darkened. Where was that inner deadpan now, you fuck? "Did she now?"

"If we're, uh, remembering the same person," Lewis added; "I think she may have been a transfer from Ole Miss. Kinda prissy. Standoffish. Not really, uh, engaged enough with others to be called bitchy, though. I don't even think the other Delta Chis liked her."

"Don't blame 'em," I said. "Did we ever get her to one of our parties?"

"Everybody comes to our parties," Dole said.

"Except you these days, Doo-dis," Bryce said.

"Gimme an invite, and maybe I'll show."

"So what do you want with The, uh, Beast, Jack?" Lewis asked. "You trying to score a hot date?"

Dole hit me with the football again, and I clenched my good fingers hard into the Nerf, testing the patience of the ones that were still screaming with pain. "Nope. Already had one. Thanks, fellas. See you later."

On my way out, I stopped beside the chapter room and looked at the doors. Against my better judgment, I went inside. Threading myself along the rows of folding chairs and the podium set aside for the president, I came up to the huge mural that adorned the back wall behind the president's and secretary's tables. A legendary Mississippi D had painted the mural years ago, spending his entire college life devoted to every pristine brushstroke. It illustrated various chapters in Sig Tau D's long history with images of the founding fathers, the fraternity mascot Leo the Lion, a famous foreign news correspondent from World War II, and a central image of Athena, the patron goddess of the fraternity. Despite what I thought of the Hattiesburg chapter and what had happened that led to my departure, I always revered the image of Athena.

Goddess of wisdom.

I sidled up to the mural and pressed my hand against Athena's face, separated from my fingers by a protective sheet of Plexiglass.

"Is this when I'm supposed to pray?" I whispered.

I heard a stentorian commotion down by Dolemite's room, beer cans being crushed and smashed into each other over bro-like screams and Bryce's deep belches. The noise broke me out of my introspection. I spared Athena one last glance and walked back to the car. Once I'd gotten in, Rick nodded his head forward at the House.

"What was that all about?" he asked.

"Confirmation," I said, and started the car.

Our next stop was downtown across the train tracks. I pulled up to the office warehouse where Duke made his home away from home and checked the aluminum carport to see if his car was there. It was, and I got out. Rick followed me, casting an eye up at the old building.

"This is your dad's place?"

"Yup. We'll go say hi in a minute."

Rick took off his glasses and wiped the raindrops from the lenses. "Where are we going now?"

I indicated with my head. "Over there."

Rick found his external deadpan, which was always on anyway. "Really?"

The house across the street stood at the corner of a dusty lot that had turned to mud in the rain. What little vegetation grew in the yard was perennially kept half-dead by the abundance of gravel and rocks in the area, as well as the sweltering heat of the Mississippi summers and springs. The house itself looked like it was about to collapse in on itself, but somehow it had survived over forty years in that same lot. As we approached, a lean man sitting on a porch rocker got up to meet us at the steps.

"I need to see Def-J," I said, not stopping even as he tried to block my way.

"Hol' up, white boy," the man said, putting a hand against my chest. "Everybody need to see Def-J. Who the fuck are you?" The man regarded Rick too, a six-foot-sumbitch on my six covering my back. "And who dis?"

"I'm the son of the guy across the street who gives you something to do when you're not getting high and fucking off," I said, letting the pressure of his hand build up against me as I pushed forward. "I got some money for your boss, if he's interested."

"You done got born with the balls, dincha, white boy?" The fellow had on a matching set of windbreaker pants and top, blue with white trim. A tennis visor rested over his brow, and a big gold hoop hung from his left ear. I mean *come* the fuck on.

"I sure did," I said with a smile. "Feel like suckin' on 'em?"

Before the guy could draw back and go for his gun, Def-J walked out of the house onto the porch. Unlike the scrappier fellow on the porch, this man carried himself with a palpable air of self-assurance and poise. He wore a simple white shirt and slacks along with a minimum amount of jewelry: a single gold chain with a Methodist cross dangling from it over his shirtfront. His bald head accentuated the thick goatee on his face. A pair of wire frame glasses not unlike my partner's sat across the wide bridge of his nose. He put a hand on Windbreaker's shoulder.

"Hold up, Marvin," he said. "Who's this?"

"Some cracker sonofabitch and his pet nigga 'bout to get they heads blown off," Marvin replied, pulling a .9mm out of his waistband.

Rick held his hands up in a nonthreatening manner. "I don't really like that word," he said.

"Jack Dooley," I said, speaking past Marvin. "My dad works in the building across the street."

"You Mr. Dooley's son?" Def-J made a face. "Hey, I heard about you. Never seen you before though. I see that Honda of yours every once in a while out front, though."

"I don't get down to this side of town that often. When I do, it's just to say hi to my dad. But I've...bought from your business in the past. Good shit, man."

Def-J grinned, showing off a full set of perfect teeth. "Put your gun away, Marv."

Marvin snorted and did as he was told. "He say he got some green for you, DJ."

"Did he now?" Def-J cast a stare my way and then over my shoulder at Rick. "Who's your friend, Jack?"

"Rick Sears," Rick introduced himself. "FBI."

Marvin and Def-J both looked at us like we were Martians. "Nigga, what you say?" Def-J said.

"Relax," I said, pushing past Marvin and putting a hand on his shoulder. "I've got a proposition to make you."

Def-J regarded both Rick and me. Marvin seemed ready to pull his gun out again at the slightest indication. Finally, the better dressed of the pair nodded slowly and held open the screen door into the house.

"Step into my office, gentlemen. But please keep your voice down. My pops is sleeping."

"I heard he's not well," I said, entering the house and waiting for Def-J to take the lead.

"He won't admit it, but he is not well." Def-J took us into a living room just off to the side of the door. A couple of Def-J's gang-bangers, the Smokies, milled around the room. At a signal from their leader, they scurried off into other parts of the rickety old house. Def-J indicated for us to sit on a sofa next to the window, and he sat down in a comfortable leather easychair opposite us.

"So what's this money you have to offer?" he asked.

"It's a job," I said, reaching in my pocket. "I need about four or five guys sent to the hospital. Preferably in no condition to ever come out again."

Def-J's face remained still. "Oh, is that *all*?"

I nodded. "That's all."

"So you figured you'd come down here and get us mercenary mothafuckas to go pop up some strange trash for you? Hmm?" Def-J steepled his hands in front of him. "Why in the name of hell and damnation would I want to risk my shit for some shit like that?"

"There's no risk if you don't get caught," Rick said. "We'll give you names and addresses. All you have to do is find these men and enjoy yourselves."

Def-J regarded me with tapered eyes. "They must be some righteous dudes to have gotten you all mad at 'em."

I pointed to the scar on my face with the fingers that were bandaged up in the splint. "They weren't very kind to me when I invited them into my home."

"All right, Jack Dooley," Def-J said, playing along. "What are you and mister FBI man here gonna provide for this service?"

I took my hand out of my pocket and set the cash on the table in front of us. "Five thousand dollars enough?"

The Smokie leader's eyes widened when he saw the money. He leaned forward in his chair to sift through the bills, counting them and checking them for indications of fraud and deception. He shook his head briefly as he satisfied himself that the payoff was real.

"You don't kid around, Jack Dooley," Def-J said. "All we have to do is fuck a few guys up?"

I waved my hand in the air. "That's all."

"Where are these fellows at?"

I took a piece of paper out of my jacket pocket and laid it on the table next to the pile of money. "Meet me at this address tonight at eleven. I'm going to see a guy here and then we'll have the names. You have a phone number I can call you at?"

Def-J reached in his shirt pocket and produced a business card. It bore only a phone number on it, no name. "Call that, let it ring, don't leave a message. I'll call you back immediately."

"One more thing," I said. "You don't happen to have a spare .357 Smith and Wesson lying around anywhere, do you?"

Def-J offered me the perplexed look he'd shown before. "Just lying around?"

"We need it for a science project," Rick said, grinning slightly.

Def-J looked at Rick then me and back again. The astonishment on his face suddenly gave way to a huge grimace, and he laughed aloud. Slapping his knee, he got to his feet.

"Well, y'all done made my black ass laugh like it ain't in a hot minute," he chuckled. "Wait here."

Def-J disappeared around a corner and into the bowels of the house. When he'd left, I looked over at Rick with a raised eyebrow.

"A science project?" I said.

"I'm still working on my tough guy dialogue," he said with a shrug. "They don't have a class for that at Quantico. Better yet, write me some."

"Blow me."

"Not in front of the gang-bangers, honey."

Def-J returned after a few minutes holding a package wrapped in a white cloth. He presented it to us like a maitre'd presenting a fine bottle of champagne and he unwrapped the pistol. Rick inspected the .357 and nodded to me. I smiled and stood up, offering Def-J my hand.

"Looks like we have a deal," I said.

"Eleven tonight?" he said, handing the gun to Rick.

"Unless I call beforehand. I've got to make sure the guy's home first, but I'm reasonably confident he will be."

Def-J picked up the five thousand on the table and started leafing through it. "We may have to do business again sometime, Mr. Dooley."

I interrupted his second go at counting by inserting my fingers between bills and pulling a good chunk of it out. As Def-J looked at me like I had just metamorphosed into a cockroach, I waved the cut at him. "I'm hoping this is a one-time deal, Def-J. You get this part of the payoff tonight at eleven. Deal?"

The well-dressed man nodded. "Don't you trust me?" he said with a smirking grin.

There was that Deadpan Man again. Finally. I was wondering where he'd fucked off to.

"I don't trust anyone," I said and winked. "Except maybe Marvin. He looks like an upstanding citizen."

As Def-J let out another throaty laugh, Marvin appeared at the door and escorted us out of the house. Rick followed me back across the street and up to the steps of the East Shipping Company, still shaking his head from our encounter with the Smokies.

"That guy could have shot you, y'know."

"You don't know Def-J," I said, opening the door. "That kid went to Southern and graduated."

"And now he's into gangbanging?"

"He's into *everything*, brother. And he's into it *well.*"

We walked through the building until we reached Duke's office. I heard him talking on the phone and shook my shoulders at Rick. We walked right in.

Immediately upon seeing me, Duke's eyes did a double take, and he slammed the phone down into its cradle without a word of cessation to whomever he was talking to. He got up from his desk and came around to me.

"Jack, what the *hell* happened to you?"

I let my dad shake me by the shoulders and give my new appearance a thorough going-over. His face got more and more white as he looked me over.

"Jesus Christ, are your fingers broken? And what did you do to your hair?"

"Dad, I'm okay!" I said, grabbing his shoulder. "I'm just a little busted up, but I'm okay."

Duke tried to shake off the shock and had a hard time of it. By that time, he noticed Rick standing next to me and blinked again. "Rick! What are you doing here?"

Rick grabbed Duke's hand and shook it. "Your son needed some help for Thanksgiving dinner, and I'm a crack shot with a paring knife."

"Settle down, Dad. You're going to give yourself a heart attack."

"Christ, I haven't seen you in weeks, you show up at my office looking like shit and ask me to calm down?" He rubbed his eyes, suddenly tired by it all, and had to lean against his desk. "Jack, what's going on?"

I sat down in one of the chairs before his desk. Rick took a flanking position behind me on the sofa.

I could see that we would be there a while.

"What do you want me to do?"

The ease with which my dad had taken everything in surprised me to no end. "Dad, I just told you about a revenge scheme. That makes you accessory enough if I get caught."

"He won't get caught," Rick said, arms folded behind me.

"Jack, he may be your uncle," my dad said, getting to his feet. "But he's *my* brother. What do you want me to do?"

I looked up at him, saw the intensity in his eyes. I'd never seen it before. Or maybe I hadn't been looking. But it was there now.

"I need you to go to a party at Doc Faller's house tomorrow night," I said. "And provide me with an alibi."

Duke crossed his arms. "What kind of alibi?"

"Just that I was at the party. I'm going to ask a couple of other people I can trust out there, too, and I want you to remind everyone that I'm there."

"Even though you're not," Duke said.

"Exactly."

"And where will you be?"

I got to my feet and adjusted the hang on my pants. I still wasn't used to being ten pounds skinnier.

"Shoving propane so far up Bill Finley's ass that he'll be heating homes with his mouth for the rest of his life."

Duke looked from me to Rick and back again. "And that Liz girl?"

I bit my lip.

"That's between me and her."

My Dad came up to me and gave me a hug. "Be careful."

Rick put a hand on Duke's shoulder. "He'll be careful."

I patted my Dad's back. "I'll be careful."

On our way out, I let Rick drive the Olds so I could talk on the cell phone. It took me a moment to remember the number, but I got it on the first try.

"Hellllllo?"

"Jeffie," I said. "Dooley."

"Jesus, Jack, did you just up and quit on us all of a sudden?" Jeffie, for all his fun-loving demeanor, had a pissy streak inside him. "Where the fuck have you been? We canceled two shows!"

"I know, I know, Jeff. I'm sorry; I owe you all an apology. Listen, I need some help. I got into a bit of trouble, and I need you to round up the guys."

There was a beat. I could see Jeffie practicing with his leg pad. "What happened?"

"Not over the phone. Look. Meet me at McAlister's in an hour, okay? And, Jeffie: I need all the guys, too. Every last one."

Jeffie's voice got a little tremulous. "Should I wear something I can dirty up?"

I grinned. "Definitely."

25.

RECIPROCITY

It was a rare day in hell when I could get even two of my bandmates to shut up at the same time, and looking at all four of them now, I absently wished I had a camera. Jeffie for the most part had sat absorbing my story nearly rock solid, his posture indicating just how pissed off he was at me. Alexei and Dave had made it only halfway through their sandwiches, pausing as I told them more and more details about the night's work. You couldn't break Steve away from his potato, but the blank look on his face told me that he had understood what I'd said to a tee. This was, after all, the guy who had tried cocaine for the first time and ruminated aloud why his heart wouldn't stop beating so fast.

"You have got to be kidding me," Jeffie finally said, sweeping his untouched turkey sandwich out of the way. "This is why you've shafted us for weeks? Missed rehearsals all those times?"

"Jeffie, look, I said I'm sorry," I said, holding my hands up and feeling peeved with his attitude. "But this is some hardcore shit I have stumbled into. And right now, I need some help."

"We can pull this off without you if need be," Rick intoned, having finished his own meal and snacking on leftover chips at a booth behind me, leaning over the divider to offer half his face and all of the sass. "But it sure would be nice to have some extra hands."

The introductions had proceeded smoothly, Rick pleased to finally meet the legendary members of 25 to Midnight. They had forgotten about him forthwith, though, as soon I'd launched into a brief recap of where I'd been and what I'd been up to. Alexei drained his glass of soda and poised a very serious stare at me.

"I don't understand what you're asking, Jack," he said in his thick Russian accent.

"He *wants* us to go *fuck* someone up," Dave supplied, trying to keep as quiet as possible and not doing a very good job of it. "That's what I'm *hearing*, right, Jack?"

"Basically, yeah," I said, wishing I could smoke inside the preppy eatery. "This guy fucked my night up, and you can see the result." I offered them a look at the splint on my forearm.

"And this is all 'cause of working for your uncle?" Steve said, sucking down the last of his Pepsi. "Sounds pretty heavy."

"It is, Steve. Listen, I wouldn't be coming to you guys like this if I didn't need the help. Badly. I've got to keep this on the downlow, and you are the only guys in town I trust to pull it off without blabbing to somebody."

"*Fuck*, Jack, I'm not a goddamned *hitman*," Dave sputtered. "I don't *even* like to *fight*!"

"Five against one?" Rick offered. "Come on, now..."

"All I need you to do is pick him up and detain him," I said. "We can leave the rough stuff to others later on."

I watched each of them mull the idea over. None of them were hardcore heavy hitters except maybe Jeffie, who indulged in more than his fair share of the building of bodies. I couldn't honestly picture Dave throwing a punch to save his life. However, these were my *bandmates.* A lot of times, people take for granted what goes on in a band. They think it's all egos and money and that the only real glue that holds a band together is their level of skill and professionalism. That couldn't be further from the truth. There's an unspeakable bond between bandmates, a relationship that defies labels. I had offered up my sofa to Jeffie after the first few weeks of his divorce. Dave routinely picked up Alexei's kids from school when he or his wife couldn't get out of work. Steve used to front me free beer at his virtual golf shop for the whole six months it had been open.

It was more than partners. Less than a brother, maybe.

It was *bandmates.*

I'd lay down in traffic for those guys.

"The last thing I ever want to see," Jeffie started, breaking the silence; "is some cockhead fucking up my lead vocalist. After all, he's the only irreplaceable guy in the group."

"Is about the principle of a thing, yes?" 'Lex said. "You do not break the band."

"Yeah, I am Spartacus, too, I guess," Dave said, shrugging.

Steve looked around at us and then back down at his leftovers. "What are we doing now?"

I fought the smile but gave up after a while. I could see from Jeffie's stone cold bodybuilder demeanor that he had made up his mind before I'd even asked. The guy could be an extreme asshole sometimes, but he was still the center of 25 to Midnight. I may be the front man, but it was he who held the band together with the beat.

"Okay," I said, lowering my voice. "Pile up into Steve's Explorer and park yourselves at the Shell station next to the Mark IV apartments on 28th Avenue. The guy's going to leave his apartment at about ten-thirty, and I'll call you on Steve's cell phone to let you know what he's driving. Tail him, find out where he's going, and call me if he comes back to the apartment. When we hook back up, we'll hit him together."

"James fucking *Bond* shit, man," Dave exclaimed. "*Damn.*"

"James Bond was a fairy," Steve said.

"Where will you two be?" Jeffie asked.

I looked at Rick. "Cleaning up the trash."

At ten-thirty, I pulled the Olds over at a gas station off Lincoln Road and went to a payphone. Unable to remember the number, I had to borrow the phone book from the clerk inside. I was lucky that Henkel kept his Hattiesburg number listed or at least had never bothered to pay the phone company the extra fee that would privatize his listing. Scrawling it down on a piece of paper, I gave it to Rick.

"Do it," I said.

Rick nodded and dialed the number at the payphone.

"Hello? Yes, is this Mister Henkel? Hi, this is Jamie over at Shenanigan's. Yes, sir! We're just calling to let you know that you've won a *free* meal and drink tonight and tonight only at our bar! Yes, sir. You bet. Tonight only, that's right. You're welcome, Mister Henkel. See you soon."

He hung up and gave me a thumbs-up. "He bought it."

We got back into the car, and I headed over to Henkel's apartment complex. En route, Rick reached into his bag and removed the cobbled-together .357 he had assembled. While driving around earlier that day, he had substituted parts from the gun Def-J had given us for the marked pieces from Luco's gun.

At one point after seeing Duke, we'd driven out to a field off of Highway 98 where Rick had me pull over behind a grove of trees.

"Can you shoot this with your hand all jacked up?" he'd asked, sliding bullets into the chamber.

Already tired of the annoyance that the forearm splint was, I'd untied the laces and slid the thing off. My wrist was very stiff, but I could move it. I could feel a deep ache in my bone, but Crys had told me that she didn't think the fracture was too bad. Working out the kinks in the formerly immobile limb, I'd nodded to Rick. "I'll manage. What do I do first?"

We had gotten out of the car and walked several yards further into the field until we were sure that we were a good distance away from the highway. There was plenty of overgrown brush and trees around, and I'd remembered from some of my driving about Hattiesburg that no one's property bordered the field. Rick had spun the chambers on the .357, flicked off the safety and presented it to me, grip first.

"It'll kick a bit when you fire," he'd said. "Pull back the hammer with your thumb."

"I can't just shoot it?"

"In a pinch, you can, but pulling back the hammer makes for a quicker, easier shot. The trigger's heavy. All right, now choose a target and shoot."

I'd found a gnarled old stump among the grove trees and had sighted as best I could. When I'd pulled the trigger, the .357 recoiled so hard that I'd felt the concussion all the way up my arm. The ache had aggravated my arm in the worst way, but I'd snapped the other five shots in quick succession in order to get used to the feel of the weapon. I hadn't hit anything, my aim was so bad, but Rick had made me walk a little closer to the stump and try again. I'd reloaded according to his directions and had fired six more rounds. That time, all six had hit the stump.

We'd driven around Hattiesburg until our rendezvous with 25 to Midnight at McAlister's. By that time, night had fallen, and it was time to get to work.

The instant we pulled up in the parking lot, Rick put a hand on my arm. "Hold it."

I looked around the darkened lot, thinking that he'd seen a cop. "What is it?"

"Let me out here. Where's his unit?"

I pointed. "Around the corner. I'm going to park on the other side of the building."

Rick opened the door and got out of the Oldsmobile. "I'll meet you there in a minute."

Leaving Rick to go do his thing, I rounded the lot and found a parking place in the visitor's section just off to the side the building across from Henkel's. I desperately wanted a cigarette, but I fought down the urge to light the flame, fearing that it could look a little weird, some dude smoking cigarettes in a car in the back of the apartment complex like a fuckin' creeper. At that point, everything started to spook me. I worried that a neighbor of Henkel's might come outside and ruin the whole thing. I worried that Def-J's posse might arrive too early and cause a ruckus big enough to get us noticed. The shakes gave way to a cold sweat that cascaded down my spine. I managed to fight them off by the time Rick returned to the car.

"Put these under your seat," he said, getting in and closing the door. He handed me a pair of license plates.

"Where'd you get these?" I asked, doing as I was told.

"There was a same-model Olds sitting in the parking lot over there. I figured we could use the cover when we got on the road tomorrow."

"Good thinking."

Rick reached into his bag and withdrew two pairs of gloves and a baseball cap. He sat the cap down low on his head and started pulling on the gloves, handing the other pair to me. "Can you get your fingers into these?"

With a wince, I pulled off the tape and splint that bound the bruised fingers of my left hand. When I pulled on the glove, tendrils of pain shot up my hand, and I bit my lip struggling to get it on. It hurt to some degree, but I closed my eyes and welcomed the pain. I would need it in a few minutes.

From our secluded spot in the parking lot, we had a pretty good vantage point on the only exit from Henkel's building. We only had to wait a few minutes before the bastard came hobbling out and clambered into a beat up old Chevy pickup. Rick scribbled down the make, model, and license plate numbers and handed me the notepad. I was already on the phone.

"Yeah?" Steve answered.

"He's coming your way. Red 1980-something Chevy pickup. License plate 3G2-DF1. You ready?"

"We're on it like a hornet," Steve replied. "Okay, there he goes! Shut *up*, Dave! Where's he going again?"

"Shenanigan's over off Broadway. He'll be in and out pretty quick if things go down as planned. As soon as he gets back in the truck and starts heading home, ring me back."

"You got it, Jack. See ya."

I flicked off the phone and set the ringer to vibrate. Looking at Rick, I said, "We're on."

We exited the car and quietly made our way up to the second floor of the building in which Henkel lived. On the way, Rick quietly unscrewed the bulbs in each of the porch lights until the light winked off, keeping each bulb in place but inactive. I put my hand in my jacket pocket where the .357 rested. I indicated the correct door and stood over to one side. Rick listened for a moment, heard nothing and nodded at me. He produced a small set of rods from his pocket and set to work on the door lock. I watched intently as he'd instructed, trying to adapt my eyes to the darkness and follow his movements. But I also kept looking back up to make sure we remained in the clear.

I heard the tumblers click, and Rick stood back up, opening up the door. We filed inside quickly, shutting the door gently behind us. A television set in the far corner of the efficiency unit remained on but muted. *The Magnificent Seven* was playing on TNT, and I elbowed Rick. He checked it out and smiled.

"Cookie jar," I said, getting back to business.

"Got it."

As Rick entered the kitchen, keeping the lights in the apartment off, I returned to Henkel's desk. Opening drawers and flipping through papers, I checked to make sure none of the stuff I'd originally seen in my first penetration into Henkel's place had been removed. Everything seemed just as I'd left it the last time, and a brief flood of relief rushed into me. I pulled out Henkel's collection of check stubs with the Betsy F. Jones signature and put them in an envelope that I found in a drawer. Then I reached into the waistband of my dark pants and removed a triple-folded copy of the document that David Novak had faxed to me in New Orleans. I stuffed the document into the envelope with the check stubs and sealed it. Grabbing a pen from a dirty jelly jar on the desktop, I wrote "FINLEY" in block capital letters on the envelope cover. Rustling around through all the junk in the top drawer, I buried the envelope under a stack of bank statements and returned the desk to its former appearance.

Rick appeared from around the corner of the kitchen holding the .44 he'd found in Henkel's cookie jar. At my prompting nod, he said, "Perfect."

"Let's go," I said.

Rick stuffed the gun and the box of bullets inside his jacket pockets and we did another quick once-over of the apartment, making sure we'd erased all traces of our existence there. Rick even went so far as dragging his feet across the carpet to hide the impressions left by our shoe soles. We locked the door from the inside, pulled it shut as we stepped outside, and headed back to the Olds. The operation had taken us a total of fifteen minutes.

We headed in the direction of Broadway, having not heard from Steve yet. I figured that it would be important to be ready just in case Henkel surprised us by not taking his usual route home. I had given Jeffie and the guys very specific information on how I wanted the ambush to go down, and we had a very small margin for error if it was to go unseen.

My cell phone vibrated against my hip about twenty minutes later, and I answered it to find Jeffie on the other end of the line.

"He just stomped out of the bar. He's pissed off."

"Good. You tailing him now?"

"Yeah, it looks like he's headed back the way he came. He's going for the cut-off through the mall parking lot."

"We're almost there," I said, stepping on the gas. "Flash your lights and try to get him to stay in the lot."

"Gotcha."

I handed the phone to Rick so I could concentrate on the driving. My arm ached as I turned the wheel sharply, shooting around residential streets to the service road on 49 South. In a few minutes, we were curving around the road's dead end into the dimly lit parking lot outside Broadacres Mall. The lot had once sported a Jitney Jungle grocery store, torn down a few months ago. Someone had told me that an Albertson's was going up in the area soon, but for the moment, all we had to worry about was a few sputtering safety lights and the storefront of SteinMart.

I saw Henkel's truck right in front of me when I made the curve. The Explorer was a few yards back, its lights flashing wildly. Henkel appeared to be slowing, maybe checking his mirrors to see what the hubbub was all about. But as soon as he saw the bright lights of the Olds bearing down on him, he jammed on his brakes fully. I cut the Olds to the left, straightening the car out perpendicular to Henkel's path and blocking him off from the service road. Steve's Explorer came to a shrill stop just behind the truck.

The second all the cars had ceased forward motion, we sprang into motion. Jeffie, Dave, 'Lex, and Steve exploded out of the Explorer, running full tilt to the Chevy. Rick and I strode quickly to join them, and I saw Rick's hand go protectively to the stolen .44 in his jacket pocket. We had cut the lights off on our cars, and Rick stood in front of the Chevy to partially block the headlamps there, also using the position to scout for unwanted visitors. For my part, I drew the cobbled .357 from my jacket and checked the safety.

Henkel had his door halfway open when Dave pulled it all the way, jerking him out of the truck. Jeffie leaned on him with a quick punch to the nose, bouncing his head off the Chevy's door. Then he and Dave pulled him up while Steve and 'Lex delivered more punches to Henkel's midsection and face. Henkel made a groaning noise as he was pummeled, interrupted only by the "bitches" and "assholes" that Dave and Steve delivered on him.

Jeffie lost his grip on one of Henkel's arms, and the trucker lunged out at 'Lex. The swing went wide as the Russian stepped easily out of the way, and Henkel fell to the ground. Dave kicked him twice in the ribs as he tried to get on all fours, and Steve leaned in for a lazy blow to the eyebrow. I waved them off as I came into the fray and administered a swift kick to Henkel's face, knocking him back against the truck and spattering bloody teeth on the asphalt. My bandmates made a protective cordon around us as I squatted down to look upon the face of the man who had mocked me.

"You *mother*fucker!" Henkel crowed, hands going to the bloody mess that was his mouth and snout. "Son of a bitch! My fucking nose *again*!"

I swung the .357 butt-first at Henkel and again smashed his nose, feeling the crunch of bone as the bandage he still wore slid off in the slick rivers of blood that began to pour out. "Shut up, Henkel. You keep whining, I'm going to shoot you next time."

"*Ahhhhhhhhhh!*" Henkel screamed, trying to stem the pain in his newly fractured face. Jeffie leaned in and stepped on one of his writhing legs, adding another source of discomfort.

"You shut the fuck up *now*, sonofabitch, or it's gonna get a whole lot worse," the drummer said.

Next to him, Steve gave a thumbs-up and grinned. "Hey, nice Bronson, Jeff."

"Man, that was *Coburn*, dude," Dave corrected.

I silenced them with a look, hoping they wouldn't get into names again. The less Henkel heard of his attackers, the better. Rick had crossed over to us and reached inside the Chevy, turning off its headlights. He returned to his sentry position, keeping a careful eye out for any approaching cars or people.

Henkel whined and writhed on the concrete ground, his whimpers making barely formed words of acknowledgment. He hadn't changed much in the three-odd weeks since I'd seen—or heard—him last. His scraggly gray hair had gotten a little longer, and he hadn't shaved in days. The paper-thin plaid shirt he wore was now splattered with blood, and his jeans looked like they had been dragged through a gravel pit. I leaned over and held the gun's barrel on him.

"You done fucked up big this time, boy!" Henkel bit out, almost a sob. "He'll kill you!"

"He's not going to do shit, Al," I said, my face stone immobile. "Worry about yourself right now."

"What do you want?" He looked from Jeffie to Dave to me and back again.

"A couple of things. But first, let me tell you how this is going to be. You're working for me now, Al. And if you even think about going to the cops or your former boss, then someone's going to find a nice envelope on their desk containing numbers, pictures, and bank statements. And then someone else is going to find out that her husband's been fucking around with a hooker in Alabama."

Henkel sneered at me. "You got nothing to prove that."

I let a glimmer of a smile invade my features. "Ask Judge Schiedle."

The weathered old trucker closed his eyes and looked away. "Fuck."

"You've got one way to stay out of jail right now, Al," I said, hefting the .357. "And that's to do exactly as I say. Do you understand?"

He hedged a moment, looking around at the parking lot ground, the truck, Jeffie's shoes. I pulled the hammer back on the .357, the resounding click loud in front of his face. Henkel looked back up and started squirming again. "All right! All right! I understand."

I reached into my pocket and withdrew my notepad and a pen, tossing them into Henkel's lap. "First thing's first. Write down the names and addresses of every one of your butt-boys that you invited over to my apartment."

Henkel paused for a moment, still getting a grip on his senses as he nudged the bruised battleground that was his face. He looked like he was about to protest, offering me a bloody sneer. Then Alexei leaned down beside him to speak quietly in his ear.

"You must do what he says," the Russian droned in a strange voice none of us had ever heard before. "In Mother Russia, before coming here... I had experience with KGB. You know of this name, no? I pay great attention to what they do. Especially what they do with pliers, yes? Pliers and...genitals."

Henkel spared a wide-eyed glance at the dark-haired Russian. Alexei remained as matter-of-fact and calm as he always was. After too many moments staring into 'Lex's dark eyes, Henkel eagerly grabbed up the utensils and started scrawling on the paper. As we waited, Alexei stood back up and offered me a wide smile with a wink.

"Jesus-*fuck*, 'Lex is a fucking communist *spy*," Dave breathed, halfway between awe and laughter.

"I always wanted to say that," 'Lex said proudly, puffing up his chest. "Like in *Red Heat*, yes?"

"Of all the cool Cold War spy flicks, you choose *Red* fucking *Heat*?" Jeffie chuckled. "Have you even *seen Hunt for Red October*?"

"Or *The Spy Who Loved Me*?" Steve supplied.

"Or *Air Force One*?" Rick added.

"*Air Force One* was post-Cold War," I corrected him. "Gary Oldman and company were playing disavowed former KGB guys and not Russian nationals. It doesn't count."

"What do you mean it doesn't count?" Rick said. "It counts. There's Russians and they're beating up on the President of the United States. What more do you need?"

"Ahh, *Air Force One* is also good movie," Alexei said, backing Rick up.

Rick shrugged at me, indicating 'Lex's reply as his proof of justification. I stood up from where I was squatting in front of Henkel and waved my gun absently. "Go back to watching the damn road."

"Th-there," Henkel said, shakily holding the notepad up to me. "That's all of them."

I took the pad and pen with my injured hand, ignoring the pain and giving the names a cursory glance. There were five men listed there, all with Hattiesburg addresses.

"You sure don't stray too far from the nest, do you, Al?" I snickered, stuffing the list in my pocket. "All right, now let's talk a little."

"What do you want, Dooley?" he seethed.

"Where is Finley's house in Jackson?"

Henkel shrugged. "I dunno. Somewheres close to the plant, I reckon."

"You reckon?" I made the .357 waver in front of him for a moment.

"Yeah, somewhere close!" Henkel's eyes got wider. "There's a subdivision off 49 that's open property. Couple of different mansions up there."

"What's it called?"

"Greyhaven, I think."

"Is it just Finley and his wife living there?"

"Yuh-yeah. I think so. They may have a maid or something."

"What about his daughter?"

I could see the glint in Henkel's eye. "She lives in the city, I think. Downtown."

"Uh-huh. She's the one who's been signing your checks for the DPI drops at Magee, isn't she?"

He looked away. "Yeah. Yeah, she is."

"You remember what you did to my uncle's plant, Al? Do you?"

He nodded, touching his broken nose again. "Yeah, I remember."

"You're going to do that again."

Henkel's bushy eyebrows pinched together. "I am?"

"Oh, yeah. Except this time you're going to do it at the PetroJet plant in Jackson."

"That place is huge, man!" he squealed. "He's got all kinds of people in there! No way in hell."

I shook my head and leaned back over Henkel, sticking the muzzle of the .357 close to his face. When he recoiled, I put the cold metal barrel against his broken nose and listened to him try not to scream. The sound reminded me of the high-pitched whimper that made Chris Tucker famous.

"Al, I'm getting a little irked here," I said. "Do you know what that means? Irked?"

"Y-yeah," Henkel said, his breath coming out on the verge of hyperventilation.

"What does it mean?"

Henkel started to ask me a question, but I pushed the barrel of the gun harder into his nose. "It-it means mad and aggravated!"

"Good for you. Now listen carefully. Wednesday night, you're going to go into the PetroJet plant and put on a repeat performance of your show at DPI. I don't care how you do it, but you're going to ruin that plant. There ought to be a front-page story in the Jackson paper the next morning with big block letters that say, 'Crippling Explosion at Finley Plant.'"

Henkel's face looked like someone had introduced him to the Devil himself. "Then what?"

"Then you better hightail it outta Dodge, Al," I said, standing back up and letting the gun fall away from his nose. "Because you'll have just committed felony arson, malicious mischief, and industrial espionage. That's a twenty-five to life fall if the right people show up to testify at your trial."

"What makes you think I won't deal for immunity? Turn you in?"

This time my smile was wide and bright. "Because you're going to have company, Al."

Rick cleared his throat. "It's eleven," he said.

I clicked back the hammer on the .357, waving it at Henkel. "Okay, get him up."

Henkel struggled minimally as Steve and Jeffie manhandled him to his feet. I gave him a quick frisk, checking his pockets, and nodded at Jeffie.

"You drive the pickup. He's between us. Rest of you follow in the Explorer. Rick, you got the Olds?"

Rick nodded to me, light from one blinking lot light casting speckles on his glasses. "I got it."

"W-where are we going?" Henkel stammered as Jeffie shoved him into the Chevy. I got in on the passenger side and closed the door, keeping my gun trained on him.

"To meet your new best friends," I said. "Let's go.

We got back to the Mark IVs only a few minutes after eleven. Rick and Steve parked their cars near the visitor's lot on one side of the office unit. I instructed Jeffie to park Henkel's truck in the spot I'd last seen it, and we clambered out of the vehicle. Jeffie's oversized hands yanked on Henkel's blood spattered shirt until he came stumbling out of the truck. I made a quick sweep over the seat, dashboard, steering wheel, and door handles with a handkerchief to eliminate any fingerprints Jeffie may have left behind. Then I locked the keys in the truck and nodded to Jeffie and Henkel.

"The office. Let's go. You make a peep, Al, and the last thing you see is gonna be my smiling face when I put a bullet between those too-close redneck eyes."

Henkel kept his head down as we walked, Jeffie looking around carefully a few steps behind him. As we got closer to the office, I saw a mass of shadowy figures hanging out on an old Chevy Nova in the parking area before the unit. I recognized Def-J leaning against the hood of the car. Marvin stood close by, still wearing his windbreaker. As we approached, Marvin and some of the other Smokies formed up protectively around Def-J, but the gang leader spotted me instantly. Steve, Dave, 'Lex, and Rick came around the corner of the office building to join us, and Marvin turned his attention to them. Recognizing Rick at the head of the group, Marvin offered up a stout and defiant "'Sup?" Rick nodded his acknowledgment to the Smokie and came over to join me. Def-J offered a couple of soothing hand signals to his bodyguards and came up to meet us, giving Henkel a dubious stare down the length of his cocoa nose.

"Didn't expect to see you taking a personal hand in all this," I said.

"Not a problem," Def-J said with a small smile and a shrug. "I'm still missing everything you waved under my nose, however."

I shoved Henkel until he ran smack into Marvin. Marvin pushed the trucker back into a throng of Smokies who immediately took hold of his arms. Henkel's eyes were as wild as an animal's, and his breath came out in rasps. My hands free, I reached into my pocket and pulled out the chunk of cash I had removed from Def-J's original payout. I had curled the bills into a tight cylinder and wrapped them with a rubber band, which made it easy to toss to Def-J. He caught it with one hand and immediately tossed it to one of his boys who began counting the roll on receipt.

"Who are the rest of the white boys?" Def-J said, inclining his head toward my bandmates. The gang leader wore the same outfit I'd seen him in earlier, only covered by a long leather trench coat. I could see the bulge of a weapon beneath the coat.

"They're cool," I said. "Friends of mine in the wrecking ball business."

Def-J glanced over 25 to Midnight, offering up no sign of whether he considered them cool or not. Steve, in his usual doofus manner, waved to Def-J and put on one of his cherubic cheeked grins. Def-J looked at me again, and I could have sworn I saw Deadpan Man in his face too.

"Damn, white boys got all *kinds* of weird shit going on," he said. He looked over at the Smokie to whom he'd tossed the money roll, receiving a curt nod with a couple wide eyes and high eyebrows that said, *"Damn, there's a lotta cheddah in this hyeah roll."*

"Gotta love it," Def-J said. "What's the score, Mister Jack Dooley?"

"There's your list," I told Def-J, handing him the notepad on which Henkel had written. I watched Def-J's lip curl into a sneer as he tried to avoid the bloodstains on the paper. "And I got you a personal tour guide as a bonus."

Def-J looked at the notepad then handed it to Marvin. "I have to admit, Mr. Dooley. The way you do business is pretty efficient."

I winked at him. "Part of my white boy charm, baby." I faced Henkel again and grabbed his ear. "Now you listen to me, motherfucker. These guys here are going to chauffeur you around to see those hard, brass knuckle sonsabitches you brought into my home. You lie to them, you give 'em any shit, and they're gonna make sure nobody finds you in the morning. You hear me?"

At the squeeze I gave to his ear, Henkel winced and tried to nod. "Yeah, yeah, I get it!"

"Wednesday night at ten o'clock sharp, Al. If I don't hear the bang, your new friends here are going to play *Operation* with that white trash ass of yours."

I turned away and nodded at Def-J. The gang leader pointed to Marvin. "Put him in the car."

Henkel started to protest then stopped as Marvin grabbed his head and pushed him into the Nova, police style. Two big black guys got in to surround Henkel on either side in the backseat, and Marvin shut the door. He chewed on a toothpick and offered me a wide grin.

"Damn, there ain't nothin' like fuckin' up some po', proud white trash," Marvin cackled.

I snickered and couldn't help but match Marvin's grin, but when I replied, I did so eyeing Rick, who couldn't help but smirk back at me. "Make him dance for you. Maybe shine your shoes. He ain't gonna smile atcha, though."

I turned back to Def-J, pointing at Henkel in the car. "That one's going to need a ride to Jackson Wednesday night," I told Def-J. "He's got a job to do at PetroJet Chemical at ten. Make sure he isn't late."

Def-J put his hands in the trench coat's pockets and offered me an affable grimace. "That wasn't part of the deal."

I withdrew another two thousand in cash from my pocket, each grand rolled into a tight bundle like the other chunk. I tossed one to Marvin and handed the other on an outstretched hand to Def-J. Def-J took his grand and started thumbing over it. Marvin skimmed through the corners of the bills in his roll and let out a "Hot *daaaaaaaamn!*"

"Will that cover your troubles?" I asked.

"Indeed," Def-J said. "You must have a righteous mad-on for someone to be throwing around that kind of cash, Dooley."

I grimaced. "You don't know the half of it."

Def-J glanced at the Nova where Henkel was shaking between his guards. "What do I do with him when he's finished?"

"Make sure he never walks again," I said and shrugged. "Leave him somewhere uncomfortable. Shit, beyond that, you guys can do what you want. Don't you have a training program or something for new guys?"

Def-J held up the list I'd given him. "And these fools?"

"Fuck 'em up. How bad?" I shrugged again. "Training, man."

The smooth leader of the Smokies nodded and held out his hand. "You're a hell of a businessman, Dooley. Easy to do when you got a bankroll like that, though." He pinned me with a duskier stare as our hands entwined in a firm shake. "Wonder what else we may get into."

"Gimme a couple weeks and maybe I'll introduce you to a buddy of mine down in Biloxi with whom you might enjoy some business," I said. "Have fun tonight, Def-J. You too, Marvin. I'll holla at y'all tomorrow for an update."

With that, I stepped back onto the sidewalk to join Rick and the rest of my bandmates. We watched silently as the Smokies' car started up and slowly pulled out of the lot. I thought I could see a terror-stricken Henkel looking back at me from the rear window, but I may have imagined that. All the same, it was a pretty pleasurable image.

"That went surprisingly well," Rick said, eyes still darting around the apartment complex to make sure no one was eavesdropping on us.

"Hey, we were the *mad fucking machines*!" Dave cackled, slapping Rick on the back. "Fuckin' *A*!"

"That stuff 'Lex pulled out of his ass was hilarious," Jeffie chuckled, shaking his head. "I swear to God, you almost made me laugh like a madman in front of that guy, 'Lex."

Alexei did his best Eastwood impersonation, substituting his thumb and forefinger for a pistol. "Make my day, motherfucker."

"So what now?" Steve said, lighting up a cigarette, his unbuttoned shirt billowing in the cool night air. "Jack, you wanna get a drink?"

"I could go for some booze," Jeffie said, looking to me.

"I think we're going to call it a night, fellas," I said, moving to shake Jeffie's hand. "Listen, I owe you guys big on this. Thanks."

"Reschedule that wedding we skipped out on, and I'll be happy," Jeffie replied, grasping my hand hard.

"Might not be able to, bud. But I'll definitely cover you guys for cutting out on you. Trust me."

"What, free money?" Dave said. "*Daaaaaayyyyaaaaaamn*!"

"I'll see what I can drum up, Dave, okay?" I snickered. "In the meantime, I need you guys to stop by a party Wednesday night. You up for it?"

"What kinda party?" Steve inquired.

"Remember that old Irish guy from Southern I was telling you about? Old Doc Faller? He's throwing a shindig Wednesday night at his place at Canebrake. I'm not going to be there, but I need people to come and say I *was* there, if you get my meaning."

"Okay. I'm game," Jeffies said.

"Can I bring Ashe?" Steve asked.

"Sure," I replied, shrugging my shoulders. "Bring your wives or girlfriends or blow-up dolls as the case is with Jeffie. But don't tell 'em what's going on. As far as anybody needs to know, me and Rick are *at* that party. Got it?"

"No problemo, Jack," Alexei said with a garbled salute. "We keep it in the family, yes? Like usual."

"No one needs to know about tonight either," Rick added. "I'd recommend against even talking about it amongst yourselves. At least for a while."

"Hey, be cool, Rick," Jeffie said, moving to shake his hand as well. "We're 25 to Midnight."

And that said it all.

We would go on to play one more show together, and then I would never see most of them again.

Everyone said their goodbyes, and Rick and I climbed into the Oldsmobile. As Steve's Explorer roared off into the night, we sat there for a moment as the car warmed up. Rick laid his head against the headrest and looked up at the roof of the car.

"I have an uncontrollable urge to listen to the *Out of Sight* soundtrack," he said.

I grinned at him, putting the car in gear.

"That's *Dooley*, not Foley."

The door was open when we got back to Doc Faller's house. Crys was stretched out on one of his plush couches in the den, the television tuned to a documentary about the making of *Key Largo* with Humphrey Bogart. When we walked in, she stood up and looked us over.

"Mission accomplished?" she said.

"Number one on the charts with a bullet," I said. "Where's Doc?"

"He went to sleep. I told him I'd stay up and wait for you."

"Sounds like a good idea," Rick said, shrugging out of his jacket and baseball cap. "I get the couch again?"

"You'll think it's a waterbed," Crys said, stretching and yawning. "I almost went to sleepy land waiting for you two to get back."

"In that case, get the hell out of my room," Rick said, turning off the TV and plopping down on the couch. "I'm wore out."

I leaned over and grasped his hand. "'Preciate the help tonight, Rick."

Rick squeezed my hand back. "It's not over yet, Jack."

Everyone said goodnight, and Crys escorted me to the guest bedroom in the south wing of the house. As soon as we were inside and the door was closed, I grabbed her roughly and met her mouth with my own. We fell onto the plush bed.

"It's going to work," I breathed, my hands making red marks on her bare shoulders.

"Do you love it?" Crys said, breathing heavily, her fingernails scratching against me as she tugged at my khakis.

One of the buttons on her shirt popped off as I ripped it open.

"I love it," I said into her chest.

26.

BETWEEN

Tuesday was spent in preparation.

Rick borrowed Crys' car and headed out to Wal-Mart to pick up a few things that we would need the following day. Doc Faller had a dentist appointment at noon and left early to have brunch with the lady friend we'd chased off the day before. Crys and I spent the better part of the morning entangled in each other. She checked the remainder of my bandages and pronounced me pretty much healed, even though I still felt the aches. The only thing I had left on me was the wrap around my ribs. I was plenty happy to finally be free of the forearm splint and the taped fingers. I put on Doc's boxing gloves and tried a few rounds in the garage, but my arms gave out early and my fingers protested loudly in throbs, still sensitive. I felt sick to my stomach. But it didn't bother me too much. I would bet good money that I wouldn't do much handwork the next day.

Crys fell into a much-needed sleep around one, about the same time that I rang Def-J. I admitted to myself that I could do for a nap as well. Rick and I both would be leaving early in the morning to get to Jackson on time. I was on my way to the bedroom when Doc's phone rang.

"Hello?"

"Mister Dooley. You rang?"

"Hey. How'd it go last night?"

There was a snicker on the other end of the line. "Well, Marvin got some stains on his windbreaker, and he's not too happy about that. Fortunately, that was just on the first guy. He had four more to work his frustration out on."

"They're down?"

"They won't be talking much anymore. Especially one motherfucker thought he was some kinda gunslinger. He'll be havin' a hard time finding his teeth where we hid 'em in his asshole."

"Cool. Henkel?"

"Your trashy white friend's enjoying a snack in the trunk of my car right now. He got a little rowdy early this morning, tried to run off. But Marvin got out the crowbar, and he shut up pretty damn quick."

"Excellent. He might need some time to prepare for his routine in Jackson tomorrow night. Make sure he has it."

"You got it, my man. Anything else?"

"Not unless you got something."

"Not a thing, my man," Def-J said. "Come by and see me again sometime. I kinda like your stupid ass."

"Me too," I chuckled. "Check you later, DJ. Bye."

With that taken care of, I went through Doc's list of guests for the party Wednesday night. Including himself and Crys, it made for about thirteen people. Not too many, I hoped. But I'd spoken to the majority of them already, and I knew Duke would be taking care of the rest once the festivities began. Shortly thereafter, my cell phone rang. The caller ID, instead of reading the usual message for unidentified caller, showed a jumble of gibberish letters and numbers. I knew who it was immediately.

"Deck?"

"We got five minutes before I gotta ditch this connection, *jefe*," Deckhead's voice came through the line. "When we're done, you make sure that phone's *destroyed*, get me?"

"I hear you, Deck. What's the word?"

"It's all set up. Transfers are going through at nine o'clock in the morning, and we've got ice worked up to keep it hid all day. After about seven at night, though, someone's gonna see. Are we on?"

"Whenever you're ready, Deck. You have documents?"

"Y'betcha. You want me to fax 'em to ya?"

"Yeah, hang on." I read the fax number of Doc's machine in the living room. "Send 'em on through."

"Cool. I'm going to code the transmission through the SouthBank branch in Jackson. Is that swank?"

"Perfect. What else you got for me?"

"Just a wet kiss on the lips when you get back to The Fort, Jack Attack," Deck giggled. "Shit, *jefe*, you mentioned something about dollar signs but *daaaaayyyyyyaaaaaaammmn*!"

"Hey, you and the gang are worth it, Deck. Listen, I'll call you in a couple days, okay?"

"Hot dog city, succotash. Spank some for me."

"You know it."

I hung up and grinned, waiting for the fax machine to start spewing out the papers. As soon as it did, I collected the records, gave them a quick and cursory glance to verify Deckhead's information, and stuffed them into a folder that Doc had lying around on his desk.

Rick got back at two. I nodded to him when he came inside.

"What'd you get?"

"Stuff," he said. "Good stuff."

"Well, that's cool."

"Yup." He went into the kitchen to fix himself a glass of milk. "What time do we leave?"

"Two in the morning. I want to scout PetroJet before we head for Greyhaven and start our stakeout. Anything else we need?"

Rick took a long sip from his glass. "Not that I can think of."

I watched him absently for a minute. "Okay. I'm going to take a nap."

"I guess I should too," he said.

"Yeah."

"Yup."

I watched him polish off the glass then methodically wash it out in the sink. He offered me a neutral smile when he passed me to head into the living room and start making his pallet on the couch. I put my hands on my hips and sighed.

He was already asleep when I walked back through and into the guest room. Crys dozed evenly on the bed, and I quietly shut the door so as not to disturb her. When I snuggled up next to her, she exhaled a long breath and settled back into the pocket created by my body. Her fingers entwined into mine and brought my arm over her shoulder. I kissed her softly on the back of the neck and put my head down.

I couldn't close my eyes.

27.

NO QUARTER

We left on schedule at 2:00 in the morning.

I'd chosen a dark pair of slacks and a forest green sweater shirt to wear under my leather jacket. Rick wore his customary pair of black jeans, dark shirt, and gray jacket. Both of us sported black caps pulled tightly down over our hair. I made sure we had all the equipment we'd need packed safely in the trunk, and Rick switched Crys' license plates with the ones he'd lifted from the car in Henkel's apartment lot.

Rick volunteered to drive for the first leg of the trip, cranking up the car. On my way to the passenger side door, I saw Crys appear in the front door of Doc's house. She was wrapped only in one of my blue button-downs, arms clasped around her midsection to fight off the early morning chill. I took a couple of steps toward her.

"I'll be back tonight," I said. "Maybe the party'll still be on."

"I'll keep it on for you," Crys told me.

"That would be sweet."

"Yeah. Hey, Jack?"

"Yeah, Crys?"

Her blue eyes twinkled at me from the glow of the porch light.

"I love you, Jack."

I paused three paces away from her, hands in my pockets.

"I think..."

"No." She came down the steps and put a finger on my lips. "You can tell me when you get back."

My eyes blinked a long slow blink as her finger slid down my lips and chin. I resisted the urge to touch her.

"Okay," was all I said.

We took our time getting to Jackson, stopping once in Collins for gas and plenty of snacks to last us. It was going on four o'clock when we rolled past the I-20 intersection on 49 and headed off toward the PetroJet plant.

"It's down there," I said, pointing for Rick to turn off the highway.

"Anything in particular you're looking for?" he asked me.

"No. Just wanted to see."

The side road that diverted off from Highway 49 coasted through a large forest of evergreens. A couple dirt roads led off from the road every so often, probably to small cottages worked back into the woods. We passed a sign that sported PetroJet's company logo, and Rick decelerated as light began to break through the limbs of the trees.

The entire plant was encircled by a large fence. No barbed wire, though. The woods in the area looked like they had been gutted in order to erect the plant squat in the middle. The ground turned from pine needles to a dusty gravel which characterized the entire area of the plant. A couple of smokestacks rose into the dark morning sky further off down the property, belching small streams of fire and smoke. There was a clear line of demarcation between the propane tanks and the refinery, as if the compound's geography was split by its respective exports. An office building stood off to our left at the southern edge of the fence. We could see a couple of tractor-trailer transports loading and unloading product from various points within the plant.

"See enough?" Rick asked after a couple of minutes.

"The Lord giveth," I said, "and the Lord taketh away."

"Amen" Rick said.

Rick dropped me off in downtown Jackson around five in the morning. We'd stopped at a Dunkin' Donuts somewhere at the I-20/I-55 interchange and gotten some breakfast, and Rick stocked up with glazed for his stakeout. Once sated, we had driven into the crumbling metropolis before us, and I headed out by myself onto the streets.

Mississippi's capital city, Jackson, exuded its old-world charm in unfortunate dreary dilapidation. Once great Deco buildings that rivaled those of New Orleans had since fallen into disrepair and disuse, classically sculptured buttresses broken and crumbling over walls sporting three coats of perpetually fading paint and a poetry book's collection of graffiti. Warehouses downtown were being reclaimed and turned into condos and business centers, hoping to attract new generational talent to an area that reeked of social decay. If you looked hard enough, you could still see bloodstains on some parts of the pavement. I don't know if it ever was and they were just lying about it, but I can't imagine Johnny and June Carter Cash would want to go to here today.

Going by directions I had scribbled down on a sheet of paper, I walked for about twenty minutes through several blocks of the west downtown area, making my way past new restaurants that would never make it and abandoned southern fried food joints until I found a gleaming new condominium complex in the distance. Confirming the street name and number, I scouted the complex and located the appropriate building. A tan Camry was parked in the residents' lot.

Snacking on an Almond Joy, I reconnoitered the complex for an hour, learning every in and out. There was a gate onto the property, but I managed to skulk close by to catch someone driving in and keying their access code. Pretending to be a groundskeeper fiddling with the bushes, I memorized the code and wrote it down on my spare notepad once the car had entered the complex. I started a leisurely walk around the block, checking my watch every few minutes.

It wasn't until a little before nine that I saw her come down the stairs from the second building. I hid myself behind a newspaper stand across the street and waited until the Camry pulled out, concealing my visage behind the morning edition of *The Jackson Star*. I waited another fifteen minutes before returning to the condo gate and entering.

Her condo was on the third floor of the second building, opposite only one other unit on that level. After listening for a few seconds at the other door, I determined that her neighbors were either absent or asleep. Turning to her door, I removed the two small lockpicks that Rick had given me and set to work. Rick had studied picking locks from a senior covert methods of entry instructor at the FBI Academy, and for all of the complaining I'd done earlier, it seemed pretty easy once you got the feel for it. We had practiced on Doc Faller's house locks several times Tuesday until I had it down straight. The key to doing it right and not bending your picks lay in feeling the all the tumblers inside the lock on a single, flexible strip of metal then tripping them in such a way that they thought they fell into the appropriate holes, thus opening the lock. As luck had it, the tougher part of the job was already done, as Liz had not thought to use the bolt lock, which would have required a different set of tools with which to shimmy and jive. I worked the tiny little devices inside the doorknob just as Rick had shown me, and I managed to get inside the condo in under three minutes.

Elizabeth Finley's flat looked about as luxurious as it could be for the location. The condos had been built only a few years before, new gentrified additions attempting to revitalize a dying downtown Jackson, and it looked like Liz had been the first occupant. The foyer led into a vast living area that adjoined a kitchen and dining room, and two glass double doors led onto the balcony outside. It was a pretty spacious place and immaculately decorated. Prints and portraits of meaningless things and anonymous people adorned the white walls, and matching maroon furniture dotted the living area along with a polished coffee table. Her entertainment center had been built into the wall and featured a thirty-six inch screen television and what looked like a top of the line stereo system. I couldn't see any CDs.

I found the bureau in the guest bedroom, which Elizabeth had converted into a study of sorts. My gloved hands moved at an even pace as I went through drawers, methodically inventorying everything she had filed. The lower drawer contained a file cabinet setup, and I leafed through the documents finding titles, insurance papers, bank statements, and other paraphernalia. Taking an empty folder from the back of the files, I sat down in the chair before the bureau and unbuttoned my jacket. I removed the faxes Deckhead had sent me from another folder I had jammed in the waistband of my pants. Arranging the files in some semblance of order, I set them in the new folder from Elizabeth's desk and replaced the folder in the files. I debated its position and ended up settling for sticking it at the extreme center of the cabinet, just behind all the other marked folders and in front of the empty ones.

I took a slow look around the condo on my way back to the door. Everything there stunk of money. Priceless vases. Original framed artwork. Upscale furniture. I was tempted to rifle through a few more closets and drawers, maybe break something. But I resisted. Ultimately, I spit on the floor, locked the door from the inside, and left.

Rick picked me up an hour later at a coffee shop three blocks downtown.

"Finley left at eight-thirty," Rick said once we were back on the road. "I assume the wife is still inside. She hasn't shown her face. A maid came by just before I left to come pick you up. Figure three to four hours for her to do the cleaning thing, and she's gone."

I checked my watch. "So let's be safe and say five o'clock. I read in the newspaper that this cloud cover we're getting is going to pick up later this afternoon. That means we should have a reasonable level of dark come five."

"How was the insertion?"

"Five by five."

"Cool. Want some chow?"

"I'm game."

The Greyhaven subdivision contained eight houses arranged on three blocks in a pocket seemingly carved from Highway 49 into the forest. The subdivision owners must have striven for a rustic look because each of the manses sported a similar red brick and wrought iron fence design. Southern Mississippians admired the classic New Orleans style, often altering their architecture appropriately to leave out the Gothic elements and create what Doc Faller referred to as the "rich redneck" style.

Rick told me that he had had a tough time locating an appropriate stakeout point. The block that the Finley home occupied was a basic square, leaving only the curb as a possibility to park the car. Unfortunately, Crys' dilapidated Oldsmobile didn't exactly jibe with the SUVs and Lexii driving in and out of Greyhaven. However, most of the homes across the street from Finley's house cultivated huge pines in their front yards. One house only two lots down sported two of the huge trees with multitudes of low-hanging branches. Rick indicated that he had driven by only twice before taking a spot in front of that home. It was only when we returned that he realized that no one was home at that house, and we took the chance of backing the Olds into the manse's driveway. We had an almost clear view caddy-corner to the Finley home.

I let Rick grab a nap while I took watch. By the time we had concealed ourselves in the pine tree house's driveway, the overcast sky had given way to great billowing clouds, coming in south from the Gulf. I absently hoped for no rain as the presence of anything wet might ruin the plan for that night. But as I sat in the driver's seat, snacking on a Slim Jim and listening to Billy Joel extol the virtues of "Modern Woman," I realized that it really wouldn't make much difference after a certain point.

"Hey." I slapped Rick's chest hard enough to rouse him. "That him?"

"What is it?" Rick said groggily as he straightened his seat.

"Looks like a Suburban of some kind."

My partner rubbed his eyes beneath the wire frame glasses and peered out into the darkness. Two large headlights came from Greyhaven's entrance, silhouetting a large frame vehicle as they turned to enter the Finleys' circular driveway. As the truck parked in front of the house, Rick smacked his lips.

"That's him."

Bill Finley got out of the Suburban, a briefcase gripped loosely in one hand. The light afforded by the porch outlined the man in his suit, and even though I couldn't see his face, I knew it was him. He had the same build as the man I'd met in Magee, the same confident swagger. I mused to myself as I watched the force with which Finley used to slam the truck door shut and the purposeful stagger with which he took the front stairs.

"He looks pissed," Rick observed.

"His wife's been home all day," I said. "Probably drinking. If Liz didn't lie about that... I'd be a little PO'd too if my honey was sucking the drinky winky all day and it was my job to clean her up when I came home."

"How should we get her out of the house? Phone call?"

"Maybe. Let's give it another couple of hours before we call, though."

Rick shifted in his seat. "Hey. Remember what Crys asked us the other day? About what we wanted to be?"

"Yeah."

"I don't think I want to be in the FBI, Jack."

I looked over at my brother. "Rick, you...you haven't been an agent that long."

He looked out his window. I could see the fog patterns his breath made on the chilly glass. "Yeah. I have."

I turned down the radio. It was only Three Dog Night. "Rick, look. If you want to scrub this thing—"

"It's not this, Jack. Not really. It's just..." His lips compressed into a thin line. "Your girlfriend's a wise woman."

I looked at the dashboard clock, thinking that Crys and Doc would just be getting ready for the party. "Yeah. But she ain't my girlfriend."

"Hey. Can I have one of your cigarettes?"

"Really? You want a smoke?"

"Yeah."

"Okay." I passed him the pack. "We should keep the windows up."

"I know," Rick said, taking the cancer stick and looking at it.

"You're starting to scare me now, buddy," I said. "Last time you had a cigarette, we were in eighth grade, and you almost had a conniption fit in the park on Hyacinth Drive."

"Consider my lungs seasoned by time."

Rick lit up and took a deep inhalation of the cigarette. After a few moments of watching him to make sure he wouldn't vomit, I struck up one of my own. It got very cloudy inside the Olds so I risked cracking the windows.

We waited in silence for another two hours, watching for telltale signs of activity from the Finley house. Every once in a while, a light would come on in some portion of the house and eventually go out after a while. After two hours, I was reaching for my cell phone when the front door opened.

A woman in gaudy accouterments stumbled uncertainly out of the house. Her heels clattered on the brick porch as she struggled to get into the Suburban. I could see a long mink coat of some sort draped about her shoulders, and a glittery purse dangled from one of her hands. Finley appeared in the light on the porch, his tie loosened and his sleeves rolled up, a glass of something in one hand. He did not look pleased.

"Thanksgiving at the Finleys," Rick said, stubbing out his third cigarette in the ashtray.

"He don't seem too pleased with his lady, huh?" I snickered.

We couldn't hear anything, but it was obvious that the couple was engaged in some kind of argument. Mrs. Finley stumbled a few more times before getting into the Suburban, and Finley himself just looked on combatively from his position inside the front door. Finally, the Suburban started up and pulled jerkily out of the driveway, making a rut in an otherwise immaculate front lawn as it skipped the curb. Finley shook his head, slammed the door and disappeared back inside.

"Good call, detective," Rick told me.

"I am a keen observer of the human condition," I said. "You ready?"

"Better now than never. Hit me with the particulars again."

"Propane tank should be buried somewhere close to the air conditioning unit on the back side of the house or sitting aboveground very obviously. If he *is* rigged for propane. Pop the concrete slab, you'll see the exchange manifold. Flip the coolant control valve off and open up the liquid compression handle to full. If it's not marked, just use your best guess. The only difference is the size of the explosion."

Rick opened the door. "Be back in a second."

I popped the trunk for him as he got out. Rick made great care with noise control as he shut the door and started fiddling with our equipment in the trunk. After a few minutes, he shut the trunk and headed out onto the street. I watched him crouch behind one of the trees in the house's yard, taking stock of the street. After a few minutes, he disappeared into the night, slinking along the fence and treeline between Finley's house and his neighbor's.

I waited for forty maddening minutes, wondering whether or not Rick had adequately pulled off the prep for the last phase of our plan. I could discern no further movement from inside the house during that time, and I tightened my grip on the steering wheel. It didn't help that the local radio station had chosen to play Stevie Ray Vaughan's "Crossfire" and an abysmal cover of "Cold Shot" back to back in that space of time.

Rick appeared again from the same shadow that he had descended into earlier. I made out the brim of his cap across the street as he surveyed the street. Satisfied that he was safe from prying eyes, he darted back across to the safety of the pines in our chosen hidey-hole. A few minutes more and he was back inside the Olds.

"Problem?" I asked.

"He was in the kitchen when I got back there," Rick said, his breathing a little rushed. "The HVAC's right under the kitchen window which faces the backyard. I had to wait until he left."

"The tank?"

"Got it. I think I got it right. Now that shit you told me to do is going to gum up the pipes in the house?"

I nodded. "It should. I'm not all that up on natural gas power sources, but the idea is that LP gas has to stay cooled in order to keep it gaseous. No coolant, ergo liquid. And all I need is a couple of drops."

"Okay, I put a slit in the pressure hose off to the side of the exchange valve," Rick said, taking off his gloves. "The buildup should be well enough to light up when the house goes. But you've got to remember to get a clear line of fire from the house to the tank cover. I strung the fuse wire from the manifold all the way up to the kitchen window. All you need to do is make sure the fire gets to that fuse, and it's the Genesis Project all over again."

I popped my knuckles. "Not a problem."

Rick shook his head, chuckled, and put a hand on my shoulder, mock serious. "This is my first arson, so be mindful of my tender pussy, baby."

"Mine, too." It was nice to smile for once. "I'll go slow."

At nine-thirty, I exited the car and dug around our equipment in the trunk. We had three guns between us: Two of the cobbled-together .357s and Henkel's .44. Rick cracked the window as I walked up, and I slid one of the .357s into his gloved hand.

"If I feel the heat, I'll put three quick shots up in the air," he said. "Make sure you can hear them."

"Deal." I stuck the other .357 in my jacket pocket and held the .44 loosely in my right hand. The fabric of the tight gloves irritated my injured fingers, but I pushed past it. Pain was a good friend of mine by now.

"Hey," Rick said, grabbing for my hand. "You be careful in there, brother."

"I will." We grasped hands tightly. "Rick... you're my man, man."

He nodded slowly, and I tossed my cap into the car. Running a hand through the matted down strands of bleached hair, I exhaled a hot wisp into the air and looked across the street. Feeling the chill of the night air brought on by the billowing clouds, I headed off toward the Finley home.

I placed four hard knocks on the door and stood close to it, the .44 held steadily in my right hand like a solitary support on a buckling ship. Oddly enough, there was no fear in my gut, no iciness inside my blood. There was nothing. Only what seemed like a low pitch of white noise in my ears and the comforting hardness of the weapon's grip in my palm.

The door opened, and he was there. Eyes wide, mouth drawn. A glass of wine in one hand. I think the tie might have been Stripling and Cox.

"Let's go inside," I told William Thomas Finley.

28.

SOUTHERN AGGRESSION

The closing of the door made a sharp snap.

"Set the glass down on the table and put your hands on the back of your head."

Bill Finley did as he was told, instantly setting the wineglass down on the oak wood table next to the door. The foyer spread widely in all directions, giving me an ample view of a den to the left and a dining room to the right. The floors exuded the sheen of brightly polished timber, light in color and covered intermittently by great Chinese rugs. More than a few portraits of the distinguished Finley clan adorned the cream striped wallpaper walls.

"Jack Dooley, isn't it?" Finley said, his voice a touch above the amused. "I didn't recognize you at first with your hair all done up."

"Shut up and turn around," I said, patting him down. I took his wallet out of his back pocket and slipped it into my jacket. The cold barrel of the gun nudged against the nape of his neck, and I could see hairs stand up.

"Take me on a tour of your house, Mister Finley."

I pushed him into the dining room and took stock of the surroundings. As we crossed the room, I started snapping off each table lamp that we passed.

"Jack, I have to admit, this is my first holdup," Finley said, the serpentine nature of his voice reasserting itself. "And in my own home, no less."

"First time for everything, Mister Finley," I said, jerking him around and pushing him back through the foyer and into the den. There, I switched off some more lights until the only glow from the front portion of the house came from the lights outside over the porch. "What's through here?"

"My study. I *was* doing a little work until you came barreling in."

"Check yourself, Mister Finley. I don't barrel."

I appraised the study for a moment, looking over Finley's shoulder. A well-crafted Indian desk took up most of the space near windows that overlooked the backyard. A fireplace resided in the brick wall to our left, bookshelves carved and molded all around it and thick with leather-bound hardbacks. A sofa and some chairs completed the homey picture as well as a large mirror on the wall opposite the fireplace. I pushed Finley through the doorway next to the mirror and found myself in a washroom. Opening doors and careful not to let the gun's barrel leave Finley's neck, I cleared the pantry area and made for the kitchen.

"This is a bit of a surprise, Jack," Finley said, grunting as I shoved him around the kitchen. "I never thought you'd have the ambition for something this daring."

"Well, we're all a little surprising under that polished veneer face we put on in the morning, huh, Mister Finley?" I jabbed the gun deeper into his neck, hearing him wince. The beats underneath my chest started to come closer together, and I had to stop for a moment to refocus. "What's upstairs?"

"The master bedroom, bath," Finley said, and I could hear the slightest trace of fear in his voice. "Guest room, library, workout room."

"Show me."

Holding him at gunpoint, I let Finley lead me upstairs and through each room of the second floor. I opened a few closet doors here and there to make sure nobody was hiding out. After a few minutes of quiet inspection, I decided that the house was reasonably clear of any occupants besides myself and Finley. I tapped the gun against Finley's skull as we headed back downstairs.

"Nice digs, dickhead. Does ripping people off really pay that well?"

"Jack, I'm sure I don't know. I'm an honest businessman."

This time I let the heartbeats overwhelm my vision, the blood in my ears, everything. I landed a quick strike to the base of his neck with the butt of the gun. Finley cried out this time, his legs buckling. I pulled him up before he could fall and slammed his face down on the cold tile of the cooking island in the kitchen. The white noise got louder.

"Don't fucking lie to me, Finley!" I hissed in his ear. "I'm *way* beyond the bullshit now, and if you haven't figured that out by now, then it's time to wake the fuck up."

"Okay, okay, okay!" Finley shouted, an edge of desperation behind the quickness of his words. "All right, Jack, you're in control here."

I shoved him back down again onto the island, seeing the stovetop just a few inches away. Keeping the gun buried in the back of his head, I reached over and flipped on the stove controls. I had to shake my head to clear the encroaching bloodlust in my eyes, but I peered close enough to see that the gas stove did not start hissing. Instead, thick droplets of fluid began to ooze slowly from the pilot ports under the grilles. I reached under each grille and ripped out the lighting mechanism, making sure no accidental flare-ups would occur. I told Finley to stay still, holding the gun on him as I moved to the window over the kitchen sink. Undoing the latch, I pushed the window up and felt around the outside brick wall below for Rick's fuse. It had been duct taped perfunctorily to the wall, and I ripped it loose, pulling it inside and re-taping it to the window sill. Shutting the window again and leaving the fuse wire sticking out from under the jamb, I moved back over to Finley.

"Okay, let's go." Finley grunted again as I jerked him up and pushed him back through the washroom and into the study. He struggled to keep his hands locked behind his head and eventually gave up when I pushed him to the floor.

"Okay, okay, no need to get rough, Jack," Finley sputtered, touching the welt I'd given him on his neck. "I'll cooperate."

"How diplomatic of you," I spat. I pulled the blinds down on the windows behind Finley's desk and went to the fireplace. I found the propane nozzle behind the faux wood setup and cranked it up to full. More droplets of congealed LP started leaking out of the nozzle.

"Jack, listen, we can make a deal here," Finley said, struggling into a sitting position on the floor. I saw that his face was neutral save for a slight curl to the left side of his mouth. "I'm perfectly willing to discuss your obvious... *grievances* with me."

"Well, that's a good thing, Bill," I said, moving over to the desk and muting the small television set up there. I checked to make sure it was tuned to a local network. "Because we've got a lot to talk about tonight."

"You're obviously angry about what happened to your uncle," Finley said, his arms out, palms flat, as he got to his feet. "That can unhinge anyone, Jack. Having that happen to a loved one."

"Easy there, Blurr," I said, hefting the gun at him. Finley froze. "Move over to the fireplace and stand there. Keep your hands where I can see them."

"Jack, this isn't going to solve anything," Finley said as he did as he was told. "You and I both know that murder isn't an option here."

"Oh, we do, do we?" I chuckled and sat down in the leather office chair behind the desk. "And what else do you know about me, Mister Finley? Hmm? Can you *enlighten* an obviously wayward and misguided young fuck like me?"

Finley's smile dripped bile, and I was tempted to shoot him right there. But I let him speak, knowing that the doublespeak I was about to hear was what I'd come for in the first place.

"Jack, you have to understand that all this mess you've gotten involved in is just business, all right?" Finley said. "You understand that. It's like a couple kids who decide the block isn't big enough for the both of them, and they race to see who's going to get the bigger piece of property."

"In your case, Dooley Petroleum is that bigger piece of property," I said. "And Wolverton's. And whoever else you've fucked over in the past ten years."

"Oh, it's more than that, Jack." Finley paused to look around him. I hefted the gun again. "It all boils down to simple economic superiority."

"Corporate Darwinism?" I said. "He who has the biggest dick does the fucking?"

"Something like that." I could see the smile start to spread on his face. "You see, it's never enough to remain competitively stable in one working environment. All that is is stagnation. You understand? It's like willingly submitting to your own apathy."

I reached into my jacket and withdrew my cigarettes. "So where does the part about stealing seven hundred grand from Carter Dooley and nearly killing him figure into the picture?"

Finley's demeanor darkened somewhat. I saw a little of the steam deflate from his posture. "Jack, I have no personal grudge against your uncle. What happened was simply a...a... misunderstanding."

I clicked back the hammer on the .44, an unlit cigarette perched between the fingers of my left hand. "Mister Finley. Let's get this bullshit over with, okay? I know you had a deal with Al Henkel to steal product from DPI. I know your stockbrokers have been filching funds from DPI's portfolio. I know you've been funneling the money through a judge named Schiedle in Alabama. And I know a few of the *paisanos* down on the coast who've been the lucky recipients of your laundering."

I let it sit with him for a moment. Finley's face remained immobile, unflinching. When he spoke, it was with a tone more acerbic than before. "There's no proof of that. Any of it. It's just circumstantial speculation."

"It may be migraine masturbation for all I care, Bill. The point is, this isn't a court of law." I pointed the gun at him again. "And Mister Forty-Four here isn't your usual jury."

Finley held up his hands. "Jack, you're upset. Listen, I understand. Let me explain."

"I'm waiting." I grinned and lit the cigarette.

"Do I engage in some illegal activities as part of my business practices?" Finley said, touching his heart. "Of course I do. Every big time CEO does. When it comes to things like gutting a rival company's stock options or—or diverting product from their stores... if you know you can get away with it, *you do it.* It's business, Jack. Your uncle does it, too."

"My uncle doesn't have one of his drivers plant explosives on competitors' bulk storage tanks and sabotage their production," I shot back. "Not to mention putting those same competitors in the *hospital.*"

"All right." Finley looked at the floor. Then he looked back up at me with a careless grimace. "All right! Yes, I had Henkel blow the tanks at DPI. It was the last thing I needed to do to ensure that Carter Dooley would sell. With enough misfortune, I was hoping he'd get sufficiently apathetic about the business and sell out."

"To you." I blew a stream of smoke at him. "Just like Wolverton."

"Yes, if you want to look at it like that." Finley pointed at me. "What you see as wrong, I see as business, Jack. This is how it's done up north, with the big companies like Transcoast and Occidentopolis. You see an opportunity, and you *take it.*"

"That's all?" I laughed, unable to contain my amusement. I opened my arms wide in a devil-may-care expression. "This is all it's about? You want to rub elbows with fat cats? In the *NORTH?!*" I said it like *"nawth,"* like Foghorn Leghorn would. Like we do down South.

"Finley, here's an insight for ya: You're a big fish in a little pond. You think you can run the local yokels around here just because you went to better schools and learned more than they did."

Finley folded his arms, grinning from ear to ear. "You said it yourself, Jack. Corporate Darwinism."

"Except in your case, you're just a Mississippi boy!" I shot back. "Just how far up the ladder do you expect to climb in *this* burnt-out place? Sure it's easy to fuck these people. I do it all the time. I'm from elsewhere, too. But at least I know where I am and *why I'm not hot shit.*"

"Is that so?" Finley's tongue touched his upper lip. "Is that what you told my daughter?"

The white noise came back.

It blocked out everything else.

I was on my feet and around the desk before I could even acknowledge the speed of its enclosure. I forced myself to ease the hammer back, to stop before the plan was completed. Finley stood stock still, savoring his victory, his eyes piercing into me and performing cannibalistic Viking rituals on the remains of the soul I used to have.

"Let's talk about Liz," I bit out. "Or Elizabeth. Or Betsy. Or whatever you happen to call her on any particular day of the week."

Finley raised his hands again and paced the length of the fireplace. "I can see she had an effect on you, Jack. You must have loved her very much."

I raised the gun again. "She's good, Finley. But she's not *that* good. At least now I can see where she gets it from."

"You know, the funny thing is how accidental all of this took place," he said, chuckling. "I really didn't even realize the irony until Elizabeth told me that you two had attended Southern at the same time."

"Yeah, it's pretty funny, isn't it?" I could feel blood start to form from where my teeth ground into the gums. "Why me? Why sic her on me?"

"You were in the way, Jack," Finley said, pausing to drive it on home to me forcefully. "After committing securities fraud, after authorizing industrial sabotage and attempted murder do you even *fathom* that I blinked twice to have you taken out of the picture? Jack, you were a nuisance. I knew it from the moment I set eyes on you in Magee. Granted, I thought mistakenly at the time that you were acting on the behalf of your father. You might even consider that something of a blessing since Duke Dooley was going to be the next person I had taken out of the way."

The hammer clicked back. Suddenly, the Bond villain in front of me became something much more. "You son of a bitch..."

"Oh, *grow up, Jack*!" The force of the shout caused me to flinch. Finley stepped forward a pace, brandishing a finger at me like some kind of warrior Roman sword. "What do you want to hear? That this all could have been avoided? That there was something you could have done to stop it? Jack, you are here right now, standing in my study, because *I had the will to see these things through*. Because I don't back down when a tough decision comes across my desk. Unlike *you* who dawdled about blindly with my daughter while I hurt your uncle."

Some of the iron in my legs went away. I had to step back. "No. No, don't you even think about putting this on me, motherfucker."

Finley took another step toward me, his arms raised outward in a grand gesture of benediction. "Corporate Darwinism, Jack. Who has the balls to do what the other man won't? It's not your fault that you weren't prepared for this. It's simply an issue of the better man holding the cards at the end of the game."

It was exactly the wrong thing to hear. The same thing I'd been telling myself for weeks. The thing that I had feared from the outset. I could almost hear the little voice inside me crying out, "Fail! Fail! *Fail!*"

But that wasn't the only voice I was listening to at that moment.

"Do you love it?"

"Dwell in the place I told you about."

"Anger management."

I lowered the gun and took two steps back.

"Back the fuck up, Bill," I said. "And get those hands up."

Finley paused, suddenly aware of the close proximity between us. He looked around for a moment, unsure of what to do. Eventually, he did as he was told, raising his hands and stepping backwards until his heels touched the brick of the fireplace.

"All right, Jack, all right," he said. "It's okay."

"Yes, it is, Mister Finley." I took a last puff on the cigarette and put it out against his desk, grinding it to nothingness and making sure no stray embers reached the pool of liquefied propane that leaked out of the fireplace. Finley was not pleased.

"That's a five thousand dollar desk, young man." His words strong, firm.

"And this was a free .44, old man," I said, raising the gun again. "I took it off your man Henkel when I beat the shit out of him the other day. Oh? Didn't know about that, eh? Wondering why he wasn't answering the phone? Too bad really..."

I crossed back around to the desk and half-sat on the edge, casting a glance at the television. "He and his friends will not be heard from again. I don't take too kindly to home invasion."

Finley's eyes narrowed. "You killed them?"

I shrugged, smiling. "Can't say for sure. I had some friends who specialize in 'personal blood vessel punctuation' see to them. I'm sure they're in good hands now, though. You should also know that your judge friend, Schiedle, is going to be out on secondary income in a few days. After all, with no one to pick up his accumulated hot money, he might make for an interesting target for a bribery probe."

I could see that he was having trouble grasping it. "What do you mean, no one picking up the money?"

"Well, I visited a friend of mine on the coast a while ago," I said, jubilant now. "Warned him that his buddies better pull up stakes soon so as not to get caught in the cloud of shit that goes flying when their partner's stock scheme dries up. I wonder how that made them feel? All cut out of the loop like that? Wow. Have you heard from them lately? Any of them?"

Finley just stared at me. His jaw was clenched quite tightly.

"No? Any?"

He remained silent.

"Well. What a shame." I snapped my fingers. "Hey! I've got a great idea."

I pulled the phone from one side of Finley's desk and slid it toward him. I picked up the unit and handed it to him, indicating the keypad.

"Why don't you call Elizabeth, Mister Finley?" I said, letting the smile envelop me. "That's right. Call her up and tell her to drag her old bones down here. It's Thanksgiving, isn't it? Families should be together on Thanksgiving."

Finley took the phone and touched the keypad. "You want me to call my daughter?"

I held up the gun again. "Call her and tell her to come over immediately. Don't tell her I'm here. Don't indicate anything more than a father wanting his Nazi daughter to drop by for some new orders. Hmm? Get it? Or do I have to shoot you in the foot first?"

Finley sucked on his lip and started dialing, averting his gaze from my glare. I kept the gun firmly in his field of vision.

"Hello?" he said, straightening. "Elizabeth, it's your father. Oh, the usual. No rest for the weary, I'm afraid. Yes, honey, even on the holidays. That's why I'm calling. Could you stop by the house for a minute? Yes, I have some... something important to talk to you about. Yes, it's very important, dear."

I nudged him with the .44. His eyes looked kind of shaky in their sockets.

"Well, you can always go back, right? I'm afraid this can't wait, Elizabeth. Yes. Right now. Okay, honey. Thank you. I love you, too. Bye bye."

Finley looked at me uncertainly as he set the phone down in its cradle. "She's on her way. Listen, we can deal with Elizabeth later, right? We should—"

I patted Finley's cheek with the gun, causing him to recoil and step back from me a few paces. My exhortations became harried and mad, the ravings of a lunatic. "Oh, come on, big daddy! Get on the love train! It's family night at the Sizzler!"

While Finley moved back toward the fireplace, I sat back down on the desk and trained the gun on him. He seemed baffled and more than a little bit on edge now. I could see a nervous tic developing under his right eye.

"Hey, I just remembered. Do you know what time it is?"

Finley looked at his watch, mindful to keep his hands open and in plain view. "Ten-fifteen."

"On the dot? Cool." I slid down the desk and grabbed the small television on the corner. Spinning it around so that he could see, I turned off the mute function. It looked like come kind of local news was about to start up.

"You live pretty close to the PetroJet plant, don't you?" I asked. "Like only a few miles? That make you nervous at all?"

"Greyhaven's well away from the danger zone of a plant accident," Finley said, his eyes darting back and forth from the TV to me to the gun. "What are you—?"

"Hush. Hush." I waved the gun at him. "It shouldn't be long now. I had your friend Henkel do up a nice little show for you tonight."

I could see from his peaked eyebrows that Finley had no idea what I was talking about. That was fine. The suspense was good enough for me.

"Bill, there's one thing that you forgot to factor into all of this," I said, grinning at him again, chatting amiably for all intents and purposes. "There was one person—just *one*—who maybe had a little bit more will to go a little bit farther than you."

The perplexed look on Finley's face deepened, and he looked at the TV again. "What? If this is some kind of—"

A slight tremor shook the house. Finley looked around in confusion as the glass rattled in its pane. The tremor rolled into a series of pops and burblings, and if one wasn't as in the know as folks like myself and Finley, they would easily pass it off as thunder. After all, there was a cloud system hanging over Jackson at that very moment.

"Wow," I said, making a shocked face. "I wonder what that was."

I could see that Finley was still trying to puzzle it out. "The news said clouds tonight, but no rain," I said conversationally. "Damn. That's some freaky ass shit, man. You have any idea what that slight disturbance was, Mister Finley?"

Something broke on Finley's face, and he looked at his watch again. And at the TV. At the gun. At me. It was 10:21. In the PM.

"You couldn't have..." he breathed.

I tipped my head to one side, eyes wide. "I dunno, bud..."

"But... but..."

I shushed him again, and made him wait. The sweat started to appear on his brow again. I sat leisurely on the desk, the gun propped up on my knee and pointed at Finley's midsection. After a few minutes, the telltale hints of sirens could be heard over the low buzz of the newscaster on the television. Finley cocked his head, hearing it a few seconds after I did. When he looked back at me, his jaw was slack and his eyes were empty.

"Not the plant..."

"Ah! Here we go!" I said, seeing the "SPECIAL BULLETIN" sigil appear on the TV screen after a few more minutes. I turned up the volume on the set and settled in, motioning Finley around so he could better see the screen.

"This just in from our emergency contacts in the South Jackson Fire Department," the anchorwoman was saying, eyes straying to a piece of paper someone had set before her. "There has been an explosion in south Jackson tonight, just a few minutes ago. Fire and paramedic sources report that the incident has taken place at the PetroJet Chemical plant off Highway 49 and I-20. We don't have any further information, but sources say that the police are on the scene and are blocking off traffic leading to the plant. We'll have more as news develops."

I glanced over at Finley. He had turned white as a sheet.

"An explosion," I said matter-of-factly. "Damn. Doesn't that just beat all?"

"You didn't..." Finley exhaled, hands falling from their surrender position. "Not my *plant*...!"

"Oh, boy, I wish I had, old son," I said, winking and snapping my lips. "But Al Henkel was kind enough to do it for me, though."

Finley looked at me again, the shock developing into something akin to abject outrage. Before he could move, I held up the gun again, letting the sound of the hammer clicking back fill the room.

"PetroJet Chemical is officially out of business," I said. "I hope your wife will understand."

"You maniac son of a bitch," Finley seethed, his teeth bared. "All this just for seven-hundred thousand dollars and a wounded uncle? Are you *insane*? The police will *find* Henkel. They'll find him and he'll talk. He'll talk, and you'll be just as far up the creek as me!"

"Actually, I think old Al's going to be having a tough time forming words from now on," I said, savoring the moment. "Matter of fact, I think my friends said something about making sure he'd be able eat through a straw? Yeah, that was it. A straw."

Finley straightened and pointed at me again. "So you think you've got this all boxed up, huh? That you're clean as a whistle? Son, you're going to—"

I leaped across the distance between us and slammed the gun butt into the bridge of Finley's nose. With all the practice I'd gotten lately, I'd perfected the strike to an art form. Finley squealed as the bone folded, and he dropped to one knee, clutching his nose and wailing as trickles of blood ruined the expensive Stripling and Cox tie and shirt.

"I'm *not* your fucking son," I said evenly. I looked down on him and spat on the back of his neck. Finley made a gurgling noise as he tried to comfort the pain of his splintered nose, and I walked back to the desk to switch off the TV.

"You... you son of a *bitch...*" Finley hissed, looking up.

"Yeah, that too," I said, holding up the gun. "You fucked with the wrong family this time, Finley. And don't think I didn't think hard on what I was going to give you in return for that fucking. I thought, well, he's a rich uppercrust gent of sorts. Maybe I could hire one of my pals of the African persuasion to come over and fuck him in the ass. Hmm? I bet you'd dearly love that, wouldn't ya, Bill? About seven... no, *eight?* Eight inches of big black dick up your ass?"

Finley glowered at me as he got to his feet, pinching his nose to stem the flow of blood. When his eyes had cleared enough to focus solidly, he saw the outstretched gun in my hand and held up a hand.

"Jack, wait..."

"Then I thought, no, that may be a tad too facile for my taste," I said. "What if I... blew up his petroleum plant? Sound good? Well, duh! That sounds fucking *great!*"

I let the gun waver before him, allowing the lunacy in my eyes to shine through. "But it just didn't seem like *enough*, y'know, Bill? So really, what else is there?"

"Jack...!"

The hammer clicked a final time.

"Well," I said, "there's always this."

"Jack, *wait*!" Finley pleaded, this time the desperation clear and evident in his tone. "I can make a deal! I can give you whatever you want! How much? Huh? I've got money. Fuck, I've got millions, Jack!"

I let the gun fall a little bit, posing a questioning glance. "Money, huh? No shit?"

"That's right!" Finley gushed. "How much? Jack, just tell me how much! How much? I can have it here for you *in cash*. Just give me a number!"

"Cash, huh?" I made a face, appearing to think it over. "Wow. Millions?"

Finley's eyes were wide as he nodded. "Yes, whatever you want! However much I've got. Look, I know you're a good kid, Jack. Hell, you've beaten me! See? I admit it. Yes, you've done good, Jack. Hell, I should have somebody like you working for me."

I rested the gun on my shoulder. "Oh, you *should*, should you?"

"Yeah!" The thought seemed to explode in Finley's mind, and his body jerkily fell into a spasm of excitement. "Yes, I could employ you, Jack. Maybe give you a nice *tax-free* salary? Huh? How much? Hundred grand a year? Two? *Three*? Come now, that's a hell of a deal, eh?"

I inclined my head to one side. "Three hundred thousand dollars, huh? Wow. That's a lot of damn money all right. More money than I've ever seen."

"Yes, you said it, Jack." Finley straightened, hands coming away from his bloodied nose. "It's your cake to eat. So what do you say? Do we have a deal, Jack?"

I scratched my chin.

"Mister Finley, you know what really irks me?"

Finley paused. "W-what?"

It popped behind my eyes.

"You haven't called me Mister Dooley all night."

The gunshot echoed throughout the wooden floored house as if a bomb had been detonated inside a bass drum. My eyes blinked convulsively as I squeezed the trigger. My arm didn't even move when the recoil from the .44 lurched up my triceps and biceps.

The bullet blew through the back of Finley's head and bore into the bookshelves around the fireplace. One semi-solid chunk of brain and skull got stuck in between a copy of James Michener's *Texas* and an economics textbook. The force of the blast didn't knock him back immediately like I expected. Instead, Finley's head snapped back along the course of the bullet, and the weight of his now-dead upper body sunk, dragging the rest of him with it. He crumpled into a pile half on top of the fireplace. His knees bent forward as his weight crushed down on top of his lower legs. The entry wound on his forehead trickled a steady stream of blood down his face.

I regarded the dead man's body for a moment after he fell. The .44 smoked briefly, and it took me a while to lower my arm. When I did, I took a few tentative steps forward and looked down into Finley's lifeless eyes. He didn't even have time to be surprised, I think. There was simply *nothing* in there. He could have been a still life portrait if not for the squirts of blood that poured out of the back of his head. The thick goo pooled on the bricks, making drippy noises as it fell in a waterfall pattern down to the floor.

I really didn't know what I was expecting right then. If you'd asked me before that moment whether or not I would really go through with it, I think ultimately I would have told you that I didn't think I was capable of it.

And yet there was the guy. Dead on the floor. By my hand.

Before the nausea could build up inside me, I sat down at the desk and struck up a cigarette.

It must have been some time past eleven when I heard the door open. A thin cloud of smoke hung in the study around me, beating down the rising smell of the decaying body a few feet away. I had made a little pile of ashes and discarded cigarette butts on Finley's five thousand dollar desk. Every time I looked at it, I kept having this weird flashback to that scene in *Close Encounters* when Richard Dreyfuss is making that mountain with the mashed potatoes. After a while, I could have sworn I had gotten up once or twice to look around for a fork.

"Daddy?"

The front door closed. A bolt was closed. Heels click-clacked across the floor.

"In here," I called out.

From where I sat behind the desk, I could see Liz when she came through the den. She had on a decent green number with stockings and a blazer. Purse over her shoulder. Hoop earrings. Hair down. She froze on the Chinese rug when she saw me.

"Jack...?"

"Hi, Liz," I said, putting out my last cigarette. "Is it Liz? What do you prefer? I'm not so clear on that. Elizabeth? Betsy?"

She took another few tentative steps toward the study. "What are you doing here, Jack?"

I wondered if the light in the room caused a shadow to pass over my eyes. It sure did feel like it.

"Ending this."

When she finally did make it into the room, she saw the gun on the desk in front of me. Before her eyes had a chance to widen, she looked the wrong way and saw the face of her dead father staring back at her. The inverted scream tore through her lungs, and her hands came to her mouth as she backed away from the ungainly mess. Finley's head had produced a decent sized blood pool on the floor. His shoes and socks were drenched in it. His hands rested in it. Yeah. He didn't look too good right then.

"Oh, my God..." Elizabeth Finley gasped, the first traces of a deep racking sob escaping her lips.

"Yeah. Looks like shit, doesn't he?" I said, getting to my feet and picking the gun up from the desk. As soon as I moved my hand over the desk, the wisp of wind left in its wake passed over and through the pile of ashes I'd created. The ash blew from top to bottom as it was caught by the drafts of the room. Long billows of cigarette waste danced across the desk and onto the floor, spilling smashed cigarette butts everywhere. I held the gun loosely in my good hand.

"But when you think about it, what really *looks* worse?" I said. "Broken nose and a bullet in the skull? Or a guy beaten up and broken apart from head to toe?"

She had stumbled back up against the sofa and could retreat no further. Her eyes welled with tears as she looked from her father to me. I stood not far from her, the .44 held down.

"How does it feel, Liz?" I said quietly. "To have a loved one attacked mercilessly in a place where he should have been safe?"

Her face started to regain its color as she looked at me and held. "You killed him."

I nodded. "I did."

"You bastard," she bit out, real anger rising inside her now. I had to give her props for that at least.

"Yup," I said. "You like my hair?"

"You bastard!"

She came at me with both her fists raised and balled up. I took two quick steps back and raised the gun again, the sight of which stopped her cold. The sobering reality of the situation struck her hard, and she froze, lowering her arms. But the anger in her eyes remained the same.

"He never..." she said, another burst of tears welling up in eyes that pinned me with roiling fury. "He didn't..."

"What?" I said. "*What?* He didn't *deserve* it? He didn't fucking do anything to me? *Huh?* Liz, what could you possibly say to make me believe that *this son of a bitch did not deserve every last millimeter of steel I put into his fucking brain?!*"

My exhortation shook me from head to toe, rocking me out of that particular plane of existence for a moment. It took me a second to reorient myself, to come back. When I returned, the white noise was there to comfort me. Liz hadn't moved but she was still seething at me, her breathing increasing to hyperventilation levels.

"You fucking...," I said, the last bit of feeling I had in me going into the declaration. "Can you even acknowledge it? Hmm? Fathom it? *Believe* it?"

She remained silent, looking at me with those same eyes I had drown myself in at Dewey's. Had become lost inside at The Beau Rivage. Had let myself believe were for me.

"I would have loved you," I whispered. "I would have. Really. Maybe it wasn't enough to compare to the dollar signs that Daddy was feeding you, but I believed it, Liz. The whole time..."

"I didn't come to Hattiesburg just to set you up, Jack," Liz broke in, trembles in her voice. "I really did like you when we met. I did."

"But that wasn't enough, was it? Daddy's pocketbook a little more tempting? Or was it something else?" I moved in close to her. "Was it just because you *could*? Because you knew I was easy for it?"

She declined to answer.

Her eyes never left mine.

"I never set out to set you up, Jack," she said after a moment, her voice regaining composure. "That night at Dewey's was as innocent as it could ever be."

"Yeah? And exactly *when* did it become not innocent? Hmm? After you casually mentioned to Daddy that you were going out with a Dooley? And what did he say? Oh, I bet that was a helluva fun scene at Finley house!" I laughed, genuinely amused by the track she was trying to put off on me.

"When I told him who you were," Liz said defiantly, looking back at me with steely eyes. "That's when he brought me into his plans with your uncle and DPI. He asked me to... *Told* me to keep seeing you, see what you knew about the DPI operation."

"Until I spelled it all out for you, right?" My eyes met hers. She had to look away after a moment. "And you ran back home to Daddy to request instructions. 'Mission accomplished, Daddy! What are your orders?'"

"It wasn't like that..." she tried to say.

"The hell it wasn't. You didn't even give me time to get a good night's sleep, you bitch. You and your father's *other* good little Nazis just came barreling in to fuck me up." I waited until she looked back at me before dropping the final accusation on her.

"You told them where I lived, Liz. *Where I lived.* You let them wreck my home and stood by doing nothing while they beat the shit out of me."

The truth hung in the air between us, and she looked down. I could see a tear or two cascading down her face. Whether or not she could acknowledge her complicity in the affair was not up to me anymore. I just didn't care.

"You are going to hell for this, Liz," I said. "Even if I was to give you this gun and let you shoot me, you're still going to burn for it."

"How?" she whispered, a plea. "Tell me how, Jack. This was my *father's* idea."

"Really?" I said, unable to make the grin I knew I should have worn. "Then he got off easy. Right now, a sizable amount of money from your father's personal and company accounts has been transferred to a bank in the Caymans with your name on it. Your name, your Social Security number, everything that points to *you*. Anybody looks hard enough, it'll seem like you've been scamming money off your dad for some time now. There's even a little account next to yours with your good friend Al Henkel's name on it."

She blinked, causing a tear to forge a trail through the makeup down her cheek. "Henkel?"

"Yeah." I tilted my head. "You know, the guy your father had you pay off to steal propane from DPI? The guy you conspired with to steal money from your father? The guy you set up to blow up DPI's storage tanks *and* the tanks at PetroJet about an hour ago? No? Doesn't ring a bell?"

I stepped in closer to her, holding the .44 up very close to her face. She shied away a notch, and I leaned in further, smothering her with the image. "How about the guy whose gun you borrowed to kill your father?"

She didn't move when I backed off, remaining frozen in time as her eyes tracked mine. I could smell honeysuckle on her neck.

"So, yeah," I said. "It's done. I'm done with all of this. I'm a changed man. That should be good, right?"

I held the .44 out to her, grip first.

"It's not so good, Liz," I said. "The way you've changed me. Now I can't go back to who I was. To my apartment. My shit. My band. It's all done."

I nudged the butt of the gun against her. "So why don't you take this gun and *really* end it, sweetheart?"

Her head moved an inch downward as she looked at the .44. Her trembling seemed to have stopped, and I realized that I didn't have to make an effort to be still before her. The white noise subsided a little bit. Not much. But enough.

Elizabeth took the gun in both hands, slipping it slowly out of my grasp. I didn't offer any resistance, letting the steel—still warm from its use on Finley—slide easily across the fabric of my gloves. When she had it fully in her grasp, holding it with both hands, I let my arm fall and took a couple steps backwards.

"Go on, Liz," I said, reaching for my cigarettes. "Do us both the favor."

I took my time slipping the cigarette between my lips and lighting it with the Zippo. When I looked up again, she had raised the gun toward me, holding it steadily between sweaty palms, fighting the shakes that accompanied her intent. I drew in a lungful of smoke and exhaled quietly from the side of my mouth.

"Whenever you're ready," I whispered.

Her finger jerked clumsily on the trigger, and the gun wobbled when the hammer clicked. She did it again with more control, trying to right her aim. A third time marked her last attempt. By that squeeze, Liz realized that no bullets were coming out.

I reached into my jacket pocket and grabbed the five remaining bullets that I had emptied from the .44's chamber. Opening my palm, I showed them to her. Her eyes took it in for a second, then her leg faltered. She tried to keep the gun pointed at me anyway as she fell back on the sofa. Tears flowed freely from her eyes now. She pulled the trigger again.

I looked at her again as I took the .357 from my other pocket and held it steadily against my leg. There was nothing left in her eyes, nothing to focus on. She kept pulling the .44's trigger, the hammer clicking on nothing but metal and empty chambers as she tried to keep the barrel pointed up. I blew out another cloud of smoke.

"Goodbye, Liz," I said. "Thanks for all the fish."

I turned around and took a deep breath, inhaling my surroundings and the handiwork I had crafted that night in the Finley house. For a moment, I wondered if Mrs. Finley would go into a psychotic episode when she came home. It probably would depend on a lot of things. Still, I had one more crime left to perpetrate.

The half-burned cigarette flew from my fingertips and landed in the pool of propane that had leaked out of the open valve in the fireplace. Having mixed minutely with Finley's brain blood, the pool took on a strange quality of gray and dark maroon. Hell, I couldn't really tell. I'm colorblind.

The propane flared instantly as the cigarette touched it. All at once, the pool flashed into a bushel of fire that reached around the fireplace and worked its way along the trail of LP gas. I had been more thorough between the time I had shot Finley and the time Liz had arrived. Using a plastic cup I'd found in the kitchen, I'd collected some of the spilled gas and spread it in a definite line from the fireplace to the stove in the kitchen. From there, I'd poured a significant amount of the flammable fuel on the fuse that I'd left sticking out of the window sill. There was a complete circuit now from the fireplace to the stove to the fuse wire that ran outside the house and down into the exchange manifold for the underground storage tank. Within a few minutes, the Finley house would be engulfed in an inferno to rival that of the fires at DPI. Maybe the explosion of the underground tank would be spectacular, shearing off one side of the house. Maybe the safety valves would kick in, and the fire would simply burn the house down. Either way, I was perfectly satisfied. There was plenty of kindling in that wooden house.

I gave Elizabeth Finley a last look as I turned to leave the study. She repeated her useless firing action with the .44, now trying to shoot her dead father. There was nothing there anymore from what I could tell. The eyes were as glassy as the facade of a snowglobe.

I tucked the .357 into the waistband of my trousers and exited the house, taking my time in opening and closing the front door and then striding across the street. Rick saw me coming and started up the Oldsmobile. He left the headlights turned off and pulled out into the street, meeting me halfway. I opened the door and got in. Rick stepped on the gas even before I was fully inside.

The clock read 11:43 PM. I started taking my gloves off.

"How did it go?" Rick said softly as he wove through Greyhaven's clean concrete streets.

"It went," I said, sinking back into the passenger seat.

"Yeah."

I noticed Rick didn't deign to look back through the rearview mirror as we pulled off.

I didn't either.

29.
MISTER GOLDEN DEAL

We took the long way back to Hattiesburg, jumping on I-20 and heading east toward Meridian. On the way, Rick tried to find some news on the radio about the night's events, and I was too tired to tell him that most Mississippi radio stations didn't have news services. Those that did usually got their stories from the same place everyone else did: the five o'clock news on the local TV affiliate. He eventually gave up somewhere around Forest and settled on an oldies station that played a bunch of good Sam Cooke.

We made several stops on the way back. About six miles off the interstate in Forest, Rick pulled into an abandoned gas station and hid the Olds behind the dilapidated structure. He got out, removed our stolen license plates and replaced them with Crys' originals. Then he used a Dremel tool to cut the stolen plates into even seventh sections. On our way out and all the way down to Hattiesburg, we would take turns tossing the pieces of plate out the window when there weren't any other cars on the road.

In Meridian, I turned off on 29th Street and looped back around to the logging farm off I-20. Numerous stacks of logs adorned the mud pit lot between the service road and 29th, and we had no trouble pulling off to the side of the highway and tossing our gloves and caps into the stacks. The sprinklers quickly soaked the garments and battered them in between the great sections of fallen lumber.

On the other side of town, we stopped at three different gas stations where Rick deposited pieces of the Frankensteined .357s in separate trashcans. He threw the remaining ammunition into the bed of a pickup truck at the last gas station. We took I-59 from there and headed south.

We pulled off the side of the road twenty miles out of Meridian and headed into the forest. Splitting up, we spread out the final pieces of the last .357, burying them under the hard earth or tossing them into a nearby creek. The rebuilt .357 that Rick had lifted from Quantico evidence control was resting comfortably in its protective camera case, awaiting transfer back to a locker somewhere up north. Just to be safe, I would later drop another stack of bills on Def-J for payment in delivering the .357 via car all the way to Virginia, where Rick would meet it and ensure its transfer back. We hadn't even needed it.

Our next stop was Laurel where we found a run down warehouse just off the interstate. While Rick went for gas and snacks, I skulked around the warehouse until I found a dumpster out back. Behind the dumpster, I took out my cell phone and crushed it to pieces with a steel mallet Rick had bought at the hardware store. I kicked some of the pieces under the dumpster, threw some inside, and scattered the rest on the street. I had placed a call to Cellular

South the day before and reported the phone stolen, electing to cancel my account instead of purchasing a new phone at a customer discount.

Forty-five minutes back to Hattiesburg. Lot of time for me and my brother to talk.

There was a blues station on the radio that was playing a Stevie Ray Vaughan marathon.

We never said a word.

Canebrake loomed ahead of us at nearly three in the morning. When the Olds finally came to rest in Doc Faller's driveway, we saw only a few cars still remained from the party earlier. I recognized my dad's Lexus, Jeffie Nils' pickup, Stevie Ray Burns' trashed out Explorer, and the Little White Honda.

"I'm tired," Rick said when we got out of the car.

"Me too," I said, working the stiffness out of my neck. "Want a drink?"

"I don't drink."

"I know."

"What are you having?"

"What else?"

"I think I will, too."

The Doc answered the door when I knocked, and it was obvious that the old Irishman had been keeping himself awake on a steady diet of martinis and wine. The circles under his eyes spoke of worry, but there was an element of the old lividity that I knew the Doc for. He smiled from ear to ear when he saw us.

"Well, we were wondering where you two fine lads had disappeared to," the Doc droned. "Everyone here's been lookin' for ya most of the night."

"I've been under a rock," Rick said, entering the house.

"I've been with him," I said, right behind him. "Just further down."

Doc laughed and showed us in. When we got to the living room, we saw Crys, Jeffie, Steve and his girlfriend Ashe on the sofa nursing half-empty drinks and watching a Mardi Gras titty show on TV. My dad's head lolled back on one side of the couch where he snored quietly.

"Jack!" Crys exclaimed, jumping over the couch to catch me in an embrace.

"Well, hello," I said, collapsing into her arms. I let her hold me for a long moment, and when we broke apart just enough to meet each other's eyes, I could see the new worry lines etched into the grooves just under her eyes.

"I was wondering where you went to," she said, a playful grin on her face.

"Rick and I went for a drive around Canebrake," I said, loud enough for everyone else to hear. "Bro-talk stuff."

Steve nudged Ashe Jackson, daughter of the man who owned MS Music. "You hear that? It means he was around."

"Jesus, Steve," the much younger girl said in a voice that sounded stolen from a Pablo Francisco act, eyes laden with drunkenness.

"What'd we miss?" I said, shrugging out of my jacket.

"Well, Dave did some Indian dance with his Indian wife," Jeffie said, tugging off an Amber Bock. "You know his voice gets more and more like helium-voice when he drinks?"

"I thought the lad was going to float off there for a minute," Doc said, stirring himself a cup of tea at the kitchen counter. Rick stood next to him trying to figure out how to pour a Crown and seven.

"Let me get that for you, Rick," Crys said.

"Thanks," Rick replied, taking off his glasses and rubbing his eyes. "Much obliged."

I crept over to the sofa and sat down next to my father. His mouth was half open, spewing forth a steady stream of snore noises. I patted his arm lightly. "Dad? Dad. Wake up, Dad. I'm back."

Duke's head snapped up into a smooth stretch involving arms, legs and every other part of the body, instantly recognizable to me. He used to do it all the time when he fell asleep in his chair back when we were living together. He saw me grinning at him and clapped my hand back.

"Hey, Jack," he said. "How was it?"

"It *was*," I said sinking back into the couch. "Everything go as planned?"

"Sure enough," Duke said, sitting forward and rousing himself. "You know me and Canebrake parties."

"What is it you're watching?" Rick asked, joining us on the sofa.

"It's a tape of these guys at Mardi Gras," Jeffie said, cackling a little. "They go around with a shopping cart full of beads and trade 'em to chicks to get them to strip on camera."

"Wow. Jack, you have to take me to this Mardi Gras thing some day."

"Ask your wife, Rick," I said. Crys delivered our Crown and sevens, and I made a thirsty noise. "Ahhhh, thank you, dear. So who all made it tonight?"

"Everyone on the guest list," Duke said, reaching for his own Crown and seven. "Dave, his wife; Alex, his wife; couple of the Jive-T's stopped by for a while; so did Vandy."

"And Doctor Faller's date is passed out on the bed in the back," Steve said, giggling like a little boy. Ashe punched him in the shoulder.

"I told her I'd only be a minute," the Doc said. "But then I forgot." He gave the nearest bottle of liquor, of which there were many adorning the house, a mean stare. "Damn you, liquor. Damn you all to hell."

"Look, folks," I said. "Thanks. I appreciate you doing this for me."

"What are bandmates for?" Jeffie said, winking at me conspiratorially. "Speaking of which, are you *ever* going to rehearse with us again? The holidays are coming up, and we're booked like a bookie."

"Probably not, Jeffie. I hate to say it, but I think it's time 25 to Midnight started to look for a new front man."

"You're quitting?" Steve said, appearing as if he didn't care one way or another. I knew better. "You can't quit."

"Sorry, Steve. I have to."

"Any particular reason why?"

I closed my eyes as the whiskey coated my throat. "A bunch of them. All the same, guys... it's been fun. Honestly."

"Shit," Jeffie said. "I hate it when front men quit."

"Can you guys talk about this later?" Ashe intoned from where she stretched next to Steve. "Steve, I'm ready to go home."

"I think I'm going to bow out, too," Jeffie said.

"Anybody need rides?" Rick asked, swirling his drink around in its glass.

"I'm all right," Jeffie said.

"We're going to her place," Steve said pointing. Ashe's parents had their own quaint little cottage on the other side of the Canebrake lake.

We all got up to see everyone off, Duke included.

"Anything we should talk about?" my father asked me as he struggled into his coat.

"Maybe," I said. "Dad... you remember that time I got caught stealing action figures from that toy store?"

"Uhhhh, I think so. You were, what... ten?"

"I think." I set my drink down and rubbed my eyes. "*After* you whipped my ass you told me that I had a responsibility to make the family proud. And that you'd do anything for family, especially me and Jeannette."

He smiled. "Well, that goes without saying, doesn't it?"

We walked out toward his car, watching the others drive off into the night. As my dad unlocked the car, I leaned up against it. My lip trembled a little.

"Dad... I don't think you'd have been proud of me tonight. I think. . .you'd be pretty ashamed."

My vision clouded for a moment, and the next thing I knew, he had his arms around me. I gripped him back, biting my lip to keep from letting the emotions inside me from burbling out onto his back.

"Son, I think I'd be proud of you anyway," Duke said. "You're my boy and I love you. Hear me? Nothing's ever going to mean a damn more than that."

When we disengaged, I snorted hard to prevent the sob from coming. "Dad, I did a terrible thing..."

He patted my shoulder. "Is it done?"

I wiped my nose. "Huh?"

"Is it over? Did you end it?"

I nodded slowly. "Yeah, Dad. It's over."

He gave me a muted smile. "Then from here on out, why don't you let me take care of things?"

"Dad? Are you sure? I mean—"

"Hey. Your old man's still got a little verve in his pipe, know what I mean?" He winked at me and put his hands on my shoulders.

"You did more for Carter than I could have. Let us handle it from here."

I nodded again, letting a shimmer of a smile appear on my face. I clapped his hand hard. "Thanks, Dad. I love you."

"I love you, too, Jack."

With that, my dad squeezed my shoulders again and got in his car. The Lexus—run down as it was—started smoothly and was soon out of my line of sight as it swerved out of Canebrake. I stood for a moment longer in the chill night air, watching hints of tail-lights disappear around tree trunks and corners.

After a while, I turned around and went back inside.

"...So I think I'm going to bid all of you good night," the Doc was saying when I went back in. He was suffering from a big yawn that distorted his words and caused him to stretch his lean body in odd ways.

"I'm right behind you, Doc," Rick said, half-lying on the sofa.

"Not in that bedroom you're not," Doc joked, winking at Rick. Rick offered the Doc a thumbs-up in return.

"Doc," I said, wrapping him up in a hug. "I owe you big time for this. For everything."

"Nonsense, snapper," the Doc replied, squeezing back hard. "It was my pleasure. Just do an old man a favor, eh?"

"Name it, Doc."

He jerked his head toward the door. "Get outta here, Jackie. Get outta this place. Go find what you need. Go back to Texas."

I compressed my lips and shook him, patting his arms. "Yeah. Okay, Doc."

Doc Faller winked at me and turned to give Crys a kiss good-night. They embraced as well, and the aging professor of all things social gave her a wide grin.

"You've got yourself a good one there, lass," he said quietly. "Take care of him. He *might* do the same for you."

"He already did, Doc." Crys smiled and kissed his cheek. "Now get in there and please that lady, huh?"

Doc blinked and laughed. Offering all of us a short bow, he started off down the hall to his room. "Don't have to tell me twice!"

I smiled after the Doc and felt Crys' fingers entwine in mine. We looked at each other for a moment; she with neutral eyes and a slight smile. Myself, I couldn't say. I didn't really feel I deserved adoration right then.

"Rick, we're off to bed," I said, looking over the sofa. When Rick didn't reply, I checked and found him already sound asleep, his hand stretched out to the table where his nearly full Crown and seven glass rested.

"Guy doesn't know how to hold his liquor," Crys said, switching off the television and the living room lights.

"It's his first," I said quietly, throwing a blanket over my brother. I carefully removed his glasses and set them on the table, then moved his hand away from the forgotten drink and onto his chest.

"First of many things tonight," I said.

"Come on, cowboy," Crys whispered, grasping my arm and shoulder. "Let's go to bed."

Once we'd locked ourselves in the guest room and undressed, I lay heavily on my back under the covers, and Crys snuggled up against me. I touched her face and brushed a strand of blonde hair out of her eyes.

"You saved me tonight," I said.

She smiled down at me. "Returning the favor. They're… gone?"

"One of them is for sure. The other..." I shrugged. "It doesn't matter anymore."

She leaned down to kiss me, and I accepted her with full fervor. She leaned over me to snap off the nightstand lamp then settled against my chest, wrapping one leg around mine. My hand snaked up the smooth creaminess of her back, coming to rest in the strands of her silky hair.

"I love you, Crys," I said.

"I know, Jack," she told me.

30.

LAST RITES

I had one more thing to do, and with everyone still sleeping off their nights at the Faller house, I headed into town. It felt good to drive the Little White Honda again, to feel the seat cushions molded to my back and legs. I got lucky, too, remembering that the last night I'd driven it, there was still a ton of lighting and sound equipment borrowed from MS Music in the trunk and backseat. None of the gear remained there currently, though, and I supposed that Jeffie and Steve must have cleaned it out sometime during the party. I hoped Chad and the rest of the gang at MS Music wouldn't be too mad. Probably not. I had plenty of money to pay for the extended rental now.

When I got in the car, I found the Kittlemeyer novel I'd bought a while back, still dog-eared down to the last chapter I'd finished. On my way into town, I picked up the novel and regarded it. *No More Solutions*, the title read. Jake Kilgore, master sleuth.

One day, I'd finish reading it.

At the nearest Desperate Guaranty, I pulled in and got an appointment with one of the bank reps and laid out precise instructions for a four-way transfer of funds. Thanks to the technical wizardry of my Fort Worth cyber-bud Deckhead, we had lifted over $500,000 from Bill Finley's accounts, not including the other half-million that went into the phantom Cayman account he'd set up in Elizabeth Finley's name. On top of that million was seven hundred grand owed to Carter Dooley which I authorized for a transfer to another new account in Switzerland. A hundred grand went to Deck and his buddies for their time and effort straight off. So after the surprised bank rep informed me after an hour's wait that all monies had been wrangled in from the other four off-shore banks, I cleanly informed him that I would be closing my personal bank account and would like the entire sum of money presented to me in cash. After the cash cases were delivered to me and the paperwork signed, the rep advised me to seek a CPA to consult with about possible taxation regulations. I took the man aside, asked him quietly to keep my business with the bank a closely guarded secret, and handed him a thousand dollars. The rep assured me that all my transactions would remain confidential and that he would see to the arrangements personally.

My next stop was MS Music where I went in to find Frank Vandy. Unfortunately, the store manager informed me that Frank had come down with a nasty case of the cocktail flu and had returned to Pass Christian earlier that morning. I made a mental note to visit my old mentor soon and set about resigning my position in the repair department. The store employees were a little shocked at the abruptness of the decision, but I smoothed things over with a promise to stay in touch.

I headed out to the post office after that, purchasing three separate boxes for priority delivery. At the service desk in the P.O. box room, I made three packages. In the first, I dropped fifty grand of the money, wrapped it up carefully, wrapped it again with a special kind of duct tape that reflects X-rays, and then wrote down David Novak's address on the box's outer cover. I scribbled the following note to David and put it with the cash before double taping the box up in another coating of magnetic duct tape:

Dear David:

I am greatly sorry for getting you involved in the events of the past few weeks. I should have been much more careful in doing what I was doing, but unfortunately, I never knew just how crazy this gig was until it was too late.

Enclosed is $50,000 of tax-free cash. Don't ask where it came from. Just do me a favor and invest a little here, invest a little there. Open an account for me and manage it however you see fit. I don't care how much it makes or how much you put into it. Just use your discretion. As for the rest of it... enjoy. I told you I'd pay you back. And before you get in a snit, this isn't a payoff.

It's back taxes.

Sinncerely,
Jack Dooley

I performed the same procedure on the second package, but lightened the cash load to only $25,000. I fished a business card out of my wallet and wrote down the address to The Dead Ringer in Biloxi. Composing a similar note to Nick Gaetano thanking him for his help and begging his forgiveness for any inconvenience I may have caused, I wrapped that one up and set aside. In the third box, I dropped another fifty grand and wrote another note. I had a hard time writing this one.

Dear Jeffie, Steve, Dave, and 'Lex:

I've now committed the cardinal sin in the music business of breaking a gig with no warning. I don't think that's going to be anything good for you guys in the long run, and since I'm bugging out soon, I thought you should all get compensated for the loss.

We played a mean tune as 25 to Midnight. I'll never forget the nights at Dewey's or the frat houses or the weddings or any of the other places we played in the last year we've been together. I hope all of you go on to making something magical out of your skills. I was the only one in the group that wasn't a professional musician. You guys should be doing better things than this. And you CAN do it. I know it.

There's $50,000 here to divvy up between the four of you. Thank you for the best times of my life and all the help you've given me in the past month. I hope I'll see you again someday.

Your front man,
Jack

I got out one of the 25 to Midnight business cards from my wallet, one with Jeffie's address on it, and taped it to the outside of the box once I'd sealed it. I took all three packages to the teller window, paid for priority shipping, and left the post office.

Doing a mental calculation to determine exactly how much money I had left in the steel cases in my trunk, I got back in the Little White Honda and headed back to Canebrake. On my way back, I stopped at the nearest Shell station and purchased a newspaper. The front page story was everything I'd hoped it to be.

EXPLOSION CRIPPLES LEADING PETROLEUM DISTRIBUTOR

Daughter Questioned in PetroJet Murder Case

JACKSON: An explosion rocked South Jackson late last night at the PetroJet Chemical, Inc. plant off Highway 49. Witnesses say the fireball was visible for a five mile radius around the plant. Sources inside the South Jackson Fire Department are still investigating the incident, but at least one member in the department suspects arson.

EPA officials called to the scene early this morning categorized the incident as a "crippling blow to the plant's refinery and storage capabilities." The detonation's epicenter has been determined to be on or near PetroJet's on-site propane bulk storage tanks. The focal point of the blast destroyed much of the plant's liquefied petroleum gas production facilities and severely damaged its oil and natural gas facilities.

No personnel were found injured or killed in the accident, sources say. EPA and DOT investigators have been called in to reconstruct the accident with the aid of the Fire Department.

The explosion at PetroJet may or may not coincide with the murder of William Thomas Finley, 53, president and CEO of PetroJet Chemical. Police and Fire Department responded to reports of a fire at Finley's residence in South Jackson where Finley's daughter, Elizabeth Finley, 27, was found inside the home. Police report that the elder Finley's body was seen dead of a gunshot wound before the house was evacuated and that Miss Finley had on her person a handgun. Miss Finley is being treated for smoke inhalation and first degree burns at Jackson County Memorial Hospital where she is under guard and expected to be questioned by police later today.

Fire Department officials reported that Finley's body was recovered at 4:15 AM this morning once the blaze was put out. Paramedics had no comment, but sources inside the police department confirm that Finley had been dead prior to the setting of the fire. Sources also indicate that the fire "was set intentionally... with no doubt." Investigations

> are proceeding immediately, but early information seems to point to tampering found on the remains of the Finley home's underground propane storage tank. Arson unit detectives would not confirm or deny this report.
>
> Police are seeking Al Henkel, 56, for questioning in conjunction with the suspected arson at PetroJet and the Finley residence. Henkel previously drove transport trailers for PetroJet Chemical. Police had no comment when asked about a possible connection between Henkel and Elizabeth Finley.
>
> In related news, Mary Patricia Finley, 49, wife of William Thomas Finley, was taken to Jackson County Memorial under sedation when she arrived at the site of the Finley house fire. Witnesses say Mrs. Finley acted in a "crazed, possibly drunken" manner and was sedated by paramedics. Police had no comment when asked if Mrs. Finley would be questioned in relation to the arsons and the murder.

There was continuing coverage on both incidents on separate pages inside the paper. But the gist of the main headline was enough for me. I put the Little White Honda in gear and headed for Canebrake.

Aunt Dee was not home when I knocked on the door, and I was thankful for that. What I had to clear up with Carter really had no business in her ears, despite what her husband may have told her. I supposed though that my uncle had learned the value of keeping his mouth shut.

When he answered the door, he was walking on a cane. As soon as he admitted me, I could see the final effects of the explosion at DPI on his face. His beard had grown back in patches, but it looked like the spots where burn marks lay were healing fine. I could see he shuffled with a different stride than before, probably due to the discomfort of whatever scarred flesh was left on his back. A little bit of the fire in Carter's eyes had died out; that I saw right off.

"Jack. Where you been, nephew?"

I held up a small folder with the Desperate Guaranty logo on it. "Getting your money back. How you feeling, Uncle Carter?"

He grunted as he hobbled through the kitchen area and into the den. I followed him at a distance, watching him walk, taking note of every nuance in his behavior that differed from the Carter I remembered before the accident. He settled down uncomfortably in a rocking chair and leaned on his cane for a moment.

"I itch all over," he said after a moment. "There's this antiseptic cream that Dee has to rub all over my burns every six hours and it itches like hell. Other than that, I'm just sore as shit and trying to get used to this pain in my leg."

I took seat across from him on the sofa. "I suppose it could have been worse."

"Yeah, that's true." Carter tried to settle back in the chair, but his face clenched in agony as he sat back. He finally settled on hunching forward, using his cane as a balance.

"Whatcha got there?" he asked me, nodding his head at the envelope.

I handed it to him.

"That's an account statement for a bank in Switzerland. It's registered in your name as an all-or-nothing account. That means you can keep it in there and add money to it over time or take it all out at once. It contains about seven hundred thousand dollars, courtesy of the Finley family."

Carter's eyes got real wide as he inspected the documents inside the envelope. "No shitting me? You actually got it back?"

"I got it back," I said, touching my chin. "Don't ask me how, but I did."

Carter set the envelope down and looked at me. The stare was neutral, probing almost. He reached down beside his chair and picked up the newspaper he had been reading, the same edition of *The Hattiesburg American* I had read earlier on.

"Does it have anything to do with this?" he asked, pointing to the headline.

"Yup," I said. I would say no more.

"Huh," my uncle grunted. "Well."

The palpable air of indecision hung between us. To be honest, I really didn't know what to say to him. He still didn't know about all the particulars, including my beating and the hit on Henkel's men.

Maybe it was for the best.

Maybe Duke would tell him later.

I was just ready to get it done.

"Do I... need to apologize?" Carter said abruptly.

I shook my head. "No, Uncle Carter. Not for one damn thing."

He nodded slowly. "Okay. You want the other twenty-five thousand now?"

"Take your time," I said, getting to my feet. "But get it to me in cash. Clear out what's left in the down payment and expense accounts, too, and just get it to me. I have a feeling I'm not long for this place."

Carter posed a querulous eyebrow at me. "You're leaving Hattiesburg?"

"Always said I would, Carter."

He put his hand up. "Thank you, Jack. You're a good nephew."

I shook his hand and leaned over to kiss his head. "Yeah. You're a good uncle, too, Carter."

"Come see me before you go?" There was the tiniest bit of sadness in his eyes.

"You bet. See you later, Uncle C. Get some rest."

I knew he would never accept it, so I found Rick's duffel bag near the hallway door when I got back to Doc's house. Making sure no one was around, I counted another $50,000 and stuffed it inside, hiding it among the clothes and other necessities he had brought along. As soon as I zipped up the bag, Doc Faller appeared in the kitchen.

"Out early today, snapper?"

"Few last things to tidy up," I said, bringing one of the heavy stainless steel suitcases into the kitchen. As Doc poured himself a cup of coffee, I opened the case and started counting out some more money.

"That's a shitload of green, Jackie," the Doc observed, adding sugar.

"Back pay for hazardous duty," I said, casting him a grin. "Where's your girl, Doc?"

"Sleeping off a rather enjoyable round of Irish aggression," he replied, sipping his coffee. "She'll be up soon. Your friend is in the bathroom cleaning up. I think he mentioned something about catching a plane."

"Yeah, I need to get him to the airport." I held out a stack of money, bound in groups by thick rubber bands. Another fifty grand from the take. "Here. Take it."

Doc licked his lips and made a funny face as he regarded the cash. "What's this for, snapper?"

"Don't give me any shit, Doc. Look, just take it." My shoulders rippled as I proffered the money again. "I want you to come away from this with something."

Doc took one of the stacks of cash, setting his coffee cup down to flip through it. "Is it clean?"

"Cleaner than anything you've ever seen."

Doc's eyes twinkled, and his mouth curled upwards. "How do you know that, snapper?"

He took the cash and set it on the counter, nodding once to affirm the righteousness of it. As he went back to his coffee cup, I found a notepad near the kitchen phone and started scrawling another note, this one to Rick.

"Did you see the paper this morning, lad?" Doc Faller asked me.

"Yup," I said. "Nice story, even for *The American*."

"I particularly like the bit about the distraught wife having to be sedated." He chuckled. "Jack, you pulled it off. However the hell you did it, you pulled it off."

"Yeah," I said, signing the note and folding it. "I guess I did. But I wish I didn't have to."

"Aye." The Doc looked at me and lightly slapped my shoulder. "Chin up, snapper. I hear it's much brighter in the Lone Star State."

This time, my smile was genuine and warm. "Yeah, I hear that, too, Doc."

The Doc turned and shuffled out of the kitchen. His Indian robe swirling with the movements of his body. He disappeared down the hallway, and I heard the door to his room crack open and shut again.

I hoped I would see him again sometime.

I counted out another fifty grand from the suitcase and set it in a small stack on the kitchen counter. I scrawled another note to Crys, letting her know I'd be back later that afternoon and that she ought to go home and check on her mother. Once done, I snapped the suitcase shut and looked over the note I'd written to Rick.

Brother,

There's nothing I can really say to make up for what I've put you through. If I'd known some other way out of it, I would have taken it. But I'm just not smart enough. Not prepared. You were always better at that. And I love you for it.

In your bag, you'll find a little present. I knew you wouldn't take it straightaway, so I just snuck it in. You deserve to come home with something for this, and I know this doesn't come to close making up for it. But at least it's something. I know you'll find something to do with it.

Now it's my turn to say "whatever you need, whenever you need it." Thanks, brother.

Down on the Upside,

Jack

Before Rick came out of the bathroom, I snuck the note back into his duffel bag, leaving it easily seen in one of the outer pockets. Just as I stood back up, Rick walked out of the bathroom. He put on his glasses and stood holding his jacket in the living room.

"Ready?" I said.

"Yup," he said.

Rick's return flight went through a relatively new airline out of the Gulfport airport on the coast. It made for an easier drive not having to go back to New Orleans, and it would cut down on Rick's waiting time. Added to that, it looked like a cool day of bright blue sky and sunshine. Not a cloud could be seen.

We didn't talk much on the way down, keeping to neutral subjects like the new Springsteen album, some comics neither of us had read in weeks, and speculation about what *The Matrix* really means. Mister Kent and Mister Wayne on a leisurely drive south down Highway 49.

We stood on the sidewalk outside the departure lounge for a moment, each of us looking around this way and that. It took a while before we could meet each other's eyes. I felt a slight tremor creep up my spine and shake me.

"Rick, I... I don't know where to begin."

Rick nodded and looked at his shoes. "Me neither."

"Brother, if there had been any other way to do this without getting you involved..."

"Hey, stow that shit, man." Rick grabbed both of my shoulders. "What do I tell you all the time? How do I sign my e-mail? Whatever you need, brother. Whenever you need it. I mean that, man."

I shook my head, feeling something well up behind my eyes. "You're an accessory now. If anyone ever finds out..."

"I'll deal with it," Rick said, smiling slightly. "Besides, I have a feeling I may be reevaluating my options at Quantico soon anyway."

"Yeah? Just because of what Crys said?"

"Partly. And partly because of this little...vacation." He shrugged. "I don't know. I just need to see my wife."

I slapped him on the side of the arm. "Then get on with it, brother. I've kept you long enough."

Our arms encircled one another in a tight bear hug, one harder than any other I'd allowed myself to experience with my brother. I felt the slickness of his jacket collar under my chin and squeezed my eyes closed.

"Goddammit, I love you, Rick. And I'll find some way to make this right again."

"We got plenty of time, Jack. Plenty of time."

We regarded each other a moment longer, probably seeing the changes in one another's physical demeanors for the first time in a long time. There were a couple of new gray spots in Rick's hair that I had not seen before, and his rimless glasses appeared to blend in with the circles under his eyes. For my part, I'd lost a lot of weight, sported a few unsightly new blemishes on my face, and changed hair color. Something had changed between us, and while the act itself was easily identifiable, I couldn't even bear to speculate on how that would unfold in the future.

Rick threw his duffel bag over his shoulder and headed into the airport departure lounge. I watched him until he vanished in the throng of people milling about, and finally I got back in my car.

It was a very quiet drive home.

31.

LONE STAR SONG

I blocked off another fifty-thousand dollar portion of the money and put it in one of the silvery suitcases by itself, separating it from the rest of the haul. No one was around when I got to the East Shipping Company warehouse. Using the security code Dad had given me, I unlocked the doors and went upstairs to his office. I set the case down on Duke's desk, not bothering to turn on the lights. Another scrawled note to my father indicated that he now had a backup stash of money to put my half-brother, his youngest son, through school and could thus rest easy about hoofing it at DCS for the rest of his life. The thought crossed my mind that I should have said all this person, but at that late hour in the day, the exhaustion was spurning me on to the very last thing I had to do. And Dad and I would have plenty of time later anyway. We always would.

I pulled into my apartment complex a little after four and parked in front of my building. When I got out of the car, I felt a mite light-headed as I approached the door to the inside stairs. Upon entering, I saw that someone had recently washed and cleaned the walls on one side of the stairs. I couldn't remember exactly how much blood I'd left at the scene upon my departure, but apparently someone had made of a note of it to the landlady. There was a note taped to my door from the landlady that said I was several weeks late on the rent and would be liable for sanctions if I didn't get in touch with her soon. I tore the note down and touched the doorknob, knowing that I would have to drop by the office later and clear up more than a few things with the owners. I absently wondered if anyone else in the building had made a complaint about the ruckus a few weeks ago.

The scene passed through me like a cold sweat when I entered. With the sunlight streaming in from the balcony doors, it looked even worse than I remembered. The small bookcase by the door had been overturned, spilling its contents all over the floor. A sea of cracked CD cases and scratched discs littered the floor, almost covering up the carpet. The entertainment center remained standing, but its doors hung from broken hinges and there were several cracks in the wood that must have been left by an axe. A forest of disconnected wires and bent metal spilled forth from the entertainment center's ruin. My work desks had been overturned and tossed, their contents mixing with the variety of broken glass, shattered wood, and paper covering the floor. My feet crunched over the collection of debris as I walked toward the kitchen, and I paused momentarily to look at a large bloodstain on the floor. A few feet away, the balcony doors let in the cool afternoon air from where the glass had been shattered by my head. A corresponding bloodstain was visible on the concrete balcony just outside. Crys had been right about the crack in the glass. Had I the attention to fix that flaw, the heavy pane glass would almost certainly have busted my skull when Henkel and his mutts tossed me. I moved the broken dining room table and chairs out of the way to peer into the kitchen. All the appliances had been ripped from their sockets and dashed against the floor. The stench of spoiled meat and cheese wafted up to greet my nose, and I saw what little contents of the fridge splattered all over the walls and floor. Maggots and ants had gotten into a split package of bacon, and they swarmed all over the exposed, rotting meat, generating more and more of their own kind to continue the decomposition.

Kicking my way back through the mess, I went into my bedroom. They had left the bathroom relatively intact, scattering only a few toiletries from my medicine cabinet all over the floor and breaking the mirror. The bedroom had fared only marginally better. All fifteen of the comic book boxes arranged in front of the bed had been kicked over and trampled on. The comics themselves sported only a few ripped pages and bends, the backboards having protected most of them from the onslaught. The chest of drawers had been emptied and its contents scattered across the floor, and I saw most of the clothes in my closet crumpled into piles on the carpet. A rich, foul odor greeted me as I sorted through what was left, and I realized that someone must have pissed on the clothes. I jerked away from the pile before it made me sick or before my hands found a lumpy turd or worse inside. They had pulled the mattress off the bed and broken the slats under the box springs, leaving the old wooden frame leaning to one side. I had slept in that bed since I was a little boy. Before that, little Duke Dooley had dozed there, too.

The dresser's seven drawers had been similarly gutted, and everything from huka necklaces to old Zippos to leftover college term papers was scattered all over the bedroom. My little red bookcases, another holdover from childhood, had been tipped over, strewing more books and graphic novels across the floor. There wasn't a poster or print on the wall, not a single picture frame left intact.

I dropped my keys, cigarettes, and lighter onto the top of the entertainment center as I walked back into the living room. Shrugging out of my jacket, I knelt down to start sorting through the rubble. After writing off a couple broken DVDs – Criterion Collection films at that – and all of the new comics I'd left on the table, I found a tiny gray figure. Brushing off some of the wreckage, I recognized it as the Marv bust Rick had given me for Christmas several years ago, the first collector's piece I'd ever received. Marv, the lead character and resident tough guy of *Sin City*. Even after all the ruckus in my apartment, he had come through in good shape. Even the cigarette clenched between his massive teeth remained intact. The rest of my collection lay in pieces all around me. John Constantine's head peered up at me from beneath the torn pages of a ripped *Justice League* comic.

"Anything worth salvaging?"

I looked over my shoulder and saw Crys standing in the doorway. Her arms were folded tightly across her stomach over the soft blue fabric of a light sweater. It looked like she hadn't bothered with makeup that morning. I didn't blame her.

"Couple things," I said, getting to my feet and blowing the dust off Marv's head. I held up the bust to her. "Marv made it."

"Good for him." Crys took a few steps into the apartment and closed the door behind her. "Jesus, Jack."

"Yeah." I felt life drain from me as I set Marv down on top of the entertainment center. "Christ, you think you have just enough stuff, y'know? Maybe a little bit of everything to keep you happy. I didn't know how much that meant until I saw it destroyed."

"It can be replaced," she said. "It's just stuff. Oh. By the way, you left this in the car."

She handed me the crushed Superman maquette that I had been holding onto since my flight from the apartment weeks ago. I turned it over in my hands, looking at the deep ruts embedded in the bright S shield, the jagged edge where his head had snapped off. I traced a finger down the length of the maquette's torso and shook my head.

"You don't know what you are until all you are is taken away." I looked up at Crys. "Or at least I didn't know. I'm not sure I like what I am anymore."

"Don't have to be sure," she said with a shrug. "I'll do enough liking for the both of us."

The smile came of its own volition, and I dropped the mutilated Superman statue onto the floor, allowing it to join the rest of the refuse. My eyes cast another long baleful look around the apartment. "Not going to be much to pack when I get out of here, I guess."

Crys stepped around the overturned bookcase and cleared out portions of the floor for her feet to stand on. "So you've decided for sure? You're going back to Texas?"

"I might as well." I kicked the coffee table over and out of the way so I could wade back to the balcony door. I stopped just over the bloodstain on the carpet, my shoes crunching on broken glass. "I think I've used up my last bit of good fortune in this burg."

I heard her moving behind me. "When are you leaving?"

"I dunno. Soon, though."

I felt her thin forearms wrap around my waist, her cool cheek press lightly against the back of my neck. "You'll need a place to stay until then. You can come over to my house."

"Your mom and dad okay with that?"

"They'll be fine. Mom's laid up in bed on antibiotics." Her breath was cool and short when she half-laughed into my neck. "Dad was pretty angry about me leaving town. He'll get over it."

One of my hands strayed to where her fingers had locked together over my stomach. She placed a kiss on my neck, her lips warm and inviting. "Jack, thank you for the money. I'm going to need it when Mom starts to get real sick."

"It's the least I could do," I said, staring out across the balcony into the fading sun. "With that, you ought to be able to take care of her and have some left over for school. I wish I could have come up with something better, Crys."

"Hey." She turned me around and put a warm hand on my cheek. Her eyes remained as clear and steady as they had for the past few weeks. "You *did* come up with something better. Hear me?"

I nodded slowly, letting her caress my check, her fingers splaying at my lips. "Crys... you could come with me. There's plenty of good medical colleges near Fort Worth. We'd be okay out there."

The caresses stopped. "You'd take care of me?"

"I would." I squeezed her hips, eyes dead set on her own. "I've got plenty of cash from the Finley run; a little over a hundred grand after Carter gives me the rest of what he owes me. We could get a place, settle in, put you through school. You don't have to stay in this place, Crys."

"I know," she said, leaning in to kiss my chin. The pecks and nibbles led to a greater frenzy of mouths, and our hands traced lover's patterns on each other's backs. When we pulled away, she took my face in her hands.

"But I can't go, Jack. Not yet."

I felt a heaviness on my eyelids. "Why not?"

She looked down at my chest. "Because I have to finish up with *me* now. I was so glad to take a break for a while, cowboy; believe you me. That time in New Orleans wasn't just spent making you better. But I still have things to do. My mother's very sick, Jack. And even after everything she and Dad have put me through, I can't let her go yet. I have to stay with her, make her understand that I'm a better daughter than before. Let her see the person she couldn't see before." She ran her fingers through my hair, a small smile playing across her mouth. "The person you saw all along."

It couldn't have ended any other way, I guess. Anymore would have been asking for too much, and I had tempted my share of fate for the time being. Even still, the abandonment fantasies sparked to life again inside me, and the cold thing inside my stomach turned hollow and hot. I steadied myself on her shoulders and leaned in to kiss her forehead.

"I meant what I said this morning," I said.

"I know," Crys replied, snaking into the embrace. "I know you did, Jack."

We stood there for a long time, bathing in each other's warmth as the cool evening breeze began to whistle into the apartment. Somewhere outside, a child squealed and birds fluttered off into the wind. Eventually, the blue sky gave way to night, and one star shone down from the azure heavens to taunt Crys and I in the wreckage around us as night fell. It was only one star, and maybe I was reading too much into that anyway. In that sea of mess around me, I thought I could hear a guitar strumming lightly. A song. Music. Whatever. Maybe I was just hearing things. It was only one night. One sky. One star.

Maybe.

"I don't know shit," I said.

Christopher Dufour
January 20, 2001
Somewhere in Texas

ACKNOWLEDGEMENTS

This book has been over twenty years in the making, originally begun in an apartment quite similar to Mister Dooley's in Hattiesburg, Mississippi. As such and foremost, I must thank all of the Hattiesburg regulars to whose likenesses, while coincidentally fictional, I owe inspiration for in the wide cast of characters populating *The One Star Goodnight.* Familiarity breeds fondness, and looking back over these past twenty years, I take heart in every fortunate moment each of you spent with me. Thank you for enriching my life, even though I may not have known it or appreciated it at the time.

At the risk of boring you, the Reader Who Already Finished Paying Their Dues Reading This Fucking Book, I'd also like to make a few specific acknowledgements to those who made *The One Star Goodnight* possible:

To Eric Semlear for providing the first swag of no-holds-barred feedback I needed to take the text from a wankfest to a real novel. Brother, I owe you more than I can express, and I appreciate you for all you've done for me over the years. We do spend most of our time together these days looking back on old days, and every one of those days is a treasure.

To my family: You put up with my shit far more than you should, and I love you for it. Thanks for letting me do this and being a constant source of support when I needed it.

To Mark Vandermark for telling me a long time ago that despite how good I was at fixing horns, it wasn't my calling. I think I finally found it, man.

To my Dad, Doug Dufour, to whom this novel is dedicated. I finished the first draft of *The One Star Goodnight* in 2001, only two years before you died, and ever since, I have regretted not publishing it in your lifetime. Every keystroke is a gift you gave me, Pop. I miss you every day.

To all the folks on the business side of things that helped make this happen: Erin Baehr for financial advice, the folks at Blue Canary Books for their cover and interior design services, and especially high school bud and fellow author Danny Tobey for answering all my questions about publishing (or not). Check out his books *The Faculty Club* and *The God Game.*

A huge thanks to Bob Reed, my creative writing teacher from R.L. Paschal High School in Fort Worth. He wrote a novel of his own called *The Red-Winged Blackbird,* which he shared selflessly with every creative writing cohort he taught, right alongside every one of us that flailed short story after short story to figure out how to write. Mister Reed, thank you for your inspiration, guidance, and aplomb. I remain ever your faithful student.

And finally, to my anonymous editor who came out of hiding to provide the final foot up my rather lazy ass that got this book made. I could not have done this without you. Especially with the thousands of tiny technical edits needed migrating the manuscript file into something that would function properly in this century. Thank you for everything you've done and continue to do to make this life a reality for me.

One last one, of course: Thank **YOU**. Each and every one of **YOU** who bought this book. Authors struggle every day to give birth to works of creation that sometimes never get read or even discovered, especially these days in the glut of attention-hoarding distractions. I cherish all of **YOU** for taking a chance on this insanity in your hands, and I hope you enjoy it. I hope you stick with me too because I'm just getting started: I have so much more to show you and new journeys to take you on. Keep up with me at du4writes.com and sign up for my newsletter to stay current on what's next. Right now, newsletter subscription is the only way to get a special, exclusive short story that will bridge *The One Star Goodnight* and the next chapter of Jack Dooley's misadventures in the great state of Texas, *Bravo Too Much*.

Thanks again, to everyone. If you've liked what you've seen so far, get ready. Shit's gettin' real.

Chris Dufour
Fort Worth
April 9, 2019

ABOUT THE AUTHOR

Christopher Dufour has worked a million jobs, from hand cream kiosk salesman to cell phone slinger to instructor in the art of open source intelligence. He loves watching old movies until the morning light and hates conditional formatting. *The One Star Goodnight* is his first published novel. Because writing don't pay no bills, he is also a national security consultant, disinformation researcher, and investigatory consultant. His nonfiction writing includes studies on digital data, information operations, and strategic influence... but those are so boring. He lives in Fort Worth, Texas, and he has a cat named Roxy.

Jack Dooley will return in

BRAVO TOO MUCH.

www.ingramcontent.com/pod-product-compliance
Lightning Source LLC
Chambersburg PA
CBHW030533260626
47157CB00006B/2018